Selected Praise for the Author's Non-Fiction Works

"Tom Corbett's *The Boat Captain's Conundrum* is a winning performance."
Forward Clarion Book Review

"Corbett takes a topic often shrouded in numbers and dense writing and turns it into an intellectual, yet conversational memoir."
U.S. Review of Books

"A long-time policy wonk delivers an engrossing look at his work fighting poverty in government and academic settings."
Kirkus Review

"I enjoy his writing style, it was comfortable yet candid, like listening to a respected relative recount their own life with unabashed honesty."
Pacific Book Review

"Corbett imparts an enormous amount of wisdom and humanity."
Clarion Review

"This is . . . a fully rendered tale. Those interested in the complexity of relationships …will find some rewards here."
Blue Ink Reviews

Reviews of *Tenuous Tendrils* (First Fictional Novel)

"Corbett has created a captivating novel. The book title perfectly describes the fragile thread that spirals around each individual…to create an enthralling story that anyone will love to read."
U.S. Review of Books

"…Tenuous Tendrils, by Tom Corbett, is a compelling journey from exile to redemption. Like its characters, the book is quite clever and features an abundance of humor. Many heavy scenes are punctuated by conversations about the futility of war and the humanitarian failings of government also feature omniscient narrative wit that keeps the text from being bogged down by sentiment and also allows the character's personalities to shine."
ForeWord's Clarion Review

"Corbett obviously loves to tell stories. Tenuous Tandrils, by Tom Corbett, is a captivating read with engaging vignettes which paint a picture of a retired professor, his life, and the connections which bind everything together."
Pacific Review of Books

Reader Reviews from Amazon

"A penetrating look into the human soul and the fragility of relationships."

"Tenuous Tendrils is a conversational and meditative look back on a man's life. I really like the depth of detail that the author brought to these characters."

"This book was incredibly personal on so many levels. Overall, I found this to be an extremely touching and educational read."

"I personally loved this book. It was refreshing and thoughtful."

"The overall story is incredibly genuine, realistic to the time limits it covers and thoughtful. Each time I put down the book I found it moderately difficult since I wanted to know what would happen next."

PALPABLE PASSIONS

by: TOM CORBETT

To order additional copies of this book:
www.amazon.com
www.barnesandnoble.com

Published in the United States of America

ISBN *hardcover:* 978-1-948000-02-4
ISBN *softcover:* 978-1-948000-03-1

I dedicate this work to those who consciously or inadvertently encouraged me to write over the years. I still recall my Xaverian Brother high school English teacher praising a short story I wrote for a class assignment, at a time when praise for my academic work was anything but a common theme. It stirred my interest in the written word for the first time. I recollect my college English Literature professor, Charles Blinderman, telling me that the one secret to good writing, and to becoming a successful writer, was the gift of storytelling. He thereby planted that small seed in me, a seed that was to germinate many decades later. I still think of "Bud" Bloomberg, perhaps the best classroom teacher I experienced at the university level, calling my writing "lush and inviting." He was praising a manuscript I wrote in India during my Peace Corps days. That was my first attempt at creating literature, a novel now lost somewhere in the detritus of a life spent in the academy. Then there were so many colleagues in my academic world who, at one time or another, offered high praise for my ability to communicate in the written form. Some that come to mind include Sheldon Danziger, Arthur Goldberger, Robert Havemen, Robert Lampman, and Charles Manski. Of course, they are all economists, a discipline known more for a command of mathematics than the English language. More recently, there have been a small number of associates and friends who remain supportive of my literary efforts. This group includes Peter Adler, Karen Bogenschneider, Carol Dowling, Todd Gosewehr, Carol Lobes, Jennifer Noyes, Stephanie Robert, Michael Simonds, and Matt Stagner, among others. Over time, the accumulated reinforcements from all those who should have known better took effect. Better late than never.

Other Books by the Author

Tenuous Tendrils (Xlibris Press, 2017)

The Boat Captain's Conundrum (Xlibris Press, 2016)

Ouch, Now I Remember (Xlibris Press, 2015)

Browsing through My Candy Store (Xlibris Press, 2014)

Return to the Other Side of the World with Mary Jo Clark, Michael Simmonds, Katherine Sohn, and Hayward Turrentine (Strategic Press, 2013)

The Other Side of the World with Mary Jo Cark, Michael Simonds, and Hayward Turrentine (Strategic Press, 2011)

Evidence-Based Policymaking with Karen Bogenschneider (Taylor and Francis Publishing, 2010)

Policy into Action with Mary Clare Lennon (Urban Institute Press, 2003)

"What lies behind us and what lies ahead of us are tiny matters compared to what lives within us."

—Henry David Thoreau

"You can chain me, you can torture me, you can even destroy this body, but you will never imprison my mind."

—Mohandas K. Gandhi

"There is no passion to be found in playing small—in settling for a life that is less than the one you are capable of living."

—Nelson Mandela

CONTENTS

PREFACE

In the dedication to my first fictional novel, *Tenuous Tendrils*, I discussed my early fascination with the art of writing great fiction. This was unusual among the younger residents of my working-class neighborhood of the 1950s and 60s. In this rough and tumble world, most vocational dreams ran toward being a famous athlete or possibly a cowboy or, for some of us guys as we hit puberty, to inheriting Hugh Hefner's emerging empire. My dream of being the next Hemingway or Faulkner eventually faded as I drifted toward academia and policy work, stimulating pursuits to be sure but not quite the stuff of my early aspirations. It occurred to me, growing up in a household where money was always an issue, that a conventional career did have some advantages. I would eat every day and have a roof over my head. Great literature would have to wait.

Now I am retired from a rewarding career at the University of Wisconsin-Madison. I have often told audiences that I was blessed, indeed. I had the opportunity to work with the best and brightest minds across the land. I flew around the country, struggling with some of society's most complex and intractable social issues. What a thrill. In addition, I had the enormous pleasure of teaching bright students at the University of Wisconsin who had to listen to me since their grades, and futures, depended on it. Not only was all this great fun, but I was paid for doing it. Not bad for a kid who, as a child, could not imagine why anyone would pay him as an adult for doing anything. I could not see that I possessed a single talent for which I might be compensated. I recall thinking that I could always join the army since they would take anyone. Little did I know I assiduously would spend my early adult years avoiding the military.

After several policy and memoir works, this is my second fictional work. Tenuous Tendrils, released earlier this year, was my first. In that book, I wanted to discover whether I could weave narratives that others might want to read. I am satisfied that the answer to this lifelong question is yes. I am ecstatic that I have had the opportunity to pursue my youthful passion at last. Thus, the theme of this work explores personal passions that are so real they are palpable. You can literally feel them.

At long last, what I have discovered is that act of writing is an undiluted joy. It is like creating a symphony. One must balance and integrate so many elements at the same time . . . the flow and pace of the narrative while pausing long enough to develop characters fully and explore the substantive ideas of interest to you as an author. What is particularly challenging is the task of blending drama, content, and humor in ways that do not come across as artificial and forced. I will leave others to determine if I have done so successfully. What I can assert, without qualification, is that I have greatly enjoyed the process of creating fiction. At long last, I have been able to immerse myself in my own palpable passion.

CHAPTER 1

PASSIONS

The young girl had been there before. The village was small, insignificant, merely a collection of baked homes where goats and chickens roamed at will. The streets were equally firm, also hardened from a harsh sun during the day and solidified further by the sharp cold that settled on the village most nights as residents huddled about their charcoal fires. There were a few small shops selling flatbreads and teas and sweets and household items that looked as if they had been purloined from someone else's junkyard. Most of the residents etched out a marginal existence from the plots of arable land or small flocks they tended on the grassy shrubs as the bleak landscape leaned upward against the taller peaks.

She had to get somewhere, but where? Was she seeking a specific destination or trying to escape? She could not decide. It bothered her. How would she know where to go next, when to stop, if no destination was known? She sometimes noticed that another was with her . . . her sister? Suddenly, this ethereal presence would evaporate, and she was alone once more. Increasingly frantic, she would rush to the end of one lane before finding another going off in a tangential direction. Each looked the same as the previous one. Desperation pushed her on. One lane simply merging into the next, the sameness was both frightening and puzzling. How could this be? Why could she not apprehend this gripping fear?

Perhaps she could find an adult to ask. She was what age, eight or ten or was it twelve. The correct number, like her location, lie just beyond her grasp. Why couldn't she remember her age, her name, this village, where she was headed? Ah, there was an adult, in a doorway. He would help. But her frantic queries were met with an enigmatic smile and a slight nod of the head. She asked another, same response, then a third who merely sneered. Something buried inside told her that not all were friendly. Danger lurked everywhere. For a moment, she sensed men behind her, threatening her with thick sticks. She was reminded of sharp pain, a terrible fear, but from when and why? Then these men, too, were gone.

These adult sentinels remained silent and remote, perhaps her inability to tell them what she was seeking was at fault. She whirled, looking for another way to go. Above the roofs were jagged mountain peaks, still covered in snow. Could they guide her out of this labyrinth? That was hopeless. The peaks looked all the same, no matter which direction she looked. There were no clues to suggest the correct path. She would have to make her own way. But she was so young, so scared.

Her father, if she could only find him, would know what to do. He would take her slim hand in his and lead her to safety, looking down at her with his kind and wise eyes. He was a fathomless wellspring of knowledge about the world, so intuitively capable of understanding what she needed. She had always found love and care within his protection. He could save her. She could not find him, though, anywhere. Where could he be? He had always been there for her. How could he have abandoned her now when she needed him so desperately?

She had always been favored by her father. Among her and her two siblings, it was clear he looked to her with a special fondness. It was a connection born of similar aspirations and dispositions. He was a physician, trained in England where he might have remained. Instead, he returned to Afghanistan out of devotion to a country in peril. He was determined to do what he could to save a people and culture he loved. His skills and training led him to a robust practice in Kabul where he was in demand by the elite and thus able both to secure a decent level of compensation and an appropriate style of living for his family. The family remained only modestly affluent since he would treat so many for free, a blessing that brought him great satisfaction. Yet, he remained discontented. His heart lay elsewhere, in the remote northern villages where his extended family had lived for countless generations.

Even as a toddler, she would follow her father around as he tended patients. He had a clinic adjacent to their house where he met those patients that were not hospitalized. She gravitated toward this office with the medical books which she gazed at in wonder but could not comprehend. He would shoo her away. After a few minutes, she would be peeking around the corner, listening as he conversed with patients and ministering to the medical and personal needs that were within his powers to treat. He knew she was there, she was always there. Eventually, he accepted defeat. Her burning curiosity would not easily be quenched. Acceding to the inevitable, he said, "Azita, come here. What am I to do with you? Your mother will be so cross that you are an idle girl who does no chores."

"But I want to learn, Papa." Her face was full of eager intensity.

"Learn what? You are such a foolish girl." He tried to sound cross but his tenderness seeped through.

"I want to be a doctor, like you, Papa. I want to help people."

"Well, you could start by helping your mother, she would like that very much." But he knew that would not satisfy her. She would not go away. She was afflicted with a passion.

"No, Papa. Do not tease me." She tried her cross look which, unfortunately, did nothing to intimidate him and always caused him to smile.

He looked at his daughter for a long time. He knew he should forbid this silly dream. A medical career for her might have been possible when he was a child. His own wife could attend school and become a mathematics professor at the university level. There was a decidedly Western feel in the major cities during the latter years of the monarchy and even through the communist era. Secular ideals flourished among the elite, particularly in Kabul and other major cities. A meritocracy was emerging in Afghanistan where talent, not ethnic nor religious identification nor even gender, determined ambition or success. Though growing up in what was considered the barbaric north, he stood out as a brilliant student and was sent to the capital city for further study. A charismatic, if quiet young man, he formed a strong relationship with wealthy benefactors who helped him to England to complete his medical studies. Now, however, the country had been wracked by civil war and religious intolerance that had crushed reformist hopes and pushed the dominant culture back into a feudal stage of development. Females had no hope for recognizing their talents or ambitions. In his heart, he knew it would be kinder to end her dream now. But he could not turn her away. He looked at her large brown eyes and a face set with a bright intensity and uncrushable hope. His heart would not go where his head lay, that spark of hope could push away reality at least for the moment.

"Okay, foolish girl, you can spend time with me but under two conditions."

"Yes, Papa," she jumped into his arms, her face beaming with excitement.

"First, you must continue to help your mother. I will talk with her. Oh, Allah, please spare me. Second, we must improve your English. It is very good for a young girl. It must be better, though, much better. And third, so I guess there are three conditions. You must find a way to make yourself useful. If you do, I will take you with me to my clinic and perhaps to some of the local villages when I venture out of the city. There, you could really get a feel for what I do, decide if you like it, and perhaps learn some medical skills."

"Yes, Papa, yes, yes. I will be your assistant."

Now she was back in those unknown village streets, perhaps the village of his birth. Here, each small lane simply became another small lane. There was no end, no suggestion as to where to turn next. It was a maze of familiarity and the unknown. She felt totally lost and helpless. Her panic rose up to her throat. Where was her papa? Why couldn't she find him or anyone she knew and loved.

She could still remember her father talking to her mother about how Azita might help in the clinic. She would listen, just out of sight. He spoke enthusiastically about her ambitions, her dreams. His wife exploded with exasperation. "Oh, you are such a foolish man! Why are you filling her head with things that cannot be? You know she cannot be educated."

"I cannot crush her hopes at such a tender age. She has that passion, the same as I had at that age."

"And you think this is kindness? It is not kindness. You will lead her along until life crushes everything inside her and then destroys her. Don't you see what has happened in this country? You could have such passion. You were a man. Even I might have dreams. Now…now, she cannot. She merely is a girl in a culture that punishes girls for no greater sin than being born a female."

"Of course, woman. I repair the broken bodies every day. I see those beaten senseless for the smallest of sins, those blown up by wars over the meaning of God. The greatest hate comes from the man prepared to die for the belief that his god is better than the other man's god. I see all the lost dreams, people without hope, people existing in desperation. No need to lecture me, woman. I know exactly what is happening to our country."

"Yet, you see nothing. Oh, you have always been such a dreamer, no matter what. And Azita, my poor Azita is just like you." Still, his wife had softened, her words had lost their edge.

"I had hoped that Majeed would join me in my profession, but it was not to be. Allah has moved Azita to follow in my path. Perhaps he has some plan for her that we cannot see. You must have faith, my dear."

"Faith?" she mumbled. "You have become a doddering old fool no better than those evil Taliban monsters." But inside his wife could not deny her delight that the youngest showed such ambition, such passion. She feared deeply for her but could easily recall herself at a similar age. She loved numbers and was encouraged to pursue that love. If denied her, her soul would have been crushed. She continued to grumble on the outside but let Azita escape from household chores and began conversing with her in English. More importantly, she tutored her youngest to improve her reading skills and, when that went so well, in mathematics and some elementary science.

"My dear," he said sadly in the beginning, "don't you think I know she is possessed by an impossible dream? You are correct. I am a fool, something I rather enjoy most days, but I am not cruel. I cannot dash her dreams at such a tender age. She has such intensity. Besides, better we let her tire of this dream on her own. I am certain she will become bored with me soon enough. If not bored, I suspect the sight of blood and exposed tissue will be enough to persuade her that her interests lie elsewhere, maybe even a boy."

Suddenly, in her reverie, it was no longer day but nighttime. The girl was still frantic and lost. No longer could she see the mountains surrounding this nameless village. Yet she still could make her way down the narrow paths. The moon cast a pale glow along with the faint light from kerosene lamps through the windows. The going was slower now. Panic rose inside her. She had to find her father, it was critical. That she knew. But why? He had been her strength and inspiration as she evolved from a child into a bright, inquisitive young girl. What was driving her blindly through alley after alley? What could possibly be wrong? She looked up for comfort and guidance. The stars were brilliant against the blackness. They always were up here in the remote mountainous region. Why didn't the moon dim their clarity? That was strange. But nothing made sense in this surreal world.

Despite her father's confident prediction, she never tired of the experience. He started her with the simplest tasks, keeping his clinic neat and bringing tea to the waiting patients. But she pestered him to do more. Soon he had her by his side, explaining what he was doing and why. But she wanted more. Finally, he allowed her to dispense pills and apply ointments and change dressings and even give injections. Still she was not satisfied. She wanted still more. He spent increasing time with her explaining the basics of the human body, what various organs did and what might go wrong. When her mother realized that her youngest daughter was not like other children, she took her aside to tutor her in math and the basic sciences. She still had great reservations about all this but could not deny the passion that burned within this fetching young girl. She had once felt that passion, for mathematics. She had assumed this daughter of hers would tire of the discipline and focus needed to master such complex material. Like her husband, however, she found her daughter's obsession with knowledge unquenchable.

Finally, she turned down a very long street in this silent village. Where was everyone? Why couldn't she find anyone to help her. There is no one to ask where her father and mother might be. She simply knew he needed her. She had to get to them, particularly her papa. It was vital, nothing was more important. He was at the end of this street, she knew it. She knew it with a certainty that was beyond human doubt. There was a simple village house at the end of the street. She could hear something coming from it but what? It sounded like groans, pleas for help. The voices were muted, however, indistinct and unrecognizable. The faint sounds propelled her forward. She tried to run but her legs were heavy. She pumped as hard as possible but progress was glacial. Her heart was bursting with apprehension.

She could recall her father turning to her one day and saying, "You are ready, my dear."

"For what?" she asked but hoping that she knew.

"You are ready to come with me to the local villages. There, away from suspicious eyes and those that oppress us, you can learn with me. You can practice some basic procedures. Since my homeland remains beyond reach, I will take you to villages nearer to us."

Her heart leapt with joy. There, in the villages, she knew she would be able to help him even more. In the villages, her apprenticeship could move to the next level. He would teach her more complex medical procedures and, after a brief period of intense supervision, let her handle such procedures as he directed. He marveled at her. She was like a sponge, absorbing all around her quickly and surely. For the life of him he could not imagine that he had been such a good student at her age. Yet, it broke his heart. How could she take advantage of her innate talents in such a culture where women were denied even the most basic rights and opportunities. He must get her out, to the West, but that thought also broke his heart. If only his son had shown an interest. But that was not to be. Not everyone would be so blessed by Allah. Only Azita had his passion to heal. Better still, she had the innate intelligence and skills to heal. She was much blessed.

After an eternity, a modest home at the end of the lane loomed larger. That must be the place but she knew not why. It was there, just a few steps away. But each yard gained demanded a supreme effort. Why could she not move faster? She was now certain that the voice she heard was that of her adored father. But it was a strangled sound, she could not make out the words. What was wrong? She had to get to him, had to? Her heart was now bursting, but the door was right there, inches from her reach. Finally, with one last supreme effort, she burst through the door.

————

She bolted up in bed, bathed in sweat. She was in England, in her room at Oxford. It was her old dream, her periodic companion. She had suffered from this nightmare for several years now, from that awful morning when her life had changed forever. Sometimes she would awaken amidst a primal scream. That was always embarrassing when she had roommates. But what was in the village house? What was so atrocious, unconscionable? She could guess the answer, she had a good notion of what was on the other side of that door. But now it was beyond her capacity to recollect with any certainty. Whatever it was, she had always been moved to unspeakable terror.

She decided to get up even though it was early. She had a big day ahead of her. She would be giving what was called a "Profile in Courage" talk. It recognized one student from the entire university who had overcome great odds to achieve their academic dreams. It was part of the graduation ceremony. She recalled some of the prior recipients—the blind girl who earned her law degree or the paraplegic who had earned a doctorate in economics. She was perplexed. Why were they honoring her? She had all her limbs. She suffered no debilitating disease unless persistent nightmares were such an affliction.

She arose and thought about the talk she intended to give. It was replete with the platitudes she had heard many times before. Don't give up. All things are possible. Believe in yourself. Hard work is the key. It all struck her as nonsense on this day. This is not what she wanted to say. She looked out into the grey of the early morning. Then it struck her. There was a different way to get her ideas across. Why not simply tell her story? Others could then decide if it were luck, fortune, the kindness of others, or the beneficence of some kindly deity that led to top honors in her pre-medicine degree. Yes, that is what she would do. She would tell her story, or a part of it at least.

With that, she crumpled up her prepared talk.

Later that day, Azita Masoud stood before a large audience, most of whom had little expectation of what this thin girl who was not blind, had all her limbs, and was not in a wheelchair, might possibly say. What had she overcome? Perhaps the university had no real heroes this year. She looked out for several seconds, wondering if it had been a wise move to put aside her talk that she had spent much time preparing. Yet, what could frighten her at this moment in her life? She had endured so much, seen so much, journeyed so far. How had she gotten here? Standing there, expectantly, it flashed before her eyes, starting in a place that was beyond her known world about a decade earlier, not long after the birth of the twenty-first century.

———

Chris Crawford became aware of a persistent ringing sound. What was it? Where was it coming from? Could it be a fire drill? Maybe a class had ended, or school was out. As he slowly emerged from REM sleep, it struck him that he had exited the academy some years back, having scored a first in Political Economy at Oxford on his way to a doctorate. This was no class bell that was disturbing his slumber. And surely his apartment was not ablaze. Therefore, no need to panic and run for his life. No, this annoying sound was his phone, a banal disturbance of this night's rest.

"Yeah," he growled, his voice thick with REM sleep. "It is the middle of the night so this better be good."

"It's Kay."

"Who?" and immediately realized his error.

"Your damn twin sister, moron, the one you shared a womb with."

"Oh, that Kay, I know so many." Now he was approaching wakefulness and tried to sound light and playful. "Hey, you don't call me during the day, never mind in the middle of the night. Wait, are you dying?"

"No, but Chuck is."

"Our brother Chuck?" He was still struggling to comprehend.

"No, Chuck the doorman." Her sarcasm was unmistakable.

A voice came from the other side of the bed. "Chris, honey, who is calling at this hour?" He could see the lithe, sensuous body turn slightly in his direction but, for the life of him, he could not summon up the name that went with it.

"Oh, great," came through the phone, "you are with another of your bimbos?"

Now he sprung out of bed, annoyed and almost fully alert. "Why don't you shout that out just a little louder, I am not sure she heard you." Walking into the adjacent room he continued. "What do you mean Chuck is dying? You mean our brother Chuck, not Dad."

"Yes, damn it, I mean our brother. Have you ever called our father Chuck? He is always Charles or maybe Mr. Crawford or Sir or even His Highness, even to us." There was anger in his sister's voice but it was tinged with another emotion.

"For Christ sakes, what happened? He was healthy the last time I saw him, maybe a bit depressed, and surely not as debauched as I . . ."

The voice on the phone cracked a bit, fear was overcoming irritation. "Chris, he was more than a bit depressed. He was fucking suicidal. He took an overdose. They don't know what yet. They are still doing tests. You have been away. You don't see it. His drinking got worse. My guess, the booze wasn't killing him fast enough, at least in his mind. He thought maybe a few pills would kick him over to the other side."

"That's a little crass, isn't it, even for you." Chris did not know why he said that.

"Don't you dare lecture me. When and if you get your ass back here you can take shots." Her voice had gone cold. "The thing is, he is in a coma. I . . . I believe it is touch and go. Even if he survives, I . . . well let's not get ahead of ourselves."

"Kay, you should have called me earlier."

"Why Chris, for God's sake, why? What would you have done, tell me?"

"I . . ." But nothing else came out. Chris stood naked in the middle of the room, his head spinning.

Then an overly sweet voice drifted toward him from the bedroom. "Honey, what's wrong? Are you coming back to bed? I think I'm ready again."

He grimaced. What was that girl's name? It started with a J . . . Joan, Janice, Jocelyn. She had to be a Jocelyn, the other possibilities were too pedestrian. But he could not risk using it. He had done that before, too often, called a woman by the wrong name. Very dangerous when in bed, naked. A man is rather vulnerable then. "Just go back to sleep, this will take a while."

The voice from the phone cut in, the anger diminishing into irritation. "I will know more tomorrow, I can call back then."

"Kay," he said to his sister. Her real name was Kristen but Kay was the nickname everyone used for her to minimize the confusion between Chris and Kris. The naming of the twins was not well thought out. Their mother thought the similar sounding names cute for biological twins while their father could care less what they were called. In truth, the nickname started out as her first initial, K, but soon became so universal that it was always spelled as Kay. Outside her family, most people thought her name was Katherine or something similar. "I am flying out as soon as I can get things organized."

"Really, don't bother, I can handle . . ."

"Bullshit!" he shouted into the phone. "Don't you dare play the martyr with me. I am flying back ASAP. Is he at Northwestern Medical?"

"Yes," he could tell the voice on the phone was relieved.

He let out a big breath. "Sorry, Kay, I didn't mean to yell. I still think you should have told me what was going on."

"Why?" Her voice was cold. "You would have done what exactly, from the other side of the pond."

"Kay, despite all the evidence to the contrary, I care about you and mother, and Kat. And Chuck, there is not a day that I don't regret not taking him with me."

"But you didn't." There was a coldness in her voice.

"Okay, let's not fight, not now. If Chuck passes, you should not have to deal with father alone . . . or mother for that matter. And if there are decisions to be made, well, I could never let you face his highness all by yourself. I may be a sorry sack of shit but I am not that heartless."

There was silence on the phone. He wondered if his sister was about to argue that he was, in fact, just such a sorry bag of shit. Instead, he heard a weak "thank you."

He continued. "It should not be hard to get a flight to Chicago in the morning. Oh, and I will be bringing Karen Fisher with me. She can use the guest room at the place I assume."

"Oh, for Pete's sake, not one of your tramps. And to think, for a moment I was inching toward a kind thought about you."

"Just shush, for Christ sake." He cut her off, sensing she was revving up for a full blast. "Karen is my right-hand here. I still have all these people around the world. I can't be totally out of touch and I think this could get ugly for us all, and maybe lengthy."

"Sorry, for a moment I forgot you were the great humanitarian."

Chris assumed her comment was ironic but let it pass. He changed direction. "By the way, how is Kat dealing with this."

"Our little sister is losing it. I cannot get her to stop crying. She is too delicate which, in this family, is not a positive."

"I am not surprised. When God distributed goodies among us kids, he gave Kat a healthy dose of sensitivity, you got all the talent in the world, me an overdose of charm and bullshit, and Chuck . . . I don't know what He gave Chuck."

"An extra shot of guilt I think and . . . the soul of an artist," Kay whispered.

"Yeah," he sighed, "you just may be right. Listen, I have a lot to do. See you soon." He paused a moment, "Oh Kay, still there?"

"Yeah."

"Love you, kiddo." He immediately regretted the expression of affection. Why had he done that?

Another pause on her end as she absorbed his sentimentality. He doubted she would respond in kind. *She was stubborn, like Father,* he thought. No, not like their father. No one was like him. She was, however, not easy with displays of affection and certainly not weakness. She had a guarded attitude toward the people in her world. It was not hostility or even defensiveness, more like a wariness born of some early hurt that could not be ignored or forgotten. He had let his sister drift away from him after their teen years. It was not a conscious thing, perhaps little more than attending different schools and then living on separate continents.

He suddenly felt alone, a sense of emotional distance that bothered him in that moment. Luxury and privilege had bought them comfort and the best educations and a host of opportunities and experiences that wealth could easily command. There was one thing it could not purchase . . . a sense of family and closeness. He lived in a family of individuals. They limited contact with one another and then danced through the forced interactions as if each conversation or touch would explode into tragedy. Family sessions were painful beyond words. He would inevitably count the minutes until he could escape. After college, he jumped at the excuse the Rhodes scholarship gave him to escape to England. He did not need the free ride, he was plenty wealthy enough. What he desired was the excuse to flee, a cover story for getting away from the pain that was a dysfunctional family. To stay in the States just might invite a closer look at matters best left hidden and beyond reach. To stay would expose him to the relentless push of his father to become a part of his world, a world that Chris had come to despise.

He was about to break the silence when she spared him the need. "Yeah, you are a disappointment but I could do worse." He knew this was the best he would get.

————

Several hours later, Karen Fisher's familiar car pulled up in front of his place. She had become accustomed to chauffeuring him around in the eight months she had been his assistant. Since her job duties were vague at best, she simply assumed it was a requirement of the position. In truth, she could not recall seeing a job description. She was "the assistant," whatever that entailed. A lot of that involved listening to him talk through issues and problems, serving as a sounding board, straightening him out when he ventured off the reservation, and most importantly deflating his ego when needed. She loved it. Some mornings she would pinch herself at her fortune in falling into a professional situation so exciting and, frankly, unstructured. Everything was unpredictable and stimulating. Her working-class family prized predictability, a steady paycheck, Guinness and some chips at the local pub, and a pension when one's labors were finished. She hated that world, and Chris had offered her a legitimate escape. She was grateful. Above all, she respected him and loved their repartee. He was quick, irreverent, and took no prisoners. Sometimes, she would forget that he was not a Brit.

He had been in England long enough to master the intricacies of driving on the wrong side of the road. Navigating the roads was one thing he decided to minimize in his life, particularly in the big city of London. He had one of those active minds, particularly when operating in work mode. He was responsible for projects in some of the most sensitive areas of the world. It struck him as wise to focus on preserving life as opposed to placing it at risk through inattentive driving. It was merely prudent, he argued to himself. Why risk finding a solution to world poverty because one was distracted by the random movements of pedestrians. He would delegate the onerous task of negotiating the London area's traffic to others. Most of the time, the task fell to Karen.

"I think I got everything you need," she said as he slid into the passenger seat next to her.

"The Afghan files? That is what I will need most of all."

"Of course, I know that's what has been consuming you of late." She was slightly irritated that he would even think that she might forget something that important to him. "And I have the reports from Eritrea, the Sudan, Liberia, and the Jordanian and Pakistani refugee camps. You can review them on the plane, we have first class tickets, all that was left on the first available flight. Hope you don't mind the extra cost."

"Not in the least. I will need the comfort. You keep forgetting, I am a child of privilege. You, on the other hand, are a product of the lower classes . . . the rabble." Chris looked at her with admiration. What would he do without her. She was the perfect woman—cutting him little slack, always keeping him honest, but somehow seeing the positive as he managed to foul up his life time after time. She managed him with ruthless efficiency and yet, in her own way, loved him at the same time.

Karen could sense he was looking at her. "Okay, one question," she said, "why take me? This is a family crisis, right? Couldn't I be more help at the office?"

"Oh, staff can handle things on that end and we can stay in touch. I just need you for support. Besides, you should see the windy city and, let me tell you, this is not going to be a fun trip."

She smiled just a fraction. "Can't stand your family? Yeah, I know how that feels."

He decided to deflect away from where she was headed. "Speaking of family. Is Alicia pissed at me dragging you off on another trip?"

"Let me put it this way, she desperately loathes you."

"But I am so charming." He protested lightly "How could she?"

"My dear," she mocked, "that only works with silly straight girls."

"Tell her I am sorry," he murmured, "but she will have to get in the 'hate Chris' queue with all the other women. The big challenge, though, is to find the end of that line. I admit, it's rather lengthy. But I do want to apologize, anything I can do to help mend fences."

It was still dark with a hint of light in the east as Karen deftly left the M system and headed toward Heathrow. "In truth, you may be doing me a favor. I think Alicia and I have been experiencing what you might call a rough patch as they say. I would not be surprised if she were gone when I return. In any case, this may bring the issue to a head, one way or the other."

"Shit," Chris exhaled, "I can't ask this of you. Really, I . . ."

"Hey," she cut in, "I'm a big girl. You know I would have bailed on this trip if I wanted."

"But . . ." he tried.

"But nothing." She slid her left hand over and squeezed his. "You keep forgetting, I am the boss in this relationship. This is a good thing, really. She and I need a bit of space to decompress if nothing else. Truth is, lately we have been fighting like cats and dogs."

"You actually fight? I am shocked, shocked." Chris smiled broadly. "Remember when you interviewed for the position. I do. There was nothing special about your background. Frankly, I was going through the motions during your interview when I threw out some hypothetical that involved how you would react if you saw me making a big mistake in a meeting. Without missing a beat, you said that you would ask me to accompany you out of the meeting room where you would proceed to kick me in the balls and bring me to my knees. Now having my attention, you would calmly explain what a fucking nimrod I was and instruct me regarding what I would do when we returned to the meeting. I decided to hire you at that moment."

"I have a confession," she hesitated but realized the die was cast, "I really wanted the job but had concluded there would be others with better paper qualifications. I figured I had to do something smashing to get your attention. The thing is, I wanted to work for you or at least for what you were trying to do. I came across your work in my last year at Durham. Well, you gave a talk at the university where you explained about the need for collaborative, cross systems efforts to really help vulnerable populations, the most desperate refugees, and those forgotten by the world. I was hooked when you used that silly metaphor about the five doctors, all specialists, treated the patient very successfully from their own perspectives. Then the patient died since no one paid attention to a fifth and fatal ailment. No matter how smart you were, you had to possess a special gift of seeing the whole. As you always say, you must see the big picture or risk not seeing anything at all. I hate to admit this, but you reached me on an intellectual and emotional level. I tried to talk to you after but there were too many people and I was shy . . ."

"Shy," he laughed. "You? You probably would have given Vlad the Impaler a good run for his money."

"I was young and naïve," she said as she pulled her hand away from his. "I have it together now." With that her now free left arm arced to place a well-aimed blow to his stomach.

"Well," he exclaimed breathlessly, "at least you didn't aim for the family jewels."

"You just wait until we get out of the car."

———

Karen awoke from a nap on the plane to find her boss perusing a report and making notes. "Where are we?" she asked.

"Oh, thirty-five thousand feet over the Atlantic Ocean somewhere. You weren't asleep that long. We have quite a way to go yet. I probably should catch a few winks myself but can't seem to shut down."

Karen looked at him closely as he focused on his papers. His features were proportional set in a strong face touched with a hint of sensitivity, even delicacy, in his otherwise rugged good looks. No wonder the girls swooned. His thick brown hair casually cascaded just over his ears and down the back of his neck suggesting a residual reluctance to embrace the corporate and philanthropic worlds in which he often found himself. She found him a bit of an enigma. Upon hearing his talk at Durham University on the east coast of England, she was smitten with his vision. She did not care about his casual sensuality that most women found seductive. Her sensual tastes, in fact, ran to women as did his. They both appreciated this convenient fact since it took the sexual tension issue off the table as they worked long hours together.

What had Chris excited in her? She pondered that conundrum for a moment. It was a desire to make a difference in the world. She wanted to do more than make a little money for the ordinary comforts life might provide. That desire to do good in the world had always been within her. She had come out of a working-class neighborhood in Birmingham, one of the midlands industrial cities. She saw struggle firsthand as the coal industry faltered in the face of environmental concerns and cheaper energy alternatives. She, however, was smart and ambitious, clawing her way to university on scholarships and grit. As she came toward the end of her studies, she was adrift. What would she do next? Then Christopher Crawford, a handsome

American with an easy and charming smile who had come to England as a Rhodes scholar, was scheduled to speak on making a difference in a troubled world. She was intrigued by the come-on in the marketing of the event. "What can ordinary men and women do to make the world a better place to live?"

She almost skipped it. Really, what could this guy say that would make a difference in her life, never mind the world. She had already embraced the cynical posture of her newly adopted culture, the educated elite. When she researched his background, her priors were affirmed. It turned out he was from a wealthy family, a rich kid with a trust fund. No spoiled shit could tell her about suffering, she was very suspicious.

At the last minute she went, mostly because her roommate thought he was dreamy looking. Almost immediately, his low-key humor and gentle self-deprecation melted her initial resistance. She saw no signs of inherent privilege or assumed entitlement. Rather, she saw a sense of commitment that was not self-conscious. He seemed naturally proportioned in his bearing and personality and, most of all, authentic. He talked at length about the fact that competitiveness and compassion were not competing ends. On the contrary, they defined a complete man and a coherent society. You needed the proper economic incentives to motivate growth and productivity. Yet, excessive capitalistic freedom, unmoored from broader societal needs, led inevitably to inequality, suffering, and a counterproductive reduction in the demand for goods and services. A little bit of greed can be good but unrestrictive greed is a disaster. He explained how we need to draw upon the successes of our capitalist machine to reach out to those struggling on the other end of the success continuum.

What really captured her was that his opinions did not appear to be clichés borrowed from radical tracts or reworked truisms from classroom lectures. He talked from personal experiences that only someone who had lived in a world of wealth and power might know. He talked about meeting Charles Koch, Richard Mellon Schaife, Sheldon Adelson, Michael Bradley, the Mercers and many others whose names she could not retain. These were economic players who were working diligently to concentrate wealth and power in the hands of the few, more specifically their own hands. They had been part of his world growing up. Finally, he explained how he had used such connections to capture resources that might offset just a little of the damage such men did by reaching out to those forgotten or exploited by the oligarchy. She was hooked. She knew what she wanted to do with her life.

Presently, he seemed to be unaware that she was staring at him, as if he were lost in his work. But something told her that was not the case. She had gotten quite competent at sensing what was going on in his head. His eyes were still on the report, but his mind had wandered elsewhere. She wanted to break in but hesitated. Why her reticence, she was wondering, when he turned to her. She jumped a fraction in her seat.

"Did you email Vicky? She would be in my personal calendar and Joseph would miss it."

"What, you now think I am your pimp?" She tried to look disgusted.

"Someone has to be, it certainly won't be me."

"Solve one mystery for me, will you." She turned her body to face him. "How can a guy with such a visionary perspective on society be such a first-class shit when it comes to real people . . . or should I say real women."

"Not such a mystery." His face betrayed no humor. "I love people in the abstract. They tend to be a bit less attractive up close and personal. Everything, I suspect, is better at a distance."

She wagged a finger at him. "You, sir, are a first-class prick. But I am gratified by the thought that you will grow old and bitter with no one to take care of you. Your dick will have fallen off from overuse and no decent woman will put up with your crap, not even though you are rich as Croesus. And, let me be clear on one point, you deal with your own bimbos. Don't look for me to bail you out."

"Come on, Karen, please." He gave her his puppy dog look. She knew it was insincere but it never failed to make her laugh. He was a charmer.

"Shit," she relented, "I emailed her in the terminal before we left, and I went into your server to make it look like it came from you."

"You are a sweetheart, I knew I could count on you." He did, in fact, look relieved.

"You think?" she responded with a mischievous look. "Maybe I didn't come up with a great excuse, do you think she will fall for the one about you needing to wash your dog, the dog you don't have. I think not. She responded with a fond wish that your penis shrivel even more and fall off and that your testicles dry up to the size of raisins. Hah! I am beginning to think this is a universal wish among all women."

"Wait, what is that?" He was losing her drift as his mind wandered elsewhere.

"Oh, the way you use your penis, all females in the Western world now share the same wish . . . that it will fall off one of these days."

He threw his head back and laughed. "Thanks, I needed that image assuming of course, it falls off from good use as God intended. But, you know, women will still love me to pieces. I am irresistible."

"How in God's name do you figure that."

"I am rich and, despite what you claim about women not giving a damn, they do! Wealth never goes out of style with the distaff side." He laughed as Karen resented the fact that his dimples were too cute when a smile crossed his face.

"Damn! You are lucky there are witnesses all around."

———

They sat in silence for quite a while. She wondered if he were about to sleep but decided to break into his personal space in any case. "Tell me about your brother. Only if you want to, really. It is not my place of course, but . . ."

"Wow," he opened his eyes to look at her. "I did not know you had a sensitive side."

"Careful there, buddy." She could see that his countenance had a darker look and wished she had not gone there. "Sorry, forget I asked. Not my place."

He said nothing for a while, long enough for her to close her eyes for a nap. "No, Karen, I think I want to talk about it, if you're still willing. I didn't waken you, did I?"

"No, please continue. Hell, I almost became a social worker."

He smiled. "No freaking way, you could never be a social worker."

"Why not?" She protested.

"I thought you needed to be nice to people to be one of those. I personally think Jack the Ripper is somewhere in your family tree."

"Ha-ha! You really think you are bloody hilarious."

"That is my contribution to the world. I leave them laughing wherever I go."

"That is only because you are a bloody joke." She thought of some other comebacks, she loved sparring with him. She chose to remain silent at this moment, hoping he might open a bit about himself.

He thought back to her university transcripts which he had reviewed in advance of her job interview. She was all over the place. There were some social work courses but guessing her vocational path from her course of study would not be a simple matter. She struck him as the quintessential eager mind searching to command all knowledge and disciplines. A huge world had opened to her and she wanted to absorb it all. He had liked that about her. It reminded him of his own restless mind. "I guess I never discussed my family with you, have I?"

"No. Nothing. You know, that hurt me a bit. For the life of me, though, I cannot figure out why I care so much." Her voice quavered a fraction which annoyed her no end. "I told you all about my sorry background as we made all those trips. But you gave me nothing back. I concluded you didn't think me worthy of that . . . trust. You know, I concluded that you were just one of those self-absorbed rich kids, except for the part about saving the world."

Chris winced. Maybe she was right. Hell, she was right. He was rather a self-absorbed prick. He knew that but you are what you are, as he often told himself. "I . . . I guess I really don't know why I have held back. I . . . I . . . have trouble getting it out."

"Oh, for Christ's sake, you open your mouth and say the words. Babies can do it." Now her voice audibly quavered. Where was this coming from? she wondered. She was tougher than that. Why would she need his approval for anything? "Sorry, that was uncalled for."

He leaned back in his seat, eyes closed. Just for a moment, she thought he was going to ignore her. "Karen, this is not easy even for a glib son of a bitch like me." Another pause as he struggled for where to begin. "You may not believe this but I am closer to you than my own siblings, even my twin sister."

"Bullshit . . ."

"Just listen, goddamn it." It came out too loud, rushed, others around them glanced over in their direction. He forced himself to soften his voice. "Please, let me get this out. From the outside I am a golden boy. All is perfect . . . rich parents, penthouse suite on the miracle mile, prep school, Princeton where I played basketball, and played damn well I might add, and then Oxford. All the best and accomplished with the effortlessness of gods."

"I bet it was not all that easy," she murmured and regretted interrupting.

He did not seem to hear her but still responded to her doubt. "In some ways, it was. But there is always the unseen story. The truth always is beneath the surface. Real life is like the proverbial iceberg. What you see is often quite lovely and not very threatening. What you don't see can sink the unsinkable. I have often seen my life like that, glittering ice on top for all to see but dangerous stuff just out of sight." He paused again. She could see his struggle, so she waited. "You will have the debatable pleasure of meeting my father . . . Charles Ashley Crawford Sr., not his real name. He was born Karol Chrezsinski in Poland right before the Germans invaded. His dad was a foreign diplomat in the Polish government, assigned to England, who got his family out in time. With a half-Jewish wife, herself from a wealthy family, returning to Poland was impossible and he surmised that the Nazis would add England to their list of conquests. During the war, the father became a leader of the Polish government in exile. Of course, the two despots who wished to carve up that hopeless country hated the government in exile."

Chris looked up at the ceiling as if trying to sort something out. "My father was forged in the atrocities visited upon his family during this period. He could easily have become a visceral enemy of both communism and fascism but the former earned his peculiar ire. Maybe it was the massacres of Polish army officers and others of that country's elite by Stalin's goons in 1940, right after he and Hitler divided up the country between them. Night after night, some 250 were dragged from their prison cells and summarily executed. All told, some 22,000 were killed and buried in a forest called Katyn, near Smolensk. The rape of Poland and killing of more of the Polish elite after the war by the Reds cemented any hate my father would develop toward Russia and the communists.

"The Germans were no better, of course. Their barbarity toward the Polish aristocracy back in the families' home country made an indelible impression on him and my grandfather could easily see the future of all the Jews they captured. When my dad's much older sister was an unlucky victim of the blitz in September of 1940, that proved the final straw. My grandfather pulled out all the stops and all his diplomatic contacts to get them to America. And the family were received as respected refugees, they had lost the family fortune and sense of inherited privilege. They never looked back at their doomed homeland, especially as things played out at the end of the war."

Karen seemed impressed. "So, your father was a self-made man, impressive."

Chris looked at the ceiling of the plane. "Better than that, he did it without his own father. The sorry history of this period, I fear, had a profound effect on my father, at least the way things were communicated to him by my grandmother. You see, Stalin was hell bent on crushing an independent Poland. You lose over twenty-five million people in a war and you want some security that it won't happen again. More than anything, he wanted a friendly buffer between Russia and Germany. I guess I can't blame him, the Commies took the biggest hit in World War II. Can you wrap your head around that, over twenty-five million?

Hell, the losses by Britain and the U.S., soldiers and civilians, came to less than one million. You have to remember that Stalin was pissed at the West, he was convinced that they delayed the second front so that the Nazis could bleed Russia dry."

Chris took a sip of a drink and kept going. "At the same time, England had declared war on Germany for the express purpose of keeping Poland free and independent. The thought of that country becoming a Soviet puppet state did not sit well with Churchill. But he was no match for Stalin. When the Red Army approached Warsaw late in the war, Stalin encouraged the Polish resistance to rebel, suggesting that his army would soon be there. The Polish freedom fighters rose up and Stalin kept his army outside of the city. He let the Germans kill off the Polish fighters before moving in since they would have opposed a Soviet takeover. No one should have been surprised by his brutality. Even the English screwed the poor Polish freedom fighters. They fought bravely for the Brits in Italy, especially around Monte Cassino, and Churchill promised them a democratic Poland after the war. It was not to be, Stalin had the divisions and the West was not ready for another war."

"Damn, you should be a college professor. This is fascinating."

"You forget that I do teach courses at Oxford."

"Yeah, but I never thought you might be good at it." She smiled.

"Funny girl, but I will still give you a nice reference for your next job."

"I am a bit lost, what happened to your grandfather?" Karen inquired.

"From my father's perspective, the worst is yet to come. At the end of the war, Stalin invited members of the Polish government back home. This was the government that the West recognized as legitimate. The purpose of the confab presumably involved negotiating the future of Poland. Stalin promised free elections and an independent Poland. The fools believed him though my grandfather hedged his bets by leaving his family in America. How could they have been so naïve, this tyrant had killed his own revolutionary friends, he was not going to honor promises to some goddamn Poles. When they gathered for lunch and discussions in Moscow, they were arrested and thrown in prison. Along with the rest, my grandfather was tortured and executed by Uncle Joe. This bit of family history explains a lot about my father, not all, perhaps, but a lot."

"Wow," was all Karen could get out.

He took a deep breath. "I guess I recount all this ancient history since it might explain my dad. He grew up with stories of social position and treasure lost. It gave him a mission in life, to become rich and thus powerful. He was driven by what he saw as a rightful place in life that had been unfairly stolen. It turned him bitter. But he inherited other things from this horrific period in history. He absorbed a life lesson that dominated his life. The weak and the naïve perish. The English and French promised to defend Poland but could do nothing when the time came. For my father, just becoming aware of things, the lessons he took away were to trust no one. Only the strong survive. Be aggressive and brook no weakness." Chris smiled but there was no humor in it. "As soon as he could, Father changed his name to Crawford and focused on making money. He would never be weak. One key step was seeking out an Irish lass who was to inherit a fortune of her own, Mary Kelly. She was the only child of a successful entrepreneur. I think she saw in my father a replica of her own father. What she got was someone who wanted her as a handy ATM. Mary's own dad, however, could spot another charlatan and set up a good portion of his daughter's bequest in such a way that Charles, my dear dad, could not get his hands on a lot of it. The bulk went directly to derelicts like me. Pissed Dad off no end but only motivated him even more, he was overwhelmed by demons only he could see. The losers in the face of his obsession to accumulate wealth and power were my sweet mother and us kids."

Karen wanted to say something but all that came out was, "Sorry."

"Nah," he went on, "part of me hates the fact that I whine about this. That is why I never mention it. When I was growing up, even I knew that crack babies had no chance for normality, that kids were being born every day who would be crippled by the time they turn four years old, their brains warped by neglect or outright stress and abuse. We had every opportunity that money could purchase except love and understanding. My mother tried to give us just a little bit of that but was too crippled herself. She was trapped within her own glass menagerie of gilded expectations and a totally loveless marriage. Charles, her wonderful husband, always made sure she would never be permitted to forget that she slipped much of her own fortune to her kids. She slowly started killing herself with alcohol and pills."

"Is she dead?" Karen asked, surprised she did not know this basic fact.

"Not yet, not technically, but inside she is. Listen, you don't want to hear this whiney crap."

Karen reached out and grabbed his hand. "Please, I do. Please."

He searched her face. Satisfied, he continued. "There are four of us. The oldest is Junior, Chuck as we call him, the one who is trying to off himself. My sister and I came next. Then Kat followed some seven years later. That seemed an unplanned pregnancy. I thought they had ceased having sex by then. Of the four of us, only my twin sister is normal. She blocked everything out and became a doctor. Dad was proud of that. He was all set to make sure she had a lucrative practice where she could bilk the well-off catering to imagined ailments. But she screwed him over by becoming an ER doctor in a Chicago public hospital. Do you have any idea what she faces on each shift? Want to save lives, that is the place to be, every night the detritus of society come in with gun and knife wounds along with accidents and those seeking basic medical care because they have no goddamn insurance. At first, I didn't understand myself. I thought she was doing it to piss off Dad. But slowly, slowly, I realized she loved it. This is what she wanted."

"Are the two of you close?" Karen had not let his hand go.

"We were, as kids. We both were precocious and loved to share books, though she was more into science. Dad tried to foist Ayn Rand on us at an early age, and books by Milton Friedman and Bill Buckley and Hayek and other right-wing advocates for capitalism. My sister and I would read passages of the *The Fountainhead* to one another and laugh hysterically. Talk about barbaric Social Darwinism. But we drifted apart by college. I went to Princeton on a basketball scholarship of all things, she to Stanford. We were a country apart. The first part of my trust fund had not kicked in yet and I didn't want Dad footing the bill. It would have been pocket change for him. Still, he would surely use this help to force me into studying business or economics."

"What did you study there?"

"History and international affairs and girls." He smiled. "That, and the physical distance between us, might explain why Kay and I drifted apart. She was so focused on her studies, which involved real courses with equations and science. I, on the other hand, remained a dilettante but I still did pretty well."

"I hate to say this, but that's because you are so brilliant. Hell, they don't give out Rhodes scholarships as prizes in cereal boxes." Karen was serious.

"Oh that!" He scoffed. "They thought I was another Bill Bradley."

"Who?"

"Sorry, that was an obtuse reference for an ignorant Brit. Bill was a great Princeton basketball player in the 1960s, and a Rhodes scholar, and then a successful professional basketball star before becoming a U.S. Senator."

Karen smiled, "So, there is hope for you. Perhaps you still can turn your life around yet."

"Ha-ha! I ain't no Bill Bradley, not even close. But seriously, I feel bad about Kay and I . . . I wish we had . . ." then he stopped.

"Maybe you can use this . . . this family crisis to put things right." Karen stopped, perhaps she had gone too far.

"Well, one can always hope." Then he sharply segued away to another topic. "Kat is my big concern. She is young and aimless. She drifted through college but has never developed any direction of her own. Kay and I were gone when she needed help. Dad has her working in one of his businesses but . . . the problem is that if Chuck goes, he will turn to her to fill the gap."

"Gap? I don't understand."

Chris turned slightly to face her. "Here is the thing. Dad wanted an heir to the business empire he built, someone with the Crawford name. Power, it turns out, is his life's passion. Chuck was it, which was great for the rest of us. He was disappointed in me for sure but could ignore my stubborn independence as long as he had Chuck to fill the expected role. What Dad never saw was that Chuck was not him. It was so obvious to the rest of us, but he had a blind spot regarding his eldest. He refused to look. The one thing they had in common was that name. My brother was smart enough but had no fire for business or making money. I think he accepted from an early age that he had been designated as the next family patriarch. Dad never even considered what Chuck might want, nor what he was capable of. He smothered him, totally. He groomed him, had him around the office all the time. When Chuck talked about going to the Rhode Island School of Design, Father exploded. No, the University of Chicago is where he would go, study economics and business, shadow my dad around the office. If he went East, he might just escape Father's control. That could not be permitted. His path was laid out, the leash held tight. Chuck's life trajectory had been set."

"I sense a big but coming," said Karen.

"No shit, Sherlock. Chuck struggled through school and followed Dad around like a pet dog. He married a blond who would serve as an adequate trophy wife. That is not fair. She is blond but I really do not know her. In any case, Father approved of her and she seems to love Chuck in her limited way. But the big tragedy is that my brother was going through the motions. He was a sweet kid, loved the arts, might have pursued an avocation in that field if given a chance. With his aptitudes and connections, he might well be a very content museum curator somewhere. Who knows, perhaps he might have created art of his own. He did paint, in secret, where Father could not discover his passion and lash out at him. He managed to escape Father for a while one summer. He visited me at Oxford, during my student days, when I always found an excuse not to go home. Chuck blossomed, painted, visited museums. He felt life for that small moment in his miserable existence."

"And then?"

"And then, he went back. It wasn't the first time I begged him to stay with me. But he could not defy Father and keeps paying the price."

"Which is?" Karen asked gently, knowing the answer.

"He periodically sinks into depressions and, my best guess, the same Irish curse as our mom."

"Addiction?"

"He tried to hide it but that is my guess. Kay sees him more. Mother uses the same escape from the pain. I am totally sure of one thing—whatever overdose he took was no mistake. It was his exit plan. And one other thing."

"What?" Karen murmured.

"If Chuck does not make it, Father will be looking for a replacement in the family. He won't let it go, it is just not him. He is an obsessive man. It brought him great wealth and power. But it has made him an unbearable man to live with. Beware of a man with an obsessive passion."

"I see, you mean a man like you," she whispered.

"Me? Passionate? Well, maybe about women."

"Tell me," she was totally serious now, "in your head, what is your passion?"

He paused, thinking about that. "I have no fucking idea. I guess I . . . prefer to think that I have vision." Then he let out a big sigh. "I despise that man and what he stands for. I suppose you can say that is my kind of obsessive passion."

Karen squeezed his hand hard and then let it go. She laid back in her seat as did he, they were both exhausted. "Chris?"

"What," he responded with a voice already fogged with the anticipation of sleep.

"I am here for you."

Now he reached over and squeezed her hand.

CHAPTER 2

CHICAGO (2000)

"Good decision." Kristen Crawford, universally known as Kay, kissed her brother on the cheek and gave him a perfunctory embrace.

"What?" Chris responded.

"To stay at a hotel rather than Father's place. I doubt your sanity would survive two hours there. And I take it this is the woman who tries to keep you in line." Kay held out her hand to Karen. "You have my sympathy, that must be an impossible task."

"True enough, but at least I am seldom bored. Very glad to meet you at last. Chris has told me so much about you." Karen wondered why she chose to lie, he had said very little about his family until the flight over.

"Hah! When we have a chance, I will set the record straight. Contrary to what he tells everyone, I haven't castrated any men in months."

"Well, let's just say I only believe half the crap he tries to sell." Karen's unease at meeting Chris's family was beginning to evaporate. She just might like this woman.

Then Kay added, "If this drama drags out, you are welcome to use my place as a base of operations. Karen is welcome for free, you Chris get my usual rate of twice what I charge friends."

"Ha-ha! Enough bonding." Chris broke in and led the group over to some unoccupied chairs in the hotel lobby. "I see I will have to keep the two of you apart."

Kay suddenly became serious. "To business, we probably should head over soon but let me update you on his situation. I exercised a little medical privilege and looked over Chuck's early test results. They are not saying anything official, but I am not optimistic."

"How much not optimistic?" Chris frowned at his fractured syntax. He felt a sudden emptiness in his stomach.

"Again, incomplete results so far but not more than a ten percent chance he will pull out of this and that I fear is based more on hope than evidence. He almost succeeded in his quest for immortality. This was not a call for help, our poor brother really wanted out. He did this at his home. However, Grace found him just in time."

"Grace is the live-in help for Beverly and Chuck," Chris murmured to Karen.

Kay continued, "Chuck planned this somewhat carefully. He hoarded pills for quite a while. Then he waited until Beverly had a bunch of charitable events to keep her out of the house and then he sent Grace away on several errands. Unfortunately for him, Grace forgot something and returned unexpectedly to find him unconscious. She got help immediately and a neighbor performed CPR until the medical personnel arrived. He had stopped breathing before they resuscitated him. My professional guess, there has been irreversible brain damage. We won't see

Chuck again, not the real Chuck. I have seen enough cases like this in the ER. Of course, anything is possible, but . . ."

Karen observed them as they continued to talk. She was struck by the lack of emotion. This was their brother and yet so little feeling. *How strange*, she thought. And how different these biological twins seemed to her. Kay was a standard beauty, statuesque and finely proportioned. Medium length, professionally coiffed brown hair, framed facial features that were wonderfully apportioned, and attractive even without any assistance from commercial makeup. Yet, something kept Karen from thinking of her as lovely as suggested by her physical features. She seemed too stern, emotionless. Was she in her medical role now? Does feeling emerge when she is alone? It was almost as if she were reluctant to be as open and transparent as others were. That would be beneath her or perhaps leave her vulnerable.

"Fuck," she heard Chris say and snapped to attention. The expletive, however, had nothing to do with her. "Dad won't let go. Chuck was his only hope. He will be firing doctors and hiring new ones in the hope of some miracle. You know him as well as I, better now I suppose."

Kay let out a grim chuckle. "You mean now that I returned to Chicago while you ran off to Princeton and Oxford, never to return."

"Hey," he retorted, "how many times did I tell you to get out of Dodge."

"And leave Kat and Chuck to Father's sadism by themselves, not to mention Mother. Someone had to care about them." Kay's voice was rising. A slight flush suffused across her face.

"Not the martyr card, Kay. For Christ's sake, not the martyr card."

"Hey, guys," Karen stood up, "what in bloody hell are you doing? Your brother is fucking dying and you two are squabbling like spoiled kids. Get it together, okay!"

Kay and Chuck turned on Karen who now wished for a convenient place to hide. "Chris, I am glad you brought her. Now I see why that foundation, or whatever it is, of yours is so successful. I just knew it couldn't be you."

Chris broke into his standard smile. "No one is fooled that I have anything to do with our success. But the thing works for me, it is a great front for scoring with women."

"Pervert," Kay and Karen said simultaneously while laughing at one another.

"I really do like her, Chris, you should just have delegated this visit to her. Then I would not have to put up with your sorry ass."

The two siblings rose to join Karen and the three walked out onto Michigan Avenue. Northwestern Medical was a short distance away but no one seemed in a hurry to get there. Karen was still puzzled by the seeming lack of real feeling for their older brother. Besides, it was a sunny, spring day. Everything around them seemed fresh and alive as they walked with reluctance toward death and despair.

"Even if the evidence is overwhelming, will Dad let go? Will he even give Mom a vote? Wow, you are right, I have been away too long. I hardly know them anymore."

"Listen, Chris, Father is only concerned about one thing—keeping his empire in the family. He will hang on to Chuck if he can. When that fails, he will go down the line. You, my boy, are the heir apparent, next in line for the throne."

"Me? Don't be absurd. I avoided business school and his empire like the plague. Why would he even consider me as a candidate?"

"My god," Kay blurted out, "after all this time you still don't get it. It is not about what you want or what you are capable of. He doesn't give a shit about any of that. He will expect you to shape up and play your expected role. The only reason he gave you a free ride so far is that he had Chuck. I mean, he was terribly disgusted with your choices which, in his mind, were totally misguided and a waste of talent. He was connected to reality just enough to see that you were smart as hell but undoubtedly deluded by Commies or someone beyond his control. But now, sweet brother, he will be coming after you if he smells any weakness on your part."

"And if I don't bite."

Kay stopped and turned to her brother. "Then, he will come after me and, when that fails he will go after Kat. Girls don't count as much but they still are in the clan. Kat, unfortunately, will be helpless."

"Well, let us strap them on," Chris intoned. "The battle begins."

———

"Christopher, good of you to make it." Charles Crawford held out a manicured hand to his son.

"Good to see you, Father, though I wish the circumstances were better."

"We can be honest here, death is about the only occasion that would possibly bring this family together."

Chris bit his lip and went to hug his mother, younger sister, and sister-in-law. It was obvious they had been crying until the tear ducts had dried out though the sincerity of Beverly's tears, his sister-in-law, was not apparent to him. "Why even go there?" he wondered. Then Chris turned and introduced Karen. The women acknowledged her while his father ignored her completely. Apparently, she was not important enough for him to acknowledge. Chris again bit his lip.

Chris went to his brother's side. He was ashen, his body connected to numerous tubes that sustained the appearance of life. A monitor beeped rhythmically next to the bed indicating that some attachment to this world remained. As Chris looked down on his brother, he could not avoid a sense of deep sadness that lined Chuck's face. It seemed as if the agony of life found expression even in his deep coma. He thought he could intuit the core sentiments embedded in Chuck's heart. *Let me go. Why are you so cruel? For god's sake, let me escape!* For a moment, he wanted to rip all the tubes out of this comatose body. He had suffered enough. Let him go, goddamn it, just let him the fuck go.

Chuck never struck Chris as a candidate for the role of heir to the family throne. He had always been delicate, even a bit effeminate. Though younger, Chris was the natural athlete and leader. Chuck would take his younger sibling to play ball with friends. Initially, the older crowd would snicker at the younger brother, not wanting to get stuck with him on their team. Soon, they realized their misjudgment as they saw this skinny and tallish kid dart and whirl around the basketball court, stopping on a dime to discharge a soft and accurate jump shot or accelerating to the basket to lay the ball in with either hand. After leaving a few defenders flat footed, he immediately became the one they all wanted on their side. Chuck looked on with bewilderment, if not jealousy.

Chris looked down on the immobile body, silent and incapable of sentient response. Whatever they say is the cause, Chris was sure it was no accident. This was his brother's desperate attempt to escape a personal hell. He was certain of that. After all this time, he wanted out. Chris remembered one evening so well. He had spent some time in Chicago after graduating from Princeton and before heading off to Oxford. In his heart, Chris knew that he might be leaving for good, he was moved to connect with his siblings one last time. Chuck asked him to head down to Navy Pier, an attractive tourist destination that jutted out into Lake Michigan. Chris knew that Chuck would want to ride the Ferris wheel that gave them a view of the city at the top. This, oddly enough, gave his brother some peace . . . looking out at the threatening city from a distance. Chuck found it preferable to seeing the grimy reality up close.

"You must understand," Chuck sighed.

"Understand what?" though Chris was certain he knew.

"He is killing me."

"You mean Dad," though Chris realized there could be no one else.

But Chuck did not answer. He walked to a railing and looked out over the lake. The sky was brooding and cloudy though the crowds were still strong, as they tended to be on most summer days. "Do you know why I like to come here?" Chuck then continued without waiting for a response. "I like the crowds, the anonymity, the happiness around me. It is a place where I can get away from . . ."

"Chuck, come with me to England. Just come with me. Get away from him."

Chuck did not seem to hear him, going in his own direction. "I also like museums but I guess for a very different reason. They are places of beauty and quiet. You can lose yourself in such places, imagine you are in the French countryside surrounded by color and beauty or the Left Bank of Paris where stimulating people discuss topics of importance."

"Chuck, listen for Christ's sake, come with me. You could have access to all the museums of Europe."

"Do you know who I spend my time with these days?" Again, it was rhetorical. "Dad forces me to spend my days with insufferable boors who are infatuated with mammon. That is all they talk about, how much they have, what they spend it on, and how to get more of the damn stuff. For God's sake, they have more than they can possibly use. Why do they want more? You know what I realized? These people are stupid and narrow beyond belief, Chris."

Chris wondered why it took so long for his brother to get this obvious lesson. He decided to stay on point. "Chuck, England . . . escape . . . your life . . . you must come with me."

Suddenly, Chuck looked at his brother as if he were surprised he was standing next to him. His voice seemed to come from far away. "Oh, you know I can't do that."

"You can. Listen to me, you are an adult. You need your own life. Come with me now or you will die, believe me, you will wither and die inside." Of course, Chris had meant that his brother would die metaphorically. Now, in this hospital room, he knew that he had been prescient. His sibling did not come with him to England and it had killed him or would as soon as they cut his tether to the machines that simulated life.

Poor Chuck, he went to the University of Chicago, his admission greased with a generous gift from his father. He struggled mightily in his business courses, however. He desperately yearned to focus on the arts but Charles Sr. would have none of that. The heir to the throne would study something practical. He would major in economics at a school known for its conservative leanings and its numerous Nobel laureates from this disciplinary department made famous by free market icon Milton Friedman. It proved a terrible experiment and soon Chuck switched to Loyola where the competition was manageable. There, at least he could pass his courses.

Chris snapped back to reality in the hospital room and leaned over his brother's body. "I am so sorry, Chuck, I failed you. I failed you. I should have dragged you on that plane with me and held on for dear life . . . yours. I killed you that day, just as lethally as whatever crap you ingested." Only Karen was close enough to hear his words clearly. She put her hand out to touch his arm and he realized suddenly that he was, in truth, saying the words aloud.

Chris returned to silent, distant memories. "I can't, I just can't," Chuck had pleaded as they looked over the lake from Navy Pier. "You must understand how it is. Dad won't relent. I am the eldest, I have his name. He will never let me go. Besides, I need to protect you and Kay. If not me, then you are next."

"What?" he had responded in exasperation. "Listen to me. Dad is obsessed. He only knows money, wealth, and power. His world view is warped by values that, frankly, are beyond me. He and his friends are mean, vicious, and totally self-centered. They are fucking sociopaths. He doesn't give a shit about you, about any of us. We are merely tools he can use to perpetuate his control of things."

"No, Chris, you are being unfair."

"Unfair!" Chris had shouted the word loudly enough that the crowd passing them on the pier turned to look. He grabbed his brother by the shoulders. "Unfair," he repeated in a lower voice. "Why do you think Mother risked her husband's wrath by establishing those trusts for us with her own money? She knew what Dad would do, what he tried to do to her. She desperately wanted to protect us from him. She wanted us to have an escape, a way out. She wanted to save all of us."

"It is not about the money." Chuck looked totally despairing at that moment. "You have not been with him very much lately. He has such a passion about the things he believes in. I have never seen such commitment in anyone else. When he talks about his plans, my future, the family's future, his eyes alight with such fervor. He needs me. He . . . he . . . would die if I didn't follow. You can say no to him. I am not strong enough."

Chris looked at him with despair that day on Navy Pier. His brother was somewhere that he could not reach. Chris could only think of the Stockholm syndrome, the prisoners identifying with those that imprison them. At that moment, he wanted to argue that Chuck was totally incapable of being what his father wanted. He wanted to throw his brother's weakness right in his face. He was too soft, and totally unsuited for the business world. His brother was smart enough, if only he had been permitted to follow his own passions. He aced the few arts courses he managed to sneak into his rigorous business and economics curriculum. Those grades managed to keep his GPA high enough to stay in school.

Everyone needs to find their own place though Chuck was assigned to a role on the stage of life for which he was totally unsuited. The play in which he was cast soon would spiral into a tragedy. And Chris knew at that moment he could do little to reverse it. He hugged his brother that day on Navy Pier. It was like sending a loved one off to a war zone from which there was no hope of return. Chris did get to spend a few more weeks with his brother while studying at Oxford but each of those days was a stab to his heart, watching what his brother could be and knowing what would await his return to the States.

He looked down at his comatose brother. What did he feel—anger or pity or perhaps even sadness? No, it was relief.

He was free at last, free at last, free at long last. He leaned over and kissed his older sibling's forehead. Then he turned to the others and looked directly at his father. "Pull the plug."

"What?" his mother, Mary, exhaled.

"No," his younger sister, Kat, protested.

His sister-in-law, Chuck's wife, simply looked away and gazed out the window.

His father stared at him impassively, his lips set in an enigmatic sneer.

His twin sister evidenced her tentative approval with a slight nod.

"Kay, what do you think? As the only medical professional in the room, do you see any hope for Chuck?"

She stammered, looking for the right words, "I . . . I . . . really need more information."

"You think you do, that is the physician in you talking. But what does your gut instinct tell you. What do you anticipate knowing with unavoidable certainty when all the data become available?"

"No, Chris, not yet," Kay's voice sounded uncharacteristically uncertain.

"Nothing is going to change much in a day or two," he said listlessly. "Father will fume and berate the attending doctors, suggesting that perhaps a donation to the hospital fund can buy a goddamn miracle. Mother will work her rosary beads desperately hoping that the Virgin Mary will intercede in some fanciful manner. Sweet Kat will weep herself to the edge of desperation hoping against hope the brother she adores will come back to life. But he won't, I guarantee that."

"You cannot guarantee anything, not a damn thing," the patriarch of the family issued the words through clenched teeth.

"Really, totally certain of things as always, Father. I have seldom met a man so assured of his correctness on all matters great and small, yet so wrong on just about everything. That truly is a remarkable ability. You should be proud. It is rare for any man to be so perfect in any arena of life . . . perfect in being dead wrong."

"Chris, now is not the . . ." Kay did not get a chance to finish.

Charles Sr. cut her off with his imperious tone, still staring at his second son. "Why did you even bother to come? You obviously have no regard for your brother or your other siblings. And we know you have nothing but contempt for me. Why did you not stay hidden from the real world in London or Oxford or wherever you have chosen to avoid responsibility? That is what cowards do, isn't it, run away and hide from the real world the rest of us must confront."

"The real world! That is fucking rich, no pun intended. Your real world is the obsequious worship of wealth and power. What is real about accumulating more and more crap than you can possibly use? What possible benefit accrues from squeezing the life out of desperate working people, selling out their livelihoods from under them since more profit is available from selling off the parts of firms they have dedicated their lives to, the products they have devoted their talents and sweat to make? Have you ever spent a moment being there with them when their homes were foreclosed, when their cars were repossessed, when their children went without medicine so that they could eat?"

"Don't be so fucking dramatic!" His father exploded. "It is called creative destruction. It is the engine that drives growth and progress and makes the real world go around. But you would have no idea about such things. You hid away in your damn artificial world of the academy where pampered elites sit on their asses in their ivory towers criticizing those of us who do the work that matters. But how could you possibly know of such things? You could not be bothered. You played games, hung around with those colored friends doing god knows what . . ."

"Colored friends? Which fucking decade are you living in, Father, the fifties?"

Charles Sr. stepped toward his son but stopped as a nurse rushed into the room. "Please," she chastised them, "this is a hospital, not a bar room. Take this down to the visiting area."

As the group walked down the hall, Karen sidled up next to her boss. "Chris, what the fuck are you doing? I just might have to kick you in the family jewels."

"Where?" Kay asked as she sidled up on the other side of her brother.

"Kick him in his balls. That is my primary responsibility, to kick him in that part of his anatomy to which he is so attached though I do worry about irreversible brain damage. I should add that I only assault him when he is acting like a total nimrod, as he is now. As you can imagine, my leg gets a lot of work."

Kay guffawed, breaking the tension a bit. The rest of the group looked back at the trio, somewhat perplexed at the sudden levity. "Karen, I can see why Chris needs you so. He really is a dolt."

"No shit," Karen responded.

"Point made," Chris said *sotto voce* as they all collected in the visitor's room.

When they settled, Kay took the initiative. She did not want her brother to pick up where he had left off and certainly did not want her father to take command of the situation. "Chris asked me my professional opinion. Okay, this is with the usual caveats since, as you can surmise, I know little about his actual medical condition. Still, I have seen many who have been deprived of brain function for as long as Chuck." She paused, struggling for the correct voice. She decided to treat them as members of a family to which she had no personal connection. "Chuck could regain some capacity to survive on his own, though that outcome is unlikely. The chance that he would return to his former level of activity is probably nil. His brain was effectively deprived of oxygen for too long. The EMTs did a heroic job of reviving him but, in my experience, that can be a very mixed blessing."

"How can you say that, Kristen?" It was Mary Kelley Crawford, the matriarch of the clan. She clung to her rosary beads as tears forced their way down her cheeks. "We cannot give up, it would be a sin. God cannot forgive everything. For as long as life remains, we must hope."

Another pause as she scanned the faces in front of her for clues to where each stood. But she knew the answer without need for explicit feedback. They had all been handed their life scripts early on. "Listen, everyone, I mentioned this to Chris earlier. I know I should let the attending physicians fill you in but I have a pretty good idea of what they will say. There will be a small chance of partial recovery but slim at best. Most likely, Chuck is gone. At best, he would remain in a near vegetative state with minimal reactivity to external stimuli."

"Bullshit," Charles Sr. erupted as Kate jumped a bit. "I am not giving up that quickly. You listen to me very carefully, I never give up. How do you think I created my financial empire, by folding at the first sign of adversity? No, that is not my way. Just remember, there are two kinds of people in this world, those that take what is given and those . . ."

Chris finished the sentence, "That take what they want. We know all the standard bromides, Father."

"Then why in god's name have you ignored them all your life."

"Stop!" Chris shouted. "Let's not go there again. Listen to me. I don't even think that survivability is the issue, not the real issue. What would he do even if he fully recovered. He would try again, and again, and again, until he failed you so spectacularly, Father, then even you would put up a white flag. You cannot control what is not yours. The truth is, Chuck wants to die. It is the only out for him. He cannot disappoint you, Father, not to your face. And he knows he cannot, no matter how hard he tries, be what you expect him to be. That is not Chuck. You cannot will into him what is not there. Not even you, Charles. I hate to be the one to break this to you, but you are not God."

"Nonsense," Charles Sr. sputtered, "he was doing better, he was getting the hang of things."

"Father, just listen." Chris took a deep breath. "I love my brother. He is, was, just about the sweetest guy I know. He also had a lot of talent, just not in that area of life where you imprisoned him . . ."

"I, what?"

"Just fucking listen, okay? Chuck loved literature, poetry, the arts, all things sensitive and beautiful. Permitted to go there, he could have thrived. As I was leaving for the Rhodes scholarship at Oxford, I begged him to come with me. You know what, he could not leave you, Father. He desperately wished to be the son you wanted him to be. Even then, I saw this day, as if it were cast in stone by the gods. It was inevitable, a classic Greek tragedy. He would write often, and more recently, email or call. I could see him in decline, desperately trying to be what you wanted him to be—heir to your empire and lord over your kingdom. But that was not him. He knew he was not pleasing you. With each year his desperation rose, his fear of disappointing you became more palpable . . . he could feel it."

"So could I." It was Beverly, Chuck's wife. "I know you all think I married Chuck for the money, the family position, the lifestyle. And you were right in the beginning. I was fine with being a trophy wife. That was what I was raised to be. But then a funny thing happened. Slowly, I fell in love with him. That shocked me, I never expected it. I had consigned myself to the role of a highly paid whore and guess what, I fell in love with my customer."

"Shut up, Beverly, you are distressed." Charles was on the verge of dismissing her.

"Sir, I will not be silent, no longer. Chris is right. You never knew your son. You never bothered to look at him, talk to him …"

"For Christ's sake, woman, I talked with him every day."

"No, Charles, you ordered him around every day. Every night he would drink himself to sleep. I would wake at 3:00 AM and find him gone. He would be in his personal office crying, crying. It would kill me to see the pain."

Chris walked over to his sister-in-law. He had never taken any time to get to know her. He merely dismissed her as a shallow and self-centered manipulator who had taken advantage of his weak brother. This bothered him, the human tendency to judge quickly based on the most fragile of evidence. People were always surprising him. Still, he never managed to fully embrace the underlying lesson. You had to look deep to understand. He embraced her as the sobs finally flowed from her. He could sense her salty tears on his neck. He heard her say something in words so indistinct he could not quite make them out. "I'm sorry, Beverly. What did you say?"

She pulled away and looked at the family. "Pull the plug."

"No, it is a sin," Mary pleaded.

"Not your decision," Charles asserted with that finality that accompanied all his positions.

"For his sake, pull the goddamn plug," Beverly repeated.

Just then, a doctor entered the room. "I am glad you are all here."

———

"Well, I'll be gobsmacked!" Karen exclaimed as she, Chris, and Kay found seats in a small Italian restaurant just off Michigan Avenue.

"What?" Kay tried to smile.

"It means that she finds our family dynamics utterly amazing and very likely repugnant. Just ignore her," Chris told his sister. "Occasionally, her working class British roots show. I keep trying to beat it out of her but you know those lower-class folk, can't teach them a damn thing."

"Bloody right, Guv," she retorted with an exaggerated Cockney accent. "But really, you guys make my family look like something out of Norman Rockwell. What was with all that? It was not the fighting necessarily. I am used to that. It was something else, as if your brother was merely a prop in a bad Eugene O'Neill play, though I guess he didn't actually write any bad ones."

"Can you explain what you mean, Karen?" Kay asked. "I think we are too close to it."

Karen wished she had remained silent but soldiered on. "I am not sure what else to say. Chuck seemed little more than a reason to dredge up old issues, to fight among yourself. The poor guy was merely an excuse to tear open old wounds, stick the knife in a little deeper."

Chris looked at his sister. "Karen is spot on. Damn, where did 'spot on' come from, been in Britain too long. Anyways, we are a tragedy in three acts and we don't even see it. I am certain the nurses sent that doc in to break us up before violence broke out. All he told us was they knew nothing and to go home, come back tomorrow afternoon when more tests would be available. They would have more to tell us then. He assured us that nothing would happen in the meantime. The whole staff is probably hoping against hope that we are all offed by terrorists before morning and that they won't have to deal with us anymore."

"I watched him closely," Kay said gravely, "I have been in the doc's shoes too many times. He was really telling us that he was not going to break the bad news until tomorrow afternoon when he had more evidence to support what he already knows. He really has all he needs now but they go through the motions of being exhaustive."

"How do you know for sure?" Karen asked.

"I'm a doc, I work in ER. You delay the bad news for as long as you can. You wait for an appropriate time so that you can say with conviction that you did all you could. He probably knew within hours of Chuck being brought in."

They all looked at one another.

"Fuck," Chris exhaled. "No more drama tonight. Let's avoid reality for a while. Tomorrow will be tough enough."

"Agreed," said Kay. "By the way, why did you ask the waiter for a bigger table?"

"Because Ricky and Jules will be joining us." Chris smiled before adding as an aside to Karen. "Old friends of mine from when I was a mere strip of a lad. And here they come now."

A black couple made their way to the table. They wore expressions caught between delight at seeing an old friend and appreciation for the somber reason for the opportunity to catch up. Karen caught her breath. She found the female breathtaking, rather light brown skin, large brown eyes, and dark hair that hung straight down to her shoulders framing a finely-structured face that could easily peer out from a fashion magazine. The male was slightly darker than his sister. Karen knew women would find him handsome and sexy. He moved with the casual grace and assuredness of a natural athlete while wearing a hand-tailored Italian suit. The two of them said power couple. After hugs were exchanged, the expected expressions of concern and sympathy were shared followed by a brief update on the situation.

When there was a pause Karen nudged Chris. "Oh my god, where are my manners?" he said as an apology. "Karen, this is my old high school friend Richard Jackson or Ricky, as we all call him. And the lovely woman with him is Julianna Jackson or Jules, as she is known by all. My favorite nickname for her is the avatar from hell."

"Chris! You are terrible, that is no way to talk about your good friend's wife. I am always apologizing for him. I try to teach him manners, but some men are simply hopeless."

Jules broke out in a laugh. "Oh, my dear, I am not married to this guy. He is my brother. I could do much better. And you are Chris's . . . what, girlfriend?"

Karen was blushing but recovered quickly. "Heaven's no, I also could do much better than him."

Chris laughed for the first time all day. "Ricky, I fear these women suffer from a case of excess hubris. No woman could do better than us."

"Now, that is a crock if I ever heard one," Kay chimed in.

"Okay, a formal introduction. Karen is my right-hand gal. I didn't know how long I was going to be imprisoned here so I brought her along to help keep my far-flung empire together. Besides, she will make a great human shield if Father decides to do me in."

"Hah! I would give you up in a nanosecond." Karen smiled.

"See, you can't even buy loyalty these days. In any case, Ricky is now a capitalist exploiter of the working man . . ."

"By that he means a financial guru and investment analyst."

Chris went on. "His lovely sister, who is getting long in the tooth, is a denizen of the media, a rising star and mediocre celebrity locally."

"A couple more ratings points and I won't even acknowledge this clown on the streets," Jules nodded toward Chris, "and watch that long in the tooth crap."

Karen laughed out loud, the tensions of the day were evaporating. "I know what you mean, I insist he wear a bag over his head when we are in public. He is such an embarrassment."

"Well, Karen, we are delighted to meet you. And you certainly have our sympathy." Jules extended her hand across the table. Karen felt a slight shiver flow through her as their hands met. *What was happening?* she thought.

Chris decided to fill in some history for Karen. "Ricky and I first met in a summer basketball camp right after our freshman year of high school. Of course, he was attending a ghetto public school and I was going to an elite academy. Still, we hit it off right away."

"Yeah, I see I need to tell this story. Here is the truth, Karen. This clown could shoot a basketball, I will grant him that. But he was a typical white boy . . . slow and couldn't jump worth a shit. For some reason, we were paired up for some one-on-one drills. I kept knocking him on his ass, started to call him 'white bread' and doing some trash talk."

"White bread?" Karen needed help.

"Soft and squishy on the inside. He probably only played with other white boys where people followed some rules. He was getting mad so I kept pushing him. Suddenly he lost it and took a swing. I am thinking, what a silly cracker taking on a black kid from a part of town he had never seen. I broke his nose with one punch."

"Hell, you sucker punched me." Chris protested.

"The revisionist history aside, I was amazed when he plugged up his bleeding nose and continued playing. Wow, I thought, this guy is tougher than he looks, just needs a little seasoning. We bonded. I would bring him around to my side of town, not too far west of here. There he got to play some real basketball and see a world he could barely imagine existed."

Chris became serious. "I am going to say something deadly serious now, some might even construe it as a compliment. Oh god, forgive me. However, you did change my life. I mean, you taught me shit about basketball except how to elbow your opponent in the gut without getting caught. Still, you did open me up to things. I loved your home, the affection, even the struggle. I understood how things mean so much more when they are not just given to you."

Jules broke in. "Dad was a mailman who slipped and severely hurt his spine in an icy fall, went on disability. Mom was
a school teacher's assistant. Money was tight, but they wanted
us to succeed, be what they could not be. They were smart, loving people. They gave us their all. But it seemed hopeless at the
time. The white world was a mile away as the crow flies but
seemed like here to Asia. And then, my brother started bringing
home prince charming here."

"Oh my god," Karen said, "you didn't fall for his line did you.
I cannot believe all the women that fall for his BS." She stopped,
hoping she did not cross some line.

But Jules laughed. "I was way too savvy for that. I was well
trained by my folks on how to resist the wiles of piggish boys,
certainly the white ones. Besides, he was shy then. The three of
us started doing things together like movies, museums, lectures,
libraries to which, I admit, Chris exposed us. I am grateful for
that. Then I noticed that it was sometimes the two of us. I suspect my dear brother was torturing me by leaving me alone with
this character."

"Hey, it was no picnic for me," Chris threw in.

"Anyways," Jules said with emphasis, "I kept waiting but he
never made a move. Here I was, ready to knee him in the you-
know-what if he ever went after the goodies but there was no
need. Rather disappointing, in fact. I was looking forward to
putting him out of action."

"How marvelous," Karen gushed. "That is how I punish him
as well, but not for hitting on me, of course, just for being a
general asshat. It is a miracle he can still pee." The table laughed.

"So, my pervert of a brother has never tried his charms on you?" Kay asked in a joking fashion. "How did a lovely woman like you get so lucky?"

"I am a lesbian. That makes it easier." Karen was pleased to get that out. At some level, she wondered if Jules might be on the same team. This woman was wearing a red power suit where the skirt stopped above the knees. Karen could not help but notice her long, smooth legs as she sat down at the table. The very sight of them sent a frisson of desire through her. "Still, I cannot afford to relax totally, I have seen him hit on the occasional coat rack when inebriated."

After a momentary pause, Jules continued. "It took me a while, but it hit me that he wasn't trying to get into my pants. I was flabbergasted. Who was this guy? Really, isn't that what they all go after? Then another hypothesis arose. Chris was trying to do something nice. He was trying to open possibilities for Ricky and me. He immediately got my brother into that elite prep school he attended. They were actually very willing to waive their fees to get a top black athlete or even an average one like my brother."

"Ha-ha! But it was a great relief not to run the gauntlet of the gang bangers every day." Ricky added, "You white folks do have it easy."

"No kidding," said Jules. "You cannot imagine what a horror it was to be studious when the other students thought that getting good grades was acting white. I will give Chris credit. He saw my pain, and my jealousy of Ricky getting out. He worked with Kay to get me into her school. I laughed at him when he raised the idea, where the hell were my parents going to get the money? He just told me not to worry. Even back then he was an accomplished wheeler-dealer but what I did not appreciate was just how rich he was. For me, then, I assumed that all whites were filthy rich. It wasn't until later that I found out some were much, much richer than others. But he made it happen and after a year where I proved myself, I got a full scholarship. But he did shell out to get me started."

"You are welcome," he said with a smile and a mischievous bow. "The thanks should go to Mother back then. I told her I knocked you up and needed money to make the problem go away."

"Of course," Jules feigned annoyance at his interruption. She assumed he was kidding about this but was never quite sure. "I still thought he only did this to get into my pants. All boys were pigs and I knew so little about white boys. I assumed they were bigger pigs. Now I was really on guard, waiting for the move. I agonized over how to turn him down while still suggesting gratitude for his generosity. I tied myself up in knots over this."

"What happened?" Karen asked, trying not to sound eager. Maybe this gorgeous woman did prefer other women.

"Well, it led to just about the most embarrassing moment of my life."

"Oooh, this sounds juicy." It was Kay. "I don't think I have heard this one."

Now Jules realized she had backed herself into a corner. "Shit, I shouldn't have gone there."

"Oh, god," Chris groaned, "you are not confessing that!"

"Get out the rubber hoses, we want a confession." Her brother, Ricky, was eager to sell his sister out.

Jules plunged ahead. "It was killing me. Why did he do this? What was he expecting from me? I finally decided to get it over with. Maybe I should give him his reward. We were alone, no one was expected back. Telling him I would be back in a few minutes, I went into my room. There I stripped down totally and put on a nightgown. I walked back and stood before him. He had this befuddled look on his face. He still didn't make a move."

"Hey, I was brain dead back then though there was this theory, one believed by all females, that my brain could be found somewhere adjacent to my penis."

"Not a theory but empirical fact, but shush, my story." Jules chided him. "Now desperate, I let the nightgown slide down my body and stood totally naked before him." She paused for effect. Giggles and laughter circled the table. "Do you know what he did? Can you guess?" No one was brave or clever enough to come up with a response. "He got up and left, without saying a word."

"No way!" Guffawed Karen. "This pervert is the world's foremost male pig. Damn, no more wine for me. He turned you down. Everyone knows he would mount that coat rack I mentioned earlier if given the chance."

"Yup, go figure. I cried for an hour. And guess what excuse he came up with when I finally confronted him."

Kay smiled. "He told you he would not accept sex in exchange for his, what shall we say, help toward improving your educational experience."

Jules was impressed. "You do know your brother."

"Absolutely, a pervert no question, but a pig with a conscience."

"No matter his motivation, all turned out well. I made it to Columbia in New York, got some media internships while there, and was on my way. Ricky made it to Northwestern, all Big Ten in basketball, several years with the Bulls, and then off to make his millions. And it all started, if my brother is to be believed, with a broken nose on the basketball court."

"It would make a great miniseries," Chris said as the food arrived.

They ate in silence for a few minutes while Karen stewed. Maybe Chris had turned her down because he knew she really was gay but she did not realize it yet. She took a deep sip of her wine and plowed ahead. "Excuse me for being so bold, but did you ever . . . ah . . ."

"Nail her," Chris interrupted. "Absolutely, she continued to stalk me until I gave in."

Jules threw her head back. "God, there never will be a shortage of BS as long as Chris is around. Truth is, we did become lovers though not until college. We were only fifty to sixty miles apart, Columbia and Princeton, and yet far enough not to risk becoming too involved in each other's lives. It proved convenient and safe. And yes, I will admit, I did want him by then.

It was not gratitude sex, more like pity sex. There really is no accounting for taste."

They ordered a couple more bottles of wine. The restaurant was not busy so they settled in for more comradeship and talk. No one wanted to leave. Karen leaned over to Chris. "Okay," she whispered, "any chance she is bisexual?"

Without missing a beat, he looked toward Jules and started in a regular voice. "Karen here wants to know if you are . . ." He never got the next word out as Karen's elbow snapped into his side. "Okay," he struggled to talk through deep breaths. "She really wanted to know if I was the best lover you ever had."

"He ruined me for all other men." She sighed in an exaggerated way.

"New topic," Chris asserted, "I want to thank you guys for joining me tonight. I needed some laughs, though perhaps I could do without the corporal punishment." A pause, then he continued. "You know, we joke about the basketball and the sex but you guys did change my life." He was looking at Jules and Ricky. There was no smile on his lips. "I could have sailed through life, unthinking and dissolute. As it is, I just focused on the dissolute stuff. It is hard to describe to others what it is like inside the bubble of privilege. You are cut off from the real world."

"Yeah, it must be horrible. Still, you were innocent, that was for sure." It was Ricky. "I recall being surprised that you would even venture into my world. You took a risk, you know. I promised to protect you, but I was not totally sure about that, whether I could do it."

"Not to worry, I could handle myself." Chris protested.

Ricky almost lost the wine he had just sipped. "Against the Blackstone Rangers? They would not have been able to find all the pieces."

"Shit, now you tell me. You know what I remember? I remember your folks. They had such love for you, hopes for you. I think that is what motivated me to help you guys. I saw how desperately they wanted you two to have a chance in life, and how shattered they were that they could not provide those opportunities on their own. It really wasn't the promise of sex, Jules. Besides, you and your brother were so pathetic, I was moved by pity."

"I definitely know that you weren't motivated by sex now," she said. "Back then, it was not clear at all. I kept asking myself, why is this white boy doing this, what is his angle? Pity never crossed my mind. I do remember that you had us over to your palace. Your folks were not very welcoming, I never got to know them."

"Hell, you were fortunate that my father did not call security when he saw your color. He probably thought you were what was left of the Black Panther terrorists. You do know that he would have an inventory of the silverware done after you left," Chris deadpanned.

"Really?" Jules seemed a bit shocked.

"No," Chris laughed as she threw an available piece of bread at him. "I ordered the inventory done." Another piece of bread flew in his direction, this one from Kay's hand.

Kay looked disappointed. "Damn, missed him again. I gotta practice my aim. However, I do agree that our lives changed for the better during those years." She lifted a glass that was joined by all the others.

Chris sighed. "It is all true. You did help me escape from hell."

"What are you talking about?" Karen asked. "You were destined for a life of yachts, limos, private jets, and caviar. Some image of hell."

"Okay, this needs some explanation."

"Oh no, here it comes." Jules feigned horror.

But Chris ignored her and continued. "When Kay and I were born, Father had already made it to the basement level of the filthy rich. But he wanted more. He also wanted power. He intuited a fundamental lesson of history. Riches help you gain control and control leads to more riches. Now that he had made it, what could he do to preserve those advantages for his family and tribe? Democracy and opportunity were ambitions for dreamers. He was a realist. You rigged the game. Why take any chances by playing fair? So, he began to drift to others who had been taken with a memo authored by Lewis Powell, future Supreme Court justice, and submitted to the U.S. Chamber of Commerce early in the 1970s. Powell decried what he perceived to be unrelenting attacks on the free enterprise system that he thought started with the onset of the Great Depression at the end of the 1920s. From his perspective, government had been way too intrusive for over four decades. There was too much regulation, labor was being coddled, and taxes on corporations and the uber-wealthy were confiscatory, at least according to the emerging voice of the right. A small group of those uber-wealthy decided that the Chamber was too public to foment a revolution, so they began to plot secretly. They were devoted to saving the free market system which they decided was on the verge of extinction. Unlike the Birchers and wing nuts of the '50s and '60s, they turned their attention away from Moscow and Beijing and toward America itself. The real enemy was within. Hell, even Nixon had vastly expanded the regulatory apparatus through OSHA and the EPA and shockingly had touted Keynesian principles. A nifty benefit of saving capitalism from all these liberals and Socialists is that they would further enrich themselves and consolidate power in their own hands. Hell, Father would argue that this was exactly what the founding fathers had in mind. The Constitution provided no voting rights to women, slaves, or even white men without property. They created an electoral college as a buffer against the people electing some radical nut job who cared about the riffraff and they had senators appointed by state legislators since this voting stuff was risky business. Democracy was fine only if you could control the outcomes. Kay, do you remember Father going on about these things even when we were young kids?"

"How could I miss it? It was constant. By the time we were seven, I remember the two of us were in deadly fear that these so-called radicals Father feared and loathed would storm our house and kill us all in our sleep. Other kids worried about the bogey man, we worried about liberals. And remember some of the people that would visit. There was Bill Buckley, Michael

Bradley, Herman Kahn, and Rupert Murdoch and so many others too numerous to mention. Sometimes we would be allowed to sit and listen as they talked about the end times that were sure to follow if they did not do more to end the rising egalitarian tide. The apocalypse was always six months in the future. To save society, and their lifestyle, the working class had to be brought into line, the poor had to be disciplined to ensure that they would work for starvation wages though they did not use that term. They talked about reestablishing a proper balance of labor's true contribution to productivity. In other words, drive compensation levels to zero. Wow, I have not thought about this stuff in some time."

Chris smiled at her. "Even by the time we became aware of what they were talking about, they had implemented much of Powell's agenda. The Business Roundtable and ALEC and the CATO Institute were created when we were toddlers."

"Alec, who is he?" Karen asked.

"Not a he, a what," Chris responded. "The American Legislative Exchange Committee was a group that began writing conservative, anti-labor, business-oriented laws for states. More right-wing think tanks followed like the Manhattan Institute, the Hoover Institute, and the Bradley Foundation, all designed to infuse free market and right-wing ideas into the public discourse. But after Reagan was elected, they were off and running. With the end of the Fairness Doctrine in the media and eventually Citizens United, they had free reign to employ their unbounded riches for their own political purposes. It was Katy-bar-the-door after that. They created Americans for Freedom in the mid-1980s, Accuracy in the Academy to go after left-wingers on campus a year later, and the Federalist Society to attack liberals in the judiciary. Oh, and I should not forget the Club for Growth. Of course, to change the political framework you need to control the media. Fox News was followed by a steady encroachment onto what had been a relatively independent media."

"And the point of this lecture is?" Jules asked.

Though the question was directed at Chris, Kay answered, "That we would have been brainwashed if it had not been for the two of you. Jules, remember how we would get together and talk. I mean, a lot of it was the usual female crap, you kept asking me if you should finally sleep with my brother . . ."

"What?" Chris seemed surprised. "Now I know why I had such a hard time getting laid. You sold me out, Kay."

"No, no, I protected her until she escaped my control by running off to Columbia. But that is not the point here. Just as you did for Chris, you opened my eyes to the real world. My brother and I had been struggling to escape Father's propaganda for years. We would pull away or at least try. It is hard, we were on our own and surrounded by adults who thought just like him. You guys got me, us, thinking about and reading stuff we would never have experienced otherwise. You introduced me, us, to people who never, and I mean never, would have passed through our sheltered part of the world. I think my dear sibling and I are struggling to say thanks. We owe you large."

"No shit," added Chris. "I would have become a financial guy like Ricky spending my days doing hostile corporate takeovers and my nights sipping champagne on my yacht. Oh my god, you would be visiting me in that hospital bed, not my poor brother." Chris noticed Ricky's expression. "What, no offense my friend. I know you don't do takeovers just to fire all the workers and sell the corporate body parts for an obscene profit."

"Thank you." Ricky nodded.

"No, you foreclose on widows and orphans to get your kicks."

"Just remember, asshole," Ricky intoned with a smile as he launched another piece of bread in Chris's direction, "I still can break your fucking nose. Maybe this time, when I break it, it will straighten itself out when it mends. Gee, still a bit crooked after all these years.'

"Right, boys, the two of you are tough guys. Tell me though, are you guys happy with where you ended up? Did you escape from your dad's world?" Jules was looking back and forth to both Kay and Chris.

Silence, then Kay spoke first. "I recall Dad trying to talk me into business courses but being okay with medicine. I think he thought there were wonderful opportunities to make a buck in medical technologies and drugs. Lots of robber barons head in that direction. You should have seen his face when I told him I was doing my residency in emergency medicine. 'You want to save people? Where the hell is the money in that?' Still, he left me alone, just wrote me off.'"

"But are you happy?" Jules pushed.

"Yes, I think." Kay paused. "I am still working on that."

"I am ecstatic." Chris rescued his sister from further revelation. "I also stick it to my father by helping people, not screwing them. I am thousands of miles away in an interesting part of the world. I successfully escaped my fellow Americans whom, in general, I find mostly boorish and narrow. I have Karen to take care of my needs." He saw Karen's eyes widen. "Professionally, only professionally."

"We knew that," said Kay, "she is far too intelligent to fall for your so-called charms."

"The big thing," Chris went on, "I am good at what I do. I can raise money. I can schmooze with the best of them. And I saw a need. There are plenty of public and private organizations there to help the least fortunate around the world. But they tend to focus on select needs. They develop their own technologies and define issues in terms of what they do. Worse, they don't talk with one another. The turf protection and institutional jealousies are ever present. All I do is put together the right teams and match them to the places where the need is the most pressing. And I get to teach a course at Oxford when I want, shape young minds."

"I have heard this pitch about your organization before," Kay interrupted, "always sounded bureaucratic to me."

"That is because, unlike my sister, I do not have this fascination with human blood, not being a vampire and all. You know, the international work in the third world is making a difference. Taking a larger view, we have seen global poverty halved in a generation or so, diseases like polio and HIV reduced dramatically and eliminated in many places, potable water brought to millions, and the list goes on. Some estimate that 122 million children have been saved in recent years. In the States, if a kid goes missing there is an amber alert and thousands turn out for search parties. The missing urchin's face is on nightly news for weeks. But save thousands of kids in some war zone and nothing. No one knows. You have to be confident in yourself not to feel bad about being ignored so totally."

Ricky didn't smile. "I . . . I want to talk to you at length about what you do, later though. I fear the ladies will be bored."

"Of course, anytime."

"In the meantime, I have a bunch of contacts for you to chat up while you are in town so call me in the morning. Most already know what you do in a general sense and they still want to see you. Go figure. Others will be new pigeons. Hopefully, your father hasn't gotten to them first."

Chris smiled without humor. "So far, he just ignores me. If I piss him off anymore, who knows. But thanks for doing this, man."

The evening was winding down. They spent some time talking about Chuck and what was coming up before all agreed it was time to go. They hugged and promised to keep in touch. Jules was reluctant to break away from her hug with Chris. "Call me if you need anything, promise?" she whispered in his ear.

"I think I need you right now." He glanced quickly toward his crotch.

Rather than responding, she moved closer and kissed him full on the lips. The others turned away, rather embarrassed.

————

Chris heard a knock on the door. He hadn't called for a girl from any service agency. He was lost on who might be there. Had Jules followed him? She seemed reluctant to part earlier.

"Chris, it's Karen."

He opened the door a bit. "I am not exactly decent here."

"Oh, for Christ sakes, I need to talk." She pushed the door open and walked past him. "She left me. I knew it was coming but still." Chris could see she had been crying. "She just sent a goddamn email saying it was over. She would be gone when I got back. No explanation, no nothing."

"Oh my god. I am so sorry." Chris felt foolish standing there in his underwear. "Should I talk with her? This is all my fault, I think. I could tell her I forced you to go."

Karen looked at him through moist eyes. "No," she said at last, "no need."

"Really, I will promise to be less demanding of your time. That's the problem, isn't it?"

"I don't want you to be less demanding of my time," she snapped, then realized he was not the object of her frustration.

"I can talk to her, let me call her," he said as he stumbled to put on a pair of pants.

"Chris, just listen. First thing, it is still night time there. More importantly, I want to let her go. I have been thinking about this. My passion is with our work. Really, it is. God, I must be weird."

"Yeah," he said softly, "you are." Then he hugged her. "But I love you for it."

Karen struggled with a thought. "Besides, if we patch things up I will just be waiting for the next blowup. I don't want to live like that. I wouldn't be able to do my job. But god, it does hurt right now. I . . . I don't want to be alone. Not tonight. Can I lay next to you?"

He stared at her blankly. "Aaah . . ." but that is as far as he got.

"Oh, for Christ sake, I am not going to jump your bones. Forget it, I will just leave."

He grabbed her arm as she turned toward the door. "No, come with me." He led her over to the bed and lay down. She slid next to him and put her head so that it lay on the side of his chest. He could feel her wet tears on his skin. After a long silence she said, "Are you positive Julianna is not bisexual?"

"Sorry, pretty sure of that," he tried not to chuckle.

"Okay, what about your sister?"

"I am not pimping out my sister, you pervert. However, now that think of it, I have no idea. How can that be? Hmmm, we haven't seen enough of each other since high school."

"That is okay, for some reason I could not imagine in a million years that your sister would be interested in me."

"Why?" he asked, curious.

"Hard to say. She strikes me as . . . unreachable."

"Funny, I get that, totally." Chris stroked Karen's head, he could feel her relax.

More silence. Chris felt himself drifting off when Karen spoke again, "By the way, I think I found a great candidate to head that new team. A Doctor Amar Singh, originally from the Punjab but medically trained in Canada. Speaks Farsi or Dari or whatever we need there."

"Handle that one, okay, Karen. I trust you."

"Thank you."

"For what?" he responded.

"For trusting me."

"Of course, I trust you. Hell, I am risking my virtue here."

With that she burst out laughing. "Virtue? You lost that a long time ago."

Chris rubbed her temple and gently stroked her hair. "I will tell you one thing. We are probably going to be fantasizing about the same woman. That doesn't happen very often." He could tell she now was relaxed, the sharpest pangs of the pain were receding. "And by the way, just so you know, if I get an erection it is involuntary. Just a guy thing."

"Gross, you pig. When you say the same woman, I desperately hope you were referring to Jules and not your sister. Don't get me wrong, your sister is gorgeous, she got the brains and the looks between the two of you. But something about her..." she stopped. He was not sure if she realized she was circling back to an earlier observation. That was not it though. He realized that she had drifted off. Suddenly, she startled him. "Oh, I know what it is. She is your sister."

CHAPTER 3

KABUL (2000)

"No, no . . ." Azita woke up drenched in sweat.

"What, sister, what is wrong?" Her older sibling asked from the next bed. "Are you having that same dream?"

"Yes, I am searching through the mountains. Which mountains, I know not. For whom, what, I can only guess."

"Well, what is your guess?"

"About what?" Azita said in a distracted fashion.

"Who or what you are looking for, in that dream of yours." Azita's sister sounded exasperated and quite annoyed.

Azita paused, then said softly, "You, Deena, and father, mother, and Majeed. But I can never find any of you, though sometimes you are there, I think, but just for a while. Then, I am no longer sure I am searching for anyone. Perhaps I am looking for a way out, for an escape. That's it . . . a way out. No matter though, I cannot find what I am looking for. I seem to be so close. Sometimes I think I am about to find it but . . ."

"Such a silly girl. We are all right here. Stop being such a nuisance and go back to sleep. Some of us have real chores to do, we are all not Papa's favorite."

Azita was stung. "I do my share."

"Hah!" Her sister exploded with derision. "You do nothing but read your books and follow Papa around all day like a puppy. You are spoiled rotten. You are Papa's favorite and why Mama permits you to waste your days with books or by learning things you can never ever use is beyond me. You are worse than spoiled. You are useless."

Azita wanted to respond and tell her jealous sibling what it was like to change dressings and clean up wounds and even suture skin that had been ripped apart by the violence that attended Kabul these days. She was certain her sister would not last a day. In Azita's mind, she was the silly girl, only thinking of boys and marriage and what motherhood might be like. Inside, she was grateful she thought of larger things even if they seemed impossible. More than anything, Azita thirsted for an education. But the Taliban had ruled that girls did not need education. It was against the Prophet's wishes. Females were totally subject to the discipline and wishes of their husband or father or brothers. They were inferior, subordinate, merely a handmaiden of their male betters. This made no sense to her. At some level Azita knew that her intelligence and knowledge were prodigious. She had always been smarter than the silly boys she had known in the neighborhood. More than that, she burned with ambition, a yearning to embrace and understand the world outside her home, the confines of the full hijab, the cloth prison of her culture. It was unfair. Why did Allah permit such ignorant men to rule over them? She felt herself getting angry as she lay in bed. If she did not curb her emotions, she would lash out at her sister. That would serve no purpose. "Perhaps you are right," is all she said.

"I am right, there is no question. What do you do around here? Nothing! I am the one always helping Mama. I go to the market, do the washing, clean and sew, and prepare the meals. You sit with your nose in a book, and for what? You cannot go to school. You cannot get a job, ever. Really, what boy will ever want you as a wife? You will be less than useless. You will wind up begging for meals on the street."

"I don't want some boy. He would just be someone else to order me around." She was getting angry.

"Order you around? That is the problem. No one orders you around. Papa should. Mama should. Your brother should. But no one does. You will pay a price. You mark my words, someday you will pay a price. If Papa somehow manages to get a husband for you, I swear that family will throw you out in a week, after you are beaten for being such an unruly and obstinate girl. You know what happens to girls who fail to be good wives? If you don't, ask Mama. It is not a pretty thing, not in the least."

Azita said nothing. What was she to say? Her sister was correct and she knew it. She looked at the ceiling of their room . . . it was as dark as her mood, as black as her future. What could she possibly do with the knowledge she sucked up from the books she read, from the rigorous lessons her mother taught when there was free time, from watching and listening to her father as he went about his craft. She could not take such things beyond the confines of her home and family. It was against the word of the Prophet, the law of Allah, at least that is what the new leaders of the land told them. Tears flowed freely down her face. How could she bear a future where there was no hope for expressing what was within, what defined her? Despair merged with a total blackness that pressed down upon her.

She realized that her sister, Deena, was still talking. "Dear sister, it is time to put away the foolish things you keep in that head of yours. You are a selfish, selfish girl. What will happen if it gets out what you are doing, learning from books and speaking English like a foreigner. Papa is so foolish, he cannot refuse you anything. But think of the risks he is taking even by letting you be with him in the clinic and going to the hospital with him. You play at just helping him out but what if others figure out what is really happening, that he is teaching you medicine, that he is putting crazy ideas in you about being a doctor someday. That cannot be kept a secret forever. I cannot believe no one has questioned him, no one has gone to the morals police. He could lose his position, we could lose everything. I would not be able to find a good boy to marry. It is fine if you want to ruin your life. But I won't have you destroying mine."

Azita wanted to scream at the voice coming from the void of the next bed. She could not believe that her older sibling had no dreams of her own beyond getting married and having children. That was the life of a slave. She would be ordered around not only by her husband but his entire family with no life of her own, nothing to look forward to but drudgery and servitude. It was an imprisonment, a life confined to home and family. She would service her husband, bear his children, meet all his needs. She could not own anything, dream anything, feel anything that was not provided by her new master. If the girl failed, the groom's family could make her life a living hell. There were stories of girls being such a disappointment that they were returned to the bride's family with future options limited at best. Sometimes, as it was told, the girl simply disappeared. The very thought of this sent shivers through Azita. She fought to control her anger. Instead, she softly asked, "Do you not ever dream?"

An exasperated voice shot back, "Silly girl, silly, silly, silly girl. Wake up. You cannot be a child forever. You must face what is real, what life has put before us. Oh, I am finished with you."

———

"Azita," her father said to her after breakfast, "you are not coming to the clinic with me today?"

"No, Papa, I think perhaps I will help Mama today."

He had noticed she had not touched her books that morning. That was not her way. She was always amazing him, rising early to study before the household stirred for the daily routine. It was her quiet time where concentration and focus were possible. Not even he had been so disciplined at her age, often sleeping late until roused by his father. It was good that he had been such a gifted child who could master his studies with modest effort, at least early on. This morning, however, he had found his favorite child staring at the wall, a sad expression on her face. Where was her perpetual smile? he wondered at the time. "Are you feeling poorly, my dear?"

"No, Papa, I am fine, really." Her smile was timid, forced. "I should help Mama today."

"Of course," he wanted to say more but it was time for him to go, patients would already be lining up, the ones that could pay and the ones that could not. "Tomorrow then."

"Perhaps."

He exited the house perplexed, with a heavy heart. He had not realized until that moment how much he depended on her presence at his side.

Azita noticed her mother looking at her with suspicion. "If you are feeling poorly, you should go back to bed"

"I am well, Mama."

"Do you want an early lesson then?"

"No, Mama, I would like to do the shopping today. I want to help you."

Her mother was perplexed. "Do you even know how?"

"Of course, I am not a useless girl, no matter what my mean sister says." The last few words uttered under her breath in a voice so low her mother might not hear. Azita fought hard not to betray what was bubbling up inside her as she struggled with her sister's words. They were vented in anger, she knew that. At the same time, she knew that they were also true. No matter how she turned over the obstacles facing her in her head, there was no escape. She was in a kind of prison. She was, in truth, a captive of her culture and her country. How could she live with that? Accepting this would kill her. Suddenly she felt on the verge of wailing aloud. But she kept her distress hidden, just wanting to escape the house.

Her mother only heard her younger daughter's petulant response. She toyed with a sarcastic response but bit her lip. Rather than chide her daughter who looked miserable to her, all she said was, "Okay, but I am sending your brother with you, just to be safe." Inside, Madeena commiserated with the misery of her younger daughter who was just coming of age. She eas-

ily recalled when things were different, when girls had real opportunities and choices. That now seemed like a fairy tale land
that perhaps only existed in her dreams. But no, her life was
testimony to what had been lost.

"You don't do that with my sister, send a keeper with her."

Her mother laughed but with felt no levity. "She is not a
silly girl." After a moment, she walked over to her daughter and
hugged her tightly. "You are such a worry to me. The things that
make you special are the very things that put you in harm's way.
Tell me what is wrong. I have seldom seen you look so miserable. Did you fight with your sister?"

Azita opened her mouth but nothing came out. Instead, she
pulled away. 'No, nothing, I just want to help. Please."

Her mother nodded and called for Majeed, her brother.

"Do you even know where the market is?" He laughed as
they started down the street.

"Don't be a stupid goat," she retorted but inside was not
certain she could recall which shops had the best deals. It had
been a while since she had accompanied her mother or older
sister on the daily market run. She loved being out and about
on the bustling streets of Kabul but now feared she would affirm
everyone's assessment of her incompetence. The day was already
heating up and she found the full burqa oppressive. Sweat ran
down her face and sides. Her mother had insisted. She was now
at that awkward age. She might yet be young enough to get
by without the required covering but why take chances. Even
if puberty had not arrived quite yet, some of the morals police would ignore legal niceties in their zeal for religious purity.

When an opportunity came to express their inborn sadism to impress their religious superiors, technicalities should never get in the way.

It was all so arbitrary and stupid, Azita thought. The Quran did not even require women to cover their heads. There were passages suggesting that women dress modestly, cover their breasts and genitals, but nothing like what the Taliban and the other religious zealots now insisted upon. The Prophet wanted to protect women from lecherous men, not imprison them in cloth strait jackets. It is these stupid men who now rule us, she fumed inside. She could not, however, take out her anger on those she despised. Instead, she directed it at the nearest target, her brother. "I don't even know why Mama made you come with me."

"Because, silly sister, you are foolish enough to start a jihad if left to yourself."

"Majeed, do you really think I am silly?" she asked, reflecting on her sister's hurtful words that morning.

"Of course, you are." His words tumbled out without consideration, as if this assessment were common knowledge and shared by all. "But you will grow out of it. You cannot escape becoming an adult forever."

"I refuse to become an adult if I have to wear this silly thing over me all the time. It is like a tomb."

"Perhaps," her brother chuckled, "but it keeps the boys from leering at you."

"And the girls do not leer at you?"

"Hah! Were Allah to permit it. But I do not worry, Papa will find me a good girl when it is time."

"Someone to cook for you and clean for you and . . ." then she realized that to go further would shock him.

"Exactly!" he said as if her sarcasm had not been apparent.

Azita mused on his words. Why was she listening to her brother? He seldom had a serious thought. She knew Papa was disappointed in him, he seemed to lack ambition and had no interest in medicine or for anything academic. Suddenly she realized that his future was as uncertain as her own. The Afghan economy was in shambles, first ruined by years of Communist rule, then chaos after the Soviets were driven out and various warlords vied for control. Now, that agony had been replaced by this Taliban craziness which had cut the country off from the Western world. What would her brother do with his future? What did he dream about? She had no idea. He was nice enough but, in truth, she hardly knew him. She wanted to ask him about such things but decided silence was better. One of these days she would reach out to him to get to know him better. He must have some of their father in him. But it would not be today. Today, she would focus on doing the marketing without making a fool of herself.

After purchasing a few items, with her brother being surprisingly helpful in reminding her what to get and what to avoid, he wandered over to a bookstore. Azita was taken aback for a moment. He had been an indifferent student. Still, he did have one literary interest, old stories of Afghan history, particularly of that era when they drove the British interests out in the 19th century. This was back in the times when local tribes were brought together in a loose kingdom known as Afghanistan. Unlike other countries, the British never fully subdued this land. Historic Afghan warriors had bested the strongest empire on earth. Now, in recent times, the same kind of warrior spirit drove out the Russians. There was much in their history to admire.

Azita's natural curiosity could not be easily quenched. She reveled in the sights and sounds of the market, the goods on display by the venders, the chattering among women and men walking in their segregated groups. How sad that the genders could not interact. It was like cutting people off from the other half of humanity. Men would not be so boorish toward women if they could talk to females from time to time, to real women outside of their own families. Azita considered whether men would lust after the female body so if it were not so hidden from them. Then they could see that their imaginings were overblown. Of course, Azita did not want to dress like the Western women she had seen in pictures. She was way too modest to put herself on display like that. However, she bridled at her current sartorial requirements.

A longish notice pinned to a wall caught her attention. "Allah Be Praised" it said across the top. Something inside told her to go about her business. Stopping to read this might attract attention to herself. But she could do no other. She was insatiably curious after all. She read the notice with increasing horror about the destruction of the Buddhist iconic figures at Bamiyan. Her father had taken the family there several years ago when travel was easier. The statues were located in central Afghanistan, not that far from Kabul. They were so beautiful, enormous, inspiring. How could such treasures offend Allah? He must have wanted them erected in the first place. Anger once again welled up inside her against these evil men. That anger spilled over onto the expression on her face.

"What are you doing?" Azita was wrapped up in what she as reading. Not paying attention, she assumed the words came from her brother returning from the bookstore.

"Look at this Majeed, this is awful. What are these animals . . ." she never got to finish her sentence.

Without any warning, a sharp pain crossed her back. She was stunned. Was it real? But words soon followed. "You, girl, what blasphemy is this, reading in public." Another blow brought her to her knees. "You would ridicule the Prophet with your sinful actions? You would blaspheme our leaders with your vile words?"

"Please, Allah, forgive me," she managed to say but the blows kept coming as she rolled into a fetal position. All she could hear was the phase "wicked, wicked girl." At first, the hurt was muted, lost in the sheer shock of her situation. But now the pain emerged in full force, searing through her back and limbs. She fought against crying out though she knew not why. Perhaps she did not want to give them the satisfaction of displaying fear or pain? They could beat her but not take her dignity. If she did not give them that, they had achieved nothing. As the blows continued, she began to question the wisdom of her stubbornness. One blow landed on her head, her world spun and nausea overwhelmed her. She was losing consciousness. What use would her pride be if she were dead. Somehow, she managed to debate that thought in her head when, from far away, she could hear her brother's voice. He was pleading with those who had surrounded his prone sister.

"Oh yes, she is such a wicked sister. We are doing our best with her. You are so right to beat her. I should not have let her alone, not for a moment."

"Who has taught her to read, who?" Came from this angry voice. "And who has permitted her to have such vile thoughts, such a wicked girl."

Her brother did not answer. "Look, let me beat her. Let me take her home where her father can also see her sins and punish her. She is so young, she does not know better."

Azita thought the worse over, her pain now pushing through the initial shock. Then, more blows. "See," she heard. "I will see that she is punished severely. Allah's word shall not be mocked, I swear. She shall respect our wise leaders." In horror, she realized her brother was now beating her. But she could not hang onto full awareness. Why had he joined them?

When she came to again, he was carrying her through the street. "Why did you beat me? Am I such a wicked sister?" she moaned.

"You are hopeless," he sputtered. "They might have killed you and then turned on me for letting you sin so. I had to distract him. If they realized what Mama and Papa were doing with you, giving you lessons and teaching you medicine, it would be the end of us. I knew you would get us in trouble. It was only a matter of time."

"Sin, my sin?" she tried to rage but only a pitiful whisper came out. "What they are doing is the sin."

"Stupid, stupid, stupid girl, one of these days you will get us all killed. One of these days . . ." For some reason, his words went deep into her heart. Her physical pain turned to a deeper despair. Consciousness left her. What she did not hear were his next words where he prayed to Allah to save the sister he bore in his arms and whom he loved dearly. "Take me, my life, Allah, not this innocent child."

———

When she awoke again, her father was applying a cold compress to her head. "My angel, how do you feel?"

"I have been better." She tried to smile but the pain returned. "Will I die, Papa?"

"No, my angel, you will not die but, to tell you the truth, I almost expired when your brother carried you into the clinic."

"Oh, the fruits and vegetables! Mama will be so mad at me. I never completed my shopping duties at the market. All of you are right, I cannot even do the simplest task. I am useless. I don't know what you should do with me, throw me out into the street. I will get us all killed." Now she was crying but she could not quite determine if it was from the physical pain or from her emotional upset.

Her father smiled sweetly. "Do not worry yourself about the food stuff. In truth, your mother is very mad but at me. And that talk about getting us all killed is silly. When Majeed brought you in, you kept going on about getting the family killed."

"Why is Mama mad at you, Papa? Everything is my fault."

"One question at a time. I suspect she is angry with herself for letting you go to the market. However, it is easier to blame me. She tells me I was wrong in not insisting that you come with me to the clinic this morning. Perhaps I should have but . . . but I had promised myself I would never force any of my children to be me, to follow my path. I thought perhaps you had changed your mind about medicine. Perhaps you had grown out of that early interest. Children do, they try something on and after a while they decide that this does not fit and this also is cast off. I was waiting for the day when you . . ." he stopped when his daughter began to cry. "Sweet Azita, is the pain too much? Perhaps I should give you another pill."

"No, Papa. The pain is there, yes, but that is not the reason for the tears."

"I know. You think you are putting us in danger. My child, the dangers are real. No doubt about that. But you are not the cause of them."

He left her for a short period and returned with two pills and some water. Lifting her head, she took his ministrations and sighed. "You will rest in a short while, but perhaps you can tell me. Why didn't you come with me this morning? That is, tell me if you wish."

"I thought, I thought . . ." She felt more tears.

"Tell me, angel." He applied ointment and topical antibiotics to where the skin had been cut by the blows. While her body would be bruised for some time, the X-rays only indicated one small fracture in her ribs. He had seen much worse when the ire of the morals police had been set off. In his mind, her brother had saved her from much worse, perhaps even had saved her life. While he did rain blows down on her as he tried to wrest control of the situation from the zealots, he aimed for her buttocks and tried to make them glancing blows that would do little harm. He would have to talk to the boy later, his son was wracked with guilt for not keeping a better eye on his sister. He knew she was headstrong and not nearly as attentive to the dangers as she should be. "Why didn't you come with me to the clinic as always?"

"I felt too guilty."

"Too guilty? I don't understand. Guilty about what?" he asked as gently as he could.

"I am too selfish. I . . . I have not been doing my share."

"And who says this?" he asked.

"It is of no matter, it is true." Try as she might, she could not turn off the tears but slowly she felt sleep edging toward her.

"Sweet angel, you should understand one thing. For better or worse, you are the image of your father, of me. I was so much like you at your age. My brothers and sisters made my life a hell, and I had many more than you. They were jealous and perhaps I was a bit selfish. But let me tell you something that I do not want you to forget. You have a gift. I was not certain when this began, when you were very young. Then I thought, perhaps you simply wanted to follow me around to ignore your chores. I thought, that is okay, I would like my favorite child to be with me even if it lasts for a few days or weeks. But you never gave up, your interest never went away. You kept showing up. You showed up day after day, asking questions and wanting to try things. While you may have thought you were overwhelmed at times, I saw something very different. You took in everything faster than I ever did. It came to me one day, you were born to be a doctor. You will be a doctor. Perhaps even better, you will be a teacher of others. There is no greater calling."

"But how?" She struggled to stay awake. "How can it be?"

"We will talk later. Sleep now."

————

When Azita awoke, she was back in her own room. She struggled to recall what had happened. She had been beaten. Yes, that is it, she had been beaten. But why? What had she done? What sin was so bad that she might have died if her brother had not intervened? But even he had also struck her. There was no doubt that her sin was great, an insult to the Prophet and to Allah. She must have been a wicked and blasphemous girl. What was it? Some of the details escaped her. Not the beating and the rage in the words hurled down upon her, those were clear in her memory. What had happened just before all the pain and venom? Oh yes, she had stopped to read a poster. It was about the destruction of the beautiful monuments to Buddha that had no place in what the Taliban had determined was pleasing to Allah. But all she did was read the poster. She displayed no emotion in that moment though she raged inside, though maybe she had said something. It was all just beyond her memory. Destroying beauty was the sin, not the beauty itself. Could they not see that? But for them, her guilt lay in being inquisitive, in simply wanting to know what was happening in the world. How could curiosity evoke such vitriol? That was not rational. But the world no longer was rational. She had paused to read a poster for a moment or two and it had almost cost her life itself.

"Ah, Allah has spared your life I see." It was her sister's voice. 'Some of His decisions are strange indeed."

Azita tried to turn toward the voice but her whole body resisted. The pains were not as sharp as before. Still, the soreness was present. "What time is it?"

"It is evening. You slept all day. I must say, you would go to any length to get out of your chores."

Azita wanted to argue but when her sister came into view she could see that her eyes were red from crying. "You have been taking care of me? Thank you."

"Mama has made me. As always, I am blamed for your foolishness." She lied. She had insisted on helping. Her guilt was great. "Are you hungry?"

"No, but I may need to pee."

"I think not. Papa put one of these things in you, he didn't want you trying to move until tomorrow."

"A catheter."

"I suppose." Her sister brought a drink to the bed. She took her two pills, raised Azita's head, and put the pills in her mouth. Then she encouraged her to drink. "I am going to tell them that you are awake. "You shouldn't listen to me, you know." Azita strained to look at her sister and thought she saw tears coming from her eyes.

"What?" Azita was not sure she had heard her sister correctly.

"Just don't listen to me in the future, okay?" And with that
she was out the door.

Azita floated in and out of sleep but awoke to see her father
leaning over her, beginning to apply more ointment to some of
the open wounds, changing the bandages as he did. "Ah, you are
awake! Good, I have some soup for you."

"I am not hungry, Papa."

"And you would send me back to face your mother with
a full bowl of soup? You are such a mischievous child. And I
thought you loved me."

"I do, Papa, I love you more than anything."

"Then you will let me finish with these wounds and we will
get you sitting up to eat. But first, move this way so I can get to
your back side." Every movement was painful followed by the
sting from whatever he was applying to her cuts and bruises.
She grimaced but did not utter a sound. She refused to show the
hurt. "You are a brave girl, my dear." When he had finished, he
struggled to get her sitting up.

Silently, he fed her a little of the soup. She immediately realized that she was, in fact, hungry. "Thank you, Papa. This is
good. I am surprised Mama is not feeding me."

"I am keeping everyone away from you. Your brother and
sister are wanting to apologize, I was afraid the shock of that
would send you into a relapse. And your mother would fuss
until you ran out for another beating just to get away from her."

"Why are my brother and sister feeling so guilty? He beat me but only to get me away from those evil men. Oh, now I remember."

"What?" her father asked.

"One of the last things I heard before losing my sense was the man who was beating me asking who had taught me to read. At least I think he did. They will come after you or Mama." Her voice revealed a sense of panic.

"Shush, my pet. Majeed convinced them you were full of pride, that you merely pretended to read. Of course, that is yet another sin. Their list of offenses against Allah is endless."

"Oh, okay. But why is Deena feeling guilt. She did not beat me."

"Don't you see," he said, "she believes she teased you so much that you went to the market instead of the clinic. Your brother, on the other hand, does not feel bad about the blows he gave you, that was necessary, but he blames himself for wandering off to a book shop when he should have kept a closer eye on you. He suspected you would do something silly and you did not disappoint him."

"Oh good." She smiled for the first time. "I think I can use this to my advantage. I will have them bringing me sweets and good things for weeks. Perhaps I will never recover."

"Oh, you are a wicked girl. Do you want your mother fussing over you forever?"

'Oh, I had not considered that. I think I will get up now."

He laughed. "We will try that in the morning."

"Papa," she turned serious, "what did I do that was so evil, so bad that I deserved such a beating? I just wanted to read about what was going on. Why is that a sin?"

"Why not finish your soup and rest."

"Please tell me what sin I committed. Why would Allah be so troubled by me."

"Dear girl, I can never imagine Allah ever being upset with you, ever. Okay, maybe if you used your wounds to take advantage of your siblings. Then you would be a wicked girl." He smiled at her but she looked at him intently.

"Please, Papa, do not treat me as a child. What did I do that was so evil? I cannot understand these men. They are supposed to be representing the Prophet and the Quran but I have read the Word, and about the Prophet's life, and Mohammed did not hate women. He tried to help the women of his time. He preached that they be looked upon as more equal than they were. I cannot understand why I am hated just for being a woman."

"I will be back in a moment."

He returned with a book about the Prophet and the early days of Islam. All she saw at first was that the author was a female. "Hide this if anyone else comes in. Your mother will scold me if she finds out I gave you something to read and that you are not resting."

"But I have things to read here, that would not be your fault. How can Mama ever be angry with you?"

"You have much yet to learn, angel. In marriage, it is always the man's fault. You should remember that for when you get married someday."

"Good rule." She laughed. Then he did as well. "I will not need it though, I do not intend on getting married. I have given this much thought."

"Truly a wise decision," he smiled, "but one you may reconsider one day."

"Never, my mind is made up."

"Okay, I believe you. But seriously, keep this book to yourself. It is considered blasphemy. If others outside this home knew we had such a book, it would not be good, not good at all."

"How can such a thing as a book be so dangerous?" Her eyes were wide, she had now forgotten all about her pain for the first time.

"My sweet, someday you will realize that books are more dangerous than bullets. They can alter a man's heart, transform the world. A great man of the West once said that 'nothing is more dangerous than an idea whose time has come.'"

"And this book is dangerous?"

"The men who rule us believe so. Let me try to explain something. When I studied medicine in England, I would discuss great ideas with my fellow students. One of them told me about something he called Omnism. I have a book for you about that, all in good time though."

"A funny word."

"But a powerful idea! This philosophy, if you will, is very simple and yet so complicated. Simply put, it says that truth is found in all religions. At their heart, all the great spiritual teachings tell us the same things. Love one another, care for one another, be good and focus on things outside of yourself. If you do such things you will be close to God."

"You must be very close to God, Papa."

"I think your mother would disagree." They both laughed again.

"Then how could those men today be so cruel?"

"You ask such good questions, my dear. Let me try this. You know what a prism is?"

"Of course, I learned from my lessons with Mama. A beam of white light, which in truth embraces all colors, is sent into it and out comes a . . . what is it? Oh yes, out comes a spectrum of different colors. It is called refraction."

"Yes, an A for today's lesson. Religion is like what happens when a bright light is sent through a prism. The beam is truth, a pure and holistic set of understandings that bring all things together. But most men and women cannot look directly at this truth. It would challenge them and overwhelm them. This truth would blind them in a way. And so, they create religions which stand between each person and God. That is the prism. Truth goes in and a set of individual colors come out the other side. In and of itself, that is not so bad except that we forget that each color comes from the same pure beam of light. Men focus on one of the colors of the spectrum. They argue that this color, the one they want to see, is the only one that counts. Soon, they vilify others that look upon another hue. Truth is green, some argue. No, it is red, or yellow, or whatever. They soon fight and kill each over such silly disputes, forgetting that each has a part of the truth within their grasp. Jews, Muslims, and Christians all trace their origins back to Abraham. We see Christ as a great prophet who also revealed truth about God. Yet, we so often descend into chaos and violence because man is obsessed with finding irrelevant differences rather than seeking commonalities that bind us together"

"That is so sad, Papa."

He started to reply when the door flew open and her mother looked in. "How is my baby? Does she need anything?"

"What she needs, Mother, is for you to go away and let her rest."

"Harrumph!" The displeased woman closed the door on her way out a bit too loudly.

"You are in trouble now, Papa."

"You would think. But I am safe so long as I can say I am doctoring you. It is the one area of life where I can find refuge and even be correct in her eyes, but only on occasion."

"Now, you are being the evil one." Laughing was becoming easier for her. He could always make her feel better. She could not imagine her world without him.

"Remember, we are not supposed to have this book. It is in English, authored by a woman named Karen Armstrong. Her writing is not always easy, very academic. But I want you to try it and I can help you if you get stuck." Until now he always had his wife handle Azita's lessons, other than his impromptu medical instruction. His wife sorely missed teaching in the classroom, something the Taliban had ended upon taking power. "Perhaps your mother is right, I should let you sleep now."

"No, Papa, just a while longer, please."

"Ah, you are a temptress. Someday a boy will not stand a chance with you."

"Never, boys are terrible. They are arrogant, selfish, dirty, smelly, and crude."

"I am a boy," he said trying not to smile.

"You don't count."

"Such a thing to say to your own father."

"You are too clever." She knew he had bested her once again. "I will be a doctor. I won't need a boy, ever." Then she burst into tears.

"What is wrong? Did I say something? I had no idea that talking about boys would be so painful."

"No, no, I am reminded of what happened today. I despaired, Papa. I abandoned my dream. It all seems so hopeless. What I want more than anything is to heal, and maybe teach. I want to be you, a healer, and Mama, a teacher. I cannot be anything less. But how can it be? We live in a place where I am beaten to within an inch of my life simply for reading a poster. How can I dream of anything in such a place? It is hopeless."

"Azita, listen to me. Nothing is ever hopeless. I was born in the northern mountains. My father was a minor leader but far removed from Kabul and the modern world. The odds of my becoming a doctor were so tiny but it happened. There was fortune involved, for sure, but there was always determination. I never gave up, never despaired. Well, there were times when I first arrived in England, I had trouble with the culture and my studies until my English improved. Many a time I cried myself to sleep for the loneliness I felt. But I would never permit myself to give up, ever. Do you know why?"

"No, Papa." She lied, she had heard variants of this story before and thought she knew but wanted him to tell her once again.

"I suppose there are two reasons. The first is an insight that the young too often forget. Life is not today, this week, or this year. It is not a sprint but a long race. It is a marathon with many twists and turns. When you start out, you cannot know where the course will take you or what the finish line will look like. All you can know is that there will be hills and troubles along the way. At some points during the race, you will want to rest, lie down, maybe even give up. That will be so tempting. But then you will never arrive at the top of the mountain. You will never see to the other side. I can still remember the day when they conferred upon me my medical degree. I had never felt anything like that in my life. I was far from my family in a foreign land. That did not matter, I had been blessed with an opportunity to follow my dream."

"Life was different then, and you were a man."

"Well, I like to think I am still a man."

"You know what I mean." But she managed a smile. "They will never let me be anything in this country, never. They'd want to kill me if I show an ankle in public or read a poster in the market square or speak to a man who is not a member of my family. They will never, never, never permit me to be educated or do anything in life. Father, I would rather die than face such a future. Do you hear me? It would have been better had they just killed me in that square today." Her smiled had melted into a sob.

"You are not listening to me. What you see is life as it is now, not as it can be. Things change all the time, they do change. Sometimes they change for the better and sometimes for the worse, but my point is simple. What you see today is not permanent." He stroked her head wishing desperately that he had some magic words to share. "When I was your age, Afghanistan was a very different place. We were at the end of the monarchy and the county was quite secular. By that I mean it was more tolerant of people with different beliefs. You would not recognize that country today. In Kabul at least, and in other big cities, women could be educated. They could pursue vocations and wear Western dress. They could even talk to boys in public though most families still had a lot to say about whom they would marry."

"This is not helping, Papa."

"Ah, you are such a stubborn child. I thought that my country would remain like that forever. I never saw the coming chaos, the Communists, the religious zealots, the rampaging warlords that were waiting on the horizon. You were born as the Russians were being driven out by the Mujahadeen using American weapons. I remember thinking that now we will return to normal. But it was not to be. We had too many weapons and too many small men seeking ultimate power. The Americans no longer cared once the Russians were gone. They are a selfish people. So, chaos descended over the country. From that the Taliban arose. They promised people stability, an end to the fighting. But it was what I call a Faustian bargain."

"A what?"

"Just one of those fancy words meaning a bargain you make with someone that you later regret. Technically, it means a bargain one would strike with the devil. I will give you some peace and security. In return, you must give me your soul in return. By the time you realize what you have done it is too late. You cannot escape the prison in which you find yourself. These devils cannot last forever. The people are not happy."

"Why are they not driven out?"

"For one very sad reason, they now have the most guns. And since America does not worry about religious zealots like they did the Communists, they do not care what happens to us."

"I hate the Americans," she said with conviction.

"I do not think so. I doubt you hate anyone, not even the misguided boys that beat you today. My point is that none of us know what kind of world you will find as an adult. But whatever it is, you must be prepared for it. You must study hard and learn all you can. You may turn a corner someday and opportunity will be in front of you. Do you understand, my child? Keep this in your heart, never give up on your dream, never."

"Yes, Papa. But you mentioned another lesson."

"Ah yes, I almost forgot. You are such a troublesome girl that you make me lose my thoughts." He leaned over her and cupped her head in his hands. Just then the door opened once again. He yelled without looking to see who was there. "Out woman, I will be finished shortly." He heard another "harrumph" as the door slammed shut again. "This is the most important thing I have to say to you so listen very carefully. You have a gift, my dear. Allah has given you talents that are provided to very few. You are so very intelligent, curious, caring, and loving. He did not shower you with such things if he did not intend that you should not use them in some way. He would not make you so special merely to bury you behind a hijab, to be a household slave to some boy. I am repeating myself now, of course. But some lessons deserve to be repeated, over and over. This one you should never forget."

"Oh, Papa, you do not care if I don't marry?" Her eyes were open with hope.

"Only if you find a boy you love. What I really care about is that you find what you are meant to be in life. I want you to be the best person you can. Do you understand me? If you can do that I will know that my life has meant something."

"Yes, Papa."

"Don't just say 'yes, Papa.' You must understand that I may not always be there for you. Someday you will be on your own."

"No, no . . ."

"Yes, my dear. I hope it is not for many years. In the meantime, you must promise me one thing."

"Anything . . ."

"Child, think about this before responding. I want you to promise that you will not give up on your dreams no matter what. I cannot repeat this enough. I may be gone, all may look hopeless, but I want you to fight for what you want to be, for what you can be."

Azita looked at him for a long time. His eyes were moist and kind. They were always kind. How could one man be so good and so many be so evil. She had so much to learn about life, so much eluded her grasp, her understanding. The easy answer was right in front of her. But that is not what her father was asking. She dug deep inside herself.

"I will, Papa. In Allah's name, I promise."

————

"Well, you are finally letting her get some rest." His wife greeted him brusquely as he left the room. "You fuss over her like an old woman."

"Shush, woman, I had things to discuss with my daughter."

"Hmm. I hope you told her not to be such a foolish girl. She not only could get herself killed but endanger the whole family. Do you think they followed her brother when he brought her back to the clinic? You know they will keep us under surveillance if they did."

"I suspect they already are looking hard at us. I have noticed young men hanging aimlessly around the clinic who seem to have no purpose there. I am sure they do not trust that I am sufficiently devout. Our surname is the same name as the man who leads the Northern Alliance, I am sure that has not escaped them though it is a common enough name."

"Oh, young men are hanging everywhere, there is little work. Perhaps you are being paranoid." She tried to be upbeat.

He looked at her with a seriousness she seldom saw in private. "I hope you are right but the lack of work is what worries me. Young men will do anything for a little money. They would create treason and sin out of innocence just to be able to report something to the authorities."

His wife knew his concerns were not to be dismissed. "Are we in danger?"

"Not tonight I suspect, my dear, but we should talk later."

"Well," Madeena murmured nervously. "We are safe for the moment. Let us join our children. We will talk more later."

"Is she still angry with me?" Azita's brother asked when he saw his father. "I had no choice. I had to beat her. Otherwise, they would have killed her for sure, I think."

"Well, son, she said she will never talk to you again unless you bring her sweets every day."

"Oh, Allah forgive me. I should go and apologize to her. But I only wandered away for a moment. I could not imagine she could get into trouble so quickly. I had to hit her, you know," he said once again. No matter how many times he confessed his sin, the guilt would not wash away.

"My son, you must forgive yourself. Your sister has forgiven you. She has never blamed you. However, she is a clever girl and I am certain she will try to get some sweets from you." The father looked at his only son, the eldest child, who slowly realized that his father was teasing him. Odd, he thought, the two older siblings were smart but neither were as quick of mind nor as innately inquisitive as was his youngest. He often mused that his older daughter had promise if she would only focus. He did, though, love them all but wondered if Allah had retained some extra intelligence and mischievousness for his final issue. "Actually, I am proud of you. If you had not intervened as you did, and had not convinced them that you would beat her to within an inch of her life, who knows what would have happened. And telling them that she was only pretending to read was very clever, my son." In fact, Pamir had long recognized that his son had much courage.

His son beamed with pride. "Thank you, Papa."

Pamir continued in a sad voice, "These animals are getting bolder by the day. They started out simply trying to enforce all these silly new rules. Now, they have become sadists. They look for reasons to beat women in the streets. And if one dies, it is merely Allah's will. They are accountable to no one."

"Careful," his wife urged.

"Mother is right. We can say such things in our home but we must never say them outside where others might hear. Many seek favor with the regime, even those pretending to be our friends. We must always appear to be devout and behave as if we support the regime. Does everyone understand? Do not even trust those whom you have known for a long time, those to whom you feel close. You cannot trust anyone. Do you understand?"

His daughter nodded, his son grunted something.

"I want to hear the words. I want to hear a promise in the name of Allah."

He looked directly at his daughter. "I promise, Papa, in the name of Allah."

Then he turned to his son. "I also promise, Papa, in the Prophet's name."

"And that is the last time Azita goes to the market," his wife added.

Pamir turned to his wife. "Mother, I need some air, walk with me into the courtyard. And the two of you leave your sister alone. She needs to sleep. We probably can get her up in the morning, okay?"

The two exited the house into a small high-walled courtyard in the back. It was a place where the females could escape to enjoy fresh air without covering up. Looking up, the sky was cloudless. He could tell by the sprinkling of stars to be seen scattered across the blackness.

They sat on a small bench looking up at the sky. After minutes of silence he took her hand. His mind wandered back to the time when they had met in school so many years ago. She was the beauty he could see across the school yard. Though it was a different time, even then the boys and girls were mostly separated. He kept staring at her until it was impossible for her not to notice. But the thought of approaching her was beyond consideration. Every time he tried to summon the courage, his feet would stick to the ground. Movement was impossible.

One day, he was sitting after school had let out, morose at his cowardice and stricken with that intensity of desire that afflicts young men with peculiar cruelty. Then he saw a shadow cross in front of him and heard a female voice. "Are you just going to stare forever? Perhaps, one of these days, you might speak to me? You can speak, can't you?" Apparently, he could not as he rose but stood mute in front of her. After a few more awkward moments, she launched into a story about herself, her family, and what she wanted in life. He heard very little until it was clear she was coming to a finish. "I like a boy who says little. From my experience, most have absolutely nothing to say, nothing worth listening to at least."

That stung. His voice returned. "You only believe that because you have never listened to what I have to say."

"Really." She smiled. "You are so confident. I find that unusual in a boy who can barely talk to a girl. What can you possibly say that will make me admire you?"

He was not confident at all, of course, but he had already fallen in love. He would try to act like the boy he wanted to be, not the one he was. He launched into a short summary of his life—coming to Kabul from the mountains to the north since his tribe had decided he had great promise. He told her he would become a doctor, he would serve his people, and make all proud of the confidence that was placed in him.

When he stopped, not knowing what to say next, she asked him one question. "You are Pashtun, then."

"Yes."

She wrinkled her nose. "That will be a problem."

"You do not like the Pashtun?"

"I could care less but my parents are a bit old fashioned. We will have to work on them."

"Work on them? What do you mean work on them? Work on them for what?"

"To give us permission to marry, silly."

All these years later he still smiled at the memory of that moment. What if she had not crossed the school yard to speak to him. He never would have summoned the courage. If up to him, they never would have talked, never married, never had a special child such as Azita. It is a good thing that Allah makes women so crafty and devious. Otherwise, men would grow old and die alone. Worse, the species would end since no procreation would occur.

"Why did you speak to me that day?"

"What day? I speak to you every day, silly man."

"No, back in the school yard when we were children. We became engaged to one another after one short conversation. At least, that is the way it seemed to me."

"Well, in truth, we did not become engaged until our parents agreed and that took a bit of doing. You did not look like a catch to my folks. But yes, I had decided after that conversation."

"But that is it," his voice rose, "why did you choose a nobody like me. There were so many other boys smitten with you?"

She looked at him as if she were deciding to share a great secret. "I knew right away that you were special. I watched you in the school yard. I saw how you treated others, how other boys responded to you. I was watching."

"I had no idea." He marveled at this news.

"Of course not, the boy is never to know. You really think you know what is going on in life. That is quite funny."

"No, my dear, I lost that illusion many years ago. But we have some serious things to discuss."

"I know." Her smile was replaced with grim determination.

"We cannot stay in Kabul. Perhaps this danger will pass but there will be another crisis, that is inevitable. I am taking such chances even having Azita around the clinic with me. It was fine when she was considered a girl but she is now on the cusp of womanhood. The Taliban will not approve. Most patients love her but, someday, one of my patients will complain, if for no other reason than to curry favor with the authorities. As with all tyrants, the Taliban become more suspicious and paranoid by the day. Someone will tell the authorities that she is doing medical procedures that only a male should be doing, not a girl."

"Perhaps we should be realistic about her future."

"No!" It was a shout, which shocked her. "My dear wife, that is the one thing I will not do. I will not sacrifice Azita's talent and promise. You can ask anything else of me, but not that."

She knew enough not to argue. "What is your plan?"

"We will go back to the mountains, to my home. The Northern Alliance is holding out against the Taliban. It is the one area that these animals have not yet conquered. I don't know if they can hold out forever. Yet, it is the only place in this forsaken country where some sanity remains. I know these people well, they are my people. Their strength surprises me not at all. Not even the Russians could beat them into submission."

"How can we do this? It will be so dangerous. There are roadblocks and spies everywhere. How can we make this work?"

"It will be very dangerous. We must plan carefully. I will try to get permission to relocate to Kunduz or wherever I can that is close to the Alliance. Maybe this will be a temporary assignment if I can find a reason that seems plausible. From there, we will have to make a run for it. It will mean leaving most of what we have behind, starting over."

"I understand."

"This is not what you signed on for in that school yard so long ago. I am so sorry."

She kissed him on the cheek. "You are a ridiculous old man. I knew what I was getting back then. I know what I have now. I will still follow you to the ends of the earth."

He laughed. "We will soon test that commitment of yours."

CHAPTER 4

CHICAGO
(2000 CONTINUED)

"Nice of your sister to let us stay at her place. This is such a funky loft, right on the river too."

"Easy for you to say. You get the guest room and I get the fold out bed." Chris was trying to sound cross. "Then again, I suppose the only reason she let me in was because you insisted."

"Well, if you were nice to her on occasion . . ."

"Shit," he responded immediately, "I treat her like a princess."

Karen laughed. "I would hate to see how you treat the common folk. Now get your ass out of bed. Kay left for her shift in the ER some time ago. I made coffee and organized the issues we need to examine. And then you are scheduled to do your money-grubbing thing with some filthy rich American capitalists. And then . . ."

"No need to remind me. Then it will be off to the pit of misery to do battle with Lucifer himself."

"Be nice!" Karen admonished him. "I know that is difficult for you but . . ."

"Maybe we can get a decision today. I think Mother sees it is hopeless now. The doctors cannot be more definitive, though they still use weasel words. Only Father is holding out for sure. Frankly, I am not certain about Kat and Beverly. What in God's name is Father thinking? He cannot possibly still believe that Chuck will return to his position in his empire. Probably just wants to piss me off."

"Okay," Karen assumed her tough girls voice. "We all know you believe the world rises and sets over your eminence, or should I say rises and sets over your scrotum. However, let me be the first to mention that it does not and certainly does not around revolve about your precious family jewels."

"Obviously you have not discussed the matter with my legion of female admirers."

"Oh, just shoot me. Now get your ass out of bed and, for heaven's sake, put some pants on. I don't want to watch you parading around in your skivvies unless you can pay for my medical care when I am struck blind."

"Little you know, my dear, women just drool at the thought of getting me out of my pants."

"Only if they are looking for your wallet," Karen responded.

"Enough, I give. Are you sure you don't want to marry me?" With that, Karen ripped the covers off his bed. "Bet you are disappointed I am wearing shorts."

A few minutes later, they were huddled over their computers looking at reports sent from their Oxford office. His initiative had two primary offices, one in Oxford where he started the enterprise as he finished his studies and the other in London where many of the essential institutional linkages were located. He almost always spent his weekends in the university town he loved. Chris preferred an academic setting for thinking and strategizing and London for raising resources and forging programmatic connections. For a while Chris and Karen worked on issues related to an Africa initiative. Many young girls had been kidnapped and forced into a life of sexual slavery. Many were now being recaptured by the provincial police backed up by the U.N. and needed intensive help that local officials could not provide. Chris had assembled a team that could help in the form of comprehensive services.

With those questions settled, he turned to his newest initiative—helping what was called the Northern Alliance in Afghanistan. They were the one area holding out against the Taliban but their hold on the region was tenuous at best. "Tell me about this person you found to head the medical team there."

Karen took a breath, hoping he would not second-guess her judgment. "Well, to be honest, she found us. In any case, she was raised in the Kashmir area of India to a medical family. So, she had a front row seat to Muslim-Hindu tensions. Speaks Farsi, did her medical training in Canada where some extended family members and her former husband live. She has done a brief stint with Doctors Without Borders but wants a bigger challenge where she believes her cultural roots give her a comparative advantage."

"Wow, she sounds right out of central casting. A former husband, isn't that unusual for an Indian gal?" Chris asked.

"Hey, Indian women don't all still live in the eighteenth century anymore. You need to get with the program here. In any case, there is no evidence of psychoses or dead bodies buried in the backyard. Just an ex-husband who is very much alive but already remarried. No children. I checked that out first thing. She is without attachments. The husband, apparently, was screwing around and not keeping it secret. That was okay until he nailed her sister. Even her conservative Indian family agreed to a divorce after that. Men really are such pigs."

"No doubt, my dear," he said, "you picked the right team to love for sure. Given the name she must be Sikh."

"For some reason I recall her mentioning in an offhand way that she was attracted to Buddhist thought but kept that from her family. Is religious preference important?"

"Of course not, otherwise I would never have hired a pagan like yourself." He seemed to be thinking of something else. "I have always been impressed with Sikhs, mostly because of their drive. A preference for Buddhism? Even better."

"Yeah, I can see why you might like Buddha, you are starting to look like him. I have noticed the start of a middle-aged spread." Karen struggled to look serious.

"Really?" He looked about for a mirror. Then he saw her smile. "Oh, bite me. So, can I talk to her?"

"Your wish is my command. If we call now, we might catch her before her day ends. I warned her you might want to call."

"I hate it when you read my mind."

"Oh, you have no idea how glad I am that I don't though clearly it would not prove much of a challenge." She chuckled. "Hell, I probably would need to carry a barf bag around with me all the time."

Within a quarter hour they had Amar Singh on the phone. After some preliminary pleasantries, Chris got down to his core concern. "Listen, I am very impressed. However, I want to know personally that you are aware of the risks. All the sites in which we work pose some danger. That comes with the job. This part of the world, however, is very volatile. You would start with refugees escaping from the Taliban in Afghanistan to camps in the Kush region. That is one of the most dangerous places in the world for foreigners. Several aid workers and journalists have been kidnapped and a few have lost their lives. But that isn't the half of it."

"I think I know where you are going. You want to develop a team in the northeast provinces themselves, where they are still holding out against the Taliban. Karen briefed me on your plans. I am in, a hundred percent."

"Good. It will take time to develop this. I want a team in there, medical and educational and community development and public health. If we cannot do the whole package, I at least want a medical team in there. We probably won't be ready to go until the end of 2000 or early 2001. But if this goes, which means they are still hanging on, I am thinking that you could head the primary care medical part of the team. You should have a good sense of what you will face after several months in the refugee camps. I cannot stress the potential dangers too much."

"If I may interject, is it Doctor Crawford? I know you have a doctorate."

"Chris, please."

"And Amar, not Doctor Singh. That is my father."

"We are agreed then."

"Chris, I did not reach out to your organization lightly. Its reputation, your reputation, is growing in the philanthropic world. I want to be where the people need me most. I grew up in a place broken by sectarian discord. I am aware of fear and violence. My father was attacked more than once. You can be assured I am not naïve. I am also at a place in my life where risk is permissible. I have no children, no husband, only myself to worry about. When I have a family of my own, things will change but now . . ."

"What about your family, parents and siblings?"

"I have discussed this at length with them. There is worry but they fully understand the woman, the doctor, that they raised. You cannot inculcate a sense of service in your offspring and then complain when they choose to do that very thing—serve others. You, yourself, visit dangerous places all the time, your parents must feel the same anxiety. Funny, my folks were more worried when I was not married and wanted to go to medical school. Risking my life is okay, risking my reputation was not. Culture is funny, no."

Chris liked the voice on the other end of the line. He glanced at her picture again that was in her file. "When we meet, I will fill you in on my family. They are the most dangerous thing I usually face. They make the Taliban look like the neighborhood welcoming committee. Welcome to the team, Amar."

"Thank you, and I look forward to working with you and . . . hearing about your family."

———

Karen and Chris walked into the ornate meeting room of the firm where Richard Jackson quickly was accumulating considerable wealth. A couple of dozen impeccably dressed men and women, all reeking of power and affluence, sat around an immense table. Off to the side stood Jules with a cameraman and portable lighting apparatus. Chris headed right for her. "What are you doing here? I was expecting a few of Ricky's wealthy friends."

"Those are the only kind he has these days, wealthy that is. Anyways, I am here to make you famous. Record some of your pitch and then interview you. We can get you a spot on the news, that will piss off your dad. And maybe the camera will loosen up the purse strings of some of these guys. Hell, they just might think you are important."

"Just make sure you get my good side on the camera."

"Hah!" She laughed. "For that you will have to turn around and bend over."

Chris leaned closer and whispered to her. "The best ass in town."

Jules leaned back, "I hope to be reminded of that again before you leave town."

Chris winked at her and walked to where his friend was waiting at the head of the table. After the introductions, Chris looked over the distinguished gathering with his winning smile.

"I suspect most of you are here as a courtesy to Richard here. I have no idea what terrible things he held over you to get you here today. I am sure, though, it was not sufficiently evil to warrant such a punishment. Thank you for stopping by. At least the food he has laid out looks good." There was an appreciative chuckle. "Let me start by being very honest. Some of you are here because you know my father, or have had the distinct pleasure of being bested by him in a business deal." The room stirred. "Don't feel at all obliged to give me a dime based on my father. It will not advantage you one whit. He rather thinks that what I do is a colossal waste of time. Knowing that, some of you may wish to leave now." Chris paused but found that the eyes focused on him now contained real interest. "As you may know, Richard and I go back a long time. I like to think that he represents one motivation for what I have chosen to do in life. When we met in high school, all he knew how to do was to play basketball and to knock me on my ass. In truth, he was better at the latter than the former." They were laughing now, maybe this would not be as boring as they had imagined. "Despite his lack of observable talent, I thought there was a glimmer of hope in this guy, particularly after he broke my nose within twenty minutes of being introduced. And despite his denials, it was a sucker punch. Today, you see an accomplished financial wizard before you. My point is this, don't underestimate people. You look out over those suffering in remote parts of the world and think, 'so what.' But you never know what talent and inventiveness and genius might be lost if some black or brown youngster is ignored and permitted to die in anonymity or merely survive in a swamp of ignorance. Ensuring everyone a chance is not only humane but a great investment. Terrorism is not bred by religion or political conviction but by the absence of hope and viable alternatives." Chris launched into a punchy, short presentation that gave the basic elements of what his initiative was about. Then he switched to his preferred Q and A format rather than guessing at what any audience needed to hear.

"Tell me again how your program is different from others. I am not sure I understand."

Chris responded with his monologue about the need for multidisciplinary teams when dealing with families torn asunder by war, famine, and the collapse of civil authorities. "If you know how to use a hammer, you believe that every problem can be solved by hammering it to death. But nothing in life is that unidimensional or simple. If everything has been taken from you, primary medical help is just a start. You need nutritional assistance, educational opportunities, security, help putting your community together. Each situation imposes a distinct set of challenges, there is no one-size-fits-all solution. What I found is that all the separate silos of help were available. They simply were not being integrated in a meaningful way. That is the big thing I do, get these different systems together to blend their distinct technologies into some coherent whole."

"Where does your money go? I am not clear how it is used."

Chris smiled. "You mean beyond supporting my lavish lifestyle. In truth, it does not go for my salary, I have a trust fund for that. But there are several areas where additional resources are critical. Most service providers are stretched beyond their limits and need additional incentives to get to the table. Oddly enough, integration is not seen as an undiluted plus for each participating program. They feel they are losing a distinct presence that going it alone provides. We don't want recipients to identify their benefactor as a single program. We want everyone to suppress the instinct to seek institutional credit. We want results and not merely to count specific services provided. To offset what we are asking, some financial incentives are initially needed. Another factor is security. We don't pick the low-lying fruit and I lose plenty of sleep worrying about the people who put themselves in harm's way. Finally, we have direct costs for medical and educational personnel and supplies. The initiative has grown quickly as have the costs."

"How do you know what you do is working? Where is the evidence?"

"This is a dagger in my heart. I occasionally teach a program evaluation course at Oxford. I know about the methods needed to assert causal connections between intervention and results. And I certainly know all about the arguments for gathering such evidence. Sometimes, however, we do not have the luxury of assessing our beliefs according to the strictures of science. Where we go and what we do is so idiosyncratic that we cannot control all the factors necessary to isolate the contribution of our specific intervention. We are, by necessity, very responsive to both exigencies and opportunities. Thus, we do not have a stable environment or intervention. That makes the isolation of impacts well-nigh impossible. Still, we have tons of data that suggest incredible results. I have some evidence to share if you want to read the material. I could argue that such data are suggestive of positive results. But such data are not the same as proof. They are indicative, sometimes compellingly so, of the good we are doing. But I am not a snake oil salesman. I am a scientist turned social service entrepreneur. At the end of the day, some faith is required by you. Some faith in me is necessary."

"Why are you doing this? What do you get out of it?"

"Wow, that is a good question. I think there are several answers, not all of them pretty. Let me start with a non-flattering response. I do this in part to upset my father. Most of you know him either through business dealings or by reputation. He defines what it is to be a capitalist, a man for whom risk, failure, and reward are the very meat of life. Those who fail simply were not hard enough or smart enough or worthy enough. Those that fail must suffer the consequences that a lack of talent or luck or whatever it is that determines the outcomes in life. Failure and suffering are not pretty but are essential if the competition inherent in the real world is to create the proper incentives for the progress that emerges from a competitive society. That is a common view in this country. I daresay, it is a common view in this room. I might argue though that we could all be more, what shall I say, authentic in our approach to the issue of proper incentivization. For example, I could argue that estate taxes, what Republicans call death taxes, should be elevated to much higher rates, perhaps considerably higher than the rate we apply to ordinary income. Now don't all throw things at me at once. But think about it. If your offspring inherit a lot of money, what is their incentive to become risk-taking entrepreneurs, the next generation of movers and shakers. They might turn out like me, a dilettante trying to save the world. Surely, an awful outcome to contemplate."

Chris paused to look over the group. He was reaching them, he was sure. "Now, I might note that this is where my personal keeper, Karen Fisher, who is standing in the corner over there, takes me out of the room and kicks me in the family jewels while asking me if I really think it is wise to insult people from whom I expect to get some money." Chuckles ran through the room. "It is not my intention to insult anyone. I merely want to stress that our view of what fairness means is quite personal. You do work hard. You take risks. Most times you reap great rewards and sometimes spectacular failure. What you do is commendable. But never forget that untold families, largely forgotten and forsaken, work incredibly hard and take risks you can hardly imagine. Their rewards often are merely to survive another day, feed some scraps to their children who sport distended tummies and cry from a gnawing hunger you shall never know. That is a reality my father will never understand nor appreciate. I guess I do what I do to remind myself of that reality, no matter how futile the gesture. My ultimate fantasy is that I might reach him with that reality."

Chris paused, wondering how he had wandered in such a direction. He noticed Karen looking at him intently when she spoke up. "You mentioned another reason?"

"Oh yes, sorry. See why I need her around? The other reason is far less self-absorbed, if that is the correct term. Unfortunately, I spend most of my time in England, a place I love but it is far removed from the people I serve. As often as I can, however, I get out to various sites. Reality is very sobering. There are days when the immensity of the challenges is staggering in their complexity. Reality often makes me question what I am doing. But there are those moments when a child's life is saved, when a family is reunited, when hope is restored, when you see a young girl's eyes light up when exposed to education for the first time." He paused. "Look around. When you wear the best clothes, eat the best foods, sleep on satin sheets, live in luxury, little touches you. Nothing stands out. When a bowl of soup means everything to a child, and you can put that bowl in their hands and watch the sheer joy on their mother's face, that can mean more than a fleet of private jets. You are giving someone else everything. Like you, I have experienced the luxury wealth and privilege provides. Believe me, all that pales in comparison to touching someone with hope." His voice had become almost a whisper but those around the table leaned forward to catch his words.

After an extended silence, another question was posed. "What does the future hold for you, your program?"

Chris wondered if they really wanted to know if he would enter the family business as all had expected, knowledge of the family crisis had to be known to some in the room. He decided to ignore that possible agenda. "Hard to say. Some things are rather clear to me. I want to spend more time in the field, not that I have any real skills to help there. But I find that people with the real talent tolerate my presence, they are very generous. To do that, I will need someone with excellent organizational and management skills to take over leadership of the organization, someone who shares the same vision. Anyone in the room looking for a career change?"

Everyone laughed but then Ricky Jackson raised his hand. "I'm in," he said but qualified that with a smile.

"Sure, Ricky, I can see you giving up your Gucci shoes." Even more laughter. "Beyond that, I probably want to return to the academy. I love teaching and the world of ideas. But we will see."

"Perhaps one final question." Ricky offered to the group.

"I have one," The voice was deep and resonant. The speaker had a full head of silver hair and the look of someone who was accustomed to power and position. "We are sorry to hear that your brother is in the hospital and not doing well. Please accept our best wishes for his recovery. If the worse comes to pass, would that alter your plans? Let me be direct. Would you replace him?" There was considerable whispering throughout the room. Obviously, some did not know the news and others had been asking themselves the same question. Everyone leaned forward. Were they looking at the next heir to the Crawford empire?

But it was Ricky who spoke up. "With all due respect, perhaps we better not get off track. It is time to wrap things up and I am sure you all want to find your checkbooks."

"No, Ricky, I am okay with any question." Then he paused for effect, thinking to himself that he should have addressed this issue early on. "If . . . if the worst comes to pass, my family will have to make some difficult decisions. We will make them as a family in due time. However, it is premature to speculate on such matters. We will see." Chris was disappointed in himself. He wanted to tell them that hell would have to freeze over and pigs would be seen in the sky on flying carpets before he would take the helm of his father's empire. But he chose to demur, leave them wondering. Why was he being so coy? Would they be more generous if they thought they were looking at a future financial icon? Some in the room knew full well that Chris was the talent in the family, except for his twin sister who had drifted off into medicine. How could he not accept the mantle of leadership from his older brother who seemed so incapable of handling this role? Perhaps a large donation to his current diversion might open big doors in the future. He desperately wanted to set them all straight, but he didn't.

"Okay, gentlemen and ladies, checkbooks out. You can make all arrangements through Karen Fisher, I presume."

Chris only nodded as applause filled the room.

Jules approached him as the handshakes were being completed and most had filed out of the room after pressing cards into Karen's hand, not that the information was necessary since she had their bios already. "Don't run away yet, while I got good stuff I want some one-on-one time, with the camera of course."

"You are getting kinky, you want it on film?"

"Film? Just how ancient are you? Anyways, you are good with a crowd. I almost pulled my own checkbook out. You are so . . . so authentic. That is the word I am looking for, authentic. Of course, I know the truth."

"Which is?"

"That you are full of crap." She grabbed his hand with a smile and pulled him to where she thought the light would be better. "Ready for a grilling?"

He smiled his 100-watt smile. "I am always ready for you."

The cameraman looked bemused. Jules noticed and said as an aside. "In case you can't figure it out, we go back a piece."

"Never would have guessed," he said with a smirk.

"Ready?" she asked.

"Shoot, show me what you got."

"Foreplay over," the cameraman chuckled.

"Professor Crawford," Jules started. "It is Professor Crawford."

"Well, I do have a doctorate from Oxford University. Unfortunately, I am not the kind that can prescribe drugs."

"Damn," the cameraman whispered.

Jules pushed on in her professional voice. "Tell us a little
about yourself."

"Well, I am six feet four of twisted steel and sex appeal. Men
want to be me, and women want to be with me. What else does
the audience want to know?"

Jules smiled. "Do you have a wife or girlfriend?"

"I did have a girlfriend, back when I was in college."

"Really? What happened, I am sure Chicago land is dying
to find out."

Chris tried to look pained. "Very sad story. I gave her my all
but in the end, she spurned me."

"I cannot believe that with you being six feet four of sex appeal and all. She must have been a naïve and innocent victim."

"No doubt about that. She always had some excuse for not
committing. She was too young, she had career to think about,
she . . ."

Suddenly neither were smiling any longer. The cameraman
simply walked away from his camera. They never intended to
get on track. "Perhaps you did not ask her in the right way. She
might have needed a little encouragement."

"Well, it was difficult for me as well. I had loved her since high school and . . ."

Jules inhaled sharply. "Sorry, please go on."

"And she kept pushing me away."

"I think she must have been an idiot." There was a twinge in her words.

"There is no question about that though, as I think on it, there is a case to be made that she was very wise indeed."

"How so?" Jules asked.

Chris inhaled, how did they get to this place. "He loved her. Commitment, though, was hard for him. She probably could see that he was not ready. She was one of the most perceptive women he had ever met."

"What about now?" she pushed.

"I don't know, I really don't."

"You don't know if she is still perceptive."

Chris started to respond but just then Ricky approached and broke the trance. "I see you guys are finished, or at least no one is recording his brilliant insights."

"Oh, that only took twenty seconds, not even that." Jules laughed. "You know, roughly the duration of..."

"Hey," Ricky said with exuberance to deflect the sexually fueled innuendo that Jules was about to use. "You knocked it out of the park. I cannot believe you can insult these guys and they still love you. There really is no accounting for taste."

"You should buy my book. The five secrets to separating sheep from their money."

"Listen," Jules piped up. "The news never stops. I must be off. Oh, I never asked. Any change with Chuck?"

"No, not really. Nor will there be. However, I think we are approaching decision time, perhaps later today."

Jules leaned in to kiss him. "Come and see me, please. I am there for you." With that, she turned and headed toward the door.

Karen watched the gorgeous woman exit the room. "Damn," she let out before covering her public exhibition of disappointment with a cough.

Chris leaned toward her. "Oh well, there is always my sister. You can always give her a shot." Then he turned back to Ricky. "I assume that your praise will be accompanied by a more practical demonstration of your appreciation."

"Maybe better than that."

"What can be better than money, particularly taking those ill-gotten gains from the one-percenters."

Ricky didn't laugh at Chris's humor. "As usual, you went right to the heart of the matter. Let's sit." The three of them sat in the now empty meeting room that, by its very design, spoke of power and wealth. Ricky looked at Chris for a moment without saying anything. Then he seemed to arrive at a place to start. "When we first met, I was at a crossroads. My athletic skills gave me some protection in the hood but the pull of everything bad there always was strong. A slip or two and I could easily have become just another gangbanger."

"But you didn't. Look at where you are now."

"Yeah, but sometimes I wonder if I am just a different kind of gangbanger, one that wears two-thousand-dollar suits."

"Wait, Ricky, I am not your confessor."

"Just listen to me for once," then another pause, as Chris glanced briefly at Karen and then settled back. "Around the time we met I used to wander down to the loop and just walk the streets. My hood was not that far away but there were many kids who had never been there. As tough as they were, they could not summon the courage to enter the turf of the enemy. The culture of white America was as foreign to them as if an alien species from Alpha Centauri had suddenly landed in West Chicago. But I was fascinated. Who were these people walking past me in their suits and carrying their briefcases? What were they carrying, where were they going? What were they thinking about? I would look up at the windows in the skyscrapers and just wonder what business went on up there. It all seemed mysterious and secret and way beyond anything I would ever be permitted to see, ever."

"And now you have seen it," it was Karen who spoke. "You really were serious when Chris asked if anyone in the room wanted to chuck all the money and power and do some good in life."

Ricky smiled. "This one is sharp, Chris. Don't lose her."

"Holy shit," was all that Chris could say. For once, he was tongue-tied.

"Listen, I had to find out what was going on in these buildings. Something powerful and mysterious remained hidden from the sight of mere mortals and I desperately wanted to know what it was. But Karen is exactly right, now I know. In the end, it is not worthy of all that much admiration. The incessant looking for edges and advantages to screw someone else becomes tiring very fast. And the social conversations, oh my god. Sometimes I want to put a bullet in my head. How often can you talk about your new condo in St. Moritz or the impressionist painting you just picked up at such a bargain or the latest broad you nailed. Pat, that is my fiancé," he directed at Karen, "goes through the motions but I am sure she is just as turned off by the shallowness as I, at least I think she feels that way though . . ." He paused. It was apparent he was not confident of this fact.

Ricky then went on with emphasis, "Who needs to display their acquisitions with such gusto? Who really gives a fuck? Why not just issue a balance sheet with your net worth and be done with it, move on to a substantive conversation for a change. You should see some of the wives, they order hundred-dollar entrees in fancy restaurants and then peck at the food because they don't want to put on an extra ounce. They buy shoes that cost $1,500 and never wear them because they forget which closet they are in or in which of their five homes they managed to leave them. And they go on and on about the how Clinton had made their life a virtual hell when he raised the goddamn tax rate on personal income. Most of them weren't paying shit anyways since they exploited that deferred interest loophole they had bought from Congress but it was the principle of the thing. They were the movers and shakers of the world and they were being inconvenienced. The world owed them, not the other way around."

"Ricky, I had no idea you were so unhappy."

"I need to get out Chris. If I don't I might snap. Hey, I like nice food and clothes but at the end of the day, all that crap leaves you unsatisfied. Well, it leaves me unsatisfied. You will pick up a paper in London someday and read about the successful black athlete and financial wizard who brought in an AK-47 to the office one day and set about reducing the excess population of self-absorbed robber barons."

"Are you really asking to join me?"

"It hit me. When you were talking about wanting to spend more time in the field, closer to the action. Maybe this could work. I am talented, I have great organizational skills and obviously have wonderful people skills. I have put up with you for almost two decades."

"You would relocate, give up the seven figure bonuses, live in a city with miserable winters."

"You mean unlike Chicago." Then Ricky broke into a broad smile that had earned him several commercials when he played for the Chicago Bulls. "I would give everything up in a nanosecond, but only if you think I can contribute."

"Well," Chris sounded doubtful, "you really sucked at basketball so, my guess is that you must be good at something. I think I can take a chance on you." The two men shook hands.

―――――

Karen and Chris found a bench overlooking the Oak Street Beach. The day was grey and brooding, a fall day where the balance tipped away from the summer days that were behind toward the harsher winter season ahead. Still, joggers were in abundance running along the cement barrier that separated the beach and Lake Michigan from the bustling city.

"Kay is going to meet us here when her shift ends, assuming no mass murders break out which is always a possibility here in Chicago. We are going to get our game plan straight before heading back into the arena."

"Good." Karen mused. "Now that I know for certain that Jules has no taste in romance, she thinks you are sexy. I can't believe that. Kay is looking better to me."

Chris laughed heartily. "Funny, I have no idea what my sister's sexual preferences are. Frankly, I always thought she was asexual. But maybe you will get lucky. Either that or she will smack you upside the head when you make a move. But maybe she reserves the smacks for me, not that I make moves on her but just in general." Then he looked out over the grey water.

"The clarification was not necessary. You are a perv but not that debauched."

"Good, you keep believing that." He gave her his best malevolent smile and then returned his gaze to the lake.

"By the way, I think we did well today. Lots of preliminary pledges but time will tell." When Chris did not respond, she tried another tack. "The thing with Ricky is good, right. I mean, while I don't know him, he seems very smart and competent. It would be good for you to have someone you trust to take over some things, you know . . . raise money and look after logistics. You could get out to the field more, that has always bothered you. I guess I would be working for Ricky then, is that what you are thinking?"

Chris didn't respond right away. "We have to push the decision tonight."

"What?" Karen lost him for a moment.

"Sorry, kiddo. I was thinking about Chuck and the family. It is time. Everyone knows that nothing is going to change." Then he turned directly toward her. "And no, after you break Ricky in, or maybe I should say we break him in, you are with me. Hey, we are a team. I get us into trouble and you bail my ass out. Do you really think I could survive on my own?" He smiled and gave her a kiss on the forehead. "Sorry, I did not pick up that you were concerned. You are stuck with me, as long as you don't mind traveling to the crappiest places in the world."

"You always knew how to sweep a gal off her feet and why, for Christ's sake, would you even think I would want to stick with a numbnuts like you." She couldn't quite keep the pretense up, though, and threw her arm around him as she whispered the words "thank you."

"Oh, get a hotel room, you two." It was Kay who walked up and sat next to her brother. "Ricky called. He told me you raised a boatload of money and recruited him to the cause. A good day, apparently. I guess the old bromide is true—you can fool the people a lot more than you would imagine."

"Well, to be honest, he threw himself at me. I was shocked, but ecstatic. I do need help."

"No shit, I could have told you that years ago."

"As far as the money goes, I can only imagine they thought they were currying favor with Father even though I was honest on that score. This is not your philanthropic crowd, at least not for the most part."

"Again, not exactly breaking news." Then Kay looked around him directly toward Karen Fisher. "I want some time with you. I want your take on what my brother is up to these days, not the propaganda but the straight scoop. Is that okay?"

"Of course." Karen found herself blushing, or feared she was, and wanted to kick herself for responding like a school girl. Kay did not see the natural charm that Jules exhibited. Still, as Karen looked more closely, she could see the woman's natural beauty.

Then Kay turned to Chris. "I am with you concerning Father. You were right on day one. I knew that. But I also know you must let people get there on their own. You don't always have that luxury in the ER. A loved one is with them one day, then some tragedy strikes in an instant and you must walk out and tell the family that they will never see that person again. It numbs you to pain, something essential to professional survival, until you know the person involved. If there is any good to come of this, I am reminded why I became a physician in the first place, why I chose the ER. Real people are involved, real lives are at stake. But in the end, reality cannot be avoided, it must be faced head on. And if people can't get there, you may need to push a little. Perhaps it is time to push."

"Thank you," Chris responded. "I was going to ask if you were ready." As he looked over at his twin sister, he saw a tear make its way down her cheek. Chris looked back out over the water. "This place never gets old for me. I suppose because it reminds me of times when everything was less complicated. Becoming an adult is way overrated. I mean, after all, this place is not that special, not really. Still, it never gets old . . . not even on a gloomy day."

Kay took her brother's hand and rose from the bench. The three started toward the hospital, with Karen hanging back to give the siblings some personal space, just in case there were intimacies and private thoughts to be shared. She watched them closely as they continued to walk hand in hand. There had been nothing until now to suggest any warmth between them. That had struck her as peculiar. Her prior had been that all biological twins were close, that they shared something special. But maybe that was only true of identical twins, those with the same genetic material. Still, it appeared now that a closeness was there between these two, apparently revealed by family crisis, though typically hidden behind shells they had erected to get them through lives far more complicated than they looked from the outside. They were whispering to one another as they walked. She could not quite hear the words but hoped they were comforting to each of them. Then she panicked. Knowing Chris, he was probably revealing to his sister that she had the hots for her. No, he wouldn't do that, would he? He was dead man, though, if he did.

As they entered the hospital, the twins released each other's hands. Both were struck with similar thoughts, how the sights and smells of these institutions evoked a mask that hid the reality of death and dying. Everything was sparkling clean and antiseptic. Still, you knew that mortality lie everywhere, the battle to prolong life was ever present and often lost. At the same time both knew that this battleground on which life and death was waged was a peculiarly American terrain. Chris could never ignore the fact that the United States spent almost seventeen percent of its national treasure on health care yet achieved remarkably modest results. He knew it was a tragedy that went unspoken, even unrecognized by most. The real winners in this contest were the providers of care, not the patients unless they were wealthy and privileged. The winners were the ones managing insurance companies, pharmaceutical firms, large care providers, and anyone else who could manipulate the price of care and ration the availability of medical help. Yet his father, even given all the resources at his command, would soon lose his struggle to keep his son alive. Even his wealth could not delay the inevitable.

Kay also looked about with her private thoughts. She saw the consequences of a flawed health care system from another perspective, the inside view. She had her choice of professional opportunities given her training and demonstrated skill set. But she chose the worst of the worst in a city known for violence and mayhem. It was her quiet rebellion against a system that clearly favored the rich and powerful who got the best of care while her patients were given marginal attention and resources and left to perish in anonymity. Day after day she did what she could to level out an inherently uneven playing field, but her efforts were washed over by a tsunami of institutional indifference and political neglect. And those she labored to heal often seemed unappreciative of her effort, blaming her for things she could not correct nor even address. To this day she smarted from the public reaction to Clinton's effort to improve access to health care in America, an effort that resulted in the humiliating rejection of his party in the next Congressional elections. What kind of country was this? Is suffering and death the proper consequence of poverty? How odd that the most passionate of Christians, the evangelicals, somehow found such a venal interpretation of scriptures in their spiritual reflections. They sold out Christ's message of loving the least fortunate among us for permission to hate the very ones that God's son would love the most.

Their private musings ended when the elevator door opened to reveal the floor where Chuck's body, sustained by artificial means, was to be found. Kat was standing there, looking forlorn and lost.

"Thank god you are finally here," Kat exploded, anxiety distorting her face. "Father is beside himself, yelling at the doctors for not doing enough."

"The cavalry is here, Kat. Sorry you had to put up with all this."

They met one of the doctors as he exited Chuck's room. He looked haggard and annoyed. Kay immediately stopped him and apologized, anticipating what the man undoubtedly had just endured.

"No need to apologize, this comes with the territory. I must say, though, that guy is a pompous ass of the first class. Sorry if you are family."

"No need to explain," Kay said with a smile. "We haven't met yet, I am Dr. Crawford, a physician myself, and the patient's sister. I know my brother's condition. There is no hope, correct? No soft words needed with me, just the facts."

"Then you will get none. There is absolutely no hope. Your brother is brain dead. I am sorry. I will spare you the clinical explanations, if you don't mind."

"Thank you for the honesty. And sorry for what Father put you through. If it is any consolation, he will be worse to us."

The attending physician finally cracked a smile. "Do you need the tranquilizers now or after the family discussion? Here is the document that needs to be signed to end things, to let him pass on. Your father refused to accept it, wanted to rip it up in fact." Kay accepted the document with which she was totally familiar. "Again, my condolences." Then he swept down the corridor, anxious to escape.

"Did you run into that quack?" Charles Crawford exploded as they walked into the room. "They must hand out medical degrees in boxes of cereal these days. What was that cereal, cracker jacks or something?"

They all ignored him and walked to the bed. Chuck lay there as he had for the past several days, immobile and at peace, or so it seemed to his siblings.

Kay suddenly wheeled around. "Everyone to the visiting room . . . now!"

Charles Crawford was the last to arrive, looking reluctant and dismayed at his sudden loss of control. He was a man who relished power and the capacity to shape events about him. But this was different. He could not demand a different outcome by ordering the medical staff around. At one point, he had blustered about going to the hospital board of trustees to no avail. Another time he suggested a generous donation if only a miracle might be forthcoming. But all was for naught and such impotence enraged him. Surely though, he could control his own family but that was not a given as he looked at the faces awaiting him.

Kay spoke first, "Time to face reality. Chuck is gone, period. When they say he is brain dead, that is it. Machines are sustaining life, but it is not a living person being sustained. Time to be adults about this, time to exercise some mercy, time to let him go." She looked directly at her father.

His eyes burned back at her with a frightening intensity. He had not expected this from her, he had prepared himself to lock horns with his second son. He had always been the openly rebellious one, defying his wishes and challenging his world view. Kristen had been a discrete rebel, going her own way but quietly, absent any fanfare or fireworks. Perhaps he had something to do with that. He never confronted her. As a female, she was less important than his two sons. Male progeny was essential to his sense of proportion and order in life. Women had other roles to play in life. Daughters, at best, were frivolous niceties. Her assertive actions threw him off for a moment. He said nothing.

"A family vote then. I vote for mercy. Kat, what should we do?"

She could barely utter the word "yes."

"Yes means?"

"Let him go," the words now came out with surprising conviction.

Kay turned to Beverly. "What do you think, dear?"

"Yes, let him go. It is the only merciful thing to do." She was surprisingly firm.

"I know what Chris believes, that makes it a majority. Is it unanimous?"

"This isn't a goddamn democracy," it was Charles, his face flushed with anger.

Kay ignored him. "Mother, I hate to ask but—"

"That is fine, dear, I understand." She was standing immobile, her eyes watery and her body trembling visibly. Everyone knew she was inebriated, struggling mightily to appear in command of herself. Her words were measured, as if prepared from a script. It was an effort to articulate her thoughts through slurred speech. Of course, the addict knows that no one is fooled but the game must be played. Slowly, she enunciated each word. "Kristen, dear, I agree with you."

"Mary," her husband roared, "you cannot be serious."

"Look at me, Charles." The woman suddenly stood erect. "I am totally serious."

"She cannot vote. She is drunk out of her skull."

"Shut up, Charles. You have humiliated me for the last time. You thought you had gotten such a bargain marrying a woman of such wealth. But it didn't work out like you planned, did it? I didn't need your support, did I? That has killed you all these years. You could never completely control me as you do everyone else. Why do you think I put all that money in a trust for the kids? I could not bear the thought of you trying to abuse them with your damn money and that obsessive demand for control." She stopped. Her lips quivered as if she had shocked herself when she realized what had come out of her mouth. Others in the room stood transfixed. No one had ever seen such defiance from her. They thought her completely incapable of such independence, such strength.

"Mary," Charles uttered in a lower voice, "you are not well."

"And who made me so sick," she seethed. "Just who do you think destroyed me, and Junior, and every vestige of affection and tenderness in this so-called family. If I were not a Catholic I would have left you years ago. I . . . I would have aborted my pregnancies before you had a chance to . . ."

She never got to finish, Charles Sr. shot out a hand that slapped her hard across the face. She staggered back, tottering as if about to fall. Kay leapt to catch her. Chris looked on, stunned for a moment. When his brain caught up with the reality before him he lunged toward his father, grabbing him by the neck and slamming him against the wall.

"You son of a bitch!" Chris exploded. His father was a strong man for his age, but Chris retained the agility and power of a man who had honed his body on the athletic field. He literally lifted his father off the ground as he spit-out venom that came from a place he never knew existed. "You piece of worthless shit. You ever touch our mother again and I swear I shall kill you with my bare hands. Do you understand, do you fucking understand?"

Words reached Chris from far away. He felt someone pulling at him, yelling his name. "Chris, Chris, please," it was Beverly, Chuck's wife. "Let him go." Then Kat grabbed his other arm.

Chris stared at his father, hate still twisting his face into something unrecognizable. But he loosened his grip and the man landed back on the ground, his knees buckling and his mouth gasping for breath. Kat and Beverly pulled Chris farther away from the object of his wrath. Kay had her arms around her mother, comforting her.

No one said anything until Kay moved to retrieve the document she hastily stuffed in her purse. She thrust the papers into her father's hand with the words, "Sign this where I have indicated."

"What?" he gasped, seemingly disoriented.

"Sign the goddamn paper," her words would brook no contradiction.

The patriarch of the family seemed to be recovering. He finally looked at the paper. Everyone in the family looked on expectantly, assuming he would rip it up or restart the battle of wills. But he slowly found a pen in his pocket and, leaning over a table, scrawled his name where it was required. "Happy now." He spit the words out.

Kay took the document back. "We are ending my brother's life. We are letting him be at peace. No, I am not happy. But I know what must be done, and I will do it, goddamn it."

Father and daughter stared at one another for what seemed an eternity. Then the father blinked as if coming back from some distant place. "You are dead to me," he said to Kay's face. "All of you, dead to me." He looked wildly around the room before disappearing down the corridor.

The remaining family said nothing as each signed the document. Later, the group sat in a silent vigil as the medical staff terminated the life sustaining machines. Within minutes the beep, beep, beep of the monitor shifted to a continuous annoying buzz until someone shut it off. Each person silently kissed the immobile form on the bed before saying their silent goodbye.

———

He could hear Jules on the other end of the intercom. "Yes?"

"It is Chris, is your offer still good?" No response, just the buzzer that permitted entrance to the secure building.

She had been about to go bed, wearing a robe when she opened the door. "Do you want a drink?" she asked.

"I suppose." Then, before she could move, he added. "It is done. Chuck is gone. Kay . . . Kay somehow managed to get Father's signature. I was useless, I almost killed him with my bare hands . . . Father that is, not my brother."

"Chris, you could never . . ."

"Jules, I had my hands around his neck. I could have . . . it scared me. I couldn't be alone tonight."

Jules was not sure what to say. She had never seen him look so helpless, so stricken. "I wish, I wish I had some magic words."

"I think . . . I think I just need you tonight. I have this need for human contact, warmth, life . . . just some kind of connection. I want to touch something positive. Now I feel foolish. I should not be burdening you with . . ."

Jules opened the robe and let it fall to the floor, standing naked before him.

"Fuck," was all Chris could get out, his emotions raw and on the surface.

"Well," Jules smiled. "I rather hoped that might be what you needed, what you came by for."

Chris permitted his primitive feelings to take hold of him. Sometimes, just before sex, he knew the mind goes blank. The anticipation of what is about to happen overcomes all sentient thought. Urgency replaces intention, movements are driven by raw need. Jules and Chris suddenly were entwined on the floor, she frantically pulling his clothes off while he grasped with consummate greed at every inch of her body. They tried moving toward the bedroom, That destination now seemed too far removed, an impossible distance to traverse. His mouth found the sweet spot between her legs which he attacked with savage hunger. He lingered there, knowing that penetration would end the erotic dance all too quickly and he refused to be greedy. But she insisted after a while and, not being quite sure whether she had already come, found his way inside her.

They were lying next to one another breathing heavily. "We should get all the way to the bed, do this right," Chris suggested.

"I don't know, I think this was awfully right," Jules sighed.

Just then his phone rang. He searched for his pants and the source of the sound. "I should check this out, could be important."

"I don't know about your priorities." She whispered. "I think what we were just doing was very, very important. Look how calm you are now. You were about ready to explode when you arrived."

"Karen, what's up? Yeah, I am with Jules. I needed . . . no, I suppose I don't have to explain . . . ah, ah, ah, okay, ah-ha . . . really, you must be kidding . . . I can't believe it . . . yes, of course we can work something out. You tell Kay we will chat in the morning." He looked at Jules as if to ask, I can stay the night, can't I? She mouthed the words "don't even try to leave." Then he spoke into his phone again. "Yes, in the morning. Oh, and tell Kay one thing for me, that I love her. She . . . she . . . well just tell her that, okay."

"So?" Jules looked at him expectantly.

"Kay wants to join me. She and Karen have been talking."

"In England?"

"Not so much. She thinks she might want to become part of my mission, in the field. She has been grilling Karen about what we really do. My guess is that all this drama got to her. She needs to escape as well or maybe it is more than that. Wow, things are happening fast. I can always use good talent to head the medical teams. Say, you interested in Pakistan, Africa? You don't know medicine worth shit but you do have some really great healing remedies." The issue of Karen joining his organization, however, did not come up again while Chris was in Chicago, which pleased him.

"Okay stud, you are getting delusional. Time to turn off your brain for a while. You need more of my special remedy." With that they arose from the floor and made their way to the bedroom.

Later, they lay in bed, spent from the passion unleashed by levels of sexual frenzy that both realized had been missing from their lives in recent times. Jules noticed what she thought of as a tear finding its way down his cheek. "Wow, I don't often make men cry," she whispered as she brushed away the wet streak.

"Well, it takes so much effort to please you . . ." Then he stopped. "No, the truth is that when we finished I found my thoughts drifting back to my brother."

"Sorry," she whispered.

"I was so focused on the battle with Father I forgot the finality of it all. My head knows he is in a better place but . . . but it is forever. The rest of me wonders if I could have done more. I tried, I really did try to take him with me but . . ."

"Don't, Chris. Don't go there. You are not responsible. How many times did you tell me, we are all responsible for our own lives. We can give others opportunity but cannot lead them to the promised land."

"My god, woman, you are going to use my own crap against me. Shit, I must be suffering from post- coital depression."

"What?" she scoffed.

"Okay, enough sadness. I have a question for you." It was obvious he wanted to go in a different direction.

"The answer is yes." She smiled.

"Yes what?" he asked.

"You are the best lover I have ever had. Or, yes, you rocked my world. Isn't that what all men want to know?"

"Other men perhaps. But I know I am the best." He knew that was a mistake as soon as the words left his mouth. Now he would pay the price.

"You are an arrogant shit," she said with a laugh as she began to tickle his sides, their bodies coming close to another bout of frantic sex.

"Wait, woman! Give me a chance to recover."

"Damn, you are getting old," she said as she rubbed his muscular chest.

"But like wine, right, aged to perfection. That is right, isn't it? Don't make be beg here."

"Oh, of course, the best I have ever had." She tried to purr seductively but they both giggled.

"Okay, a serious question. Why haven't you ever married?" He waited but nothing came back. "No, I would like to know. I mean, you are a pain in the ass, that is clear. Men are stupid, however. I am sure you have knocked out many a guy, in a good way, not by whacking them over the head with a vase."

"Oh, I don't know." She tried to avoid his query, she looked away. He had raised himself up on an elbow so that he could look in her eyes. Slowly, he used a finger to trace a pattern over her beguiling facial features before wandering down to the nipples on her breasts. She could tell he was getting erect again and considered avoiding the question until they would start up again. She sensed though that he was determined to wait her out. "Yeah, I have turned down guys, some who were real athletes, not Ivy League pretend ball players like you."

"But why?" He was not backing off. "I don't understand."

"It doesn't matter." She tried one more time.

"No, tell me. Why?" He was not backing off. "Wait, I know what's going on. You're a lesbian who is kind enough to have pity sex with me. That's it I bet. Good, Karen will be ecstatic, she has the hots for you."

"Sorry, she is out of luck."

"Then why? I am not giving up."

"No," she protested again.

"Sorry, I am not giving up. No sex for you."

"That is your threat? How will I survive?" She chuckled. Damn him, he always made her chuckle.

"I can wait forever." He sat fully up and crossed his arms.

She stared at him. "Damn you, because none of them were you." The words just came out and she could not take them back. "Happy now?"

"What?" He wasn't sure he caught her words.

"Oh my god, you are going to make me say it again." The next sentence came out in measured terms as she turned slightly so that he could not see her moist eyes. "Because none of these other guys were you."

Chris laid back on her bed so that they both could stare at the ceiling. After a long silence, he whispered, "Oh my god, you love me."

"Don't be silly." The words caught in her throat.

"You love me," he repeated.

She was silent so long that he was certain the next thing he would hear would be gales of laughter. "You really are a moron. You never got it, did you? I . . . I have loved you since high school, from the moment you walked out and left me standing naked and mortified that day I threw myself at you."

He sensed unusual feelings coursing through his body. His instinct was to get up, maybe escape. But she sensed that and moved closer to him. Almost absentmindedly she began to stroke his penis which immediately responded. "I see you know the way to a man's heart," he murmured.

"Well, it's not exactly a big secret." She wanted to change the subject, this suddenly had gotten too deep, way too personal. "I probably should have made some crap up, for never getting married that is, taken it off the table right away."

"I am thinking," he said quietly. "Maybe we should get married."

"Be serious."

"I am deadly serious. If Ricky and Kay join me, I want you there as well. We could be like a family again. Really, this is not silly at all. If what we have, whatever it is, has lasted this long that must mean something."

"What it means is that we are idiots, or maybe that no one with any sense wants us."

"That is bullshit, I know many girls that would be thrilled with a big loser like me. And you really are a catch, even I can see that. You even have a good job. Come on, let's get married. I am serious."

She paused for a long time. He was certain she was going to say yes. But a different word came out, "No."

"No?"

"No, not now. Listen, Chris. I do love you. We have been best friends for most of my adult life, wonderful lovers, confidants, just about everything two people can be ..."

"These are shit arguments for avoiding marriage. What is the but?"

"Your brother just died, your family is broken, you are facing all kinds of changes. Let's wait six months, a year at most. If you feel the same way, maybe we can go ahead. I am not saying no forever, just for now. I don't want you on an emotional rebound of sorts. And I have a lot of stuff to sort out myself—this career of mine. I worked hard, there might be a network opportunity on the horizon. I am not sure I can break into the media over there." Then she let her words dribble to an end.

"Shit, there is nothing there we can't work out. We can make this work."

"Well, there is one other thing."

"Ah," Chris moaned, "the one more thing."

"Listen to me, dumb shit. Most guys struggle against making a commitment. That comes with the macho guy crap. But they fold when the right girl comes along. It was all bullshit to begin with. But you are believable. When you, as you have said so many times that I consider it your middle name, assert that you are not settling down, I believe you. Everyone has believed you. In fact, it is the only crap that comes out of your mouth that people do believe."

"Maybe my time has come."

"Hah, and maybe I will get a movie role opposite Denzel Washington. Listen, I am not going to trap you into something that is not you."

"But . . ."

"No," Jules asserted in a way that would brook no retort. "However, there is something that you can do for me." She tried sounding sexy as they both realized he was fully erect once again.

"You are going to kill me, woman." He smiled pulling her on top of him.

"Good, my plan is working." She returned his smile but inside she was awash with confusion. "Chris, I am up for a network position. I cannot say more than that. This would be the worst time to complicate things personally. Do you understand?"

"A network opportunity? Did you just make that up . . . to let me down easy?"

"No, really. I am deadly serious about that. It is a secret at present. Not a word, not even to your sister. You got that?"

"Damn. Keeping this secret will kill me. I really want to brag to all my male friends that I nailed a future star."

"Wait," she looked suspiciously at him. "with all your legions of lovers you never managed to nail someone famous?"

"I might have. I never asked them what they did."

At that, Jules laughed out loud. "And you wonder why I won't marry you."

CHAPTER 5

THE FIRST HEGIRA

"Come in, Abdul, as you can see, my clinic is not busy these days." Dr. Pamir Masoud took his old friend by the hand and led him to the area he used as a private office. "What brings you here? I hope not an ailment."

"No, no, I am well, physically. It is more a heavy heart that afflicts me."

"My good friend, please sit. We are long overdue for a good chat. Azita, go and get some tea for us, and some sweets. Then you can go back to your studies."

"Yes, Papa." She dashed off.

The two men exchanged pleasantries until the girl returned from her errand with the refreshments on a tray. Rather than leave the men to have their discussion in privacy, she lingered in the background, hoping that her continued presence might go unnoticed. She wanted to hear what the adults were about to share with one another. Her curiosity, as ever, remained insatiable.

Pamir, however, noticed. "Azita, go back to your books, such an impish girl."

"But Papa . . ." she tried to protest.

"What are you trying to do," the good doctor tried to sound cross, "put more grey hairs on top of my head?"

"Yes, Papa . . . I mean no, Papa." With that, Azita hung her head and slowly exited the room still hoping that her kind father would relent and call her back. He had trouble being firm with her. This time, however, he remained firm.

Dr. Masoud took a sip of tea and then asked his companion, "I love her dearly, but she can be such an exasperation. Tell me, what makes your heart heavy these days."

"You, my friend. You are the reason."

"Abdul, how can this be so? Have I done something to offend you? If so, it was not intentional in any way."

"No, no, my dear friend. You have always been kind and generous with me, with everyone in truth. Surely Allah looks with much favor on you. I cannot think of anyone in your acquaintance that finds fault with you or thinks of you in any way other than with the highest esteem. It is those who cannot look inside your heart that are having trouble with you, those who would not understand even if they could."

"The authorities?"

"Yes, my friend, our religious overlords, the Taliban. You must see that fewer people come to your clinic. Have you asked yourself why that is? They are afraid. There is talk at the mosque, among the Imams. Such talk then spreads to people in the shops and on the streets. These evil men, they have spread their fear everywhere. Now, even those who have been coming to you for medical assistance all their lives ask themselves whether it is safe now to do so. If I go to Dr. Masoud's clinic, will I also fall under suspicion? Will my family be endangered? These are questions and concerns not easily dismissed. They may love you, my friend, but they love their own families more."

"And yet you are here. Are you such a foolish man that you come to me despite this, that you would risk being seen talking to me?" Pamir looked deeply into the tired and concerned eyes of his friend.

"I suppose I am. I can do no other." His friend, Abdul, looked up at the ceiling, his expression was troubled. Perhaps he was questioning at last the wisdom of what he was doing. More likely, it was the sad nature of his message.

"Pray tell me, what kind of talk is this you hear about me," asked Dr. Masoud, though he knew the answer already. "What apostacy can they possibly believe I have committed?"

"You must know already. In your heart, you must be able to guess." For reasons Abdul could not quite locate, he did not want to say the words. "It is painful for me to even say such lies aloud."

Dr. Masoud leaned over and took his old companion's hands in his. "This is not a time for niceties. What is it?"

"It is said that you are not favorably inclined to our new leaders and the changes they have brought to our country. You are not demonstrating the required fervor in your heart and in your actions." Abdul looked pained that he had to utter such words. "Word is spreading that you are not a believer."

"And these men know what is in my heart? They must be wiser than the Prophet himself." The doctor tried to sound light in his response. He knew, though, that only a kind of desperate necessity brought this man to his door.

"You must take this seriously. These are not men to be ignored. Once you fall under suspicion, it is almost impossible to escape their attentions if not their wrath."

"But I have done nothing to them," the doctor complained, his voice elevated in exasperation. "I tend to my profession and my family."

"I can only tell you what I have heard," Abdul added softly. "You know I do not share what they say about you with others, only you. The word on the street is that you are failing to raise your daughter correctly as a good Muslim girl. Rumor is that you are teaching her things not suitable for a girl."

"Azita, I suppose. That is outrageous." He exhibited real anger, rare indeed for the good doctor. "I am sorry. I don't mean to be cross with you. You are merely a messenger. Even coming to me is an act of some courage on your part. That is obvious to me and I appreciate your great courage or is it foolishness?"

Abdul smiled. "Not so much courage, more out of affection and respect for you."

"I am so fortunate to have you in my circle of friends, dear man. You have been like a brother to me, which is important since my own extended family is so far away. Please tell me what you have to say. And be most direct with me. Tell me what I need to know."

"Yes, this is what I have heard. Some of the talk also concerns your wife. She has been heard to complain about the way women are treated nowadays, she is outspoken in her words though what she says is obvious to most of us. She says such things only among her friends and acquaintances but, I am sorry to say, there are no longer any safe places. Truly we are now imprisoned within our homes."

"I find that hard to believe, she is very careful. We have talked about this on many occasions." The doctor wanted to argue more, he wished to convince his friend that he and his wife were not naïve or foolish people. But held his tongue, that would be excess pride speaking. "Please, I apologize, go on."

"I suspect it is less what she has said than who she is." Abdul found this discussion harder than he thought it would be.

"I don't understand."

"She is an educated woman. She taught mathematics at the university level in her younger years. This alone makes her a dangerous person to these fanatics. I agree with you, Pamir, she has kept her counsel in these troubled times very well. She has not flaunted her education or her intelligence, at least not on her own behalf. However, even the slightest slips on her behalf is interpreted in the worst way."

"I understand what you are saying. In any case, I suspect the real problem is not with Madeena." Dr. Masoud looked infinitely sad.

"Yes," his friend responded in a low voice. Abdul hung his head. He knew how close his friend was to his youngest child. She had inherited the attributes that defined him as a special person. She was the intelligent, inquisitive issue of his line. More than that, she had his sensitivity and warmth. She cared about people and their wellbeing though she was more than capable of exasperating him by becoming preoccupied with her own insatiable curiosity from time to time. "Yes, it is Azita."

"But I have been careful, she has been careful."

"Oh my friend. You remember the beating she received so many weeks ago. They have not forgotten what they consider blasphemy against the word of the Prophet. They have been watching, talking to people. They know that you let her help you, that you are teaching her the medical arts, how to speak English, which they see as the language of the sworn infidels."

"But I do this in the privacy of my own home, my clinic. I have wanted to take her to the hospital, but I have not." The good doctor knew how foolish his protests were. "Even here, I am careful, usually only involving her with people I know personally. I try not to flaunt her talents and I have talked with her repeatedly about being careful. And English, why it is the universal language, even many of the Taliban speak this language."

"For such an intelligent man, you can say such foolish things. You know that they have spies everywhere and that what is innocent to a normal person is not seen as innocent to them. They have been talking to your clients ever since that day. Most say nothing, you are well loved. But some speak out of fear, or simply want to curry favor with the new regime. Some will fabricate sins that never happened just to look good to these fearsome tyrants."

"Yes, of course you are right. I am so naïve, so trusting. But tell me why has nothing happened yet then," the doctor asked, suddenly feeling concerned.

Abdul leaned in to give his next point emphasis. "They have been reluctant to come after you because you are so popular among the people. They know you are considered a just man.

But I am afraid any reluctance they feel is evaporating. The longer they remain in power the more emboldened they become. They are feeling more untouchable with each week. But something else is happening." Then he paused.

"Which is, tell me everything."

Abdul sighed and continued, "Azita is about to become a woman. When she was considered a girl, things could be overlooked. That is no longer possible. They now expect her to become a good Muslim woman and retire from public life."

"A good Muslim woman," Pamir almost spit out the words. "How could anyone torture the teachings of the Prophet in such ways."

Suddenly, there was a sound from the adjacent room which served as a waiting room for clients. It was faint and neither man was certain that they had heard anything. Pamir considered whether it was in his imagination, then stood and walked to the other room. But he returned quickly. "I am thinking this discussion has made us paranoid. There was no one there."

Abdul wiped some perspiration from his face. *That was odd,* he thought. It was winter. The temperature was quite cool. The moisture collecting on his neck had nothing to do with the weather. Suddenly, he feared for his own safety, for his family. It was so easy to be painted with the broad brush of being overly familiar with someone suddenly designated as an apostate. If you know the sinner, you have sinned yourself. "I am afraid you will have to tell Azita that she must be a good Muslim woman. It must happen now. It must be very public so that the morals police are satisfied. It is not too late, I pray, but time is running out. I cannot press you on this enough. Do you understand?"

"Yes, my friend. I understand, and I thank you."

Abdul had a sinking feeling as he looked upon his friend's face. "Oh, I don't like what I am seeing in your eyes."

The good doctor put his face in his hands for a few moments. Abdul felt a frisson of hope. Perhaps his friend was accepting the reality of his situation. He could not bear the thought of losing his longtime companion, the man with whom he had spent almost a lifetime sharing hopes and fears. He knew the penalty of those that defied the regime. At a minimum, it was torture and loss of livelihood. Perhaps it would be longer term incarceration under such conditions that one's survival was not assured. In extreme cases, people merely disappeared, sometimes their battered bodies were returned to the family, sometimes not. In the more gruesome circumstances the remains were displayed publicly to guarantee that all understood the consequences of defying the rules of Sharia law as defined by the Taliban. When a lesson was deemed necessary, a public beheading would be carried out for all to witness, including family members. They would be forced to watch.

Finally, Dr. Masoud looked up as if he had come to some conclusion. "No, these men shall not have my soul. They shall not rob my daughter of her dreams."

"My good friend, please think . . ."

"No, Abdul, you listen to me. I shall not sacrifice the dreams of my child, her passion. When she first started following me around I found it charming. I was flattered as any father would be but did not take it seriously. She was a child. Soon, something else would catch her fancy. Then, my friend, slowly I came to understand something. She has the gift. She has intelligence and drive and compassion and all the things a great healer should possess. She might even become a teacher of others, the highest calling. One day I asked myself a simple question."

Abdul began to shake his head, trying to interject, "But—"

"Let me finish, my good companion." Pamir was not to be interrupted. "I asked myself a simple question. What if the gift is real? Why would Allah give her these things if He did not intend her to use them? How can I thwart His will, her passion?"

"And you are so convinced that this is some divine intention?" Abdul was becoming frightened for his friend. "Is this not presumptuous on your part? Would He not have given such gifts to Majeed? That, at least would make some sense. I hate to say this but it is far too easy to believe what we want to believe."

Pamir extended his hand and placed it on his friend's arm. "I know, I know all the thoughts in your head and heart. They have been part of my agony for many months now. I am an analytical man. I was trained in science in England. We were discouraged from letting our passions, our heart, dominate our head. Whatever impediment or obstacle you can suggest, I have considered it, usually at great length."

"Then you are a fool," Abdul's words exploded from him, not in anger but desperation. He had not expected such resistance from a man known for his probity and common sense. He bolted upright and started pacing the room. "If you do not put an end to this foolishness, you will be tortured and probably killed, your family ruined. And there will be nothing that we, those who love you, will be able to do."

"But there is," the doctor said in a calm voice, rising and taking his friend by the shoulders. "There is something you can do. Listen carefully, I am about to ask for your help."

Abdul calmed down a bit but could not imagine what might be coming next. "Just as the Prophet fled persecution, I want you to help me escape, help my family escape, to the Northern territories. You know that is where my family is from. But not many others are aware of this. I have been in Kabul a long time. This will be the start of my family's personal hegira to freedom, this escape to my family's homeland."

"But how, what can I do?"

"This is my plan. You have retained a government position. Even the crazy Taliban leaders realize that they cannot drive all competence from public service without seeing everything collapse. I am going to request that I be allowed to move north, perhaps to Kunduz. That is near the front lines where the Taliban and the Northern Alliance vie for control. I can argue that I realize my sins, that I want to make amends. How can I expiate these sins against the Prophet? Easy, I am prepared to journey north, to where the forces of good battle Satan's minions. I will offer my medical services to help heal God's warriors. I know they need such help. Frankly, I am surprised they have not ordered me into their service, other than the fact they are deluded enough to believe death in this cause is a good outcome. Such insanity. Once we get that close, it just might be possible to cross the lines. I have family in that area."

"This is insanity." Abdul was trying to process what his friend had just shared.

"I know the risks. So much can go wrong. But I cannot sit and do nothing. Obviously, I am taking a chance just by sharing such thoughts and intentions with you. I have not lost my senses. I understand that you would be foolish to help us. In fact, prudence dictates that you should run away from me straight away, perhaps go directly to the Taliban and turn me in. I would not think less of you if you did such the wise thing. In the end, my friend, necessity makes heroes of us all, or fools. Only time will tell."

Abdul looked stricken. "How can you even suggest that I might betray your confidence? You darken my heart with such words."

Pamir looked more stricken. "My friend, accept my apology. These desperate times make us all paranoid."

Abdul leaned over and grasped his friend's hand. "I do understand. Still, we must be careful. It is true that there are spies everywhere. This is a regime that pretends a pure faith in the almighty but thrives on fear and hate. Even children turn in their parents as blasphemers and sinners and for no action worse than reading a book for enjoyment. I considered that you might turn me in for this conversation but only for a moment. How did we get to such a place, my friend? You and I, we remember when this country was sane, when men and women could dream and be whatever their talents permitted. There are times, dear Doctor, when I reflect upon what collective sin we must have committed to deserve such a punishment from Allah."

"I cannot imagine such a sin, Abdul. In my heart, I know that no such sin so black and unforgivable can possibly exist. I believe God is testing us. Can we survive and achieve amidst such insanity? Are we strong enough? It is like Job who is found in the Christian Bible? We can better appreciate what we have when it is not given freely and when it is achieved in the face of challenge."

Abdul sat across from his friend in silence for several minutes. Each man had retreated into his own conscience, that private place where fundamental decisions are settled upon. Then he grabbed the hands of his good friend. "Whatever I can do, I will do. You can count on me."

"Do not promise with light and ill-considered words. I do not want to place you or your family in any jeopardy. I could not live with such guilt." Dr. Masoud looked in his friend's eyes with a special intensity.

"Listen to me carefully. Perhaps, if this was only about you I would not promise anything. I would think of my family and what any resistance to the regime might mean. But this is about more than you and your family. These tyrants are destroying our country, they are perverting Islam. Yes, I want your Azita to realize her dream. I also want my daughters to have futures that involve more than serving some man. But I am thinking of more than that, much more. It is time to stand up and say no, in whatever way we can. The Northern Alliance is not perfect by any imagination. But they are holding out against these madmen. If you can help them, that would be a contribution to me, to our families, to our nation, to our faith. I am convinced, my good friend, that the world is not just changed by great men doing great things. It is also transformed by small thing done by insignificant people. It is like a snowflake falling on the mountain snows. It is lost among the millions of other flakes. Soon you lose sight of that one flake. It becomes the spring streams and rivers that nourish the crops of the plains. It somehow affects the whole community, sometimes in ways we cannot detect. But it does. I am certain of that. And with respect to the dangers I will inevitably face, I also have a plan."

Pamir smiled. "Thank you, my friend. Let us put our heads together and make our plans."

———

"Where have you been, silly man?"

"And this is how you greet your husband whom you have worshipped all these years?" The good doctor had on one of his favorite facial expressions, a hurt look that was clearly insincere.

"I know you were not taking care of the sick and wounded. Azita told me that once again few people came to the clinic today. You must have been wasting time with Abdul. I know you were. You and he are always chatting like two old women."

Pamir could not resist. "So, you finally agree with me that women gossip all the time."

"Harrumph, your favorite daughter told me that he came by at the end of the day but then she ran off to her room. Something is wrong with her. Did you scold her? The only time she looks like this is when you are cross with her."

"I did make her leave, she wanted to stay with Abdul and me. We had important things to discuss, however." Then his expression changed as if he stumbled on to a secret truth. "Ah, I fear the little imp was spying on me. That is not good."

"What, you are sharing secrets with Abdul that you keep from the family? What kind of evil are you up to?" She tried to maintain a cross look, but it faded when she saw concern on his face. "I will tell you later when we are alone. First, I must go find our little girl. I fear she has more on her mind than any rupture in my affection for her."

"Oh, you fuss so over that girl. She will be so spoiled. Someday, not long in the future, she will need to listen to a husband and will have no idea how to do that or what to do when he gives her a command. She will be such an obstinate girl, arguing with him and getting into such trouble with her new family. She has such a will about her."

"You mean, unlike yourself and how you handle your own wonderful spouse." He smiled.

"Oh, you are such an insufferable man. I should have listened to my mother."

"Hah, how soon you forget. Your mother loved me. She was so frightened that you were way too independent, that no man would want you. Then I came along and she said, 'Ah, this one is so foolish he will take Madeena off our hands. He hardly knows any better, that poor, ignorant boy from the North.'"

"She did think you ignorant and rather backward." His wife gave out a hearty laugh. "I was very popular. Many of the young boys were much taken with me when I had my beauty. And I know for a fact that my mother thought you were not worthy. To think I fought them off to get you as a husband."

"And yet I won your heart. How did it happen that I would have such fortune? You still have that beauty that bewitched me. You have never lost that."

She gave him an exasperated look as if to chide him for such a transparent and insincere piece of flattery. "I was young and naïve, and didn't know any better." She then fussed with the food she was preparing. She never could hide her affection toward him for long. "I saved some food for you, the children have eaten, except for our spoiled child who said she was not hungry."

He leaned over and kissed her on the forehead. "You made a good choice, woman. Someday, perhaps Azita will make a good choice, if she is as lucky as you. Now keep my food a bit longer. I will go talk to her first."

"Hah, off with you then," she barked. She kept her head down. The problem was that she knew she had made a wonderful choice and that he was aware of that fact. How could she win any dispute with him when they both recognized this fact?

His daughter was lying on her bed, her head buried in a pillow. He sat next to her and began stroking her head. She refused to respond to his touch. She was tortured by the very thought that he would see her tears. For a while he said nothing. In his way, he was thanking God for giving him such a gift. It was a blessing he was not sure he deserved.

Finally, he shook himself out of his reverie. "Sweet girl, you listened from the other room. You were the one that made the noise Abdul and I thought we heard." She said nothing. He continued to stroke her long black hair. "You probably heard me discuss our problems with my friend." She started to sob ever so slightly, her body heaving as gulps of frustration and remorse grasped at her body. "Oh my sweet, sweet girl, you are blaming yourself . . ."

She suddenly startled him by bolting upright and throwing her arms around his neck. "Oh, Papa, it is all my fault. We would have none of these troubles were I not such a willful, selfish girl. You should put me over your knee and whip me for my sins."

She continued to sob as she buried her face deep into his neck. Her salty tears began to course down under his shirt in craggy rivulets. "Azita, you know I would punish you if you were guilty of any such sin, but you are blameless my lamb."

"But I am selfish, and vain, and willful, and guilty of bring- ing terrible things down upon all of us. This time, Papa, you cannot talk me out of it. I am decided. I shall be a good Muslim girl, no more thinking about things that cannot be. I will learn what a girl needs to be, a good wife and mother. I am fine with this. It obviously is what Allah wants, what must be. You will see. From this day forward, I will be a good girl."

He pushed her away so that he could look upon her face. Her eyes were swollen a bit and red with grief. He grasped her by the sides of her face and redirected the angle of her head so that she faced him directly. "You listen to me, young lady. You listen to me very well. You are a wonderful Muslim woman. If you give up on what you are capable of being, you can be certain of one thing. There is one thing I can guarantee you."

"I don't understand, Papa."

"You give up your studies and I will put you over my knee for sure. You will get a beating from me that even those Taliban monsters would not dare to give you. Do you understand me?"

"No, Papa, no." She had never stood against him so. Her defiant words shocked him.

"You would refuse me?"

"I must, don't you see. It is not only about me and you but Mama and Majeed and Deena. I cannot put them all at risk. I cannot. And your practice, what will happen to you if no one comes for your help. You will die, slowly, and it will be my fault. And those to whom you minister without pay, what will become of them? Where else will they find such a wonderful physician? No! I cannot permit that, I refuse to permit that. You can beat my body black and blue. You can refuse to feed me. You can throw me into the street. But you cannot make me do what will put us in harm's way. You cannot."

For some reason, she thought he might strike her and braced herself for a blow. Of course, it never came. It never did matter what mischief she brought to the family. He only smiled. She immediately felt foolish for her suspicion that he might discipline her. "Now you listen to me. You can be such a silly, stubborn girl. You promise not to be stubborn and willful by becoming even more stubborn and willful. We must review your logic lessons. Someday, I think, Allah will punish you with your own children for being so terrible to your father." He shushed her as she tried to open her mouth. "I am going to share something with you. But it is only for your ears. You cannot tell anyone, not your brother and sister. These are things that Abdul and I talked about after you finally fled my clinic. Are you listening to me?"

"Of course, Papa, but my mind is set."

"Yes, I understand that. But first, understand that we are going to escape these people." He waited for his words to reach her but all he saw in her eyes was uncertainty. "This is what Abdul and I discussed after you left at last. He will try to help us by using his position and contacts with the regime to get us papers to make our escape. He thinks the religious fanatics will want us out of Kabul, I am an annoyance to them and popular enough to stay their hand for the moment. He will convince them that it is better to send me north where I can help mend their soldiers fighting against those holding out against them."

"Would you, Papa?"

"Would I what?"

"Mend their soldiers?"

He looked at her with a smile. "That is the blessing of being a healer, you heal. You do not ask which man is worthy and which is not. All are worthy of your ministrations. Simply by possessing life, you are obligated to help. I have always thought that those who must distinguish the worthiness of individuals have such an impossible challenge. You must remember this if you are to become a healer. It is a promise, an oath, you must make."

She absorbed his words as she often did, storing them for the time being so that she could consider them at length in the quiet of her bed. His words typically were a source of comfort and, at the same time, stimulation to her. At the same time, they often were a challenge, making her rethink what she thought she knew. In the end though, his wisdom was a source of revelation, growth, and peace. Then another current of concern made its way to her chest and stomach. "You are making this sound too easy, Papa. This will be dangerous. Moving about the country these days is not easy. Leaving the security of Kabul, such as it is, would put us all in danger. You see, I am putting us in danger no matter what soothing words you use." Tears welled up in her eyes again.

"Aaah," he moaned. "I am within an inch of putting you over my knee. The world does not revolve around you, my dear. If you learn anything from me, it should be this. The sun does not rise and set because of you. Yes, it rises and sets over you, but the cause of such actions is way beyond what you would presume to affect. Each of us, in the end, are small players in a very large drama with many actors. That is something a very famous playwright penned one day a long time ago. I must acquaint you with Shakespeare with whom I became familiar with in England. I so want you to get an education, a proper education. You must get to know The Bard. Your mother is good with numbers but there is so much more out there, poetry and literature and history and philosophy. You should have it all."

"Are we running away to England? Is that your plan? There I can get an education like you did, be as wise and knowing as you."

"My girl, there are moments I feel you are beyond me already. Perhaps someday we can get to England. But for now, I am thinking we might get to the mountains of the north, where I came from a long time ago. Then we will see."

She sat up and looked at him for a long time. "In England, I could get the kind of education you wish for me."

"Yes," he said, "you could get the best education possible."

"Tell me, Papa, why do the men that rule over us hate it so when a woman uses her mind?"

He paused to think. "I believe I have a short answer and a longer answer to that one. The short answer is that these men would soon find out that women are much smarter than they are." A broad smile broke across her face. "The longer answer goes back to our discussion of a prism. Do you remember that?"

"Of course, I never forget anything you teach me."

He suddenly realized that this just might be true. He would have to be careful about what he considered casual conversations with his daughter. Then he had a cold insight. Someday, probably on a day not far off, she would no longer look upon him as a font of knowledge. The pedestal on which she had placed him would crack and crumble away. But he still stood on that pedestal today and that was good enough. "I know you read that book I gave you back on the day of the beating. You asked me enough questions about it. Well, the answer to your question lies there and in our discussion of the prism. Light or truth goes in and interpretation comes out. The problem with all religion, as opposed to spiritual truth, is that men shape it after their own dispositions."

"Dispositions?"

He sometimes forgot that she was still so young, barely beyond childhood. Often, she exhibited a level of maturity and comprehension beyond her years. "They take the word of God and twist it into something that looks correct to them because it fits into how they look at the world. If they are bad to start with they will rework what is good and holy into a message of hate and violence. It is not that the message is flawed, but the messenger. That is human nature, men use religion to affirm their prior beliefs."

"Wait, does that mean that faith itself is evil?" She gave him a quizzical look that mutated into dismay. "Or perhaps faith is irrelevant to whether men are good or bad."

"Some, many, have concluded such things. But I do not believe that to be the case. The trick is to look beyond what these so-called messengers of God say. You, each of us, must look behind the curtain to discern the truth. When you do that, you will discover that there is a common message behind each great religious tradition. This core is found in Islam, Christianity, Judaism, Buddhism, Daoism, Confucianism, and all such traditions. It is that message of love, caring, and community I have mentioned earlier. It tells us that we are custodians of the earth and of each other. Embrace that and all the rest is merely for show."

"Why cannot the Taliban see that, it is such a simple lesson, such a powerful message."

He smiled ruefully. "These are small men. All the original sources of religious insight were set down centuries ago, typically using the oral tradition, for a simpler people in an even more contentious period than ours though it is hard to believe that times were once worse. They often are vague because their purpose was to move a people from where they were then to a newer understanding of what was about them. Jews were told not to eat pork or other products from a pig. Do you really think that God would care about such things? No, more likely the early religious authorities saw that disease came from eating such things, that it would be safer for the well-being of their tribe to use God as a way of keeping people healthy. Now, of course, that makes no sense. Unfortunately, literal people draw lines in the sand over such silly things. Do you understand?"

She smiled brightly. "Yes, I think I do. The Taliban do not want people to think for themselves. If they did, the people would reject them. They also know in their hearts that women are, indeed, smarter than they are. If given a chance to be educated, women will see what silly men they are and make great mischief for them."

"So, my dear, we will first get to Kunduz, then my homeland in the mountains. After that, we will see where we might go next. If Allah wishes, perhaps you can get that proper education in England and come back to educate all of your sisters as well as heal their bodies."

Azita held out her hand. "We have a deal."

"And what deal is this?" Pamir asked with suspicion.

"I will obey you without question and you get me to a place where I can be educated properly. I want to hear more about this Shake—"

"Shakespeare." He took her hand.

"Yes. Then, when I am educated fully, I can come back and tell these Taliban what fools they are but in a nice way of course."

"My brave and foolish girl." He kissed her on the forehead. "Now come and eat some food with me. Remember, we must keep this conversation a secret between you and me."

———

Later, he lay in bed with his wife. "I see you worked your magic with your daughter. She went in her room weeping and, after your visit, came out smiling and happy. What lies did you fill her head with?"

"Nothing much, I promised her a proper education in England," he said the words quickly hoping she might let them pass.

To his dismay, she bolted upright in bed, looking at him as if he had just lost his mind. "Oh, you are such a foolish man. As you went about making silly promises, why not suggest a place to live on the moon or a vacation villa in the Alps. She still believes everything you say, she will be crushed when you cannot deliver on your hopeless dreams. You will be the death of me yet."

"After all these years, you have such little faith in me. When have I failed you?" He thought she might soften in the face of his obviously light, witty remark.

But she was not to be mollified. "Ah, you don't want me to start on that. You would be ancient before I finished with no teeth left in your mouth to eat your food."

"True enough," he said softly to her. "You must admit, though, my heart has always been in the right place."

She let out a small groan of exasperation. "You must have used that same charm on your younger daughter. You are the devil himself. But I am not so innocent as she. What in Allah's name was I thinking in that school playground so long ago?"

He knew she was softening and changed his tone. "Here is what I did tell her. We start our journey to England or at least safety by making our way to Kunduz on the pretense of helping care for the wounded Taliban fighting in that area. From there we somehow make our way to Fayzabad or someplace where the Alliance retains control. That way we can get to the protection of my extended family. I am sure if we get to Kunduz, we can make it the rest of the way. In truth, I agree England is a dream. Perhaps all we can hope for is Pakistan or India. There are good schools for her in India."

"No matter where you have in mind, I have one thing to say. Are you mad?" Now she was angry again. "Do you understand the risks involved? Just asking for permission to move north might spell the end for us. We are not exactly favored by our current rulers as it is. Then we must make this journey. It will be perilous, indeed. There are so many pretending to be loyal Taliban but who prey on those they come across on the roads. Even if we make it to Kunduz, how will you reach out to the other side? How can a whole family make it across the lines without capture and death? And who knows if this whole crazy scheme is for nothing. Can the Northern tribes hold out against these monsters? Who is helping them, the Americans? They don't care. Why don't you write to that president that was just elected, this Mister Bush. Tell him that our new leaders are

Communists in disguise. They only pretend to be religious fanatics but secretly are being ordered about by the Kremlin. That was the only time the Americans cared, when we were headed by some Communists." Her voice caught. Fear was replacing anger. "Oh, my husband, we would be giving up everything, all that you worked so hard to build."

"My dear, everything I really care about is in this house—you and our children." He then took her face in his hands as he did with his daughter earlier. "What you say is true. There is great danger in all this. But what if we do nothing. We already have run afoul against the regime. How long will they leave us alone? They demand victims and use public displays of their violence to keep the people afraid and in line. Just how long will they leave us alone. I fear not much longer. How much longer before Azita lapses again and does something, something so innocent to us but not to them. It is bound to happen, you know her. She will try her best but . . . once again, they will be aflame with indignation and seek revenge upon us. She will be imprisoned every day. She needs to fly, to be free, not in some invisible cage the remainder of her days."

"She is foolish like her father. But even she will come to terms with what needs to be." Madeena was crying now. "I have become accustomed to that cage."

"Which kills me a bit every day that your imprisonment endures." His words were soft, but they penetrated her heart. "Dear wife, do you know what agony it is for me to see what you have been forced into? You are meant to be a teacher, a shaper of young minds. You were a great teacher. The young women at the university would flock around you, they wanted to be like you. Some of them could have been like you. Now, you would be tortured and executed for doing what you are meant to do, to be. I can no longer stand by helpless and watch you die little by little. I cannot consign my girls to such a fate. I would rather we all die quickly trying to be free again."

His wife arose from the bed and walked about the room. It was as if she was having a silent conversation with herself. Suddenly, she stopped, no longer weeping. "Okay, my dear husband, you are right . . . crazy but you are right. I despise the cage in which I and my daughters fester. How do we start our hegira?"

———

Pamir was encouraged and concerned. Patients were returning to his clinic in some numbers. At the same time, he had not heard from Abdul in some time. Had the regime been resistant to Abdul's entreaties on his behalf? He was uncertain about what to do. Should he approach the authorities himself? He had thought that the notion of his relocating north ought to come from someone else, someone the regime not automatically suspect of duplicity.

He was catching up on paperwork at the end of the day as Azita came in with tea. At that moment three men burst through the door their long scraggly beards, swords, and rifles announcing to all that they were the Taliban.

"You are Dr. Pamir Masoud?" They swaggered with an authority that had been earned with fear. Their eyes cast about the room as if evil lurked in every corner.

"Yes," he said as he glanced at his daughter. He was relieved that she obviously was serving him tea the moment they burst into the room. If she had been helping with a patient, as she had begun to do again, that might have caused a problem. One never knew what would be a problem with these people. The law seemed rigid and unyielding in principle but random and subjective in practice. In any case, the men ignored his daughter as she shrunk back toward the waiting room.

"You will come with us."

"Where?" he asked, his mind racing.

"No questions, just come with us. It is not for you to question."

"Can I inform my wife when I shall return from the police headquarters?" He asserted his hypothesis aloud so that Azita might know where he was going if they did not contradict him. Men were summoned in this fashion never to be seen again. Their final trip always started by disappearing into the local police headquarters.

"We do not know how long you will be there, just accompany us now." Pamir glanced at his daughter, mouthing the words that she need not worry as he left with the men. His daughter scampered across the courtyard to the main house, her heart racing with apprehension.

Pamir soon realized that he was correct, he was led to the local police headquarters which were always manned by a mix of the traditional police and representatives of the regime. The latter were easily identified by their wild dress and appearance, while the remaining officers from the old force dressed in their traditional official uniforms. He was immediately ushered into the office that had to belong to a high-ranking official. Pamir was relieved when he spotted Abdul seated next to the official's desk. *That was good*, Pamir thought, unless they are both to be executed at the same time.

"Finally, I am to meet the famous Dr. Masoud." The official was dressed as the guards he had sent to fetch Pamir, his face framed with the required scraggly, unkempt beard. As he finished his greeting, he signaled that the guards should exit the room.

This relaxed the doctor for some reason and after the customary greeting that involved a praising to Allah, Pamir added that he was gratified that he was famous and not infamous. He immediately regretted his attempt at wit. These men had no humor. That, too, was a sin. But the official indicated that he was to sit across from him and poured tea that was already on the desk.

It was Abdul who spoke next. "Good to see you, Dr. Masoud. It has been too long."

As the official offered Dr. Masoud a cup he got right to the point. This was unusual, one seldom went straight to the business at hand. However, Pamir was happy to avoid the usual circuitous chatter that accompanied all business meetings. "We have been discussing your intentions. You wish to help us in the north where the infidels still trouble us, is that correct, Allah willing?"

Pamir tried to look enthusiastic. "Yes. I have given this much thought. I have been selfish, thinking about my career and not about my nation nor about the renewal of faith you have brought to our great land. I cannot fight for truth in battle, I am afraid my age would make me a poor soldier. However, I can heal those who are soldiers for Allah."

"I wonder, Doctor, is it not better to be a martyr for Allah. Perhaps it is His wish that they not be healed, but sacrifice themselves as a testament to His greatness."

Pamir could easily see the old trap. "I cannot imagine that my meager medical skills could alter His will. Those destined for the glory of being a martyr will find a way to be at His side. However, those not so graced I can repair so that they might fight another day. Allah needs healthy soldiers. That shall be my contribution"

The official smiled. *A worthy opponent,* he thought. "Tell me, Doctor, why now. It has been brought to my attention that you have not been such a staunch supporter of our movement. In fact, there are rumors that are troubling, rumors about your family."

"Yes, I have a most troublesome daughter. You cannot begin to appreciate the headaches she has brought me. Such a headstrong girl. But I have beaten her well, as Allah would wish. I think that taking her away from the temptations of Kabul would help. She is about to become a woman. Her mother and I strongly feel that she must begin to act like a good Muslim woman. No more nonsense will I tolerate."

"Is it as he says, Abdul?" The official looked to the doctor's friend who had been sitting in silence, not reacting, but inwardly admiring the disingenuousness of his old companion.

"It is, sir, totally as he says. He has come to me on occasion, asking for advice on how to bring his headstrong daughter into line. We agreed, she must be punished, severely, and he has done so. On one occasion, I witnessed such a beating. She is quickly becoming a good Muslim girl." Abdul looked directly at the official as he told his lies betraying no guilt whatsoever. He had become practiced at evading the truth.

"That is excellent. Nothing pleases Allah more than a good Muslim girl and displeases Him more than those who try to emulate these evil Westerners, such shocking immorality as they display their bodies wantonly. No wonder their culture is collapsing. Of course, you can cut the cancer out from the body and turn this girl over to us, we have ways . . ."

Pamir tried not to betray his horror at the thought. "I will keep your generous offer in mind. Without doubt, this is one of the greatest of your accomplishments, ensuring the propriety and modesty of Afghan women." Was he laying it on too thickly? He decided to stop there.

"One last thing that bothers me."

"Bothers you, I don't understand." Pamir looked disconcerted.

"Well, let us say we are curious about your past. You come from the northern provinces, where the infidels are strongest."

"Yes, that is true." Pamir assumed a casual look.

"So, you have contacts back there?"

"Extended family members . . . uncles and cousins. But I have been away a long time. I studied medicine in England and have practiced in Kabul since my return. I have not been back in a long time. It is something that shames me, to be so detached from my family. But they are not educated people, we have little in common." Pamir smiled as he finished, hoping against hope that his lies were not betrayed by his demeanor. He had been back from time to time. He even ministered to people during his visits though not since the Taliban rose to power. If the Taliban knew of such visits, he would be caught in a lie. Then his only hope would be to engage in a semantic discussion about the term "quite a while."

The official looked at him for a long time without expression. Pamir stared back at him, trying not even to blink. Finally, as the doctor thought he might explode, the official smiled as he reached for papers on his desk. "Thank you, Doctor. We look forward to your service to our cause. I am signing the papers that will facilitate you and your family's trip north. They are good for three months so please make all arrangements quickly. Besides, if you wait, the fighting may be finished. I am sure you would then be disappointed. We were considering only permitting you to go. But I am convinced of your sincerity and Abdul is most persuasive."

When Pamir arrived home, his family rushed to him. His wife threw her arms around his neck and hugged him tightly, tears flowing from her eyes. "We thought we had lost you."

"Not to fear . . . I remain among the living and with the papers that will permit our *hegira*."

———

The caravan started out early one morning. There was the family car driven by Majeeb with his mother and Deena, his sister. In an older truck that Pamir had bought especially for the trip to carry what he thought they would need to relocate, he and Azita sat in the cab. He had sold his home and much of the family belongings they had accumulated over the years. That decision had been a matter of much discussion. Might they return? Could the Taliban last for the remainder of their lives? He believed that the authorities thought that this relocation would not last longer than it took for the Northern Alliance to be defeated and Taliban rule to be extended to the entire country. Might selling their goods signal a different intention and result in their papers being revoked? In the end, Pamir decided that they were now off the Taliban's list of suspects and no one would care. With good fortune, they would make it all the way to England. If not, he had decided that returning permanently to his childhood home and family would not be such a bad idea. Still, he reflected on how every decision had become so calculated.

It was primitive up north, the cities modest and less sophisticated. Many of the people lived in smaller towns nestled in the valleys framed by rugged peaks. The land was beautiful, breathtaking in Pamir's mind. The crusty earth was broken by rock thrust into the sky eons ago as great land masses collided. The resulting terrain was harsh and unforgiving, breeding a tough brand of tribes that banded together and fought together to survive both the unyielding elements and a host of invaders. Most recently, such fierce warriors had driven the British out in the nineteenth century, the Russians in the twentieth century, and now were holding out against the Taliban at the beginning of the twenty-first century. By nature, they were suspicious and insular. However, once you had gained their trust they could be generous and devoted to the final measure of their blood. Yes, they might not be highly educated but these were Pamir's people. He could easily see himself living among them.

In good times, the journey might be completed in a day. But these were not ordinary times. There would be several roadblocks to traverse. At each roadblock, papers would be checked and some discussion, if not searches, might ensue. The further they moved away from Kabul, the closer they would be to those the Taliban saw as infidels and the more scrutiny they might receive. He worried that his papers might not be enough to persuade overzealous would-be soldiers that their journey was appropriate. Undoubtedly, the car and truck would be scrutinized for contraband that might be made available to the regime's enemies or sold on the black market. Paranoia was everywhere.

Still, the early part of the trip went well even though the light of day was not yet present. They were stopped at roadblocks a couple of times but a review of his papers and a brief discussion was sufficient to allow them to proceed. Pamir began to relax. "So, my daughter. Have you finally realized that you should not blame yourself for this flight?"

"No, Papa. I have given the matter much thought."

"Oh, oh," her father moaned, "it is never good when you give a matter much thought."

"You should be happy to have a daughter with such deep thoughts, not like Deena who thinks only about boys and getting married."

"And you have never thought about such things?" he asked with a smile.

"No, never. As far as I can see, boys are annoying and smelly. I can see nothing useful in them."

"So, the logic of your position is that your father is annoying and smelly."

"No, not you, silly, and I am now aware of your trick. It will not work again." He now realized that she was annoyed with him at that moment.

"Then you are saying I am not a boy, not a man." He persisted.

She thought for a moment. She knew there was a way out of his logical conundrum. "Here is what I think. All smelly and annoying creatures are boys but not all boys or men are smelly and annoying. You are the exception."

Pamir laughed aloud. "Such a philosopher, the ancient Greeks would be proud of you. And you think there might not be another exception, a boy that you might love someday?"

"No, I doubt that is possible. Besides, I will be too busy. I must work hard now if I am to study medicine in England someday."

To that, Pamir fell silent. Madeena had been right. He had put a foolish thought into his daughter's head. In truth, he had little idea of how he could make such a thing happen. He tried to shift the topic. "My studious daughter, I am hoping that once we get to Kunduz, and certainly beyond, that we can accelerate your learning. You should be able to help me in many more ways, without worrying that we will be persecuted by the authorities. In my home area, they are Muslim but not fanatics. I am thinking that you might even encourage young girls to study, become educated. You can be what we call a role model. They can see what is possible."

Azita did not respond as he thought she might. She stared at the countryside, still flat and bleak but the higher country looming ahead. Soon, the terrain would change. Finally, she whispered, "Papa, I know you cannot make miracles happen. I will not study in England. I know that. It is okay."

It was as if his daughter had taken a knife and stabbed him in his heart. He wished more than anything to lie and say he would make it so. No matter what, he would make it so. But he held back, fought against any such impetuous promises. "Sweet child, I will not make any promises that are impossible to keep. England is far away, thousands of kilometers as the crow flies but much further in reality. It would not be easy, so I will be very honest. I have no idea how to get us there, how to get you from this ravaged country to that blessed place. It was different when I was your age, so different."

"I know, Papa. And you are not a smelly and annoying boy." She tried to smile, sensing his heavy heart.

"Child, listen to me. Never give up. I have told you this before. And you will hear it from me again. Never give up. Life is a mysterious journey. The one certainty we have is that no one can take away our dreams, our passions. They can take away our freedoms, inflict pain on us, fill our heads with nonsense, but they cannot take away what is in our heart unless we let them.

Keep your dream, your passion. I can promise that I will do my best. I will do my best."

"I know you will, Papa." She put her hand in his. She knew she had been a selfish girl and had caused him pain again. She wanted to erase that more than anything.

"There is more. You must promise me that you will never give up, that you will keep your passion alive no matter what, no matter how awful and hopeless things look. Do we have a bargain? I will try my best and you will never despair."

"Yes, Papa. I promise."

"Good," he said. In his mind, he did have a vague plan of eventually escaping over the Kush into Pakistan and from there somehow to England, particularly if the Northern Alliance were to collapse as likely it would unless more foreign assistance was forthcoming. But what could possibly happen to cause such a fortuitous turn of events? He decided not to share any glimmer of hope with his daughter. Madeena was right, he did tend to raise false hopes in her.

"But I still won't marry one of those smelly and annoying boys." They both laughed aloud until they saw another road-block ahead.

"Out of the truck, everyone." A rough looking man sporting an AK-47 ordered. There were no niceties or smiles. He did not even look at the papers offered by Pamir, instead ordering his compatriots by gestures to search both vehicles. Pamir could not help but sweat despite the cold winter weather as the guard stared at him with ill-concealed suspicion, if not contempt. An hour later, they were permitted to repack their vehicles and start up again.

They were heading to higher ground, the mountains looming closer especially off to the east and northeast. Pamir started talking to his daughter about his childhood growing up in the rugged terrain that was his homeland. His family was relatively well-to-do in an area where few had any appreciable wealth. They were merchants and larger farmers and local leaders, if not by official office then by reputation. Family name and respect was critical where kinship played such an important role. Among his larger tribal connections, there were bureaucrats and teachers, those who had a rudimentary education and who had made it into the lower levels of respectability.

"I wonder how they are doing."

"Who?" Azita asked, surprised by her father's unclear utterance.

"I am sorry, Azita. I was thinking about my family. I have been so bad, not keeping in touch as much as I should have after my parents passed away. With all the troubles in the land it has been so difficult. I do not even know how many have been caught up in the fighting or whether any have been killed recently. I wish you had met my parents, your grandparents. My father was killed during the fighting with the Russians and my mother soon died of a broken heart. They had been brought together in an arranged marriage but fell deeply in love. He is another boy who was not smelly and annoying."

"Okay, Papa," Azita seemed to agree with great reluctance. "That makes two good boys but they are all my relatives and I cannot marry into my own family. Still no boys for me! You and Mama had a love marriage, that is right, isn't it?"

"Oh yes, your mother chased me shamelessly. She did not think boys were annoying and smelly."

Azita laughed again. "That is not what Mama says. She told me that you chased her shamelessly and that she married you out of pity. I think that makes more sense to me. And she agrees with me about boys. So many times, I have heard her say that all men are worthless."

"Oh, Allah has not been kind to me. He has cursed me with such a wicked daughter." He loved this time alone with his favorite daughter. "Assuming the best, I want you to get to know my family. They are good people. You remind me of them."

"How is that, Papa? Are they also troublesome and headstrong?"

"Well," he laughed, "now that you mention it, some of them are. But they are also kind and generous. If a neighbor needed food or shelter or help with their flock or crop, they would do what they could without question. I have come to think that such traits, such blessings, are either in a person or not. Some people are given such gifts. Some are not."

Azita looked up to the mountains to her right as the truck strained to keep going. "Do you think I have such gifts?"

"Allah blessed you with an abundance of them, my dear. I think sometime that He realized that he had given me so little that when you came along He decided to give you so much."

"Hmm." His daughter seemed to consider that comment seriously. "Yes, I can agree with that." But she could not restrain an impish smile.

"Oh, my sweet troublesome daughter. You will not have to worry about the boys. None of them will want a girl with such a wicked wit."

"Good, such smelly and annoying things." She laughed aloud.

They continued talking about his home and family for some time. The journey seemed to be taking longer than planned. The truck was old, sputtering and wheezing on occasion. If it failed, Pamir wondered what they would do. In addition, it was getting darker. In his mind, he wondered if it might be better to stop and seek a family that would put them up for the night. This was a custom in the land. If travelers needed assistance, it would be provided without hesitation. It was tradition and thus more certain than the written law. At the same time, he sensed they were getting close to their goal, they should press on. If this damn truck would keep going, they could get there this very day. If it failed, he would not have the slightest idea as how to fix it. Too bad learning about the complexities of the human body did not translate easily to the workings of the internal combustion engine. He always had patients who would barter services for medical help but that was far away, in Kabul.

Another roadblock loomed. Pamir cursed under his breath. Once again, they were made to get out of the vehicles. Several men immediately began to look through their belongings but in a desultory way. A fierce looking man glanced at the papers

Pamir handed him but seemed uninterested. It struck the doctor that this man was probably illiterate. His authority came from the weapons he kept close. "I am thinking we have a problem here," the fierce one finally said.

"No problem, I am Dr. Masoud and have permission to journey from Kabul to Kunduz to help care for Allah's warriors in the fight against the infidels."

"But we are not in Kabul, are we? As I said, I think we have a serious problem here."

Pamir watched the man closely. He saw no softness in his face. It was hard, etched by a life lived on the edge where survival was often a close-run thing. The doctor made his decision. "I believe we can clear up these problems to the satisfaction of you and Allah." He reached into his pocket and pulled out several bills, pressing them into the man's hand.

What he got in return was a fierce unbending stare. "What is this?"

Pamir did not blanch, he looked steadily into the eyes of his adversary. Had he been wrong? Would this be the end of the road, an aborted run to freedom? He decided he had no choice. "This is a contribution to your important work on behalf of Allah and the Taliban. I will be sure to report to the top Taliban officials on the diligence with which you are carrying out your duties." He pulled out a few more bills which he pressed into the man's hand.

For a moment, Pamir thought the man would raise his gun and arrest him. Instead, an unsettling grimace crossed his face, it might have been confused with a forced sneer. "Yes, of course.

I appreciate that you can see the good work we do. You can go. May Allah be with you."

"We all appreciate your cooperation." Pamir hoped that the man opposite him would assume that the word "all" referred to the powers that be who would have authority over such men. In any case, Pamir amused himself as he reflected on the fact that he had established the price for securing the blessings of Allah.

As darkness was complete, the small caravan made its way over one last hill and the city of Kunduz lay ahead. Pamir felt exhausted, drained. He had not fully appreciated the strain under which he was living. He had no choice, however, nor could he display doubt or weakness to his family. They so depended on him. The first leg of their journey was complete. They had made it this far. The real danger, Pamir knew, lay ahead, on the next leg of their flight. That, however, must await the right moment.

CHAPTER 6

OXFORD ENGLAND
(2001)

The group entered the front door of the Hairy Hare establishment. "This is my favorite pub in Oxford," Chris exclaimed with a broad smile.

"Bloody nonsense," Karen murmured to herself but loud enough for all to hear her.

"And I am sure you are about to enlighten us regarding your decided lack of enthusiasm," Chris feigned to be hurt.

Karen adopted her superior smile that preceded any effort to correct her boss. "Look at this." Her arm directed the group toward the mahogany colored bar. "It looks like an authentic English pub bar but, I bet, it is no older than ten years. It is a fake authentic English pub bar. And the name, the Hairy Hare! What is with that? No self-respecting pub would concoct such a name. It is simply a lame attempt to poke fun at some of the village pubs that have names like The Wild Boar and go back to the days of Henry the fifth and the battle of Agincourt. You would have to be a really dumb American not to see this is a tourist trap for gullible foreigners."

"You mean idiots like me." Chris grinned.

"You said it, not me." She laughed. "However, I think your self-awareness is quite admirable. Most American men are totally clueless."

"You know, my dear," Chris rubbed the top of Karen's head, "you just might want to check on waitress openings here. Keep it up and it is very likely you will be needing a new job."

"Promises, promises," she responded. "You would be lost without me."

Chris grimaced in an exaggerated fashion. "Curses, she is right. I hate when she is right. Fortunately, it does not happen that often. In any case, as I was saying, I like this place. The Guinness is warm, the fish and chips are overpriced, and you won't run into too many of those bothersome Limeys. All the locals crowd into contemporary-styled wine bars and coffee shops. Hell, it has gotten so bad here that you might as well be in Seattle."

The group made its way toward the back where they might enjoy some privacy and be able to hear one another talk. Chris raised his glass of Guinness when the drinks arrived. "To good friends . . . Jules, Ricky, Kay, and I suppose my favorite pain in the ass . . . Karen. It really is great to be together again and under better circumstances."

Chris picked up the conversation. "I want to thank Kay and Jules for taking the same flight in from Chicago that made it easier for us to pick you up this morning."

"No problem," opined Kay. "It gave Jules and I time to compare notes on what a colossal shit you are."

Karen chuckled aloud. "Yeah, I finally have some allies to support me." She looked directly at Kay. "You will notice that he uses the royal us when he means me."

"We, my dear Karen, are inseparable. You know that." Chris gave her a quick peck on the forehead. "And Jules, you are looking even more fetching than usual, that network job must agree with you."

Jules laughed. "I bet you say that to all the girls. He does, doesn't he?" Her query was directed toward Karen. "How women fall for his crap remains a mystery."

"Hey, I am not his pimp, why women fall for him is a mystery to me as well," she responded quickly as she made a big deal of wiping the spot where he had kissed her. She did not want to get between two people she knew to be lovers. In the end, though, she could not resist. "If I were responsible for his ability to get laid 24/7, I would have no time for real work." A groan went up around the table as Karen blushed visibly. She realized that did not come out as intended. She was nervous. She tended to force the humor when anxious. Why?

"I am a realist. My money is the secret to my success with the distaff side. Alas, even I must admit we males are a sorry lot and I am the sorriest. We are creatures of our base desires. I was reading a study that explored the differences in how males and female perceived one another upon initially meeting. Men inevitably focus on the prospects of scoring some sex while women start through an inventory of tests to see if this guy is marriage material, sex is the last thing on their minds. But neither side can appreciate where the other side is coming from so the dance of the absurd begins. One experiment, using controlled circumstances, had women approaching men they did not know to suggest a no-strings sexual liaison. Some three out of four men agreed and started to undress in the middle of the street.

"Don't listen to him." Kay insisted. "He is making this up. I hate to even think of the garbage he spreads about in his classes."

"Okay, the undressing in the street part is an exaggeration." Chris then finished his story. "However, when the situation was reversed, males propositioned females, virtually none of the women agreed. In fact, the percentage of females agreeing may have been precisely zero. Venus and Mars here, the sexes are so far apart. So tragic."

Jules laughed the loudest. "Oh my God. You do make this crap up, don't you, and I once thought you were so smart."

"Hey, this is science I am talking." Chris protested.

"Poor Karen." Ricky noted. "You are a saint, my gal. I am surprised that this guy can even dress himself in the morning. Surely, you are wise indeed to leave him to his own devices when it comes to women. He is pathetic. My kind sister provides pity sex. I have no idea why, but she does. She is a saint."

Jules gave an exaggerated sigh. "I am stocking up good deeds for my judgment day. You know our parents grounded us in the principles of Christian charity, taking us to church every Sunday. All I remember is the part about suffering in this life helps you into heaven in the next, particularly if the suffering is accompanied by good works. I gave this a lot of thought. What could I do that would put me in the good graces of the celestial powers than take pity on such a sad excuse for a man. I would both suffer myself, thus earning god's grace, and at the same time help one of god's most unfortunate creatures . . . this pitiful thing."

A round of assent circled the table.

"I have to change the topic here." Chris tried to take control.

"But we are having so much fun." Karen tried.

"You checked those waitress jobs out yet?" He tried to look cross. "First, I want to say that Ricky has had a successful start as my co-conspirator in crime. He hasn't been here that long, yet he is quickly becoming indispensable as we expand our operations. Welcome again and thank you. You have picked up on stuff remarkably quickly and people seem to like you. Truly, there is no accounting for taste."

"Following on you, looking good was no big challenge. You have set a remarkably low bar." Ricky smiled.

"A low bar . . . that is my forte." Chris smiled.

Glasses were raised and clicked as Karen added. "What a relief to have someone on board who knows what he is doing."

"And what a relief it is not to need an administrative assistant anymore," Chris said without a smile.

"Oh my god, you are going to fire me. Wait, I don't think my bosom is big enough to get a job here." Inside, though, a bit of her wondered if she were pushing him a bit too far.

"Your bosom is plenty big enough," Chris exclaimed.

"Wait everyone, he doesn't know, really he doesn't." Inside, Karen was relieved he was still kidding her. She really did treat him terribly, she should be more careful.

"Don't worry Karen," Kay offered. "We know you are way too sensible to fall for this guy's so-called charms."

"And I am not," Jules feigned outrage.

Kay loved this banter at the expense of her brother. "What can I say, Jules, but don't forget you are racking up all those points for the hereafter. And speaking of racks, yours is plenty big enough, Karen. You could compete with that barmaid any day," said Kay looking at Karen's chest who was blushing visibly. "Listen, this is a good opportunity to bring up a topic that has been on my mind since Chuck passed . . . a possibility I mentioned before but somehow never finalized when you were in Chicago. I have been thinking and no wisecracks, Chris. I . . . I want to finalize my decision to join your mission as a field physician or whatever you call them." Her pace picked up as if she were afraid Chris would cut her off. "As you all know, I have labored as an ER doc in the worst of the worst conditions. On a typical summer weekend, I am up to my elbows in blood and gore. And as for danger, I have stared down gangbangers after they just learned that I failed to save their brother. I am ready for this."

Chris looked at her with a blank expression while the others joined in a chorus of approving responses. Finally, he found his voice, "I knew you were thinking about it, Karen mentioned. But I thought you had come to your senses. Have you thought this through, really thought it through?"

"Listen, wherever you put me it will be a step up in my situation and surely the quality of the clientele. You cannot imagine how bad Chicago is. Sorry to just spring this on you, Chris. You probably thought I decided against this. I have been thinking about this since Chuck died and have been chatting with Ricky and Karen over the past several weeks." She blanched. "Oops, that slipped out. Damn, why am I so nervous. Don't be mad at them, I swore them to secrecy until I could decide for sure. I wanted to tell you face-to-face. I feared you might try to act like a protective big brother. I mean, that would be a first but . . ." Then her words petered out. She looked directly at her brother as Ricky and Karen stared at the table.

Ricky broke the silence that followed, "Well, good thing I am heading back to London today. I mean, we have talked about how difficult it is to get good doctors for the field. It just seemed like such a good idea to me." When Chris did not immediately respond, Ricky tried a light tone. "So, should I clear out my desk?"

"No, you should be so lucky though I am not the happiest camper in the world . . . all this secrecy." Chris continued after a pause, "Ricky, I guarantee that there is no way your bosom is good enough to get a job as a bar maid. This just caught me by surprise is all. Should have guessed. Wow, I am losing my touch." Chris paused again. "I think it is a great idea." Then he shifted into serious mode. "Okay, let me be honest here. I am not ecstatic about this, not really. It feels like cold water being thrown in my face. I mean, I guess I never faced up to the fact that I, or we, really do send people into harm's way. When Karen and I were in Chicago, I recall a doctor we took on. Her name was Amar Singh, right, Karen?"

"Yes."

"Well, she volunteered for one of the Pakistan sites dealing with the refugees from the Taliban. That was dangerous enough and I worried a bit since she was a female and not a Muslim, an Indian . . . a Sikh in fact. Still, I figured she is an adult and we never sugarcoat the risks. If she wanted to take it on, that was her decision. We would give her all the protection we could but no guarantees. That we could not promise. That I cannot promise even you, the risks are unavoidable. Anyways, now she is arguing to be posted in Afghanistan itself, near to where the conflict still rages. I am trying to talk her out of it, but she is insisting. I keep stalling her that we need her where she is. In the end, I know I will let her go. But you . . ."

"Me what, Chris. You probably have talked to this Amar person more than you have with me in recent months." Her voice quavered just a bit, they were on the cusp of a topic that scared them both. "Don't fight me on this one. I will simply go to Doctors Without Borders or one of the other services. I am going to do this. Besides, if I take over in the Pakistan site, she can get her wish."

"Great, then I can worry about the two of you." Then he paused and sighed deeply. "Okay, then, it is a done deal. We will discuss details later." Then, before anyone could add anything he quickly went on. "Next announcement. Karen, you are fired. Fortunately, for you, I agree with my pervert sister that your boobs are plenty big enough for the barmaid's position, particularly after the guys get liquored up a bit."

"Wait, Ricky also kept her secret." She wasn't totally sure he was joking.

"Boy," Chris responded with a wry smile, "you sure threw him under the bus quickly enough. No, I am firing you as whatever I call you, it is administrative assistant I guess. I'm giving you a real title, something like field operations officer or FOO. Then you will be our FOOey."

"You are on fire today." Karen laughed uproariously.

"No kidding. I already cleared this with the board."

"Oh." She eyed him suspiciously. "Do I get a raise?"

"No."

"How about an office with a window?"

"No."

"Do I still have to listen to you?"

"Even more."

"That's it, I am stuffing some toilette paper in my bra and asking for a job here."

"Wait, okay. You get the raise and the better office."

"But I still have to listen to you?"

"But that is such a joy."

"He is an arrogant prick, isn't he?" Jules could not resist.

"Better be a big raise and a really nice office," Karen added as they all laughed. "And thanks, I guess." When no one was watching, she quickly reached out and touched his arm.

He leaned toward her and whispered, "Be careful, people will think you like me."

The food arrived and they all focused on that task for a few moments.

"Chris, you were right," offered Kay. "The beer is warm, the food does suck, but the fake ambiance saves this place. It is so... so inauthentic." She paused before adding, "And we will talk more about me later, right. I am sorry I sprung this so suddenly and so publicly. No, I'm not. Wow, this proved hard for me, like begging my heartless brother for a favor."

"All is okay. This just took me a moment. We will work something out," he smiled weakly and then spoke quickly to change the topic. "But listen, I want to get back to the Jackson home. Now that the two of them are here, there are some things that I want to get out, that have been on my mind since Chicago."

"Okay, since you did not fire me I guess I will have to listen," Ricky smiled.

"Well, it is funny as I remember things. Once I sprinted past the addicts and rats to actually get to your place I always found your home so idyllic."

"What the hell are you talking about?" Jules seemed genuinely perplexed.

"No, listen, this is important. I really have been thinking about this a lot over the past few months. It might explain how some of us got here."

"This should be good," Jules murmured.

Chris did not smile which, by itself, caught their attention. "I would watch how your family related, the way you two got along and how your folks talked with you and with each other. There was always this quality of respect and affection. That had to be hard for them given what a wild child you were Jules. Yeah, they complained to me about you all the time."

"What?" she scoffed.

"Sure, running around with bad guys, except for me of course. They loved me."

"Hey fellow, you were the only loser among the multitude of boys chasing me and I made sure you got nowhere."

"Really, taking off your clothes to seduce me . . ."

"Okay, that one moment of weakness."

"You are not fooling me, Jules, we all know your folks adored me. They desperately wanted us together as a couple. I was their last hope."

She scoffed again with more emphasis. "Now you are totally delusional. Do you really think my folks wanted me paired up with a loaf of white bread like you? See that bosomy barmaid there?" Jules said seriously.

"Of course. Why do you really think I like this place?" Chris responded.

"Keep it up and she is your best bet tonight, your only bet."

"I doubt that very much," Chris said above a round of laughter, "she already knows me all too well. I doubt I have a shot in hell with her."

"Don't listen to Jules," Ricky broke in. "My folks thought the world of you. My god, you had them totally fooled. I can remember ma talking you up to Jules, what a nice young man you were, and why wasn't she trying harder to . . ."

"One more word, dear brother, and you will be singing in that Vienna's boys choir. Got that, Benedict Arnold!"

"Okay, children, settle down." It was Kay, relieved that they had strayed away from any further discussion of her. "I did not spend nearly as much time as Chris in our home, but I know exactly what he is talking about. You cannot begin to understand the advantages you had."

"What?" Ricky and Jules said simultaneously. They were shifting to a theme that never failed to excite a vigorous debate among them. Then Ricky responded, "Hey, the only challenge you guys faced in life was when your limo had a flat tire on the way to your fancy school or maybe which resort to visit over school holidays."

Chris suddenly looked serious. "Seeing Jules and Ricky together always reminds me of what was special about the Jackson home, something I did not see in the homes of my more affluent friends."

Ricky smiled. "Are you sure you are not talking about the crackheads you had to sprint by to get to it or the rats that shared our meals."

"It wasn't that bad," Chris countered. "Bad, but not that bad. I would just throw a few twenties into the curb and dash for your apartment when the street crowd scrambled for the dough. Of course, then I realized that Jules was beating up the neighborhood kids to get the biggest share. The rats were easy as well, a few well tossed pieces of Wisconsin cheese."

Kay picked up the thread at this point. "No, I know what my brother is saying. From the outside our lives looked like paradise. It was far from it as you well know. You saw all that tension again at Chuck's funeral. Let me tell you, it was worse when we were growing up, far worse We were already broken at the funeral."

"What was it like? We never spent much time at your place." Jules had always been curious.

"When Chris and I were younger, two things were different. For one, we were still kids and didn't know how to defend ourselves. And two, our dad still thought he could shape us into his image of what we should be. He still saw us as lumps of pliable clay while he was the master puppeteer."

"What," Ricky asked. "he wanted the two of you to be junior fascists?"

"More than that. He wanted us to be leaders of the movement, junior Fuehrers."

"What in god's name are you talking about." This time it was Karen, thinking back to all the emotion she witnessed in Chicago.

Chris and Kay looked at one another before Chris started, "We haven't talked about this in a long time so just chime in if I get something wrong." Then he took a deep breath. "You know my dad as an arrogant, headstrong hyper-conservative. And all that is true. He was a poster boy for the far right. But he also was something far more sinister. As he came of age he was drawn into the conspiracy-warped world of the Bircher tribe, the John Birch Society. That crowd of wackos grew quite strong in the 1950s as the Communist paranoia swept the country. People really thought the Russkies were winning or at least that they suddenly would drop the big ones on New York and Chicago. People, otherwise sensible people, began looking at their neighbors with suspicion. Whom could you trust? They would see these Congressional hearings on television where Hollywood movers and shakers were accused of being pinko sympathizers. If they were Reds, then what about that guy with an accent down the block or the one reading a newspaper in a foreign language? Anything could get you tainted."

"This sounds like a stretch to me," Ricky tried.

"It should have been, but it wasn't. Remember, Stalin had taken over Eastern Europe, China fell in the late '40s, Cuba in 1959. The Reds were pushing the envelope in Korea and Vietnam, several South American and African nations looked iffy. Names like Patrice Lumumba, how suspicious is that, were on people's lips, at least people who collected in our home for the political autopsies. A lot of stuff we absorbed later, having been born too late to see it firsthand. For many, the domino concept made sense. Nation after nation either fell or was teetering on the edge. To the true believers, the Commies were this monolithic pseudo-religion that held sway over people's minds. Once a Commie, always a Commie. Worse, a Commie in Vietnam was the same as one in East Germany. Cultural and national influences played no role whatsoever. It was an international cult where the puppet strings were being manipulated in the Kremlin. I knew people who were convinced that sleeper cells had been implanted in America after the war as European refugees streamed in. These families were raising children who would, one day, worm their way into significant posts in government and industry. Then, when the word came from Moscow, they would rise up and destroy America from within."

Karen looked puzzled. "But what does this . . ."

"Getting there," Chris said without missing a beat. "Our dad was part of the Bircher movement in his younger years. As I told Karen on the way over to Chuck's end game, his family came out of Poland at the start of Second World War. That poor country was swallowed up by Hitler and Stalin. For some reason, Dad chose Uncle Joe to be the bad guy though neither were blameless. This inchoate sense of betrayal slowly sifted down to an intense hate for the Communists. They were evil incarnate. This was not exactly an irrational position, the Moscow contingent had little to recommend itself. But he saw Reds everywhere and in everything. Not such a surprise, the fascists had been crushed. That was Dad and his friends, wild with paranoia."

Kay jumped in, her brother's words triggering her own memories. "Wow, I can remember Father talking about Eisenhower as if he had been a lackey of Moscow. This was long after he was out of office, maybe even dead but as a little girl this image that Ike was some Red monster who had fooled the American people found a way into my brain."

"Ike, for Christ's sakes," Ricky was astounded, "the very man who saved Western civilization?"

Chris now picked it up. "You have no idea where his paranoia took him. He had all the usual conspiracies. Public schools had been taken over by leftist propagandists, fluoridation of the water supply was a way to poison us or our minds, the specifics changed weekly, civil rights for Blacks was only an excuse to undermine legitimate authority and weaken the control of the rightful rulers of this great land."

"As a little girl," Kay's turn again, "they drummed into me a sense of imminent dread. The apocalypse was always six months in the future. If my dad and his friends didn't do something drastic to change everything, then civilization was doomed.

Of course, six months would pass, nothing would change. All would go on as is, so the doomsday date would just be extended another six months. It was a rolling horizon, but the validity of the underlying world view was never questioned. He never said to himself, 'Maybe I am wrong about things. Maybe I should change how I think.' That never occurred to him."

Kay paused for a second and Chris continued. "While he never crushed the Red menace, he did do one thing very well. He made a lot of money, tons of money. He embraced capitalism with a passion, the uncaring acquisition of wealth no matter the costs to others became his personal deity. It certainly did not matter to him if the niceties of the law and ethics had to be circumvented and even subverted. You could exploit and cheat others. That was not a sin. That was the primal struggle out of which progress emerged and a better society evolved. In his mind, society was a little different from what we saw in the wild. Male stags fought one another for preeminence in the pack. The biggest and toughest male got to breed with all the females. That made sense. They had the best genetic material. Perhaps that is what Father took from the carnage and slaughter of World War II, as it was related to him as a toddler, that you only made it if you were sufficiently cunning and ruthless enough. He could have picked either Stalin or Hitler as his role model, they both savagely dismantled his beloved Poland and decimated the ruling class there. But he picked the Fuehrer to be his role model. Maybe it was the fact that Stalin ordered the slaughter of the Polish elite after they shared Poland in 1939.

Some of those killed were grandfather's and father's friends. Stalin tried to blame Hitler but that never stuck."

"My guess is that Father could never pick a Communist to idealize, that would interfere with his greed. He always wanted more opportunity to exploit and control others economically. God, he was so dark." Kay had picked up the theme, it was as if they had rehearsed a team lecture. "As Father became a business icon, he added another component to his hyper-conservative philosophy. Really, it was a world view, not just a philosophy. A philosophy sounds like something outside of yourself that you might embrace or discard if something else came along that better fit the evidence. No, my father embraced a view that was unshakable, an immutable sense of right and wrong that went beyond reason and analysis. We are talking about something that was a part of himself, something that defined him as a man. He began hanging with what would become the economic oligarchy that persists today, an elite that soon committed itself to the control of our society."

"Wait a minute." Karen was clearly skeptical. "This sounds like a B movie plot."

"All right, all this sounds a bit sinister here but believe us, we do not exaggerate. There is a bit of history to support this conspiracy theory and a whole lot of personal experience. The hard right in the '50s were mostly anti-Communists zealots that had a lot of clout but quickly fell into disrepute as Senator Joe McCarthy went too far as he plummeted into alcoholism. With them were the racists who hung on to a vision of an apartheid America with all their might even as media coverage made it increasingly untenable. There was no coherent right beyond the crazies. Government was a good thing back then. It had taken us out of the Depression and won the World War against fascism. The economy was booming and the middle class was growing by leaps and bounds. By the sixties, Americans were ready for an expansive government. There was no hyper-partisanship because some of the most conservative member of Congress were southern Democrats and some of the more liberal were northern Republicans. President Johnson never could have gotten the civil rights legislation passed without northern Republican support. Even Nixon was on board with an expansive government agenda, passing numerous liberal bills and exclaiming that 'we are all Keynesians now.' Goldwater had tried to rally a conservative counter revolution in 1964 and was crushed at the polls. It looked like the right was finished with only people like Bill Buckley out there crying in the wilderness and he was too polite to attack the establishment."

"Wow," Ricky whistled, "for a doctor you know your political history. You are making me hot."

"Okay cowboy, keep it in your pants." Kay laughed. "Besides, I have a confession to make. I learned most of this from Chris. God, I hate admitting that."

"But you learned your lessons well. And all these years, I thought you were ignoring me."

"No," replied Kay, "what I always said is that I should ignore you."

"But then you would be just another unlettered doc, little more than a mechanic for the body," Chris quickly picked up the narrative before she could respond. "Kay has nailed the early story. But it gets very interesting after the Goldwater debacle. First, we had the ideological restructuring, the south went Republican where they belonged and the north drifted to the Democratic side of the spectrum as the GOP drifted further to the right. My guess is that a core constituency of the Republican Party, the economic right wing, finally saw a chance for a comeback by joining with and then exploiting your garden variety racists . . . those who feel a good lynching is perfect family fun on a Sunday afternoon. As moderate GOPers left the fold, there was a chance to remake the party and expand its appeal. Whatever their thinking, I still can remember Father showing me this now famous memo written by Lewis Powell, who would soon be on the high court. It was written to the U.S. Chamber of Commerce and basically argued that the free enterprise system in this country was in danger. We were being swamped with high taxes and government regulation. Someone had to retake America from those liberals who were sapping the entrepreneurial spirit that had made this country great."

"Been there, heard that tired refrain before," it was Jules offering her cynical take.

"Aha," chimed in Kay. "But there was something in this memo that was different. It didn't just argue ideology or end with a call to elect the right people to office, no pun intended. What it called for was a revolution in thought, in the underlying political dialogue in this country. It was not enough to capture people's vote, you had to shape their hearts and minds. The political culture in any country starts with foundational premises that shape the dominant consensus across the land. For example, you go to Europe or our neighbors to the north and suggest that access to health care is not a right of citizenship or even not a basic human right, and they will not understand what you are talking about. Such a statement won't make sense to them since they believe in their hearts that some public goods are sacrosanct and beyond questioning. In America, the dialogue about access to health care starts from a totally different position, it gets you accused of being a Socialist at best or a Communist at worst."

"And so . . ." Ricky murmured softly, as if asking for the punch line to a joke.

"And so," Chris stated with emphasis, "my father and some of his friends took that memo and ran with it. They set about the task of remaking the very way that Americans framed the way they thought about government. They set out to erase any positive sentiments about community and the public good and replace them with a different normative good, one that stressed individual freedom and social competition. Compassion was weakness. Struggle was good. And success bred innovation and progress. America could not afford to coddle the weak and the frail. Society could not afford such misplaced charity, which was not charitable at all since it simply served to enable counterproductive behaviors. Not to embrace this vision of struggle and conquest was to ignore the very rules of social existence. Even the concept of fairness had to be reworked in the American psyche. It had nothing to do with outcomes. You were not being fair if you took anything from the rich to help the poor and vulnerable. That misplaced sense of giving merely extracted what rightly belonged to those with who employed their intelligence, work ethic, and risk-taking spirit to achieve and be successful. Tinkering with the game of life risked undermining the game for all. They saw that as the tragedy unfolding in America."

"Who would buy that crap?" Karen seemed incredulous.

"Oh," Karen jumped in, "they knew it would not be easy. The memo laid out the semblance of a larger plan. You had to infiltrate and rework all the major institutional systems in the country. It was a multidimensional, decades-long commitment to change."

Ricky tried one more argument. "But I know this world. These guys don't play well together. And their frame of reference is very short term, the next quarterly statement to the stockholders, keeping the goddamn stock price up so that they can score their yearly bonus."

Chris responded, "All true, my friend. But I think it was a little like Lucky Luciano and the Mafia. He convinced his fellow thugs that it was better to cooperate than compete, at least on this macro-political level. The potential rewards would be enormous. And look what happened. Starting in the 1970s, the economic right created a bunch of think tanks to develop and push conservative ideas, they created philanthropic entities to fund the right kind or research and thinking, they started taking control of the media through hundreds of right wing talk shows and by scooping up print media or creating things like Fox News. They created an arm to develop legislation to enact at the local level, something called ALEC, they created a Federalist Society to take over the legal system, they started going after universities by attacking free speech, and the list goes on. While the liberal side was content to publish their ideas in academic journals or mainstream outlets read by other elites, my father and his friends sought to publish their ideas in thousands of outlets in every hamlet across the country. Mainstream think tanks thought it good enough to get an idea out there under the naïve assumption that brilliance would be recognized. The new elite pushed their think tanks to put as much money into broad dissemination as into the creation of knowledge in the first instance. They focused far more on emotion than on intellect, always looking for wedge issues to keep people riled up and, more importantly, suggesting whom to blame for all their problems. Eventually, they moved to tinker with democracy itself. Starting from the ground up, they worked on gerrymandering voting districts to favor their candidates. As they saw the demographics shift away from them, more minority and non-white voters, they worked hard to suppress voters they don't like through the purging of the rolls, new voter ID laws, and manipulating voting machines."

"Oh, that sounds like a first-class conspiracy theory, my friend. Been drinking Kool-Aid lately." Ricky struggled.

Chris looked at Kay but she said nothing. He continued, "Perhaps, but think on this. Republicans now control much of government, state legislatures, governorships, Congress, and now the presidency. Why this level of control when the natural constituency of the Democratic Party has done so poorly of late? Since Jimmy Carter the top one percent of the population has seen their share of the annual income rise from less than ten percent to well over twenty percent, soon to be a quarter of the total pie if trends continue. Wages are stagnating for most. The middle class is suffering, perhaps heading toward extinction. Yet, the white working-class stiffs who are being hosed every day are flocking to the most conservative assholes in the public arena. Just think about that."

"Why are we talking about this again?" Karen asked. "I am lost."

Now Kay piped up. "Well, I cannot speak for my dear brother but of course I will. I think this has everything to do with why Chris and I are here, in a kind of personal exile if you will. You see, our Father saw us kids as the vanguard to carry on his revolution. We were not children to him but recruits in a holy war. His abiding passion was for us to follow in his footsteps. He yet saw Armageddon around every corner, maybe no longer six months down the road but soon enough if his vigilance ever wavered. He desperately wanted us to be foot soldiers in this war against the evils of the left. That was his abiding passion and oh what a passion it was. When we were still young he gave us these things to read that were well beyond our age level . . . the writings or Locke, Hayek, Rand, Buckley, and so many others. Then he would drill us on what we had learned. As we got a bit older. Then he would have us sit around and listen as he plotted and conspired with fellow right-wing revolutionaries. He assumed we would absorb these truths by osmosis and it never occurred to him that we would ever reject his universe. The verities in his universe were self-evident."

"But you did, didn't you? You rejected them. Quite amazing, really."

"Amazing as it is, we did reject him and his world. I am still not sure why, but we did. Someday I will figure out how. And here we are, in our self-imposed exile since we fear what might happen if we went back. First, I escaped and now my sister is with me. Remember, Kay, how we would whisper in my room at night? You would sneak in and we would turn out the lights. You would ask me if I really thought Ike had been a Communist. I think early on we realized we were wired differently. Maybe it comes from our mother, I don't know. Maybe we missed the Nazi gene. Chuck is dead, Kay is now here and heading to some remote part of the world and Kat . . ."

"Is lost, I fear." Kay suddenly looked infinitely sad. "I tried to convince her to come with me, much like you tried to talk Chuck into coming with you years ago." She reached over to touch her brother's arm. "She was furious with me. She said I didn't understand father. She went on and on about how hurt he was, how cruel we had been to him. When I tried to explain she just shut me down, asked me to leave. I never saw this coming. I thought she was reachable. Frankly, I am devastated. My one hope is that she has not thought things through, that Chuck's passing is still raw. I cannot believe she is like Father, not inside. I cannot believe that."

"Shit, she is likely lost," exclaimed Chris. "I thought we had a chance to reach her as well, save her. We should have tried harder."

"We . . . what is with this we?" Kay's look transitioned from sadness to anger. "Sorry, that was uncalled for. Sometimes I get a bit resentful that I was left behind to deal with the family, not that I did much of a job at it."

"Yeah, well, we both failed but I never tried." Chris lamented. "I never gave it a fucking try. You are right, dear sister, I am guilty as charged."

There was an anger in his voice that Karen had never heard before. She typically saw only the easy smile, the charm, the wry humor that melted many a woman's heart. That was why she was taken aback by the fierce emotions bordering on violence in Chicago. She broke the short awkward silence, "But now you and Kay are together again. You escaped whatever evil was planned for you. You escaped your dad."

Chris looked at his sister. "Have we, Kay? Have we escaped?" She only shrugged her shoulders. "Funny, Karen, I was taken aback by your calling Father our dad. We never call him that, never. Dad implies some affection, caring interest in who you are and what is becoming of you. No, we had a father. He was an autocrat and a patriarch who never expressed an ounce of affection toward us. He had a passion in life but it was not for us. It was for his vision of the future. We were supposed to be his pawns in this titanic struggle against whatever demons haunted his dreams at night and we failed him. Poor Kat thinks he is hurt. Fuck that, he is a goddamn sociopath who never felt anything for another human being."

"Is that what pushed us away from him? Maybe it wasn't that we rejected his world view early on, perhaps we saw the monster in him. You know, he did see the world as an ordered, hierarchical, structured thing, much like the popes saw the Catholic Church. Maybe that is why he stayed connected to the church, not for the religious teachings but because it reflected a world order he admired. He saw the family as a natural aristocracy, the chosen ones who were ordained to run things. That was how that whole crowd saw the world. They were to use their wealth to make sure they commanded things in the future. Democracy and community were sops for the losers, the weak sheep who needed to be led. Let them have their illusions of participation as long as the elite controlled the levers. It reminds me of a saying attributed to Stalin that went something like 'I don't care whether and how they vote as long as I get to count those votes.'"

"Well, dear brother." Kay raised her glass. "I officially join you in exile. I salute our cowardice."

"To abject cowardice." Chris saluted and clicked her glass. "We have officially abandoned our designated position in the aristocracy of the new world order. Hear, hear."

"Well, this sounds like bullshit to me, but it does remind me of Thomas Cromwell."

"Who?" Jules asked, vaguely remembering the name.

He was a commoner, the son of a blacksmith but he was probably the smartest guy in the realm during reign of Henry the eighth. That innate genius and hard work made him the most powerful man in the kingdom, next to the king, of course. In the end, he still lost his head. The nobles of the land could never forgive him for not being one of them, for getting above his station. Then he went and pissed off the king by pushing religious reform too hard. Henry never abandoned Catholicism, he just hated the Pope telling what he could and could not do."

"Great story, but . . ." Chris looked puzzled.

"Maybe it has no connection at all. Maybe it means more to me than to you guys, someone trying to rise above their station while you are trying to escape your destiny. I associate with Cromwell, the commoner seeking power and esteem in the realm. You had access to power and are running the other way. I grew up with nothing and always wanted a bit of that action. My guess is that where you sit might depend on where you start the race."

Ricky was thoughtful. "I know what Karen's vignette means. I would never be allowed into the inner sanctum. In the world of finance, they might tease me, play with me, let me fool myself that I was one of them. In the end, they would never invite me inside where it counts. Maybe that is why I am here."

Chris looked pensive. When Karen was not being sarcastic, she often shared provocative insights. He had grown to admire her intellect. "Maybe Thomas Becket is a better historical analogy," Chris offered. "He stuck to his principles even when commanded by his king to do otherwise. Cromwell always tried to suck up to Henry though it did no good in the end."

Karen looked grim. "I thought of Becket but didn't like the outcome." Looking around the table, she decided an explanation was in order. "The king asked in front of his knights who would rid him of this meddlesome priest. Off they went to slaughter the archbishop in his own church. It was never clear whether the king really wanted his advisor dead. Unfortunately, for Thomas, he was not clear enough regarding his intentions."

Chris looked at Kay, trying to smile. "You don't think Father would have us knocked off?"

Kay shrugged. "Well, that is not why I left though I considered hiring a food taster. I could not take him anymore. He was becoming a bit unhinged in my opinion. Mother had retreated into her own world and Kat had given over to the dark side. I had to leave."

"One thing is certain. Father's assassins will never find me in a church." Chris tried lightening the mood.

"Shit," exclaimed Jules. "How did we get on this depressing topic?"

"You're right," Chris found his smile again. "I only wanted to thank the Jackson siblings for bringing me into their home. You have no idea what it meant to me, to see what a loving family could be like. I mean this, thanks," his voice quavered.

Kay wanted to rescue her brother. She switched topics. "And what has brought the rest of you to this table. Karen?"

"Shit, I was this young and naïve student who was swept away by your brother's rhetoric. That was before I knew he was a perv."

Then Ricky spoke up, "You know. I grew tired of making money and enjoying life. Besides not feeling totally accepted in my new Chicago world, I had to see firsthand what Chris was up to. It seemed romantic and, more to the point, relevant."

Sensing that was all Ricky was going to share, the table turned to Jules. "Hell, I am just here to jump Chris's bones. I need some more credits for the afterlife. Oh, I suppose I wanted to see how my brother was doing. I am panicked that he is being corrupted by Chris, a known derelict."

"Okay, enough obsequious praise for me, I am too humble for that," Chris said with his typical wry expression. "Jules will stay with me to sate her carnal desires, Kay with Karen because it is convenient. Ricky will head back to London where I exile him after he pays the bill. We all will join him in the morning to get Kay's new life organized."

Kay reached out toward her brother. "I do want to make one thing clear. I am . . . I am not just running away from Father, from the endless sea of blood in a Chicago public hospital ER room. I am looking forward to doing this work and even, boy I hate admitting this, to helping you."

Chris squeezed her hand.

————

"Thank you." Kay spontaneously gave Karen a quick hug as they finished unpacking some of her things and got her settled in what served as an office and quest room. Visiting field workers, the females at least, often stayed with Karen, so she had the drill down pat.

Karen responded to the hug uncertainly. "What was that for, I do this a lot for visitors, at least the females that Chris has not seduced."

"Sorry." Kay smiled broadly. Karen had not seen that smile before. She liked it, the way it softened the woman's face. There was a warmth that had been hidden to that point. "It's not the free digs, I can afford the best. I wanted to thank you for taking care of my brother."

"Oh, for heaven's sake, I don't . . ."

"Don't even go there. He adores you and he needs you. The moron would be lost without you. Despite the bravado, he is vulnerable, really."

Karen sat on the edge of what would be Kay's bed that night. "He is rather sad, isn't he? I mean, I know he is brilliant but he does have these flaws. Tell me something. What is it with all the women. Yes, men are pigs, we all know that. But I thought by now he would have worn his favorite organ out and be ready to settle down."

"What?" Kay laughed.

"Oops, where did that come from? Sorry, way too familiar."

"No." Kay smiled at her as she also sat on the bed. "It just caught me off guard. I guess I wouldn't mind sharing notes. Jules is the only other woman he confides in and, for some reason, I can't quite be open with her. I don't know where they are relationship-wise so I keep my counsel." Suddenly, Kay looked at Karen with concern. "Wait, you are not in love with him, are you?"

Karen laughed out loud. "Hell no. I am as advertised, a lesbian." Then she paused as if considering something. "I suppose, though, I do love him. I . . . I think of him as something of a brother, the one I never had. I mean, I do have two brothers but we have nothing in common. Also have two sisters who are very straight and have no bloody idea what to make of me. I am an outsider, the only one that went to college. Guess what, I hardly ever talk to my family. I had not thought about this before. Chris has filled that need I suppose, the need for family."

Kay assumed a faraway expression, as if she were seeking memories lost in time. "That is funny. I envy you."

"For god's sake, why? I am just a working-class kid from Birmingham who was gritty enough to get an education and fall into a great job. You, on the other hand, are accomplished and smart and beautiful and . . ."

"Lonely."

"How can that possibly be? Really, I cannot believe that! Guys must be crawling all over you unless you intimidate them. Some accomplished women do that I hear."

"Karen, can I tell you a little about myself?"

"Of course. Shit, it took me forever to get Chris to open up."

"Well, I am easier than he is." Karen was happy to see Kay smile at this point. "Chris and I were never naturally close. We had different personalities and interests and goals I suppose. He was carefree and undisciplined. I knew what I wanted. Maybe that is because I am the older sibling by some fourteen minutes or so. No matter, the thing is that we were friendly but not confidants as kids. Then our world got complex. Father started on his crusade to turn us into Hitler youth. We had to find one another then. As we did, you already know that we would hide at night and ask each other questions. Chris was way more into history and politics than I even at a young age, and he was the one that planted seeds of rebellion in my head."

"Seeds? What kind of seeds?"

"That our Father was insane. Oh, not insane in the conventional sense I suppose, but I am not a psychiatrist. He was, however, fixed on this tortured view of the world. Father lacked some basic elements we see as essential to being human. He could not put himself in the situation of the other. His world was the only world. He could not feel anything—a classic symptom of a sociopath, no fucking empathy. To the outside world, he could be charming and eloquent. Inside, he had a venality and viciousness that was palpable. Other than Mother, no one seemed to see this. I could never figure out what Chuck or Kat saw. They clammed up. It was just Chris and me. We were allies but never got closer than that. We preserved each other's sanity but seldom offered love or emotional relief to one another. I have thought about that many times."

"And the answer?"

"I don't know, only many thoughts. I usually conclude that we had no role models at home. No one taught us how to love. That is why Chris is so thankful for the Jackson home. I think he got an injection of caring and compassion from them. I still need my shot."

"But you save lives every day." It was yet difficult for Karen to see why this lovely, accomplished woman could be so sad.

"As a technician, not as a person. I think . . . I think maybe that is why I am doing this. I want to find my heart, my passion. Oh, this is silly, you should not have to listen to me whine so."

"No, please, please." Karen reached out and took Kay's hand. They looked at one another for several seconds, not a word was spoken.

"One more thing, something I never shared with Chris, with anyone really." Then Kay froze.

"Please . . ."

"Father raped me," it just came out, hard and fast.

"What . . . when? Recently?" Now Karen was lost. This was the last thing she expected from this woman whom she viewed as an older authority figure.

"This was years ago, when I was a young teenager. The abuse went on for a while, quite a while. It was around the time that Chris and I pulled away from him and eventually one another. Sometimes I think Father was punishing me for being a bad daughter, unfaithful to him if you will."

"Did Chris know?" Karen managed to get out.

"Oh, heavens no. He would have killed Father or tried. And then I would have lost him as well. Mother knew but said nothing. For all I know she has repressed the memory. I think she probably knew it was inevitable, that is why she set up the trust funds for us with her own money so that we could escape when the time came. But I am just guessing at that. All I know is that I withdrew from people, even Chris. We were never as close again as we were during those earlier nights we dissected Father's world in secret and determined he was full of shit."

"You should tell him . . ."

"No . . . no! And you are not to say a word to him." Kay wiped a tear from her cheek. "I cannot, for the life of me, figure out why I confessed this to you right now, we hardly know one another."

"My guess," Karen leaned over to hug her, "is that you now feel like you are out of jail. And I am safe I suppose."

Kay looked at her as if Karen had just solved the alchemy challenge. Then they sat holding one another. Karen could feel slight tremors course through Kay's body but was paralyzed about what to do. She felt a nimbus of conflicting emotions around her—pity and awe and a raw, inexpressible sensuality.

"Thank you," Kay suddenly said as she pulled away. "This was silly of me."

"No . . ."

"Time for bed." For a moment Karen wondered if Kay were inviting her to stay in the same bed but immediately dismissed that possibility. "I am beat from my trip and I really want to talk with you about some possible assignments. I know my brother will stick me someplace safe, or at least he will try."

"I am certain of that," Karen confirmed.

Kay leaned over and kissed Karen on the cheek. "Thank you and good night."

As Karen headed toward her own room that familiar sense of need and anticipation coursed through her. She managed, somehow, to pushed these feelings away. *Don't do anything stupid,* she told herself. Karen lay in bed, sleep was difficult to find. Then there was a soft tap on the door. It was so soft she was not sure it was real. "Come in."

Kay stood mute just inside the bedroom door, framed in the light from the outer room.

"Anything wrong?" Karen asked, puzzled while knowing at the same time.

After another awkward pause, Kay spoke in a soft voice, "I always loved the story about Jules trying to seduce my brother in high school when he turned her down. Of course, she probably was happy he walked away and he probably regretted doing so. Talk about the kind of miscommunication that mars relationships. It took great courage on her part."

Karen looked at the lovely image before her, a woman that seemed beyond her wildest aspirations. She was not sure she could get any words out. Then she thought the vision would evaporate if she remained silent. "You know, I guess there is something to that old aphorism about never knowing if you can win unless you run the race."

Kay let her night gown fall from her shoulders. "Are you going to run away like Chris did?"

"Do I look as crazy as he is? Besides, this is my place, where would I run?"

They both laughed, breaking the tension. Moments later, they began to embrace and kiss. Karen could not resist one question, "Kay, I am not sure why this is happening. I am not that attractive."

"Nonsense," kay responded, "you are beautiful, especially in all the ways that count." Kay slid onto the bed next to Kay taking her face into her hands as she peered deep into her eyes. "I am empty, Karen. I need someone to help fill the emptiness. Please. And you are lovely, better than that barmaid at the Hairy whatever for sure."

"Never in a million years would I have guessed you would need me, or anyone. Are you certain I can help, you know, fill the void."

"I am sure you can," Kay's words were soft yet assured.

"How, how could you possibly know that. We barely know one another," Karen whispered as Kay's caresses fired up her senses in ways not experienced since Alicia had abandoned her.

"Simple. My brother loves you, that is good enough for me."

———

Chris took Jules on a short tour of Oxford. Oddly, she had never visited him there, their meetings typically taking place in London. He had always thought she would find this academic town provincial, boring. But she seemed charmed by it, the medieval feel and the broad greens behind the colleges. Eventually, though, they made their way back to his place, a rather charming cottage with a poorly tended garden on the edge of town.

"Do you want a drink?" he asked, uncertain what to do now that they were alone. *Why am I so nervous?* he thought. Before he completed the thought, she pushed him back to the wall where their bodies started a desperate erotic dance. Hands started clawing at clothes as grunts and groans replaced words as the means of personal expression. He swung her around as he grabbed her by the buttocks and she wrapped her long legs around his waist. He slowly ground his pelvis into hers as her mouth greedily found his.

"Damn," Jules moaned, "I miss this so, miss you so."

"You had your chance, we could have been together." Then he immediately realized that his choice of words was ill-advised.

"You want to start that now." She tried pushing him away to no avail. Mutual need overwhelmed them.

Their struggle descended to a plush rug near a fireplace. Remaining clothes flew in all directions. He poised above her, his body taught with anticipation. This was always the best moment of the sexual dance, when you knew it was inevitable and yet still in the future, but only barely. He smiled. "You are just as beautiful as you were in high school, but savvier."

She was breathing heavily. "That is your idea of sweet talk, no wonder Karen has to pimp for you. But what I need is for you to get inside me or I will explode."

Sometime later, they lay in each other's arms. He could feel her breasts heaving and pushing against him. That always excited him, and it was doing so now as well. "Maybe we can make it to the bed? What do you think?"

"How far is it?" Jules responded. "I am not sure I can move, you wore me out, kiddo."

"Really, so I am getting better with age."

"Oops," she said, "no, I meant you are getting heavier, just a few extra pounds there."

"Oh, no, you are not fooling me. I still ring your bell. In truth, I believe that was too rushed, always a problem after a lapse in time. So, time for plan B." With that he started to tickle her around the waist as she giggled and squirmed.

"Stop that!" she protested. "You are still a little boy at heart, aren't you?" She tried to look cross.

"And you love it, don't you?"

She laughed. "Goddamn it but I do. What the hell is wrong with me?"

"Nothing at all. You show exquisite taste that is all, except you were not smart enough to say yes when I offered to make you an honest woman."

She grew quiet. "I do wonder about that. I do wonder."

"Are you happy?" Chris suddenly asked.

"Absolutely!" she exclaimed too quickly.

"Really?" he stared at her.

"Of course, what is not great about my life? My career is taking off. I am affluent, healthy, and, if the rumors are to be believed, very hot."

"Who started that rumor?" Chris scoffed and then returned to his serious look.

Jules realized that a light jest might not suffice. She rose to a sitting position, her legs crossed, and she looked back at him while composing her thoughts. "Do you remember when you were finishing at Princeton and I was at Columbia. If you recall, we talked about me joining you here when I had finished up."

"I remember." Chris looked up at her closely. He had always loved her soft eyes, softer lips, dark hair that framed her smooth, copper skin. "But you never committed. You came close, as I recall, but . . ."

"I came very close, oh so close. If you had pushed a little . . ."

"I couldn't push. That was not me. I assumed you knew what you wanted. I simply was not good enough."

"My god, you are such a sad sack of idiocy. How many times do you want me to tell you that I have loved you since you turned down my body in high school. My god, the boy who was known to mount a coat rack if given the opportunity turned me down. Maybe I am not that hot."

"Jules, stay serious with me here."

"Okay, Chris. Here is the thing. There was a deal breaker. There has always been a deal breaker. When we had those talks back then about a future I would mention children. You know, it is the woman thing, the ability to create another life is a heady prospect. Well, it was for me. The thing is, you never responded."

"Wait," Chris protested, raising himself up to look directly at her. "I can't recall never saying I didn't want to have children, not once."

Jules got up and circled the room. It was as if she were searching for where to go next, both physically and emotionally. "This is the thing about women, Chris, we are intuitive. I knew, I knew with all the certainty in the world, that you did not want children. I did not understand, I think you would be a great dad, but nevertheless I knew."

Suddenly Chris flushed with a bit of anger. "Jules, how could you not know? How could you possibly not know? My father! My goddamn father. I could not bring a child into this world. I could not possibly expose them to the same suffering . . ."

"Oh, for Christ's sake, Chris. Do you know how silly you sound? Look at me! You are not your father. Do you understand? You are not your father. You are as far from that man as you can get. You would be a goddamn great dad."

"Yea," Chris whispered. "My head tells me that. But my gut is not so sure. We are not talking reason here. I am sorry."

Jules looked at him for a long time. Her lips quivered until she forced them together. Then she walked to him and threw her arms about his body, drawing him to her.

"This is my punishment?" he tried to sound light but a heaviness forced its way into the words.

"Yup, you are to be my sex slave until I am sated."

"Oh my god, woman, you will kill me."

"Good, two birds with one stone."

———

Kay and Karen arrived late the next morning. They had agreed to meet at the small office that Chris used while in Oxford. Normally it was manned by an office manager but found it useful to keep it going for his occasional use. Karen was known to be tardy on occasion, a sin for which he never dared to reprimand her. Kay, though, was never late. She approached life with precision. He had even bought scones in case they were hungry.

"Where is Jules?" Kay asked.

"Where were you guys? This is no way to impress your new boss, being late on the first day."

"Oh god," said Kay, "you really don't consider yourself my boss, do you? Well, we will deal with that later."

"All my fault, boss," said Karen as she grabbed a scone to eat with the coffee she had bought on the way over. She always thought the office coffee too weak. "I kept us back."

Kay smiled. "Actually, this is true. She insisted we have sex one more time this morning."

Karen spit out the coffee she was just about to swallow. "Oh, no, I . . . we . . ."

"Don't have a cow, Karen. I would sooner believe that George W. Bush is a Rhodes scholar than you and my sister made love last night. I did not fall off a turnip truck, at least in the past week. Hell, my bet is that Kay is still a virgin."

Kay walked over to her brother and pinched his cheek. "You just keep believing that."

Karen continued blushing profusely and kept her eyes focused on the scone in her hand.

Chris looked puzzled but then came to an internal conclusion. "No, you guys are just screwing with me. Come over here, Kay, here is the place I have in mind for you."

"Yup, Karen, exactly the place you said he would pick, boring and safe."

"You guys have been plotting." He looked back and forth between the two of them. Kay had a determined look on her face while Karen was still blushing and oddly reticent.

"You bet your ass, buttercup." Kay was in her take-charge mode. "By this time, dear brother, you should know I am going where I want to go. You don't need to protect me. You must know me by now."

Chris looked at Karen who shrugged and continued to stare at the floor. Then he turned back to his sister. "The thing is, Kay, I don't know you, I really don't. I think I did a long time ago, when we spent those nights hiding from Father and trying to figure out the world together. Yeah, then I felt very close to you. But somewhere I lost you and never knew why. The bottom line is that I don't know you and I feel bad about that."

Kay took a deep breath. "Yes, I suppose that is true. Listen, Chris, my best guess is that you are going to want to protect me, am I right?"

"Of course, I love you."

That seemed to startle her. Kay paused, either to digest his assertion or decide how to respond. "I . . . I love you as well." She walked across the room to him and put a hand to the side of his face. "How come Jules never snatched you up. You really are a catch, and not bad looking either for a debauched and aging pervert that is."

"Well, I am figuring that out . . ." Then his expression changed. "Wait, you are playing me, trying the flattery scam."

"Damn," Kay expelled the word. "I thought for sure you would fall for it." She walked to the map and pointed her finger at a spot in Pakistan. "There, that is where I want to go, right there."

"You want to work with the Taliban refugees?"

"Yes, those Taliban monsters represent everything I despise, the way they treat women. You have no idea how I despise men who abuse women the way they do. I see these women coming into the ER on weekends, beaten and abused and miserable out of their minds. But they won't press charges. They make up the most ridiculous stories. I would want to scream. Some men... some men deserve to be in jail. They are...never mind."

Karen's head popped up, as if she had to drag her stare from whatever on the floor had mesmerized. She looked at Kay as if she knew her meaning precisely. "Chris, I have briefed her on the mission and dangers there. We spent the early morning talking about it."

"Hah," cried Chris. "I knew you were plotting to screw me and not one another. You know, Karen, they still need a well-built barmaid at the Hairy Hare."

"Give it up, Chris. I have been staring down Father these past months, years. I did not run away, remember, at least not until now. Karen has filled me on all the risks. That is where I am going. Besides, the chief of medical services there, Amar Singh, sounds amazing."

Chris sat down and put his head in his hands. "One of these days I am going to find a way around the 'I stood up to Father while you ran away' gambit but I have nothing today. Listen, Kay, I will agree but please be careful. You get hurt, or worse, and I swear . . ."

"What?" Kay asked with a wry smile.

Chris got up. "I swear I will come and find you in whichever part of hell St. Pete puts you. Then I will dispatch you a second time myself before I drag your sorry ass back to the land of the living. Don't you ever, ever forget that. Damn, I need you, kiddo. You are all I have left from our sucky family." Chris could see genuine surprise in his sister's countenance. She had not expected such genuine passion from him. Sensing he had the upper hand, he decided to keep control of the conversation. "Okay, we will have a lot of work getting you ready, some language and cultural prep. Lots of resources here in Oxford for that kind of stuff."

"Thanks." Kay hugged her brother before looking in his eyes. "Dammit, I love you too."

CHAPTER 7

THE SECOND HEGIRA

The door opened and Azita spun around to see who had entered. But her face sank into gloom again. It was merely her brother, Majeed, returning home from the position that his father had secured for him with the local development agency, a catch-all ministry that purportedly initiated projects designed to spur economic progress in the area. The mission sounded important but, with meager resources and almost no political support, there was little they could do in practice. The rulers were suspicious of change and Allah, not science, would show the way in any case. What he did there was not clear to the family, but he greatly enjoyed any excuse to be out of the house where things were not going well. Azita looked back to her book on the table but soon her eyes shifted back to the front door.

"Azita, staring at the door will not bring your father home any sooner," Deena chided her sister.

"Why do you assume I am waiting for Papa? I am doing my studies here." Azita glanced back down at the book in front of her.

"I will tell you why. You have been staring at the same page for an hour. Perhaps if there were a picture of a handsome boy on it I would understand but there is only all this writing in English and these numbers. Perhaps the problem is that you are not as smart as you think you are. Can't you understand what you are looking at?"

"And if you did not waste all your time reading trashy romantic novels you buy on the black market, perhaps you would amount to something," Azita shot back, immediately regretting it.

Deena added her anger. "Majeed, you should have let the morals police beat some sense into our little sister back in Kabul. Maybe then we would not be exiled in this hell hole now."

Majeed rolled his eyes. "Mama, the girls are at it again. I am only home a minute and they are pecking at one another like two hens. You know that if Father would permit me, I would beat some sense into the two of them."

Madeena worked at the kitchen counter. The days had become tedious in the several weeks they had been in Kunduz. They did not have a circle of friends here to pass the time. At the same time, tensions ran high in the city and surrounding area. They were close to what was considered the front lines between the area controlled by the Taliban and the mountainous regions generally held by what was called the Northern Alliance, a loose group of tribal clans and powerful warlords that resisted the harsh rule of the new religious fanatics. This northeast portion of Afghanistan had always resisted what it considered foreign domination, even from Kabul. It was here that the mujahedeen fought the Russians with incredible ferocity and bravery against all odds until American weapons clandestinely shipped to these brave warriors tipped the battle. As their casualties mounted, the Communists finally admitted defeat and retreated north by

1989. It proved to be their Vietnam. The costs to the Afghans had been horrific, with untold numbers slaughtered, maimed, or driven into Pakistan as desperate refugees. Still, the warriors of the northern provinces would remain unconquered.

But the notion of control was a loose one. Taliban sympathizers were found everywhere, as were those who opposed the new regime. As a result, geographic location did not always guarantee safety from your enemies nor that you were among friends. It was a battle where the so-called front line did not exist. Thus, suspicion and anxiety were ever present. You were always on guard, continuously sifting every conversation and every facial expression and bodily movement for clues about the allegiance of the other person. The Masoud family was feeling the tensions.

Madeena sighed deeply. "You know, Majeed, if you raise your hand against any woman you will have to answer to me. I will not have you acting, or even thinking, like those animals out there."

"Oh, Mama." Her son smiled. "You know I am joking. I love my sisters no matter how silly they are."

"My dear son, watch it." She brandished a large knife in his direction but with a smile on her face.

"You girls are lucky. I am outnumbered now but wait until Papa is home."

"Hah," cried Deena, "Papa will spank you like he did when you were a little boy." But then she stopped. In truth, she could not recall her Father ever striking any of them. All the parents she knew disciplined their offspring in such a manner but never her father. He was different in so many ways.

Madeena decided it was time to take charge. "Okay, enough. Majeed, you go check on the livestock. See that they are fed and watered and perhaps you can get some goat milk for us. Deena, you go to the market, there are a few things I need. And Azita, come away from your studies. I need some help with the evening meal."

After the others left, Azita slowly made her way to her mother's side. "I miss the old days," the girl murmured with a touch of petulance.

"We all do. Now cut these and no whining. And be careful, I don't want the tips of your fingers in the salad. The way you daydream . . ."

"Yes, Mama." The girl started cutting the vegetables though without great enthusiasm.

After a while, Madeena finally broke the silence, "You know, you could be better company to your poor mother. My life is so difficult these days, putting up with ungrateful children who squabble endlessly and your father who is so unhappy. It is such a drain on your poor mother who is, as everyone says, a saint."

Azita broke into a tiny smile. "You are right, Mama. You really are a saint and Papa is so lucky to have you. Tell me, tell me again about how you fell in love with Papa."

"Oh you foolish girl, you have heard that story so many times. We met at school, when girls were permitted an education. For some reason, he pursued me. Of course, I was a proper young woman and would never flirt with a boy. Yet, he still sought me out and begged for my hand. Eventually he won my heart and we got married. No big thing."

"So, a real love story, how romantic."

"I suppose so. It was possible back then." Madeena smiled.

"Unfortunately, that is not how Papa tells the story." Azita had her mischievous smile now.

"Really, what does that evil man say?"

Azita tried to erase a tiny smile. "He told me that he had many girls chasing him but that you chased the hardest and, in the end, he felt sorry for you."

"Is that right." Her mother laughed. "Well, perhaps I will serve up chopped Papa for dinner tonight." She waived the knife in her hand menacingly.

Azita squealed with laughter. "I only repeat what he told me. We all know that Papa never lies."

"That is true, almost. He doesn't, which is quite odd for a man since they are all well-known liars. You remember that, dear." Madeena stopped cutting. "Hmm, perhaps you are old enough for the truth. I did chase him though he did not run very far. In fact, he did not run at all. Funny, I could tell from across a school yard that he was a special boy, unique. How can we tell? I am not sure we can really. But I knew."

"I will never be as fortunate." Azita grew somber.

"I should not say this. I know I will regret it. But the boy, the man, that wins your heart will be the luckiest guy in the world. You are special, my dear."

"Hmmm, that is not what Deena says. She insists no boy will ever want me, which is okay as far as I am concerned. I think they are ..."

"I know." Madeena laughed. "You think they are smelly, obnoxious, rude and all things disgusting."

"So, am I wrong?"

"Let me think." Her mother paused as if she were thinking very hard on the matter. "No, I guess not. You may be right. Still, it can be nice to have one around."

Just then, the door opened and in came Pamir. His face broke into a broad smile at the sight of his wife and daughter. Azita dropped her knife and sprang across the room to his arms.

"Ooph," Pamir grunted, "you are gaining a few pounds, my girl. Too much studying and not enough exercise. We will have to see what we can do about that."

"Oh, yes, Papa. I should be in the clinic with you and making home visits. That would take the pounds away, not that I have put on any." Then she ran to a mirror to look. "No extra pounds, I am sure."

"See, mother, for a girl who cares nothing for the boys she is quite vain I believe."

The two adults laughed while Azita blushed.

Majeed walked in the door just then. "What is the joke?"

Pamir could not resist. "Your sister thinks she is putting on some weight and the boys won't like her."

As she tried thinking of a good response, Majeed spoke out, "You are right. I have noticed this myself. I am thinking she needs some more exercise, like looking after the livestock and our garden. All she exercises is her brain and sometimes her mouth."

"Perhaps something you could have done more of, exercising your brain that is," Azita finally found her voice.

"Aiii, here we go again. Father, your children have been at it all day, sniping at one another. Where did we go wrong with them?"

"Yes, it is so sad to watch your children grow up to be such disappointments." But the smile never left his face. He knew how to quiet them, seldom needing to raise his voice and never bringing a switch to their backsides. Azita noticed and stored this in her brain. She would never have children, she was sure. She would be too busy as a doctor and besides, boys were too obnoxious. But, if she did find a boy, get married, and have children, this is how she would raise them. Her parents were perfect, she thought.

Deena soon returned from the marketplace. "I hate this place," were the first words out of her mouth.

"And this is how you greet your father after a long day?"

"But it is true, Papa." His older daughter was not to be dissuaded. "There is so little in the marketplace. Everything is dirty. The people are suspicious and surly. And look what you are forced to do. You must spend your days fixing up these fighters who probably got hurt killing and maiming your own family in the mountains. We should be back in Kabul."

"Well, it is not that easy."

"No," Majeed chimed in, "my sister is right. Quite astonishing but she is correct. I see the Taliban looking at me. I can read their eyes. They are wondering what is wrong with me, why am I not with them fighting for Allah."

Pamir almost snapped the words out, "These men are not fighting for Allah, never forget that."

"The problem is, Father, that they believe they are and feel that anyone who has not joined them is a traitor of some kind. The good people at the ministry protect me as well as they can. But we have so little to do, there is no money and those at the top care little for our mission. They only care about their fanatical beliefs and conquest."

"And I, Papa, so miss being with you when you tend your patients. I love my books but . . ."

Pamir raised a hand to cut her off and then sighed. The look on his face was so sad that his children immediately felt shame at their own selfishness. "My children, you are right. This is not easy for me either. In Kabul, I could treat my fellow citizens, those that needed my ministrations whether they could pay or not. And most did in one way or another because they were grateful. Here, I must give priority to those who are in the business of killing and torturing and maiming others. They feel entitled to my services and never thank me. But I have no choice. That is why we were permitted to move north, the promise that I would help them. Of course, there usually is some time to help the citizens in need unless some battle has taken place. That keeps me going. But when I must work on someone that has returned from fighting my own clan my faith is surely tested." His face was in agony now. "You have no idea the cost I am paying. I may be saving the life of a man who will go back and kill a relative of mine. It is a thought I can bear only with enormous sorrow."

"Then you must not do it," cried Majeed.

"How easy those words are said," Pamir responded. "And how will I feel when I am tossed in prison and I know my family has been cast into the street or worse. Besides, I have taken an oath. I am a healer. It is not up to me to judge the individual before me. I must do my best to repair their broken bodies. It is up to someone else to examine the worthiness of their lives and pass judgment on their sins."

"But I can, Father. I have taken no oath. I shall not fight for them, these barbarians who almost killed my sister. I cannot. But I feel they will come for me any day now. They are not doing well against the Northern Alliance. Some of these fighters are from Pakistan and god knows where, sent here by their mullahs. They do not care for us or our country. They are ablaze with religious fervor but that does not last. Now they are up against people who know the cause for which they fight and die."

"And I, Papa," it was Deena's turn. "I am also afraid. What if one of these powerful men come for a wife? I am already well beyond the proper age. How can you turn them down if they claim it is Allah's wish? I cannot marry one of these animals. They will rape me every day and beat me mercilessly, even if I do nothing wrong. Is this what you want? You want to see me so desperate and crazed that I might kill myself?"

"My children . . ."

Before Pamir could continue, Deena turned on her younger sister. "She is why we are here. Everything is for precious Azita.

If you did not coddle and favor her so much we could still be in Kabul. There, it is big enough to have a real life. Here, we are trapped and visible and thus in a kind of prison. You cannot do anything without fearing someone will notice and tell. You are so afraid, Papa, you do not take Azita with you during the day. We must watch her mope around all day, the useless cow."

"Stop it, just stop it," it was Azita, tears streaming down her face. "I know it is my fault." With that, she ran from the room in tears.

"See what you have done, wicked girl," Madeena regretted the words as soon as she said them. "But I understand, we are all stressed."

"Listen. We will all talk after supper. But first, Deena, come with me." He took her by the arm and led her into a small room he used as an office. Once there, he embraced her and held her for some time. "There is one thing I want you to understand, that I want you to accept without any doubt whatsoever."

"What is that, Papa," she could barely get the words out through her sobs.

"I love you, my dear. I remember you when you were a tiny baby. You were so beautiful. Everyone said that you would grow up to be an extraordinarily beautiful woman. I beamed with pride. How did an ugly man like me create such beauty? Now that was a miracle. Maybe it was because I had such a beautiful wife, what do you think?"

"I think . . . I think I have the most handsome father in the world."

"Oh Allah, how did I raise such a brazen liar?"

Deena managed a tiny smile as the tears flowed copiously. "It is no such lie."

"Just remember this. Each of my children has a gift and I treasure you all. Azita will never have your beauty. I only ask you to treasure what you have and accept what she has. Can you do that for me?"

"It is hard," she forced the words out through heaves of her body.

"Remember this, sweet Deena, your sister does not have a choice in the path she has chosen. It is a passion that Allah has cursed her with. You can easily see how difficult this journey will be for her. The chances of success are . . . are small at best. Think about what must be inside her heart, to want something so bad yet which is so impossible to possess. If you wanted a boy with all your heart but he had eyes only for another."

"I would smite him with a curse."

"And you know these curses? I think I had better be nicer to you." He smiled at her as he took her face in his hands and looked kindly upon her. "I admit, it is difficult to imagine that any boy would not be swept away by your beauty. But I want to ask a favor of you. Go to her. Talk with her. Would you do that for me?"

Deena said nothing. After some moments, she heaved a big sigh and shook her head to indicate that she understood.

———

Azita looked up as the door to the bedroom opened. She looked up expecting to see her father. Instead, she saw her sister standing tentatively in the doorway. "Sister, can I come in?"

"No," Azita barked. "Go away."

"Well, I am not going anywhere. This is my bedroom too. You are going to listen to me." With that, Deena walked over to the bed where Azita lay and sat on the edge.

Azita turned her body toward the wall and tried to put a pillow over her head. "I am not listening to you. I hate you."

"That is fine. In fact, I understand and…I do not blame you at all. So maybe I will just talk. Whether you listen or not is irrelevant. Allah will hear me, and His judgment is worth more than yours." She looked to see if there was a response but saw none. "I have come to realize something. Okay, maybe Papa has helped me realize something. I have not felt kindly toward you for a long time. I knew this to be wrong in my heart but it was hard to push away such feelings. To me, you were a spoiled and selfish girl who thought only of herself and what she wanted."

"This is to make me feel better? Just go away."

Deena ignored her. "I could not understand why Mother let you avoid your chores to study your books and why Father spent so much time with you. After much time, I concluded that they loved you the most and that hurt me. That hurt me very much. I am not sure you can understand that."

Azita slowly turned her body to look in her sister's direction. "Deena, I…."

"No, shush. I want to say all that is in my heart," the words were sharp but without anger. Then she said nothing for a few moments. Azita turned slightly more to look at her and saw that she had been crying, that the tears were still falling. "Even as a girl, I knew I was considered a beauty. The relatives would ooh and aah over me, telling me what a good catch I would be and how lucky some boy would be to get such a lovely girl as a wife. Of course, this was before the Taliban and things were not as strict. Even love marriages were possible in large cities like Kabul and you could go to the cinema and dream of romance and love. Mama took me to a few Bollywood films which lose something when dubbed in Dari but you still could see the dances and listen to the music and see the heroes fall in love. I thought to myself, 'My life could be like one of those in the movies. I would come home and dream of meeting some boy and capturing his heart.'"

"But you are beautiful, so beautiful." Then Azita remembered she was not supposed to talk. "Sorry, I promised silence."

"No, that is fine. You can talk if you say nice things like that." Deena smiled. "Slowly, as the Taliban took over and I approached the age where romance was possible, my dream began to die. I wanted to find a boy to love on my own, to capture his heart through my own efforts and form a bond that would carry us through life. I wanted to be a mother like ours and raise wonderful children that would bring pride and admiration to us all. I wanted a man like Father to be at my side throughout life." Deena thought Azita was opening her mouth. "Before you say how stupid such a dream is, I want to say that no matter how commonplace it is, that is my dream. That was my dream. You think of things that are beyond my imagination but that should not matter between us. I think . . . I think I am finally understanding that each of us can have our dream. Each of our dreams is worthy of who we are and want to be. Does that make sense?"

Azita rose in the bed with such suddenness that Deena drew back a bit. After a moment's hesitation, she threw her arms around her sister. "I understand, I understand, I so understand." The two girls wept. Each felt the tears of the other. "I want you to know that I was jealous of you."

"Of me?" Deena was incredulous. "How could that be?"

"Don't you think I cannot see how beautiful you are and how plain I am? Why do you think I say such nasty things about boys? I know I have such little chance of getting some worthy boy to pay attention to me, even if it were permitted. Maybe I should thank the Taliban. They are giving me an excuse for being ignored."

"For what?" Now Deena had a big smile. "They almost beat you to death."

"True, but now I can blame them if I go through life alone. I will simply tell myself that I would have gotten the handsomest boy in the land, but they would not let me flaunt my sexy body."

Both girls laughed deeply. "I had not thought of that." Deena added, "If I end up with some fat, smelly husband that Mother selects, I can blame the Taliban as well. It is good that they take such decisions away from us. It does make life easier."

"This is good. If I never become a doctor I can blame them as well. I would be the best doctor in the country except they would not let me go to school. That takes so much pressure off. I must confess something. This is what I fear most, that I will have a chance and fail. I won't be good enough. I will let Papa down."

Deena looked at her with amazement. "It never occurred to me, not ever."

"What?" Azita asked.

"That you would doubt yourself. You seem so confident, so sure of who you are and where you are going. And believe me, you are very beautiful. Any boy that captures your heart will be lucky indeed. I think just a little make up, maybe? Azita, you are a beauty about to blossom."

"I hope Allah forgives you for such an outrageous lie."

Deena said quietly, "How can you doubt your beauty?"

"My doubt comes easy, you are not in here to see what goes on in my heart, dear sister." With that, Azita put a hand on her chest. "In here, I am full of doubt and fear."

They hugged again. "Let us make a pact," Deena offered.

"What will this pact be?"

"Let us face life together. Let us pursue our dreams together. If we ever become cross with one another, let us always be open and talk things through. By the way, I don't really blame you for being here. It is not your fault. Father would insist that we escape these people no matter what. They strangle the life out of everything they touch."

"I do love you, Deena. You have always been what I wanted to be as a woman."

Deena laughed. "Your dreams are small indeed. I can say one thing. If I had a brain like yours, you would be my inspiration, my hero. There is little doubt of that. I would not be a doctor though, I could never stand the sight of blood. I went to Father's clinic once before you started going. I had to run outside where I threw up."

Azita tried to stifle her laugh. "One more thing, Deena. You are much smarter than you let on. I can tell. You read all the time, and not just romantic novels. You flaunt those to hide the fact that you have a fine brain. You should join me in my studies. I would help you."

Then they both heard some noise at the door. The two girls looked at one another. "I think we are being spied on," Deena whispered. "We should play a trick on these spies."

"How?" Azita asked with a sly smile on her face.

"Just follow my example." Then in a much louder voice she started yelling while continuing to look at the door. "Damn you, sister. If you don't do your share around here, I will throw you to the Taliban. Let them try to beat some sense into you since Mother and Father won't."

"As if you would even try that. I would tell the Taliban that you lust after the boys and read forbidden books about romance. We will see how you like their beatings."

"No," Deena cried. "Don't hit me."

With that the door opened and in rushed their mother as the two girls laughed uproariously and fell back on the bed. "Such girls," Madeena tried to sound angry. "I should give you both to the Taliban. Come, dinner is ready."

———

After dinner, Pamir went to the windows and looked out each one. The moon was brilliant that evening, getting close to full. It was easy to see if anyone was lurking about. Satisfied, Pamir walked to the center of the room. "Everyone gather around. I have something to discuss." After everyone was settled, he took a deep breath. "This is one of those discussion that cannot leave this house, this room, no matter how much you might trust someone. Does everyone understand?"

Murmurs of assent rose from everyone.

"Okay then. I think that it is time we make our move. Majeed is correct. His time may be up." The look on Pamir's face reflected his seriousness. "I cannot protect him. They will press him into their unholy war. I think we are not being watched as closely as we were in the beginning or perhaps I should say that I am not under such great suspicion any longer. The authorities knew of my background, where I came from. Being suspicious of everyone and everything, they could not help but consider the possibility that I came here only to get to the Northern Alliance. I could tell at first. They were watching very carefully. Azita, that is why I could not even consider bringing you to the hospital or the clinic. We could not afford to raise any doubt in their minds."

It was Majeed who spoke up, "Oh, I am feeling bad about this. I am putting the entire family into danger. I can take my chances."

"No, no, we are all in this together. I know Deena and Azita are miserable. I am miserable. I talk about oaths and commitment to my patients, but I cannot escape that I go through the motions some days. That is not me. I want to feel the passion of my craft again. I wonder, can the rest of you understand my agony?"

"Yes, my husband. I understand. I can feel the sadness in your body each night. You try mightily to hide such things from me. Do you really think I can be fooled? After all these years, there is no way you can fool me." Madeena knew in her heart that her husband might be exaggerating a bit to remove some guilt his children felt. Healing was healing after all. But she had no doubt that he was miserable indeed.

"No, my wife, I cannot hide anything from you. We are one. I want one thing for all of you to understand. No one, by themselves, is responsible for us making this dangerous move now. We are all in this together as a family. We are a family, never forget that."

Deena and Azita looked at one another, each reached out to the other. "We understand," both of them said simultaneously.

Pamir smiled. "Good. Now I want to ask each of you individually. Are you ready to try now?"

Madeena spoke first, "You must have a plan. First tell us your plan."

"Yes, very good, my dear. Well, I have been working on this for some time now. In truth, events started without any action on my part. If you are not well known, it is dangerous but not impossible to move from one side to the other. There are many spies from the Alliance in Kunduz and word of my arrival made it to the other side. One frequent visitor to the clinic aroused my interest. He came in with minor complaints and seemed more interested in talking than in medical help. Was he Taliban or was he from home. While I did not recognize him, he was Tajik and knew the mountains well. One day, I simply asked him what he really wanted. It turns out he had doubts about me. In truth, he wanted to know if I would come to the other side, help them with their medical needs. They desperately needed doctors, nurses, anyone who knew what they were doing. In hindsight, this was one of those large moments in life. It was one of those moments when everything was in the balance. If I had guessed wrong, who knows what fate would befall all of us. I would surely be beheaded in the square but for you . . ."

"What happened?" it was Majeed.

"Fortunately, I guessed right. Since I still have my head attached it turns out that he was from the Alliance and we started to talk about what it would take to get all of you out of here. He talked with me about various routes from here to the other side. We discussed which might be the best way and what to look out for. He has a pretty good idea of where the Taliban are located but his knowledge is not complete. Besides, things change all the time. You cannot imagine the weight that was lifted from me at that moment when I knew he was not Taliban. I am not cut out for this intrigue and danger. I am just a doctor who wants to do his job and protect his family. That does not seem like such a large request but perhaps it is in these days."

"Pamir, you shall always be my hero," Madeena said softly to her husband.

"Yes, well, we shall see if I am worthy of such admiration. In any case, when the time comes, we are to drive east as far as we can go. I am working to get a truck that we can load up with what looks like medical supplies. The women will have to hide in the back, under the supplies, if we are stopped. Still, we can only go so far on the roads. Then, as we approach the rough dividing line between the Taliban and the Alliance, we must make our way off road. With this man, I have worked out an escape route." Pamir then walked into his office and came back with a map which he laid out before them. "Look, we will use the road to about here, then into the lower hills until the land becomes too rugged. That will be somewhere here."

"Then what happens?" Deena asked, fearing she knew the answer.

"Then we start to walk. You know what that means of course. We must leave all behind except what we can carry. It means starting over."

When he paused to let that sink in, Deena spoke up once more, "Do you think that should matter to us?'

Pamir stammered, "I could not be sure. I thought you, Deena . . ."

"Yes, I know. I am the thoughtless one, the girl who fills her head with empty thoughts of boys and romance, who is only concerned with her own comforts." She took a deep breath. "I want you all to know that I care about this family, and what Father does, what service he provides. I also care about this country and what has happened to it. I want you all to know I am ready."

Azita reached out for her sister's hand. They looked at one another as the rest of the family looked on in wonder. What was happening here?

"I must emphasize," Pamir added, "there is great danger here. Perhaps my effort to get a truck and talk of doing medical work closer to where the fighting takes place will trigger their suspicion. If that does not, there will be all manner of unsavory men out in the countryside looking for mischief in the name of the Taliban. Every fanatic and thief, every insane mullah invokes the name of Allah to pursue their own twisted ends. I must say this though, it may not be pleasant. It is possible some brigands will come upon us, take whatever we have left and . . . violate you." He looked at his wife and daughters.

Everyone looked at one another. Then Madeena spoke up, "Perhaps we should think on it overnight, discuss it again in the morning."

Azita then turned to her sister. "I want to go but I cannot put you at risk. I would rather die."

Deena smiled. "What kind of life would I have here, watching you mope day after day. And then I could never enjoy my food because I would be watching to see if you cut off a finger while trying to help Mother prepare the meal. These men can have no horror worse than watching you wither and die." She had been smiling but now her face softened. "Everyone is right. You have a gift, a passion, and we must see that you have a chance at it, or we can die trying."

Pamir wanted to say something at that moment but found it difficult to talk. Rather, Majeed broke the awkward silence that followed. "Oh, no, my sisters have stopped fighting. This is not good for me, I am doomed."

"That is okay, my son. Though we men are outnumbered, we shall stand together."

"And fall together, Father."

The tension had been broken and all laughed. "Still, I want to make sure everyone is okay with this. Let me ask each of you in turn. We all must agree, or we will not go. One final thing. There is no guarantee that the Alliance will survive. They are stubborn fighters but poorly equipped. We might find ourselves back under the control of the Taliban even if we can make it."

"We could then try for Pakistan, could we not?" Deena asked.

"Yes, that is a possibility. We would be wretched refugees, but it is a possibility."

"Perhaps the Americans would come to the aid of the Alliance?" it was Azita's hopeful voice.

"Ah, yes, the Americans. That would be nice. I do remember when they brought in the rockets that knocked down the Russian helicopters and blew up their tanks. It saved our country. You cannot imagine what the Russians were doing. They would butcher the boys of military age, rape the women, sometimes bayonet the girls who were obviously pregnant. They would leave explosive devices disguised as candy or toys that would entice the children. Can you imagine putting back together the body of a five-year-old who would not have his arms again? I still have nightmares."

"Pamir, must you relive that horror?" it was Madeena.

"Yes, I must. The children should know of the world's cruelty. Would the Americans have helped if we were not fighting the Communists? I doubt that very much. They were not moved by compassion or care for our country or the people. We had fighters who would kill Russians. That is all that counted. When the Communists took their tanks and planes and soldiers and headed north, the Americans abandoned us. We were of no use to them anymore. They will not come to the aid of the Alliance. Can you think of one thing, anything, that would make them care about what the Taliban is doing to us?"

"I cannot, Father," Majeed affirmed.

"Neither can I, my son. However, that is not the point here. I simply want everyone to consider everything before deciding. So, let us vote, Majeed?"

"Yes, Father, more than ready. I want to join the Alliance and fight these monsters that beat my sister without mercy and terrorize my family."

Pamir blanched at his son's sentiment to become a soldier but moved on without comment. "Deena? I believe you are ready."

Deena held her sister's hand in the air. "We are ready, Father."

"Oh my, now I know that the age of miracles is not past. Our daughters agree on something. And mother?"

Madeena did not speak for a moment. Pamir thought that her courage might be failing her. That fear evaporated when she did speak up, "Father, you know how I feel. I would follow you to the end of the earth and beyond. I made that pledge when I picked you out on the school playground so many, many years ago."

"Good, I hope. But I must clear one thing up. It was I that selected your mother back then."

"Yes, Papa," the two sisters said laughing aloud.

"Do any of you believe that such a beauty as your mother would choose such a boy. Seriously," he went on as his smile evaporated, "we must get ready over the next few days. Look through what you have. We must select only what we can carry. And please remember that our path on foot will not be a leisurely stroll to the market. It will be difficult. Fortunately, it is almost summer. The weather will be warm. We will walk at night. If we are fortunate, the moon will be bright enough to guide us. We will need to prepare food for the journey, things we can carry, which will not spoil. Majeed, you and I will discuss what equipment we might need, there may be some items to be purchased."

"Weapons, Father, we will need weapons."

"I think not. Do you think I will go up against trained fighters? It would be a short fight indeed. It is more than that, however. I cannot go from saving life to taking life. I would rather put my fate in Allah's hands."

"Allah has not been kind to our country," Madeena added sadly.

"No, my dear, He has not. But perhaps all of this goes in some large circle, we suffer to appreciate better the good times when they come. Absent the suffering, we cannot appreciate how rewarding the good times are. In any event, let us start the preparations. I want us ready to move in a moment's notice."

Azita stirred in her seat, then stood up. "I want to make sure of one thing. I know why I want to take any chance for the possibility of some freedom. I yearn for the day when I can walk outside without a burqa, can sit in the sun and read a book, help Papa heal others. I desperately want to taste those freedoms so many others enjoy simply by being alive. Still, I would die inside if harm came to any of you only because I was a selfish girl. I love you all desperately. Every day I thank Allah for giving me this family. I arise some mornings when I sleep in and hear your voices first thing. It is simply the day's chatter, of no consequence, but it means the world to me. I know I seldom say this, maybe never say this. You are my world. Each of you are my world. I would give up my dream without a second thought to keep you with me."

"What a vain girl," Deena said with a smile. "Where would you get such a silly idea that we walk about thinking of your silly dream."

"Why would I do this for you?" her brother quickly added as if the idea was preposterous.

"Thank you, thank you all," was all Azita could say, the words barely audible, wiping away a tear.

Then Deena broke into a smile. "Now my dream is one that is worth pursuing, not like yours dear sister. I have decided to go to India and become a Bollywood star. And if you are nice to me I will pay for your doctor's education." At that, Azita broke into laughter and chased her sister about the house.

———

Several days later Dr. Pamir was treating a patient at the hospital. Three men with long beards and sporting automatic rifles barged into the room. They had to be henchman from the local mullah representing the Taliban. The doctor's first thought was, *I could have sworn we had just a little more time.*

One barked, "Where is Majeed Masoud?"

"My son?" the doctor stammered trying to think.

"Do you know another Majeed Masoud?"

Dr. Pamir regained his composure and almost smiled. *They are such caricatures,* he thought, *almost as if they were hired from central casting for a bad movie and dressed up for the part.* He wondered if they ever thought about being polite, asking nicely, or saying please and thank you. Apparently, being a faithful servant of the Prophet excused you from common decency.

"My son would not be here. He is never with me at the hospital." The doctor worked to control his breathing and remain calm.

"He is not at home. We went there first. The women said they did not know where he is. How could his family not know his whereabouts?"

The doctor tried to look aggrieved. "You went to my home when I was not there? I certainly hope you did not enter when neither my son nor I were present. Only the women were there and likely not dressed appropriately. If you had, that would be most insulting to my family. I might be required to bring such a matter to the mullah."

"Never mind that," the man tried to sound aggressive, but he had been thrown off just a bit. "Where is your son?"

Pamir's response was calm and measured, "it is no secret. He works at the Ministry of Development. He is a very clever boy. I suspect he is out at one of their sites. Yes, now I recall. He mentioned that he might not be home until the morning, until tomorrow morning. He sometimes spends overnight when working with locals outside of the city. He is a very hardworking young man."

"Perhaps, but now he is being called to a higher duty."

"Ah yes," the doctor now smiled broadly. "He is such a diligent young man. I suspect you wish him to join the warriors in battle with the infidels. Yes, he is ready. In fact, just the other evening he was telling us how much he was looking forward to taking up arms against what he called these 'monsters.' Of course, we are concerned for him, particularly his mother. You know how women are."

"That is of no matter," the man barked again. "He must do his duty."

"Of course," Pamir said. "Were I a younger man I would join myself. But I suspect my contributions are better met by healing our brave warriors to continue the fight. In fact, I am about to move my practice closer to the front so that I can do my ministrations near the battlefield. I have been preparing for such a move over the past week." For Pamir, this was a desperate attempt to develop a cover story in case his recent actions were generating suspicion.

This seemed to stop the man in charge. He looked about to his companions for support. They, however, also seemed uncertain about what to do. When the large man apparently in charge spoke again, his voice was a bit more accommodating. "Very well. Here are his papers. You must bring him to the barracks tomorrow morning, is that clear?"

"Of course, it is surely Allah's will." Pamir hoped he looked sincere.

"Tomorrow morning, no later. We are preparing to rid ourselves of these infidels once and for all. It will soon be over and done if it is the wish of Allah."

"As Allah wishes," Pamir responded.

"As Allah wishes," the man said as they swept out of the door.

Moments later, Dr. Pamir was taking his leave, arranging for the rest of his patients to be seen and promising that he would be back in the morning. It was a lie, of course. He would not be back. He would be escaping the Taliban, in prison or dead. In his own mind, escape or death seemed the preferable options.

————

His family crowded around him as he entered the door. "Oh Pamir. We are so glad you are back. The men were here for Majeed. I tried calling but the phone service was down again. Nothing works well in this country anymore."

"You can be assured that they found me. Deena, you run to the ministry. Try to find your brother and tell him to hide until dark. Then he is to make his way back here carefully. The rest of us will get ready to leave tonight. I put them off, but they will expect him in the morning. But I don't trust them. If they see him, they may not wait. Knowing them, they will be back early. They trust no one and with good reason in this case."

About forty-five minutes later, Deena slipped into the house and nodded that all was fine. She had located her brother. The family said little to one another. They had talked about this night many times over the past several days. They went about packing clothes and other essentials into boxes that were labelled medical supplies. As they went about their work, panic hit the doctor. How could this possibly succeed? He had no idea what he was doing. If they were stopped and searched, his pretense would surely be discovered. And even if they made the hills, could he lead them at night? He had grown up in such terrain, knew the stars and the directions that they suggested but that had been decades ago. He was no longer conversant with the outdoors, with the wild country in which he was raised. What if he led them into disaster? But he could not betray his doubts now. He must be strong.

Later, as darkness fell, Pamir walked casually around the neighborhood as if he were taking an evening walk. Seeing nothing suspicious, he returned home. As he approached the house, he heard a whisper from the shadows, "Father, it is me."

Moments later, father and son entered the home. They all hugged and a few tears were shed. "Do you have the list, Mother?"

"Of course," she responded.

"Let us go over it one more time. Then I believe we should wait. We will leave during the darkness but not so early as to raise suspicion. If we are to leave now, they will demand an explanation of why we are starting a journey so early in the morning. Later tonight, we can argue that we are merely starting early. I will argue that I am anxious to get an early start in the morning treating the soldiers. I will try to convince them that I was asked to get there early as I could. And remember, if I hit the horn, take cover under the bundles. It will mean that I see someone in the road. It might be nothing or we might be checked." Then he didn't know what else to say. They all looked at him with wide trusting eyes.

"We will put ourselves in Allah's hands," Madeena whispered, "and yours."

"Your trust is better placed in God, I fear." He thought of covering the risks and dangers they faced but decided against it. What was the use of that. So, he began to reminisce about his childhood, how he would roam the hills and mountains. He talked about the magnificent peaks, snow covered and majestic, about how the spring warmth resulted in rushing streams and profusions of bright desert flowers. But he missed the people most. They were hard, forged by challenge and deprivation. But they were also loyal. If you needed help, they would provide it, without question and hesitation. Most of all, they were independent. They resisted domination by anyone, whether the Communists or the Taliban. Their clan or tribe was paramount. All loyalty was directed to those with whom you were connected by blood or affinity. Beyond that circle, you were tested, trust grudgingly awarded. Once that bond was formed, they would sacrifice all for you, including their lives. He loved these people, he told them. They would as well. As they listened to his uplifting sentiments, all they could hope for was the opportunity to find out if his words were truthful or not.

No one found sleep that night. In the dark, they quietly began to fill up the truck with the few possessions they might carry and the boxes and materials they would use as subterfuge and hiding places if they were stopped, questioned, and searched. It was cloudy, which Pamir was thankful for at that moment. It would make their actions less visible. Later, he would be less sanguine about the cover which would make navigation more difficult on the road.

They were tense. Occasionally, someone would drop a box in the back of the truck or stumble in the dark, making some noise. They all would freeze, wait, look about. They were not quite sure what they were scared about. If a neighbor saw them, what were they likely to do? But everyone was afraid these days. Suspicion and terror were the bread of life throughout the country. God had been rendered a horrific tyrant in the hands of men who knew no sense of morality or spirituality.

Twice, they saw lights flick on in nearby houses. They waited to see if anyone would emerge, Pamir had his story prepared but he found his mouth dry with tension. Why was this so hard? They had not even begun their journey. Perhaps it was because they were so close. He could taste some possibility of freedom, of not pretending things that were not him. His family might escape the prison to which they were confined, not total freedom to be sure, but enough to blossom more fully. That was so desperately needed for Azita. She had to be given a chance to find her gift, her passion. If not, he was sure that this flower of his would wither and die. The lights were extinguished. No one appeared. They completed their clandestine endeavors.

Later, they made their way down back streets and alleys, avoiding the main arteries until they were at the periphery of the city. Again, Pamir was not sure why he was doing this. Surely, trucks went about their business at night. His presence on the roadway was not an automatic signal of guilt except that he knew what they were about. He knew and that was what counted. He would see an occasional pedestrian and his heart would leap. Was this someone from the police, someone from the army of God? But all he could see was a disinterested glance, perhaps some surprise at most.

As they reached the periphery, he saw the unmistakable evidence of a roadblock. It surprised him. Why was that? Of course, they would have some security on this side of town. He tapped his horn and heard quick movements in the back of the truck. Pamir slowed as they approached a sleepy looking guard who stood and peered at him. Pamir was sure he would raise his hand. Still, his heart fell when the man stopped them. He had hoped they might be more concerned with anyone entering the city from the east, not leaving. Apparently, their suspicions knew no bounds. He looked at the man who had stopped him, it was someone he had seen on his trial runs to the front.

The guard smiled upon recognition. "It is Dr. Masoud, is it not?"

"Yes, my good man, you are on duty early."

"As are you, good Doctor, so many trips to the front these days."

"Yes, I have word there are many wounded and that my help is needed."

"You are a good man, Doctor, please go ahead. We will crush these infidels soon, Allah willing." The guard waived his weapon towards the east.

"Allah willing," Pamir said and gunned the engine. He should let the women know it was okay to come out of hiding but realized they had no such signal. He had not thought of everything. Perhaps he would let them hide, just to be on the safe side. Apparently, they would escape the city. No need to tempt fate at this point.

The truck ambled on mile after mile. It was a relic, but available and cheap. The engine would sputter and make ominous sounds from time to time. If it failed now, they would be in trouble. They had not reached the hills and places to hide. Yet, they were far enough away from town that explaining what they were doing would not be easy. Worse, it would be a long and dangerous hike to anywhere that might provide safety. But the truck kept moving. What bothered Pamir more was the difficulty in seeing.

A harsh rainstorm hit them at one point. Fortunately, the downpour was brief. He knew the women would not be comfortable. Then again, neither was he. The strain of seeing the road and lack of sleep were catching up with him. He forced himself to stay alert, talking about anything with Majeed and focusing as hard as he could on the road in front of him. But he was losing the battle. He should stop and take a nap. The thought scared him, however. He was torn. Perhaps anxiety and fatigue now affected his judgement.

The rain had ceased as suddenly as it had begun. He could see stars overhead and the sky taking on a different hue toward the east. Dawn was approaching. He felt revived. Then, his easing mood turned as he saw another roadblock, this one fully manned. It was situated just as the road started up into the hills and the mountains beyond. Beyond this point, he concluded, control by the Taliban was not certain. People were fighting in small skirmishes and terrorist attacks that left the countryside bleeding and in fear. He tapped the horn and slowed as he saw the soldiers raise their hands and point weapons toward the truck.

"Allah be praised," Pamir greeted the soldiers.

"Allah be praised," came back to him. "What are you doing here?"

"I am Doctor Pamir Masoud. I had relocated from Kabul to help with the fight against the infidels. Still, I have talked with my superiors about coming closer to the front. There, I can do better medical work. This is my son, Majeed. He wishes to join in the fight." Pamir panicked. He had talked with his superiors, that is true. But he had no papers and what if they checked with Kunduz or worse, searched the truck.

The soldier stared at him with disbelieving eyes. "What is in the truck?"

"Medical supplies, so that I may cure our warriors."

The man in charge barked to a subordinate to look at the back of the truck. Pamir forced himself not to blink, not to betray any emotion. His mind raced for a story. Perhaps he could persuade them that he was selfish, that he wanted his family with him. Would they buy that? Then he realized the head man was talking to him. What had he said? "I should check with the hospital in Kunduz but it is so early, no one in charge will be there I suppose."

"I am sure you are correct. I left early because the need is so great for medical help." Pamir could see a man jump down from the back of the truck and signal to the head man. What had he found? "It is good to see you are so diligent in your duty. We must all contribute to Allah's will and my medical services are needed greatly. Allah's warriors are wounded, some may die without attention." Pamir's mind raced. That would work with rational men but perhaps not here. Death is martyrdom, a good thing, not to be regretted.

The head man said nothing about that. Instead, he smiled. "Perhaps your son could join us, we could use another good soldier."

"I am sure he would be honored. However, he is set on killing some infidels for the glory of Allah. He wants to be closer to the fighting. I am sure you understand the young. He so wants to fight." Pamir regretted his last thought. Had he implied that these men were cowards, too far from the real fighting. That fear ceased when he heard the men at the back of the truck yell again in a louder voice. What had they said? Were the women discovered? Why could he not understand their words, had his brain ceased to function?

The man staring at him from just outside his window just laughed and nodded his head toward the eastern mountains. "Allah be praised."

"Allah be praised," Pamir responded. While they were stopped, the engine had stalled. When Pamir turned the ignition, the engine merely groaned. *Not now. For God's sake, not now,* he thought. He tried again and again. All this and it ends here. One last time and the engine coughed and turned over. "Apparently, Allah has blessed my mission."

Now the road began winding up into the hills. The medical mission to which they were ostensibly were heading was about twelve to fifteen kilometers ahead. They would get close and then veer off into the rough countryside, continuing to move east until the truck was no longer a feasible method of transport. He knew the general area where he wanted to walk with his family, his contact in Kunduz had promised that help should be available. In his heart though, he had concerns. These were troubled times where allegiances and fortunes shifted often. They could easily walk into disaster.

The truck whined and coughed and struggled up into the hills. The road had never been good but now became merely a rutted and rock-strewn terrain. He felt bad for the women in the back. Occasionally he saw men with weapons. Each time his heart would miss a beat, but they barely paid any attention. He realized that two men driving a truck was commonplace. It was merely assumed that they were delivering supplies to the so-called front. Eventually, he reached a plateau. He knew the base camp was not far ahead now though he could not he see it. He stopped the truck. And looked around. Nothing but bleak high desert. This, he decided, would be the place where he would head north and further east to either a bit more freedom or much personal grief.

They crawled up into the low mountains at a snail's pace. Later, after what seemed like an eternity, Pamir looked ahead. There was nothing but craggy high ground ahead, no opening appeared before his eyes. As he looked ahead for any possibility, the engine coughed and died. "Majeed, I believe the vehicle is telling us it is time to walk."

"So far Allah has blessed us with fortune," his son responded.

"Well, I doubt that God wants you to fight for these apostates. I don't know what I would have done had these men drafted you into their service back there. How would I have explained to your mother that I lost you along our way. I suspect I would rather have joined you than face her." Father and son laughed and stepped out to start the next leg of their journey.

———

The sun was rising in the eastern sky. After they had secured what they would carry, it was largely a matter of finding a place to stay for the day. Though the full effect of summer had not yet settled on the land, the days were quite hot. If they had been rural people, they would not have hesitated to start on their journey. However, they were sedate city folk, elite professionals. They would try the journey at night. In truth, while the journey would be more difficult, there was less chance of discovery.

After walking a while up and over a rise Pamir noticed an overhang a short way ahead. *This would be a good spot,* he thought. They settled down for some food, rest, and protection from the sun.

"Dear husband," Madeena growled with a smile. "Did you aim at every pothole? My poor body is bruised all over."

"But we are still together," Deena added.

Pamir walked to his daughter and put an arm around her. He could hardly believe how much she seemed to mature over the past few days. It was as if she had turned on a switch, transforming from a pouting girl to a young woman. "You are very brave, my daughter. You all are."

"Father is the hero," Majeed added. "I was almost lost to the Taliban at the last checkpoint."

"Yes," Azita commented with her wicked smile. "You would be a great addition to them. You could become head beater of young girls who read in the public square."

Majeed took the bait. "Azita, stop that. You know why . . ."

"Son, you should know your sister by now, she is just teasing you."

"I know." But he hadn't.

"I think I will heed the call of nature," Azita said as she wandered off to find some privacy.

The others chatted amiably for a few minutes until they heard a blood curdling scream come from the direction in which Azita had gone. "Stay here," Pamir said to the women. "Majeed, come with me."

The two men ran over the rise to see Azita standing still, frozen in apparent fright. The two men scanned the horizon looking for any sign of threat. They saw nothing but rock and sand and craggy heights but no sign of life. "Azita, what is wrong?"

"At my feet," her voice quavered.

About ten feet in front of her a snake had curled up in front of the girl. It was a standoff, reptile and human. It was difficult to determine which was more frightened. Majeed slowly circled beyond the snake, selecting a large rock as he went. Silently coming up behind the coiled assassin, he raised the boulder high and slammed it down on the reptile. Azita screamed again as her brother dropped to his knees and slammed the snake again and again until his father calmly suggested it was probably dead.

When they returned to the protective overhang, Deena was outside looking anxiously. "What happened?"

Majeed responded, "Now my sister and I are even, I saved her life . . . again."

"How?" asked Madeena. "I was so frightened."

Majeed smiled, he was enjoying the moment. "She was being threatened by this enormous reptile, like a dragon. But I single handedly confronted this monster and slayed it. Dear Azita, you can thank me now."

"It was just a harmless little snake, it startled me," Azita was clearly on the defensive.

"Hah," Majeed chuckled. "You were paralyzed with fear. I hope you had already done your business or your fright would certainly have helped you along."

Before Azita could respond and their small sibling battle escalate, Pamir intervened. "Azita, thank your brother."

She opened her mouth but had trouble getting the words out. "Thank you, Majeed," she finally managed.

"Was it poisonous?" Deena asked, now concerned.

"I don't know. By the time Majeed was finished with it there was no evidence left." Pamir knew it was a poisonous variety but had determined that such knowledge would not do his charges any good. To his surprise, Majeed supported him rather than emphasize the bravery of his act. Like his slightly younger sister, he was quickly becoming a man. During their travails, they had not turned on one another or fallen apart. No. They became stronger and more supportive. He felt his eyes moisten. He reflected on the odd fact that parental pride should arrive as they were wandering the desert seeking a new life.

Hours later, Pamir woke with a start. He had slipped in and out of sleep, afraid he would miss the opportunity to start out during the cool evening. He checked his watch. All was fine, he had only overslept an hour at most. Walking from under the overhang he looked up into a cloudless sky. *Allah had blessed them,* he thought. The moon was bloated just above the horizon. Soon, it would rise and turn into a bright orb, casting a ghostly light over the harsh surface of the land. Moonlight both softened the terrain but gave it a harsh edge where shadows hid possible dangers. Above him though, was found God's majesty that never failed to suffuse his heart with admiration and wonder. An endless field of stars twinkled, sharp against a blackness that knew no end. How could one doubt the divine in the presence of such infinite mystery? Then he smiled, perhaps they would make it after all.

They soon were winding their way through defiles and up steep inclines, generally climbing higher into the hills that seemed endless. Pamir would stop on occasion to permit them to rest and to gaze intently at the sky.

"What are you looking at, Papa?" Azita asked at one of their stops.

"Come here, child." The whole family gathered around him. "See that group of bright stars above the horizon over there. Can everyone see them?" Soon, everyone had found the brighter arrangement of stars. "I can no longer recall the name of that constellation, but it always is toward the east this time of year. I knew the stars well as a child. We had few distractions in my village, so I would study them when I was not reading my books. Not surprisingly, my siblings also thought I was lazy and useless. In any case, if we follow them, we will get to our destination."

"This is like the eastern star and the wise men in the Christian Bible," Madeena added.

"I had not thought of that, my dear, but you are right." Pamir looked at her with admiration though his expression was lost in the semidarkness.

"You were not the only child to have read everything she could get her hands on and not the only one who received angry taunts from her siblings."

Sometime, in the early hours of the following morning as the faintest glow emerged in the east, they reached another hilltop. Ahead of them, though, was not another hill. Rather, the land flowed down and away. In the distance they thought they could see flickering lights. These pricks of illumination seemed a far distance but suddenly they no longer felt alone and abandoned. Perhaps that far beacon represented safety. But they would not know whether that far point represented hope or despair until they made the remainder of the journey. Still, their pace picked up, their hearts beat faster.

Eventually, the terrain began to flatten out and the distant beacon was not always visible to them. Eventually, they came to a gully that clearly would direct rushing water to the valley floor after any heavy rain. The sun was coming up and Pamir hoped they might find friendly faces before the heat of the day and exhaustion would force them to stop. He could only push them so far. The physical and emotional strain was taking its toll though Pamir was astounded by the lack of complaint.

Suddenly Pamir was aware that they were not alone. He looked up to see a half-dozen men pointing automatic weapons at them. He could sense that others soon realized what was in front of them. They all had stopped, paralyzed by uncertainty. Pamir suddenly found his voice gone. Had they come this far and raised their hopes so high to have them dashed at this point? He could think of no story that would satisfy the Taliban at this point.

"You," one of the men said, pointing at Pamir. "Come forward and keep your hands where I can see them."

"We come in the service of Allah," Pamir finally managed to say, thinking this could offend no one.

"Who are you? What possible business can you have here? There are enemy everywhere. They try to infiltrate our lines, causing great mischief when they do."

The man looked angry and suspicious. What had happened in his country that had turned everyone so surly. Then Pamir decided. There was no longer any need for deception. Even at this moment, Pamir considered the man's words but found them ambiguous. However, there was nothing else to be done. "I am Doctor Pamir Masoud and this is my family. I have come home to help mend those fighting against the Taliban."

There was a burst of chatter among men that Pamir could not quite hear though he could sense the fear and uncertainty in his family. It was palpable.

The discussion among the men was over, the man in charge smiled and lowered his weapon. "Welcome home, Doctor Masoud. We have been expecting you."

CHAPTER 8

THE PANJSHIR VALLEY

The helicopter circled over the camp a couple of times. It was late in the afternoon and the sun was beginning to hover with lazy reluctance over the western hills. Chris Crawford looked down to get the lay of the land. Mostly, the landscape reminded him of what the moon must be like, harsh and devoid of obvious life. Still, there were roads and buildings and tents and, when they got lower, patches of green and flocks of animals tended by real people. Soon they approached a larger collection of human activity. He could make out discrete sections of a prepared layout . . . the refugee camp, what appeared to be a crude military section, and several tents with red crosses over the tops. That is what he wanted. He needed to get to the medical program that he had a part in supporting and staffing. It was now considered the most dangerous place his people worked, though that honor shifted depending on circumstances. Of course, he would have been highly concerned in any case. Now, he was beside himself with anxiety.

He recalled the afternoon at his London headquarters when Ricky and Karen were chatting on the other side of the room and looking over at him. They had that peculiar look on their faces suggesting that they were in deep debate about what to do next. Perhaps Karen was commiserating with him, perhaps this had nothing to do with him. Pat, Ricky's longtime girlfriend and sometimes fiancé, decided not to join him. In fact, she ended the relationship, an event he confronted with only modest suffering to date. Perhaps the relationship had been tenuous at best and his move to England simply hastened the inevitable. It was, of course, always possible that Ricky was suffering internally and that Karen had sniffed this out. Chris tried not to look in their direction but noticed out of the corner of his eye when they slowly headed in his direction. Nope, this was not about Pat, this definitely involved him. Internally, he prepared himself. He knew they were about to drop disturbing news on him and he was girding himself to react calmly and professionally.

"Hey, Chris, how is it going?" Ricky asked with excessive bonhomie.

"Cut to the chase, my man, you look as if you are about to birth a cat."

"Okay, here is the thing." Ricky took a breath. "As you well know, Kay joined Amar Singh in Pakistan despite your vigorous objections."

"Oh, you noticed that I wanted to wring her neck." Chris tried a grim smile. "Wait, did something happen?"

"Oh, sorry," Karen chimed up. "Kay is just fine, happy as a lark."

"That, I do not like." Chris was losing his smile. "If she is happy, I know damn well that I am about to get much less happy."

"Wrong attitude boss," Karen tried. "You should support your sister. She loves you very much."

"Oh, bull hockey," he retorted looking at Karen. "I know that you and my sister are talking all the time like two hens. What is with that by the way? When did the two of you become such bosom buddies?"

Karen blushed. "Okay, Ricky, you tell him."

"Shit, I thought you . . ."

"Just fucking tell me." Chris surprised them with his anger. He seldom lost his temper and this reaction overtook him despite preparing himself for unsettling news. They were being way too circumspect for his taste and he knew this involved Kay.

"All right," Karen chose to share the news. "Kay has joined Amar in Afghanistan, they are both working in territory held by the Northern Alliance."

Now Chris's prepared control was gone. His face went white, all expression gone. Not even he expected this. "What the fuck! I specifically told her that she could go to Pakistan only if she remained there. That place is dangerous enough. I allowed Singh, and only Singh, to go into the northern territories just to check things out. Even that I hated doing but she threatened to quit if I didn't relent. Don't I control anything in this goddamn program? Did either of you okay this?"

"Of course not, this was some scheme that Amar and Kay cooked up between them, some bullshit about being where the need is greatest." Karen tried to look outraged herself. "After all, we did increase staffing in Pakistan and . . ."

"Don't you dare patronize me . . . no rationales, period. This is horrific. I lose Chuck and now she is going off to get herself killed. Cancel everything. I am going there to drag her ass out."

Ricky put on his 100-watt smile. "Chris, be sensible. You know Kay. She is stubborn. She is going to do what she is going to do."

But Chris was still seething. "Bullshit, what if it was Jules. No, not on my dime. Is she on some fucking suicide mission? Has she been depressed? You talk with her more than me. God, I spend way too much time raising money and mending fences across programs. I am losing touch with the field. Just tell me this, Rick, what if it was Jules. Would you sit on your fucking ass and do nothing?"

Ricky was silent. He had not seen such anger in his friend before. Chris had a point, Ricky admitted to himself, and no reply came to him. It was Karen that took over, grabbing Chris by the shoulders. "Listen, just listen. You let Amar go in there. Whatever the rationale, Kay saw that as evidence that you simply were protecting her because she was your sibling. She saw that you were playing favorites and assumed that it wasn't that dangerous. There was no way she was going to let her older brother treat her as a child. So, just calm the fuck down and think. You don't want to go off half-cocked."

"I am the younger brother," Chris said quietly.

"What?" Karen was not sure of the point he was making.

"She came out of the birth canal first. I came a few minutes later. God, she always had to be first, never has let me forget that she is the senior twin. And try to tell her anything. I would have a better chance convincing a rock that it was really a tree."

"Well," Karen tried a small smile. "She does seem to be the wiser one."

Chris glared at Karen but his words proved not as bad as she expected. "No shit, but I am still going, if nothing but to check firsthand on the situation."

"I am going with you," Karen said firmly.

"No way, not this time. Too dangerous."

Karen turned to Ricky. "Please leave, I want to speak to the boss privately." Ricky saw the expression on her face and exited quickly. After he had left the room, she turned back to Chris. "Remember my promise from my interview. If you ever said or did something galactically stupid I would knee you in the family jewels. Well, I am about to kick you in the balls so hard that you can kiss what you think of as your love life goodbye for the next six months. Maybe forever."

Chris looked at her for several moments. Then he spoke, "Start making the arrangements for the two of us."

"I knew you would see it my way." Karen smiled.

Now Chris looked down from the helicopter as he pointed were he wanted to land. There were tents and buildings with crosses emblazoned on the tops. They must be medical in character or being passed off as medical to fool the enemy. The blades beat up the dirt and sand when the copter settled to the ground. Karen and Chris alighted as the pilot retrieved their gear. The two stood there, no one appeared to greet them or much care that they had arrived. He was sure that their arrival time had been forwarded to the base. Chris found the lack of interest disconcerting. Usually, people scrambled to please him. After all, he was the man who was in charge. Well, he was not technically in charge of anything. In truth, he was more important than that. He provided a lot of the resources, especially in forward bases like this where the mainstream programs were reluctant to risk their staff. He said the word "doctors" to a local passing by and was directed to a nearby building. Entering it, all he saw was a young girl, no more than eleven or twelve he estimated. That was disappointing. There was no brass band, no welcoming committee, not even a crummy banner.

"I bet Kay is hiding from me," he said to Karen.

"Do you blame her?"

"Okay, I am going to try my advanced language skills on this girl." In a slow and labored voice, he tried his limited Dari which, in truth, consisted of a few memorized phrases he had learned on the plane. "Where are the doctors? Where is Dr. Singh and Dr. Crawford?" The girl merely smiled at him. "Damn, she doesn't understand me. I practiced that phrase."

The girl smiled even more broadly and then in excellent English began to speak, "Your Dari is not bad. It is not good, but I have heard worse." Karen chuckled as the girl continued. "You must be Professor Crawford and Miss Fisher." No one called him professor though he was an adjunct professor at Oxford where he tutored at least one course per semester.

"Aaah . . . aah." But he got no intelligible words out.

"That was brilliant, chief." Then Karen decided to rescue him. "Yes, we are here to see the doctors, Amar Singh and Kristen Crawford. And you are?"

"I am Azita Masoud. I am the daughter of Dr. Pamir Masoud, who has been working with your two female doctors for many weeks now. In truth, we escaped from the Taliban to help the Alliance. My father is originally from this area and life under the Taliban was awful."

"Oh," Chris said, seemingly at a loss.

"Yes, and I help the doctors with many medical procedures. I used to help my father when we were in Kabul, and now I get to help the two lady doctors. That is such an inspiration for me, to see female doctors."

"Yes, that is fine." Chris finally uttered a sentence. "Where are the lady doctors now?"

"Your sister is working with my father, out in the countryside where there was some shelling earlier today. They might be back later today but probably in the morning, there were many wounded. Dr. Singh is attending to some of the children from that shelling who were in very bad shape and needed the kind of help we can only provide here. They were brought in by truck, some died on the way. She told me to keep you company until she can join us."

"Can I ask you something?" Chris suddenly was curious.

"Of course," Azita responded.

"Where did you learn such good English? I did not think the Taliban permitted girls to be educated."

"Oh," Azita laughed. "They don't. They almost beat me to death for reading in a public square. But my father and mother have schooled me. My mother once taught in the university when that was permitted, she taught mathematics. They usually speak English at home so that we children will be able to communicate in it if we get an opportunity to study abroad. They say it is the international language."

"Wow," was all Chris could say. It was not what he was expecting. He finally looked closely at the girl. He found her fetching, with her dark hair pulled severely back into a braid and the usual copper-hued skin. Her features were pleasant enough though one was immediately drawn to the eyes. They were large and bright, suggesting exceptional intelligence. These eyes seemed capable of unusual expression. By their dominant presence, they communicated a deep capacity for embracing and understanding the surrounding world.

"I am impressed," offered Karen. "You speak English better than my boss here."

Azita laughed aloud, her face lit up in an inviting way. "I have accomplished nothing yet. Someday, I will become a doctor like my father. He is a great man and it is my passion to be like him someday. That is why it has been so wonderful to have the women doctors here. Dr. Singh has been so wonderful to me and then when your sister was able to join us we have become such a team. Now we can get out into the countryside and help the villagers. And we are doing so many other things now, like starting up a school for the girls. That is a favorite of mine. Nothing hurt me more as a child than not being able to go to school and learn with other girls. And this has been so good for my Papa. He is such a talented man, but he had not been able to improve himself in recent years. Our country is in such agony. All of us here are so happy to have such wonderful lady doctors with such advanced medical knowledge. We have others who spend time here like those from OXFAM and the Red Cross but Dr. Singh and Dr. Crawford are the best and most loved.

Amar, I mean Dr. Singh, was most happy when Karen called and said you had agreed for Doctor Crawford to remain with us, at least until you could visit of course and see that all was okay."

Chris quickly glanced at Karen with an inquisitive glance before exclaiming, "Oh my god, I am getting a propaganda pitch from a little girl."

Karen laughed. "We are so happy to meet you, Azita, is it? Can you show us to where we will be staying and then give us a tour?"

The girl beamed. "Of course."

After they had a chance to freshen up and get settled, they found Azita waiting for them. "Are you ready?"

"Yes, of course. This is so kind of you. We are both grateful," Karen spoke up when Chris remained silent. He was perturbed at being snubbed or at least he thought that was the case. "By the way, I noticed that I will be in a room with someone else. Who might that be?"

"You will be with Doctor Crawford, she suggested it." Karen smiled.

Meanwhile, Chris grumped in a low voice, "I am surprised they did not decide to have me sleep in the latrine."

In a low voice, Karen growled at him, "Keep acting like an ass and I will drop you in the crapper myself."

Azita seemed not to notice his mood, remaining cheerful, even ebullient. "I will skip the medical facilities, I am sure that Amar will show you them herself when she has a chance. And this is not the best time for a tour since many activities are done for the day. At the least you will know where everything is."

"This is so kind of you and Mr. Crawford is very appreciative, I am sure." Karen then poked Chris in the ribs.

"Yes, absolutely. I am very thankful. And by the way, Azita, you can call everyone by their first names. You should hear what my sister calls me."

"I have," Azita said before looking directly at Chris. "I know you are disappointed to have me as your guide. Really, it could not be helped. Dr. Singh, Amar I mean, and another doctor are working hard to save some children who were seriously injured by shells that hit their village this morning. I don't know why the Taliban believes they can win by maiming and killing children. It is a mystery to me."

"To me as well." Chris softened a bit.

"About your sister," she went on, "she told me to tell you that there would be plenty of time for you to yell at her later. However, she needed to make this trip. My father needed help. He often makes these trips to the countryside but there is way too much work for him in such an emergency like this. I would go with him but there is only so much I can do. Your sister is such a good doctor for the terrible wounds suffered in such a shelling." She paused at this point as Chris looked for a response. His glib tongue had failed him so Azita spoke up again, "I want to say one thing to you. This is from me, not from your sister. She hopes you will forgive her. I hope you forgive her. She has said so many wonderful things about you, what a great man you are. She only wants you to trust her and her choices. Well, she said these things but not for me to tell you. I overheard her talking with Amar. Perhaps it is wrong for me to share such things but . . ."

"Thank you, and I will keep this our secret," Chris said with real softness now. "You are a special young woman, aren't you?"

Azita seemed relieved, she had obviously struggled about whether to share what she had heard. "I do my best. And now for the tour." Inside, she was much relieved that this man, about whom she had heard so much in recent days, had seemed to soften.

She walked them past several buildings where people ate, gathered socially, and conducted military planning and local administration. This had been the site of regional government and a large school and hospital. Now it was one of the main sites from which a loose confederation of tribes and clans fought to keep independent from the Taliban. As they walked, Azita explained the ethnic background and history of the area, going into some detail about the difficulties the Alliance faced from internal dissention and the lack of external support. Then she stopped walking. "I fear for the future. These are proud people, devout Muslims. But they are not fanatics like the Taliban. They treat others with kindness, respect women, and permit girls to be educated. They care for the country, not merely the power they can wield. They would never destroy beauty like the Buddhist statues at Bamiyan. However, it is not clear how long they can hold out. If only the Americans . . ." Then she caught herself and continued with their tour.

"Here we have the rooms where we teach school. The boys and girls are kept separate in classes but at least the girls have an opportunity to learn. They are so happy to have this chance. I think they would walk through a minefield to get here. And being separate from the boys is not a problem I think. Boys are silly, the girls are better students, they are learning more."

"True that," whispered Karen,

"What?" Chris looked at her suspiciously.

"Oh, I just said that Azita probably helps with the learning. Don't you, dear."

"I do, I love being with the girls, helping them learn even some English but only when the work in the hospital permits. My mother also teaches here. She is so good as a teacher, she has taught me so much. I will bring you here when the classes are taking place."

Outside the main set of buildings, they came to what clearly was a refugee camp. All he could see were scores of impoverished people wandering through makeshift tents. "I am confident that Amar and Kay will show this more carefully when they can. It is so sad."

"How have these people come to be here?" Karen asked.

"For one reason or another, they found it necessary to flee the Taliban. Some were not devout enough. Others fled so that their sons would not be drafted into the fighting. Many because their daughters were raped by these religious zealots for breaking some real or imagined rule. They risked their lives and willingly endure such privations for a bit of freedom. But it gets late, let us return."

Chris finally spoke up as they walked toward the main buildings. "What will happen to you and your family if things go poorly?"

Azita walked with her head down. "Maybe Pakistan. In my dreams, we will get to England where my father studied medicine. I would so love to study at a real school." Then she changed the topic as if she were embarrassed. "Professor Crawford . . ."

"Chris, please. I only insist that Karen call me Professor Crawford or your highness."

Azita paused and then laughed. He liked her laugh. "Chris then. You might try that building there, Professor Crawford. Oops, that will take some time. You might find Dr. Singh in there. I will take Karen and we will find something to eat. We will have it ready when you return."

After some fractured conversations and much pointing, he was finally ushered out a different door. There, he saw a woman holding a baby in her arms. It was Amar Singh, he knew her well from pictures. She was facing the setting sun, singing a soft lullaby to a child, the words he could not comprehend. *Hindi,* he thought. This tableau puzzled him. What was happening? He took a few steps closer and stopped again. It hit him. The child was dying. She was providing comfort during its last moments. He looked at her closely. She was wearing loose-fitting army fatigue pants and a surgical scrub top that was littered with what looked like human blood. Even at this angle, she looked infinitely weary, her eyes sad, her demeanor worn. The desert wind was blowing a fine dust over her and the child in her arms. He could see a track from her eye down her cheek, made by one tear, one expression of the sadness that had taken hold of her. The doctor had stopped singing. Apparently, the baby had died and could no longer hear the words of comfort.

Chris waited, transfixed by the tableau in front of him. Finally, he spoke, "Dr. Singh," he said softly, "Amar."

She was startled and turned. "Oh, I did not know you were there." She had been retrieved from some private place. It took her a moment to recover. "I am sorry not to greet you. It has been so . . ."

"Not to worry, Azita explained everything. By the way, she did a marvelous job."

"Azita is so precious. She brings me great joy, to all of us really. She has become indispensable. You should put her on salary though she could care less." Amar realized she was starting to ramble, perhaps she was nervous. In silence, she led him back into the hospital ward where she handed the dead child to an aide who went off in another direction. "Let us head back. There is nothing more I can do here."

"Do you face these . . . horrors every day?" Chris asked as they walked.

"Not every day, but too often. We can save some and we lose some. There was nothing I could do for that child so I gave it some human contact and warmth at the end. It is a small thing, such a small thing."

"No," Chris said with meaning, "it is everything."

Amar gave him a quick look. She seemed taken with his aside. When they reached the main building, Amar stopped and looked directly at him. "I want to get one thing straight. I will have some demands of you for more supplies and equipment. We can negotiate about those. But you are not taking Kay away. That is not negotiable. She goes, I go. Do you understand?"

Chris looked in her eyes. The sadness that he had seen earlier had been replaced by a fierce determination. Still, they remained red from emotion and weariness. Suddenly, something hit him, a raw sensation in his chest, gnawing at him. He wasn't physically sick. This was different. This might not pass. "I understand," he said. Inside, though, he realized that while he understood her words, he had no idea what was happening to him. One thing he did understand all too well, there was no way he was taking his sister back with him.

———

Later, Amar and Chris were alone, the food indifferently eaten. Azita had been sent off to her family and Karen decided she needed some sleep.

Chris looked at the woman opposite him, that strange gnawing sensation still clawing at his chest. "You do know why I reacted the way I did to Kay joining you here, aside from everyone going behind my back."

"Of course. She is your sister and you love her."

"Well, sometimes I love her. On the other hand, she can also be such a pain in the ass."

Amar smiled, and Chris gulped. It was such a fetching smile and he was seeing it for the first time. "Karen also told me to ignore you. She is most useful. If you give me any trouble, she told me what she does to you or at least threatens to do. I imagine her threats would strike fear into any man. Just remember that when we negotiate over the next few days."

"Do you have anyone here that knows how to reattach a broken penis?"

At that, Amar laughed out loud. "I could try but only without an anesthetic. We need all we have for the patients who count."

Chris was captivated by the way her face transformed when she smiled. It was no longer the weary and clouded face he first saw just an hour earlier. He tried to focus on the conversation, not her. "Let me be honest with you. When I first heard about this I was furious. Partly it was because it seemed like everyone worked so hard to keep me out of the loop like I was the idiot child who could not handle anything bad." Amar opened her mouth but then changed her mind. "But mostly I was scared for Kay. I, we had just lost our older brother. Another loss …"

"Yes," Amar responded in her soft vice, "I am sorry for your loss. Kay told me about Chuck. On the secrecy thing, not telling you, perhaps that was my fault. Kay wanted to be honest but I suggested we take the evasive route where it is better to ask for forgiveness than permission. That was childish, I suspect. Neither Karen nor Ricky knew anything until it was a done deal, you must believe that. The thing is. I really wanted her here. There is so much to do and, frankly, I was lonely."

"Wow, you must think me an ogre." When she did not contradict him, he continued, wondering in the back of his mind whether there was more than a professional relationship between this beautiful woman and his sister. In truth, he long had harbored questions about his sister's sexuality. "Amar, I am a realist. I know I cannot tell Kay what to do. I just want to know that she will be safe, that both of you are safe."

"Thank you." She looked at him in a way that made him blush slightly. "Kay is right, you know."

"About what?" he asked.

"You are very handsome. She warned me about you."

"Do you want my side of the story? I can imagine what she told you."

"No, not really, I rather like her story. Besides, I have corroboration." Amar smiled in a way that reached him.

"I can guess as to the identity of your other source. Hmmm, I wonder if there is still a job opening at the Hairy Hare." Then Chris realized that was incomprehensible. "Never mind, that was an inside joke."

Amar looked at him pensively, as if deciding something. "We have a busy morning and I am a bit fatigued. It was a difficult day. The military men will brief you on the security situation, I will bring you through the refugee camp and the medical facilities, and I know Azita will want you to visit the school for girls. She is so proud of that. Then Kay should be back by late morning or early afternoon at the latest I suspect. I want to give you plenty of time for you to yell at her."

Chris sighed and looked at the ceiling. "Why does everyone treat me like a child?"

Amar let that bit of self-pity slide. She stood up, looking a little uncertain he thought. That struck him as odd since she came across as self-assured. "Chris, I was raised as a good Indian girl. Beside my ill-fated marriage, it is never a good thing when your husband sleeps with your sister, I have had only a couple of other rather disappointing liaisons, if that is what they are called. The thing is . . . the thing is, this is hard, that I need a human touch. There is so much death here. I want the feel of another person, someone I can at least pretend is caring. It does not have to be real. Please understand that . . . it just has been too long."

"Amar." He broke in to end her discomfort and then didn't quite know what to say next. "As debauched as I am, I have never made love to someone who worked for me. Even if no one listens to me, including you, technically I do sign your checks. I . . ."

"No, don't say more. I need a shower now. I will see you in the morning." She turned to leave the room but stopped, not turning back to him. "I only suggested this because I thought you were safe . . . no chance of any romantic involvement and soon you would be thousands of miles away." Then she was gone.

Chris sat for some time staring ahead. His mind raced. This was the last thing he imagined happening. He had thought Amar Singh was rather contemptuous of him. She struck him as confident and competent, thinking of him as merely an out-of-touch administrator and minor nuisance to be handled. She had seen so much in her short life.

For a moment, he had to convince himself that she had, in fact, propositioned him. That was a proposition, wasn't it? Had he misinterpreted her words? Was this real? Next, he started mentally reviewing why this would be a very bad idea. He could only think of one positive against the many, many negatives. His analytical side gave him clear instruction. In the end, therefore, it was an easy decision. He slowly rose from his seat and made his way to the sound of water.

An hour later, Amar cuddled next to him, her head on his chest. "I am surprised at your heart rate," she offered.

"What, are you surprised I am still alive? I admit, it was touch and go for a while." Chris began gently rubbing the side of her head.

"No, silly man. I was thinking that, with all your experience, I must be such a disappointment to you. Your legend does precede you. Thank you for being so considerate and not making fun of me."

"Amar, you took my breath away."

"Don't," she replied, "no need to spare me."

He decided not to argue at that moment. Rather, Chris lay there trying to make sense of what transpired over this last hour or so. It all was rather ordinary in a conventional sense. A man and a woman made love. For him, though, it struck him as so unique that he could not quite embrace the reality of the experience. This sensation inside must be arising from his deepest desires, a place he had not visited in a long time, perhaps never. Yet, he focused on these immediate experiences as if they were real. He had experienced them, they were real. He was sure of that. Yet, they seemed the stuff of fantasy and dreams. The whole thing left him disoriented so he dug into his memories to recapture the reality, if that is what it was.

After deciding to accept her offer, he followed the direction of the water and surprised her in the shower. She looked startled. For one last time, he considered the possibility that he had imagined the prior conversation and almost fled in embarrassment. But she recovered immediately and looked at him with wide inviting eyes. Then she held out her hand as he finished disrobing, shuddering perceptibly when their bodies touched. He took her face in his hands and gently kissed her forehead, her nose, and her mouth with the barest whisper of kisses. She continued to tremor slightly, her breathing becoming deeper with anticipation or apprehension, he knew not which.

"Are you okay with all this?" he whispered in her ear and then nibbled at it.

She squirmed as he explored her ear and then her neck with his mouth. "Yes, yes really. It is just that it has been some time for me."

"Same for me," he whispered back.

She looked up at him and immediately saw the smile spread across his face. They both laughed hard and the tension broke. "Kay told me you were an irredeemable shit and I won't repeat the warnings Karen gave me."

"Well," he said, "give me a chance and I will share with you my most redeeming and unforgettable attributes."

She laughed again. "Yes, insufferable egotist was on both of their lists." Then she leaned in to kiss him and pull him toward hers as the water cascaded down their intertwined bodies.

When they made it to her bed, Chris took much time to kiss and caress and employ his tongue with all the experience and sensitivity forged by his considerable experience. When he felt that she was wet with expectation he pulled her on top of him, positioning her so that she could lower her body in a way that she might control the way he entered her. He was taken aback how tight she felt to him. Undoubtedly, it had been a long time for her. As she lowered herself onto him, she gasped, and gasped a second time. Her head fell forward onto his neck where he sensed gentle sobs and salty tears.

"My God, Amar, am I hurting you? We can stop."

"No, please no. Let me just feel you inside me for a moment."

The next hour was a blur in his mind, all thrashing and groans and arched bodies shivering in sensual delight. Now a kind of exhaustion overtook him along with her expressed fear that she had disappointed him. How could she possibly believe that? Could she not sense what was inside his head and heart? But how could she miss the reality of her desirability. He could not figure out his own sensations and feelings. They were new to him. He felt paralyzed and speechless.

When he did not respond to her murmured statement about disappointing him, she pulled away and stared at the ceiling. "I am so sorry. It is just that I have so little experience. I never should have imposed . . ."

That broke him out of his reverie. "What, wait, you are apologizing? For what?"

"Please, Chris, don't patronize me. I am terrible at this. Hell, I drove my husband into the arms of my own sister, among many others. I am so inexperienced. I'll bet a month of that generous wage you pay me that Karen and your sister will fare much better tonight. You have been with so many women, I must be like some child . . ."

Chris jumped out of bed so suddenly that she stopped mid-sentence watching him with wide-eyed surprise. He walked quickly across the room and back to the bed where he pulled her up toward him. "Okay, now you listen to me."

"Please, Chris, there is no need to lie."

"Lie, me, to a woman? Perish the thought! You can ask anyone, never happens."

"Nice try guy, but I don't have to ask. They all volunteered the information. Let me see, how did Karen put it, something about you being a lying son of a bitch but adorable, even lovable."

Chris grabbed her by the shoulders and looked directly into her eyes. "Listen very carefully. This is from the heart. Amar, I am totally sure that you could command a thousand dollars an hour."

Her eyes narrowed as she tried to decipher what he was saying. It was not what she expected. Then the meaning dawned on her, she tried to look cross but chuckled despite herself. "You are worse than they said you were."

He pulled her close again and started kissing her. "Give me another chance and I will show you how good I can be."

"Okay, I will give you another chance but remember one thing."

"What is that," he murmured a she nibbled at her neck.

Her response was a seductive whisper, "You already have run up a tab of fifteen hundred dollars and the meter is still running."

"Worth every penny," he said pulling her down on to the bed as she squealed with delight. "Do you accept checks?"

Then he stopped suddenly. His mind whirled back to an earlier comment of hers. "Wait, what did you mean by Kay and Karen doing better."

Amar's eyes widened with concern. "Oops," she said as she tried to start kissing him again.

"Nice try." Chris looked at her quizzically. "Do better at what and I am turning the meter off, at least until you fess up."

Now it was Amar that looked puzzled. "Surely you know." But he did not respond. "Really, you did not know that they got together in London?"

"You mean became lovers?" His words sent a slight frisson of anxiety through Amar. "I . . . I had no idea."

"Wait, I am confused. Are you trying to tell me that you didn't know about Kay's . . . about her interest in women?" Amar knew the answer when she saw him fall on his back and stare at the ceiling.

She waited. After some time, Chris found his voice, "We haven't been close. As kids we were, but we drifted apart in our teens. Then we spent so much time apart. We were cordial most of the time. She did resent that I ran away to the east coast and then England. That created some friction. She knew it was my cowardice, I didn't want to face Father and his world."

"Yes," Amar said gently, nuzzling her head on to his chest. "Kay has told me a lot about the family. I have a few problems with mine but nothing like you."

"Still, I always thought there was more. There were times when she seemed on the verge of saying something. She would look at me as if there was some internal debate raging inside. I would wait expectantly on the verge of trying to pull it out of her. But then I could see her retreat, the glimmer of openness gone. Later I would kick myself for letting her retreat. Why was I so reticent? She was my goddamn twin sister after all. We were supposed to have this bond and we did, for a while. Was she embarrassed to be gay? I cannot believe that is it. Why would I care about that? I am pissed that she kept it from me."

"Oh *Pagwan*, I fear I am in such trouble." Amar looked dejected. "It just never occurred to me that you didn't know."

Chris noticed that when stressed, Amar shifted from a British accent to a more Indian lilt. "No problem," he said. "Really, who gives a shit about that now? Why the secrecy on her part? I just don't get it. It must be something else."

"Don't be so sure. I have a cousin that committed suicide when his parents found out the truth. He was such a sweet boy. I still become so sad at the thought."

"Yeah, but you come from such a backward culture." Chris had second thoughts immediately.

Amar smiled though. "You are not very smart, are you? You keep forgetting that I know Karen's secret torture technique and you are very vulnerable at present."

"So true, I have been told that I am dumber than dirt many times."

With that, Amar positioned herself on top of him, saying with a shy smile, "I only have one thing to say. I am not a lesbian and I am ready to turn the meter back on."

"Great," he said as he sought out her breasts with his mouth.

"One thing though," her words were broken by small involuntary grunts. "The hourly rate has gone up."

"Whatever, as long as you accept worthless checks." He sighed softly and then passion took over once again.

———

Chris, along with Karen, followed Amar and Azita through the makeshift camp for refugees and asylum seekers. At first, his mind kept straying back to the morning's briefing. He had done this alone, not wanting any complications from including women in the conversation. This was not the Taliban but still, military and security matters were viewed as a male prerogative. The three commanders, each representing a distinct tribal group, tried hard to reassure him that they had things under control. But the more questions he asked, the less certain he was that this was the case. They were starved of the most basic military hardware, mostly using hand-me-downs from the Soviet era though some Chinese weapons were filtering into the area. Pakistan would not help, believing that the Alliance had little hope of holding out much longer and not wanting to stir up even more opposition among their own religious zealots. At present, the situation seemed in kind of a homeostasis. The Northern Alliance had fierce warriors and were defending their homeland. The Taliban had fanatical devotees, but many were not even from Afghanistan, migrating to the jihad in search for glory and martyrdom. What most impressed Chris was the argument that the tribes of the Alliance knew the rough terrain. It was their home field, rugged and mountainous with all types of opportunities for surprise and mayhem.

Occasionally, the conversation would turn to what Chris could do for them in addition to medical and humanitarian assistance. It was painful for him to be firm in explaining he was not in the war making business. He felt guilty. Both he and the men briefing him well remember America's role in recent years. When the Soviets were battling the jihadists for control of the countryside, Congressman Charles Wilson wheedled support for full bore covert mission on behalf of the freedom fighters. It was something America might support, anyone who would kill Communists. Once the Soviets fled north, deciding that they were mired in their own Vietnam, America lost interest. The country was awash in weapons with a disturbing power vacuum in Kabul. Too many guns and no effective central authority was a prescription for civil war. The Taliban eventually came along with promises of law and order. Their notion of law was fanatical, and their sense of order was enforced with a special brutality. In the beginning, though, it seemed a good bargain to the chaos that had overtaken the land.

"We do not blame you, Mr. Crawford. However, your country cared only when we killed the Communists for them. For that, they spent a fortune. To rebuild our shattered country, they gave us virtually nothing. They were not wise men."

Chris wanted to go on a rampage of sorts, tell them that he could not agree more. His countrymen were the worst sort of selfish hypocrites. If you asked the typical American how much their country gave in foreign assistance, they would guess in the range of fifteen percent of the annual federal budget, maybe more. They also thought it was for humanitarian assistance, to help people about whom they were suspicious. In truth, America spent a tiny fraction of that and most went for military assistance to essential allies. They spent much less on humanitarian aid, when adjusted for national wealth, than their peer countries. Americans are, in fact, very stingy. They are the restaurant customer the wait staff hate to see come in the door since they leave no tip. Chris wanted to tell them how disgusted he was with his homeland but knew from experience that honesty did not work. They would not believe his sincerity, assuming he was being disingenuous for political purposes. He sat mute. It killed him every time.

Once they started to move through the desperation of the camp, his mind snapped into focus. On every side were faces emaciated by want and despair. Thin children hung to mothers who had long abandoned hope. They seemed everywhere. "So many," was all he could say.

"No," Amar responded, "this is a small camp. In fact, it was never intended to be such. It just happened. Many seeking asylum head for Pakistan as they did during the Soviet occupation."

"How did they get here? Why?" At that moment, Chris longed for the comfort of London or Oxford. He always told himself that he wanted more time in the field, to make what he was doing real. This, however, was too real. For an instant, when he thought no one was looking, he grabbed Amar's hand. She squeezed it for a moment before pulling it away. Karen appeared to look ahead but still noticed. Her antennae were alerted. Something was up, her lecherous boss was at it again. She just knew it.

Amar separated herself from Chris. The temptation to touch him was strong and not advisable. "Azita," she asked the girl who would serve as translator. "Ask this family why they are here." Amar, in truth, could speak broken Dari and fared well with the more educated Afghanis but the local dialects remained challenging to her.

A woman holding a child and probably only in her early thirties but looking much older, responded at length to Azita's query. As she did, she occasionally wailed and shed copious tears. The young translator spoke quickly to keep up with the tale of woe. Her husband had been beheaded by the Taliban for some unnamed crime. One son had been drafted into their army and killed in battle. Another had fled. She did not know where he was or if he were still alive. Without male protection, her oldest daughter had been raped as had she. She could do no other than flee. Azita murmured what Chris assumed were words of sympathy and encouragement and they moved on.

She next asked an old man his story. He sat alone, which was odd. Most of these refugees were families. He had offended the local leaders and was accused of blasphemy. He thought his sin slight but was told by friends one night that they would come for him in the morning. He was certain of his fate, a beheading in the public square as a lesson to all others who might be similarly tempted. In the middle of the night, he fled, not even telling his family. Now he was in such despair, not knowing their fate and full of guilt for his cowardice. Amar returned to Chris's side and whispered, "This man will soon die, perhaps by his own hand or from a black despair. Most likely, we will come to the camp one day and he will be gone. We will never know." As she completed her judgment of his likely fate, she took his hand for the briefest moment. Karen again noticed.

They came to a group of children. At first Karen asked if they were from one family. Inside, Karen marveled at the stamina that any mother would need for such a brood. But that was not the case. They were all orphans who had been rescued in one way or another. In some cases, the fate of their family was known, in other cases it was impossible for the circumstances to be determined.

Chris looked over the children ranging in age from about three years to twelve. They all seemed too thin but had smiles. A couple had the distended stomachs that spelled greater medical problems. Funny, he thought, children are so easily pleased. Provide them with a little food and security and they can find happiness. Perhaps adults expect too much, want comforts and opportunities that life cannot always provide. Then he looked closer. One child was missing an arm, another an eye, another a leg. How could so many children be maimed. How could life be so cruel. How could there be such an indifferent God. He knew such atrocities existed. He had read the reports, listened to the briefings. Somehow, looking in the eyes of a crippled child with no hope for the future, yet with sparking eyes capable of awe and excitement. Suddenly he was ashamed of his own selfishness.

Azita stopped to talk with a teen girl, by herself but with a child attached to her hip. After an animated conversation, Azita started to walk on.

Karen called after her, "Wait, Azita, what did she say?"

When the girl turned around, her eyes were moist. "I am sorry, perhaps it is because she is only a couple of years older than I am."

"That is all right, we can move on," it was Chris.

"No, I can talk about it. It is not such an unusual story I fear." Then Azita took a deep breath. "She was by herself in the marketplace. Some Taliban found an excuse, some sin in their eyes, to take her off where they all raped her and just left her. Her own family was appalled, not at these monsters but at her for somehow allowing this to happen. How can a family be so cruel? I cannot understand this." Then she got control of her anger. "Dr. Amar, have you told them about tonight?"

"I was saving the news as a surprise. Chris and Karen, we are dining with Azita's family tonight, you will get to meet Dr. Masoud. He is such a fine man."

"I think that is why such stories as that of this girl touch me so. I am so fortunate to be surrounded with love. But you will love my family, though you will not meet Majeed, my brother. He is off fighting with the Alliance. Father and Mother are very upset about this, but he was determined. I pray for him every night."

"Azita," Chris said, "I look forward to meeting your family. Now I believe it is time to see your school for girls."

As they walked from the refugee camp to where the rooms used for classes were located, perhaps a half-mile walk, Chris worked his way next to Azita and put his arm around her shoulder. Karen, and particularly Amar, looked upon this gesture with interest. They hung back a little to give Chris and the young girl some privacy. Besides, Karen had an agenda she wished to cover with Dr. Singh.

Azita remained silent as she walked next to Chris. Then he finally broke the ice. "Are you all right?"

"Yes," a monosyllabic response.

"You know," he tried, "I hardly know you but even I can see something is wrong. You are always so full of life and joy."

"I am okay. Really," it was a longer response but unsatisfying to Chris.

"Listen. I am not the Taliban. I will not beat you with a stick. However, I have been known to put stubborn girls over my knee and giving them a good spanking. How do you think Dr. Kay turned out so good? I had to spank her so often when she was your age."

At this, she finally looked up at him with a reluctant smile. "I think if you had spanked her she would have given you Karen's punishment."

"You know about that." Chris was genuinely astonished that this came from such a young girl.

"We all do. We talked about it if you caused us trouble, if you tried to take Dr. Kay away." Now she smiled fully but it was not a happy smile. "At the camp, with the young mother, that might have been me. I have been so sheltered, so protected, but once I did a thoughtless thing and the Taliban beat me mercilessly."

"My god, what could you have done?"

"I read a notice in the public square. Girls are not supposed to read or be curious." Azita took a breath, looking up into the hot sun. "If my brother had not come to my aid they might have dragged me to someplace private and attacked me in the same way they raped that poor girl. They could have violated me and who would bring justice. Majeed beat me that day so that they would stop, he did it out of love. I never have thanked him properly, only when Father demanded. I must do that when I get a chance."

"I am sorry." Chris squeezed her shoulder.

"But the thing is, I am so fortunate, so blessed by Allah. I have a wonderful family, even my sister and I get along these days. But things could have turned out differently that day. What if I was attacked and got pregnant. I do not think my parents would permit an abortion."

Chris struggled to find something positive to say. "At least you would be a wonderful mother, of that I am certain."

She stopped and spun on him. "No, you don't understand. How could I become a doctor with a child? No, I would die."

Taken by the desperation in the young voice, Chris did not know how to respond. "Wow, I doubt anyone, or anything, will keep you from what you must be. Come, let us go and see your students."

When they entered the first room, Chris was surprised at how many girls were crowded into the space. They obviously were expecting him, arising in unison as they chanted in a sing-song manner, "Welcome, Mr. Crawford." He could almost make out what they were trying to say and broke into a broad smile.

"I am happy to be here," he said in that loud, exaggerated way that people employ in the erroneous belief that others who speak a different tongue will then understand them. "Will they understand me?" he asked Azita.

"None of us understand you," she said with a big smile.

He whirled to look at the girl who looked back with a smile. *Sarcasm,* he thought to himself, *what is the world coming to.* He leaned over to Azita and whispered, "I am thinking that you have been hanging out with my sister for too long."

Azita now laughed fully. "Some can speak a bit of English, they will try to explain their lessons and I will translate or fill in when needed." Azita brought him to a small group that was arranged about a larger table. It struck Chris that this was a somewhat older and advanced group, perhaps ten to twelve years old. "Okay," she whispered to Chris, "ask them what they are studying."

In a louder voice, he parroted her, "What lessons do you have today?"

They giggled a bit but finally one spoke up, looking very hesitant. "Today, we are doing our reading lesson, our writing lesson, and our numbers. We are working so hard. And we thank you."

Chris stood as the several of the girls tried to show what they were doing. The lessons were elementary, well below what children their age would be doing in London or even Chicago. Still, he cautioned himself not to judge. The miracle was that they were learning anything at all.

After about twenty minutes, Chris asked if he could watch a class in action, a normal lesson. A young woman of about twenty-five approached the front of the room and said something first in Dari and then in Pashto. All the girls scrambled in their seats to pull out a book. A second teacher took over with about a quarter of the class.

Azita started to explain, "We start them off with the language they are most familiar with. We want them able to speak and write in at least one language but hope they can learn the two main languages. We must pull our people together. Ideally, some will learn English. I give lessons for those interested. But you must understand, only a few had any lessons before this. Some were taught in their homes but not enough."

"They seem to really want to learn."

Azita looked at him as he looked out over the sea of activity. "It means everything to these girls. Cannot you see that?"

Chris looked away from the class and at the wide eyes of this young girl beside him. "Later, Azita, tell me what you need to do a better job, books or equipment or whatever."

"You can provide such things?" she asked with genuine surprise.

"I guess my sister failed to mention that, despite my many faults, I am a miracle worker."

Azita then looked across the room. "I am thinking your sister might be back. I saw someone from the hospital come and take Karen away."

———

In the medical facility, Chris noticed Kay leaning over a patient. "I see the prodigal sister has returned."

"Oh, it had been such a pleasant day to this point," she said without looking up. After she finished a minor procedure she turned and walked to her brother, giving him an indifferent hug.

"Where is Karen?" Chris asked. "I thought I would find her here."

Kay cracked a small smile "She was here, we talked. But she said that she didn't want to see us fight."

"No fight."

"Good," Kay responded. "Karen did give me a refresher course in where to kick you. Actually, the prospect of causing you a little pain sounds delicious to me."

Chris stepped back. He was uncertain suddenly. Kay seemed distant and irritated. He also thought moving beyond her kicking range might be a prudent move. He decided to skip any small talk. "Okay, let's cut to the bottom line."

"Good," she cut in, "I love the bottom line."

He tried to ignore her set, impassive face. "You obviously know how pissed I was when I found out you were here. You went behind my back, for Christ's sake. Perhaps if you had just been honest and up-front."

"Bullshit," she said with terse conviction. "You don't micromanage your programs. That is partly what makes this effective.

You pick good people, and give them the freedom to do what they see needs to be done. Most of the time, from what I hear, you support their judgment. It was my assessment that this is where I need to be. Okay, you are here now. You can see for yourself."

"Need was never the point."

"No, it wasn't. You were okay with Amar being here and some of the support staff. Suddenly it was a problem when I came."

"Listen, goddamn it. I said it was the way . . ."

"Oh crap. Chris, just be honest. You were trying to protect me, keep me out of harm's way. Well, I have a news bulletin for you, dear brother, I am a big girl now. I can take care of myself. You certainly didn't hover over me when I was putting up with Father's bullshit as you hid in England all those years."

"Oh my god, not that again," his voice betrayed real anger. "Do you want me to grovel? I will grovel, but that is it. I refuse to be a whipping boy for one sin the rest of my life."

"One sin?" Kay laughed cynically. "My word, you have an elevated sense of your purity. I hope the papal commission doesn't interview me when you are up for sainthood. But let's get back to the bottom line. Are you going to try to send me back?"

"No, of course not. Do I look like an idiot?"

"Really want an answer to that?" Kay yelled.

"I am quite sure you are about to tell me."

"Damn right I am. You are a total idiot."

Chris fumed. "Why are you busting my balls like this? It is not about you staying here. I gave up on that already."

Kay still simmered. "You really want to know why I am pissed?"

"Yes, goddamn it."

"You are fucking Amar and I think that is utterly despicable."

"I . . ."

"Not another word, you reprobate. I never cared one whit about your bimbos or whether you wanted to ground your penis to a stub from overuse. But Amar? Sure, on the surface she is a tough, competent doctor. Underneath, she is an innocent, vulnerable woman. You can't just sate your lust and move on to the next conquest. This is not business as usual. She is special. Jesus Christ, how could you even think of seducing her like that?"

"I didn't, she came on to me." Chris knew that sounded lame.

"Oh, like I am going to believe that. She is not that stupid."

"Hey, just because you don't like men, that doesn't mean . . ." Chris stopped. He hadn't meant to go there. Now it was too late. "Amar let it slip last night. She was shocked you kept your lie a secret from me. So am I."

When Kay spoke, her voice was softer, with less anger left. "Fuck, there goes my moral high ground."

"Just listen." Chris was on the verge of real anger, an emotional place he did not find often. "There is no moral high ground between us. I think each of us squandered any advantage away a long time ago. I am guessing we just better call it even. But I do want you to know I don't care who you love, just find some. Okay, I am just a little surprised at Karen. She doesn't seem like your type."

"And sweet Amar is yours?"

"Point taken." Chris managed to smile. "Still, if you knew what is inside me . . ."

Kay also relaxed. "And it is not so surprising about Karen, by the way."

"How so?" Chris asked.

"You obviously love her in your own way. Am I wrong there?"

Chris just smiled. "She does make both of us smile. But let us get back to the original point before the others catch up to us. Amar and that girl, Azita, wiped away any doubts I had about whether you should remain here. This is the kind of place I had in mind when I started all this, a place of real need where others were reluctant to be. It was just . . . just . . ."

"I know. I know. You worry about me."

"Yes. Why in God's name does that surprise you so? We just lost Chuck. Kat seems beyond our reach. Mother is checking out, killing herself with liquor and pills and despair. Some days I wake up and just think, 'If I lose Kay I will have nothing left of family.' Maybe Beverly but I hardly know her. You are it and I cannot bear the thought of being without you."

Kay looked a bit stricken, not grief but confusion. "You are lonely, aren't you?"

"Can't fool you. I guess that is why you were always at the top of your class. All the time I spent at Jules and Ricky's home. That is what I desperately wanted, that kind of unconditional love. You could take all the money, who gives a shit. What is really priceless is a family that cares about one another."

"Then we have a surprise for you."

"Meaning?" Chris pushed.

"Wait till you meet Dr. Masoud and his family. They exude love. I think they pattern most Hallmark cards after them."

"Oh goody, that should make me even more jealous about what I am stuck with."

Kay moved closer to her brother. She became very serious, it was obvious she had something to share. "Chris, one more thing to share, now that we are into this honesty thing. All those years, it was not just your running away, at least that is how I saw it, that bothered me." Now that she was on the edge, she was having trouble jumping. "It was more than that. Back in high school, middle school really . . ."

"What, Kay. Say it."

"Father . . . Father raped me, many times." It was out, she breathed deeply. "For some reason, I could never bring myself to tell you and I was furious you never figured it out. No, I know that is silly, a silly female thing I suspect. The man is supposed to intuit stuff that is never expressed. For some reason I just blurted it out to Karen. Perhaps it was the moment where running away would no longer work. Maybe she was someone safe. When I told her, I had no idea our lives would remain connected. Now, maybe it is getting easier for some reason. I had said the words once, perhaps I could say them again."

Chris didn't say anything. He took her in his arms and she wept softly.

"Oh look," it was Karen at the door with Amar and Azita. "She did not kill him, but he did reduce her to tears."

"No, my dear," Chris looked at Karen with his fake scowl, "but you might want to call the Hairy Hare to see if the barmaid position is still open."

———

"Welcome to my home," Dr. Masoud said with a slight bow. "I am so honored to meet the man who has put this wonderful program together. I wish I were here to greet you upon your arrival but the fighting does not always honor our wishes."

Chris looked over the thin, smallish man in front of him. He somehow expected someone larger, more prepossessing. Then he quickly realized that this man's power was not in physical strength but rather in his character and intellect. "This is my honor, sir. I have heard great things about you. And let me introduce Karen Fisher."

"Oh yes, I have talked with Karen several times by phone but of course we have never met. She has always been most useful."

"Dr. Masoud, you will be happy to learn that she survived a near-death experience earlier today." Chris quickly found a way to indicate his comment was a joke though Karen did wonder how many figurative lives she had left.

"Please call me Pamir." His smile was broad and inviting. "Now, let me introduce the rest of the family. This is my other daughter, Deena. She has the beauty of her mother. My son, Majeed, is off with the warriors. He is a brave, but I fear a foolish boy. We pray for his well-being every day. And this is my good wife Madeena. She has been my rock for so many years.

You would have met her at the school with Azita earlier but she had much work around here with my return."

Even at this age, it was obvious Madeena had been a beauty in her youth. "I am so excited to be teaching again even if it is with girls just learning their numbers and basic arithmetic. I will say one thing. They are so enthusiastic. I doubt my students back at university had such enthusiasm. These girls are desperate to learn. It is as if they appreciate at some level that the world out there is much bigger than they had been allowed to see."

Chris smiled. "Your daughter, Azita here, was the first person we met upon arriving. I thought she was a local girl who was just happening by and tried my few words of Dari. She surprised me by responding in perfect English, better than mine."

"Now Azita, don't become too vain." It was Amar. "You have to remember that his English is not that good. Americans are not that good with the Queen's English."

"Hey, don't lump me in with my brother." Kay laughed. All joined in. It would be a nice, relaxed evening.

They chatted amiably for a time, sharing bits and pieces about their backgrounds and the situation in which they now found themselves. Then Madeena gathered them in a large circle in the living room. "We have no table large enough for such a group. We will do this traditional style. We shall sit on the floor and share from common servings. You scoop up the food with the flat breads." Once seated, Deena and Azita started bringing out serving after serving of lentils, vegetables, hummus, goat meet, and the ubiquitous flat breads. There were olives of various kinds and some homemade sweets. As they ate, Pamir talked at some length about their escape from Kabul to Kunduz and then to the Alliance territory.

Chris grew more impressed as the story unfolded. "You took enormous risks. Life under the Taliban must have been intolerable," Chris noted.

"Yes, they were becoming more intolerant and fanatical as their power increased. That is the way with tyrants I fear. But it was more than escaping from them. I wished to get closer to my own roots, my own people. For some reason, I always missed the mountains, the simple life found here. I doubt my family shares my enthusiasm, but I have the upper hand at present." He laughed. "The alternative is to go back to the Taliban. When things settle a bit, I have a home being prepared further into the mountains, where my family can be found. We will spend some time there where Azita and I can tend to the medical needs of the area."

Azita could not stay silent. "Deena is most unhappy, she fears there will be no boys there, no good boys, just goat herders."

Deena shushed her in Pashto which did not need any translation. Madeena then silenced her squabbling daughters with a word and a look.

Pamir just laughed. "Daughters, they are inflicted on fathers to punish us for our sins. But I must warn you, Christopher, I think my daughter is already casting eyes in your direction."

"Azita? I doubt . . ."

"Oh no," Pamir quickly protested. "Azita only has eyes for her books and medicine. But Deena . . ."

"Papa." Madeena scolded him while wagging a finger. "You will embarrass the girl to tears."

"Yes, yes, I am very bad. Let me change the discussion. What do you think of us so far, what we are trying to do here."

Chris knew what the man was really asking. He wanted to know if Chris were there to take Kay away. As sophisticated as the doctor was, it seemed quite natural for a brother to exercise control over his sister's life, especially an unmarried sister. Obviously, the good doctor thought highly of his sister's medical skills.

"Yes," Chris responded slowly, "let me first reassure you that Kay will remain here if she wishes." Chris noticed that the other man relaxed a bit but showed no overt reaction. "Just as you worry about your son, I will continue to worry about her safety but that would be the case if she were in Chicago which, as it turns out, is almost as dangerous as Afghanistan. Our greatest acts of love involve letting those we care the most about be themselves." Chris noticed Kay blink, was she fighting off a tear?

"Thank you," Pamir responded, "both for providing the answer we wanted and for not requiring that I ask outright."

Chris had something else on his mind. "But also let me answer the question you asked. I am impressed by what I see. Obviously, the medical staff is doing great work. But it goes beyond that, something that touches me deeply, makes it all worthwhile. I visit places where bodies are being healed or minds are being strengthened and that is always a good thing. But I sense something more here, I have been trying to put my finger on it. The best I can come up with is that I see you providing hope. People arrive here literally with nothing, ripped from their history and their culture. They are met with love and healing."

Chris turned to Azita. "That sense came to me in your classroom. Those girls. Yes, they were learning some basic skills. But the joy on their faces. Given what they had experienced, what their lives looked like, you are all to them. You are giving these people everything. I have done some good things in my life, some not so good things as well." He glanced at Kay quickly. "But no matter what I have accomplished, I have never brought everything to another person, never replaced despair with hope. I think for the first time, I am taken aback by what that might feel like. Looking at those girls in the classroom, I understand why Kay and Amar want to be here, even with the risks. I have never given another person everything. You do."

"Do you understand now?" It was Karen looking directly at Chris.

"Understand what?" He looked perplexed.

"This is exactly why I put up with your shii—stuff."

Chris laughed. "Before my lovely assistant betrays just how uncouth Western women can be, I want to ask you a question, one for all the Masoud family. From what I see and hear, the Afghan people are much to be admired. How can the Taliban have taken over? How can they be so cruel?"

There was silence and Chris blushed a bit. Had he relaxed too much, had he embarrassed his hosts? He need not worry, they were merely collecting their thoughts. He was surprised just a bit when Madeena responded first.

"People forget that we once were a rather Western culture, in the cities at least. I could study at university and teach at the university. I could wear dresses, even rather short dresses, and chase after the man of my dreams." Then she reached out to take Pamir's hand. "You must understand he was much younger and still very handsome then." They all laughed at her joke, especially Azita.

"Madeena, you are very bad, he is still very handsome." It was Kay, she obviously had much affection for them all.

"Perhaps," Madeena responded with a smile before continuing. "In the 1970s, however, the Communists assumed power and chaos began to descend over the land. By the end of the decade, the Soviets invaded as the local Communists were fighting among themselves and losing control. It took a decade to drive them out, we have not had peace since. The fighting left too many weapons behind, and too many young men who knew nothing else besides war. Chaos appeared across the land giving men with fanatical views a chance to rule. They took it. It is not so different from Hitler taking power in Germany when it was facing economic collapse in the 1930s."

Pamir had been reflecting on his wife's words. "I suspect it is not so different in America. You have so many who cling to fanatical religious beliefs. They praise your Christ but then act as if they had never heard his message. Some of them wear robes and hoods but most of them do not. If they faced a threat to their way of life, it is possible that they might convince others that devotion to some rigid beliefs was the way toward peace and stability. If your most fundamental white Christians thought they were losing control of America, might they not convince others to take a stand, protect some imaginary virtues that turn out to be vile and disgusting. Hate and fear are powerful motivators. The Taliban promised stability after two decades of war and conflict. I once explained to Azita what a Faustian bargain was. That was the bargain into which we entered."

"But they are so unpopular, are they not?" Amar asked.

"They now have the weapons, it all comes down to power. Without help from the outside, who will drive them from power? I so despair for my . . ." Pamir was looking at his daughters and then caught himself. "Still, I have lived long enough to realize we cannot predict the future. Did you know that the Taliban is giving refuge to a terrorist hated by the Americans, Osama Bin Laden?"

"I have heard the name," Karen responded. "He has attacked American interests before."

"Perhaps he will attack America directly, even we hear talk of that, and then they might come to our assistance, to get at Osama. It probably will not happen. Still, one never knows."

The conversation went on for some time as Chris and Karen were drawn into the warmth and intelligence of the Masoud family.

Later, Chris, Amar, Karen, and Kay stood awkwardly outside their various living quarters. No one seemed to know quite what to say. Chris broke the silence. "If things fall apart here, I intend to get that family out, the whole family, to somewhere they can live in peace, thrive."

Kay walked over and kissed her brother on the cheek, this time with affection. "I am glad you are here. Each time I get to the point of wanting to clock you over the head, you go and do something to make me love you again."

"I did something nice? Damn, didn't mean to." He smiled and kissed his sister on the forehead. "Won't let that happen again, but I am glad I came to see you, even if it was to kick you in the butt."

With that, Kay took Karen's hand and walked toward her quarters. There was no reason to hide anymore.

Amar looked at Chris. "Are you okay with everything?"

"I think so, I may be getting too old for so many surprises in one day."

"I hope you are not too old for some more sex with an exotic Indian girl unless you are tired of her already."

Chris turned abruptly on her, no smile on his face. She was startled at his abrupt words. "Sorry, but don't say that again, ever."

His sharpness had surprised her. "What thing?" she stammered.

His face turned soft, his words softer. "That thing about me being tired of you."

Then he took her hand and led her toward her bedroom.

CHAPTER 9

CHICAGO
(SEPTEMBER 2001)

Jules was waiting for Chris at O'Hare Airport. She smiled broadly as he emerged from the crowd, walking briskly to him and wrapping him up in her arms. Something immediately struck her as off, his response was not as affectionate as usual. Her reaction, however, evaporated as being overly sensitive. She had been thinking of him a lot lately. Perhaps it was the fact that she was getting beyond the first flush of youth, hitting an age when settling down becomes more attractive. Or perhaps she had now reached a position in her career where she felt somewhat satisfied and secure. She had a network affiliation yet was fortunate enough to be able to remain in Chicago. Her face and reputation were sufficiently well known now that additional possibilities were available. Just maybe she could find something in London, perhaps it was time . . . then she caught herself. Best not get ahead of the game. Despite her cautionary words to herself, the thought persisted. Hmmm, she could pop the question to him this time around, that was a delicious thought.

She grabbed his arm. "I was delighted when you got in touch, that you were able to get to the windy city even for a few days. Ricky tells me you have been traveling a lot of late. Of course, I hate having to get the news from my brother, but you have been a naughty boy recently. I don't hear from you enough. I have no idea what mischief you have been up to recently."

He smiled weakly. "Yeah, it has been a rough patch, very busy and somewhat distracting. Listen, your brother has been a godsend. I am not sure what I would do without him. He really is taking over most of the logistical crap that I hate."

She laughed. "Funny about Rick. He really is organized for a guy, more organized that I am. However, I am not buying this too busy to stay in touch crap. You can get by with that bullshit with all your other women but not me. Do we understand one another?"

"Yes, dear." He put on his best whipped husband look. He did that often when she chided him no matter how gently. She sometimes hated the fact that he was so charming. Maybe her new fantasy about him being spousal material was misplaced. Girls would always be throwing themselves at him.

Jules pushed any negative thoughts away. "I am going to get you to my place, feed you, bathe you, and then ravage your body. Everything still works, doesn't it? You haven't broken anything essential from overuse? Damn, everyone uses that joke now, I need new material."

Chris ignored her attempt at levity. "Jules, you could have put me up at a hotel, I don't want to be a burden. This is not a fun trip."

"Nonsense, I won't hear of that. None of your trips are about fun. When was the last time you took a real vacation? That is something to think about—you and I on a real vacation."

"High school I think. But that was to get away from Father. When I did get away, vacations seemed less necessary."

She caught the fact that he did not respond to her suggestion. Deciding to ignore his evasion, she leaned up and kissed him as they walked toward her car. "Well, I will take care of you now. What's up on your agenda?"

Chris grimaced at the thought of his agenda. "Most of it comes from what you have been telling me. I want to check on Kat and Mother. What you tell me about Mother is disturbing. I also want to check in on Beverly, see how she is doing. Then, of course, I will be doing fund-raising. I stopped in Boston and New York already. I am good at it but rather hate it. You can see it in people's eyes—here comes the bloodsucker. Has to be done though."

Jules chuckled. "I have that same feeling when I see you and you don't even ask me for money. Listen, let's get back and I will fill you in on the family tragedy."

When they got back to her place, she took out some salads and made drinks for each of them. As they ate, Jules brought Chris up-to-date on family matters. She had become his source of information now that Kay had fled Chicago. He listened carefully to what she had to say.

"It sounds as if Kat is doing better and Mother is failing fast."

Jules reached over to touch his hand. "That is how I see it. Of course, I don't have anything to say about your dad. He does not permit me into the inner sanctum, not even the outer sanctum. Perhaps it is that 'no Negroes permitted' sign he posted. I even tried setting up a media interview with him but he did not bite. Perhaps if I were with Fox News . . ."

"You have done great. Father is a lost cause. He would never trust you. For one thing, you are the wrong color. For another, you like me." Then Chris paused. "You do still like me, right?"

"No, asshole. I don't like you, I love you."

That caught Chris off guard. He stumbled over his next words as he changed direction. "Well, I . . . I need to see him. I have something to discuss, confront—" then he stopped. Chris looked stricken and uncertain. "I need to ask you something. It is difficult."

"Hey," she tried to lighten the mood, "you have already been to my promised land many times. I think we can share any-thing." Then she waited until he was ready.

"Jules, I wonder . . . I am curious if Kay ever confided some-thing personal to you, about her and Father, when she was young, early teens."

"Ah, I didn't know her until high school and—"

"This would have been something that she might share with another female. I know the two of you were not super close and Kay was rather a loner. Still, she was as close to you as anyone."

Jules thought carefully. "No, nothing other than she could not stand him, same as you, and that you were an asshole of course that I should avoid like the plague. What—"

"Nothing, you would know if she had. No big thing."

Jules knew that conversation was over. She also was ready to move on. "Chris, get comfortable. I will be back in a few mo-ments."

He ambled over to one of the windows that looked out onto the city. You could see both Navy Pier, Grant Park, and the twinkling lights of the city. *Wow,* he thought, *this is nice.* Soon, she had returned wearing a robe. Chris's mind went blank. She stood in front of him with a seductive smile. "Okay, let's see if this works now." With that, she let the robe slide from her body to stand naked in front of him.

He flushed, he sensed himself getting hard, need taking over. Then, he pushed the feelings back with a heroic effort. He opened his mouth, but at first nothing emerged. Then, with words he could barely utter. "I can't, Jules. I am so sorry. I can't."

"Oh my god," she stammered. "I am back in high school. Why, what is wrong this time?"

He looked at her with infinite sadness. "I met someone."

"Oh." She looked stunned. She was stunned. This was, of course, always a possibility but she never thought it would happen. He met girls all the time. It had never mattered in the past. They had something special.

"Shit, my next comment was going to be something like I never meant this to happen. Wow, how trite can you get. I am supposed to be a clever guy. You might expect I could do better than that."

"Chris, no, no need to explain. We . . . we were never exclusive or anything. Hell, I turned you down how many times?" Then her lips began to tremble as tears flowed down her face. "Shit, damn it. Why am I doing this?"

The space between them disappeared and he embraced her. "Never in a million years did I . . ."

"Do I know her?" Jules asked.

"No, she is a doctor, the one with Kay in Afghanistan." Then he paused as he fought off the sensations her naked body imposed on him. "Jules, I am closer to you than anyone else. I am going to ask a big favor. Can I talk about this, her, with you? It might be a lot to ask . . ."

"Of course, I think . . . yes, of course, it was just the shock." She broke away from him and put her robe back on, leading him to the couch. "Maybe, just maybe, that is why this has never quite worked between us."

"I don't understand."

"We have been too close. We shared too much. Maybe we have been more like family than lovers. I sometimes thought this. You don't have a real family. Ricky and I have been like siblings to you. Can't really marry your sister now, can you? What do you think?"

"Hmmm, all I can say is that I never had such sex with anyone in my own family. Never proposed to a family member either. I can assure you that Kay has never turned me on, nor Kat." Chris smiled at his little joke. "Still, maybe you have something. The thing is, and this is what baffles me, I knew right away that she was the one, on my first sight of her. I saw her from a distance, maybe a hundred feet. She was holding a child who was dying, singing to it because there was nothing else to do. I just looked at her, could make out this one tear that slowly made its way down her face. She was disheveled and covered with sweat and blood and looked like shit frankly. But I knew, even before we spoke a word. Well, we had chatted on the phone, but does that count? How many women have I been with and there was nothing like this before though you were awfully close."

"Not sure I want to know," Jules threw out quickly. She was trying to be there for him. It was proving harder than she imagined.

"My point is, I knew immediately. How is that possible?" He looked at her for an answer.

"She feels the same about you?"

"To be honest, I have no fucking idea. We made love that night and I have no idea why she did. She really is quite innocent and took great pains to convince me that this was not going to get complicated. She said that Kay had warned her about me and that she expected nothing from me. Kay was furious with me, still is."

Jules looked in his eyes. "You really are screwed up. Aren't you."

"Just a bit."

"I have a big favor. Will you sleep next to me tonight, not with me, just next to me. You owe me that."

"Yeah, that will be okay. Funny, I did that with Karen once, after her lover dumped her. Maybe I have a future as an asexual escort. What do you think?"

"Don't get carried away with yourself. I just don't want to make up the guest room."

A few minutes later, they were in bed, Jules leaned into him, resting her head on his chest. How many times had she done that before. It now saddened her immensely that this might be the final time. Why had she let him slip through her fingers? They lay in silence for a while. Then she broke the silence.

"I want to know more about . . ."

"Amar, Amar Singh."

"Indian then, there are some stunning Indian women."

"Yes, but that is not it, I don't think so, at least. Yeah, she has the dark hair and dark complexion that draws me in, the large eyes and soft lips. So, there is that physical attraction. But there is more and that is what baffles me a bit. I think it has something to do with contradictions."

"What do you mean?" she asked.

"Hard to say, exactly. She is innocent yet quick witted. She is tough yet vulnerable. She is competent yet never betrays an ounce of arrogance. She is reserved and shy, yet she walked right into harm's way. She is quite inexperienced sexually. Still, she seduced me that first night. I never would have . . . she said that she could handle it, sleeping with me."

"You believed her?"

"Not for a second."

"But you slept with her anyways." Jules was skeptical.

"Because I knew that I loved her, that I was in love with her."

Jules raised herself up on an elbow. "I am sorry but that is stupid. How could you possibly . . ." She stopped herself, looking in his eyes for some time. Then she sighed deeply. "Amar is a very lucky woman." She put her head back on his chest. "But you get back to her and tell her how you feel. If she is as you describe her, she is regretting her actions and probably not happy these days."

"I thought about us on the flight over. I never regretted asking you to marry me. We would have been a wonderful couple I think, compatible and comfortable. But I think you knew something when you turned me down."

"I have no freaking idea what that might be."

"We loved one another, still do, but were never in love. You sensed that, but I never did, not until now. I was convinced I would never love anyone as much as I did you, but you were not on the same page . . . the old unrequited love thing."

Jules thought about that for a while. She was not sure she could accept it. Neither could she refute it. She was still forming a response when he broke the silence.

"Jules, he raped her."

"What?" She popped up on her elbow again.

"Father raped Kay, that is what I was getting to earlier. Remember I asked if Kay had confided something in you? That was it. I recently found out. That really is why I am here, I guess, though I did want to tell you about Amar in person. I am burning up inside, I loathe that man."

"Holy shit." Jules looked at him in amazement. "I never . . ."

"Remember that I told you that Kay and I drifted apart around the time we started high school? I thought it was because I went to this boys-only place and she to her elite girls' school."

"Yeah," Jules murmured in a distracted fashion, "I always did think it was good to separate you, and my horny brother, from vulnerable high school girls. Sorry, no more jokes."

"No, no," he quickly said, "I appreciate the effort to lighten me up. This is eating me up inside. I need the distraction."

"What are you going to do?" she asked.

"No fucking idea."

Jules rubbed his chest. "In the old days, I would know how to comfort you."

"I can't Jules. I can't. You have no idea how much I want to right now. If I do, I would not be able to go back to Amar."

She stopped rubbing his chest. "Let's get some sleep, I am guessing you have a big day tomorrow." As Chris started drifting off, he heard the soft voice seemingly from far off. "You might be right. I am not entirely sure I was 'in love' with you, until tonight."

He did not respond.

———

The next morning Chris walked into the ornate offices of Crawford Enterprises. It had been a long time for him. If it were possible, the place looked even more opulent than he recalled. The textured carpets, the richly upholstered chairs, the artwork on the walls, everything spoke of affluence and power. He was ushered past two secretaries into the inner sanctum. He arrived at the desk of yet another efficient looking woman.

"Hello, I am Christopher Crawford, I am here to see the person in charge."

"Oh, yes, the son of Mr. Crawford, the one who lives in England."

"Guilty as charged."

"Very nice to meet you at last and my condolences regarding your brother. We still are all in grief about that."

"I appreciate that. It is Ruth, no?"

"Why, yes. You do know that your father is in Washington though we expect him back later today. We have you on Ms. Crawford's calendar. She was delighted by the fact that you could stop by to see her."

The middle-aged woman, pert and reeking of quiet efficiency, pressed a button before rising and ushering Chris into a door that clicked, signaling that it had just been unlocked. He was in a large office with more opulence and artwork. He wondered if one of them was an authentic Cezanne and then quickly realized that many of them might well be originals. Kat was already standing in front of her desk. She walked quickly to him and embraced him with enthusiasm.

"Oh, Chris. I am delighted to see you."

"It is good to see you, Kat." He pulled away so that he could look more closely at her. She seemed to have matured a decade in the past few months, at least in appearance. Some of the apparent newly accreted years of poise and presence were undoubtedly attributable to her formal business attire and new hairdo. He wondered though if some of the new years were the early effects of crushing responsibilities and worry.

"You are staying with Jules I assume. You didn't ask to stay with me and I know you would not ask Father. I see her on TV all the time now, she is doing increasingly important stories for the network, traveling more, getting great exposure. She is a star.

You better grab her up before she will be too important to even see you."

Chris made a quick decision to skip his news about Amar. "I keep trying. I think she knows I am a loser."

"The playboy of the Western world, a loser. I suppose. Still, it is very funny. You were always very funny. How I miss you." She hugged him again. "Oh, before I forget. A little something for you, well for your work."

Chris glanced at the cashier's check and saw the amount of four point five million dollars typed in. "Kat, this is too generous."

"Nonsense. It is not enough. This is from corporate funds, we have a philanthropic fund. Just spend it on Kay's work. You cannot imagine how much we spend on so-called charity though ninety percent is for Father's so-called causes. I kept it under five million because that is the amount at which he might ask questions. Better we keep this between ourselves for a while."

"Thank you very much. I was there not that long ago with Kay. The work she is doing, they are doing, is amazing. I have pictures."

"Come, let us sit over here where it is comfortable." They sat on a luxurious leather couch as Chris retrieved some pictures. "Oh my god," Kat exclaimed, "this looks like a war zone."

"It is, in a way, too close to the front. I worry about her every day."

After a few more, Kat grew quiet. "God, I worry about her as well. Why is she there? Damn, we had such a row just before she left. She thinks I am a sellout, you probably do as well. But let me say something. Father didn't want me in this position. You left, Kay left, and Chuck really left. I was it and I think he put me behind that desk just to have our name at the top. Good thing I have no plans to marry and change it, the name that is. Father would be apoplectic. My position probably was ceremonial at first. Quickly, I discovered something. I can do this. I was shocked. I do have the talent and, more importantly, the instincts. More than that, I had absorbed tons just by paying attention all these years. No one noticed but I was. Chuck was terrible, he hated it. He was an artist, not a businessman, and certainly not a schemer. He was way too transparent. It was only Dad's sexism that blinded him to reality. But I am learning tons every day. I have a long way to go but—"

Chris cut her off. "But do you want to run his empire? Are you really with him?"

"We are not going to fight, Chris. I won't permit it." He looked at steel gray eyes and saw a strength he had never seen before. "Besides, I have a plan. But first, show me these pictures again. Who is this young girl in so many of these pics. She is even too young to be one of your trollops, I think . . . I hope."

"Ha-ha! I am not such a total pervert." Before she could correct him, he went on. "This is Azita, the daughter of Dr. Pamir Masoud, a local physician. You can see him here. He does amazing work. His family is lovely, how people survive such horrors without losing their humanity is a miracle. Such love. Anyways, Azita is kind of the mission mascot, and a lot of help."

"And this woman, she is gorgeous."

"That is Dr. Amar Singh. From India originally, also a British citizen, educated at Cambridge and then medical school in Canada. There are other doctors who are available but the three of them, Pamir, Amar, and Kay are permanent and do the most amazing work. The lives of people fleeing the Taliban are so desperate. Azita even organized a school for girls which the Taliban hates. The risks they take, that is what hit me when I was there, Kat. What they do is so meaningful. They touch people's lives totally. I could not do it. What I do I do well but—" then he stopped. "Ooops, I am getting on my soap box. Sorry."

Kat got up and crossed to her desk. She brought back a checkbook. "Here is something from my personal account. Don't try to talk me out of it or even thank me."

He looked at the sum and blanched. "I am speechless."

"Then it was worth every damn penny. Should have done it years ago. But don't cash it until the date I posted. I will have to move resources around. You know, I hadn't given much thought to what you were doing. Like Kay, I just thought you were running away from Father, thought you were being a coward. Kay believed that, I know she did. She was rather disappointed in you."

"She was downright pissed," he corrected her.

"Okay, she was pissed. So was I. But then Ricky followed and then Kay herself. I started checking your website and talking to some of the fat cats who donated. I realized it was more than running away."

"Why did you and Kay fight when she left?"

Kat grimaced. "I was scared at the time. Father was drawing me in. I didn't know if I could handle it, if I wanted to handle it. I just wanted Kay to be here for me. I felt she also was abandoning me, as Chuck had, as you had. There were lonely, scary days for a while."

"Kat, I feel like a shit. I could have stayed in touch. We kids were never close, not even Kay and I except early on. We never had a family. That is why I grabbed on to the Jacksons." Chris paused to pick up a picture. "Look at this one. This is the full Masoud family. His wife had been a mathematician, one son is missing because he is off fighting against the Taliban. They have been through a bit of hell, more than a bit. What gets me is the love. They love each other dearly."

"I would have given anything for your love, Chris, for Kay's. I didn't know how to ask." Her lower lip trembled slightly but she controlled it. "I had been too wounded to ask, and way too insecure."

"Okay," Chris took a deep breath. "There is something I must ask. It is difficult."

"I'm a big girl now. Just ask."

He looked intently into her eyes. "Did Father ever molest you sexually?"

Kat stared back at him. She betrayed nothing though Chris could tell her brain was racing. She stood up and walked toward the window. For a moment, Chris regretted the question. Was she going to have him escorted out by security? However, she stared out at the city, toward Lake Michigan in the distance. He rose slowly and walked over next to her. Finally, a word escaped her, "Yes."

For a moment, he wasn't sure he had heard her. "I thought so. He is nothing more than a serial pedophile." He put an arm around her and she lay her head on his shoulder.

"All I wanted, Chris, was a normal family. We had every advantage, every luxury we could imagine, not that we were spoiled at all. Father did his best to see that we developed character. No reward without effort, remember that. He always talked about values, about principles, and the eternal virtues. Tell me one thing, Chris, where are the eternal virtues in screwing your own daughter. Answer me that one, can you?"

He pulled her to him so that she could collapse into his arms. She let herself go, first softly and then with more abandon. He could feel her heave in his arms as pent up feelings poured out.

"I've no answers for you, never understood that man. I suspect he comes from a place in hell that simply is foreign to me for sure and I suspect unknown to decent people."

Kat sighed heavily. "Ever wonder why I don't date often? Rhetorical question. I still can't get close to men. They come after me. Hey, I'm rich. Thing is, I cannot trust anymore. Maybe I never did . . ."

"I am ashamed. I never even thought about that. We have to be closer now. We will be closer." He paused for a moment to let that notion sink in. "But listen, my question did not come out of thin air."

She pulled away to look at him. "Yes, why . . ."

"The thing is, he did the same thing to Kay. Did he attack you in your early teens?" She nodded affirmatively. "That was about the same age he went after her. You never knew, did you, about Kay? I'll bet you never talked about it."

"No, I wondered. I wanted to ask her. I could never summon the courage. I know what you're going to ask. Why didn't I tell someone? Well, why didn't Kay? You have no idea about the shame, what you do to yourself. You think it must be your fault. You must have done something. Besides, our esteemed father seemed more powerful than God. Who do you complain to about God?"

"But that is—"

"Stupid!" she yelled. "Yes, it is stupid, beyond stupid. Don't you dare judge me, or Kay. You have no idea."

"No, Kat, I don't. Believe me, I don't. Now I get why Kay was so damaged that she withdrew even from me. We used to huddle under blankets as kids and talk through what Father was feeding us. We banded together to hold on to our sanity. And then, she shut down. I thought it was puberty or something. Now I know. Do you think that Mother knew?"

His sister sighed deeply. "Sometimes I think that she must have. Now that I know Kay suffered as well, I cannot believe she didn't. But who knows. Why didn't she say something, do something? Why did she stay with him? Yeah, she is Catholic but still, to stay with such a monster."

"I want to talk with her, before Father gets home."

Kat walked to her desk and pushed a button. "Ruth, call Mother and tell her that Chris will be visiting later today. She won't be surprised, she knows he is in town but not when he might stop by. It would be better if he did not show up without warning. Thanks, Ruth."

Chris could read between the lines. "She is declining, isn't she?"

"Yes, so be careful with her. She is so vulnerable. Losing Chuck hit her the hardest. Just be careful."

"Of course."

"She will likely be drunk when you get to her. She is by noon every day, seldom leaves the house. Her life has become small. Knowing you are coming by might keep her presentable." Kat looked at her brother intently. He was sure that she was going to tell him not to be a klutz in dealing with their mother. "Okay, let me get back to this plan I mentioned earlier."

Chris smiled. He could not help himself. He thought of an old comedy where the Gene Wilder character kept saying he had a plan that would never work out. "Good, because my plan is to kill Father which is what Kay feared when she told me."

"My plan is much worse for him. Sit." They walked back to the couch. "Chris, have you checked your trust fund recently?"

"Not really."

"When you do, you will find that you are even wealthier than you thought."

"Okay," he said uncertainly.

"Here is the thing." She became very focused. "Mother has been using her own wealth to funnel shares of Crawford Enterprises into our trust funds. Now we realize that Chuck had planned his end for some time and for what would come next.

He shifted his shares to Mother who has given them to us. Same with her accumulated shares which are substantial. Father is the biggest single shareholder, but this is key. He does not hold the majority of the outstanding shares. He is sufficiently short that a hostile takeover is feasible. Chris, I think we can take control. If we collect enough proxies, and all of us vote the same way, we can oust him as chairman of the board and CEO. We all thought he had an iron grip on his empire. He doesn't."

"What?"

"I have been discretely reaching out to shareholders, not Father's ideological allies but those in it for the money. A lot of them fear that he is spending too much on the firm's resources, particularly on his quack causes. I have been buying up shares. If I can get enough without him knowing, we can take over, turn it away from his warped vision of things. Chris, his crazed right-wing vision is as frightening as ever. I know you thought I had bought into his shit. And I came close, I suppose, mostly just drifted in that direction before I started reasoning for myself. I didn't have a sibling in which to confide though I often wondered why Kay and you fought him so. Maybe I never would have broken if he hadn't raped me night after night . . ."

"Are you asking me to join you, commit my shares, maybe bring Kay on board?"

"Yes."

"Kat, you amaze me! I remember you being shy, uncertain, even vulnerable. Now you are thinking about taking down one of the right-wing titans of the Western world. What the fuck happened?"

"Aside from the fact that a man I thought to be just your ordinary garden-variety asshole turned out to be a top-shelf sexual predator and first-class asshole—"

"Wait," Chris stopped her as she appeared to have more to say. "There is something I have to ask, something personal."

"Shoot." Her eyes were now clear, the tears fully passed.

"You never married. I am wondering, like Kay, if you are—"

"A lesbian?" She laughed. "Wait, Kay is gay? I didn't know that."

"Damn," Chris exhaled. "I thought you knew. My bad. I thought girls shared everything."

"First, asshole, we are not girls. Second, we don't sit around gossiping all day. Don't be such a sexist. No, I didn't know but I had my suspicions."

"I thought maybe because of Dad . . ."

"My god." Kat laughed. "For a brilliant guy, you can be dumber than dirt. Being raped doesn't turn you gay. And if you are so nosey, I get laid on a regular basis. As I said, I just don't trust any male bastard. But I guess I have to trust you."

Chris blanched. "Okay, too much information about that getting laid stuff."

Kat laughed even louder. "I am being flip here. I have been tempted by the thought of settling down. Every women's dream, right. It never happened because of Father. He never approved of any candidate, and there were a few. Rich girls get lucky, as you can imagine. Somehow, they all failed the daddy test. You think that a couple of the best ones were Jewish had anything to do with it? I thought the drop-dead handsome Italian stud might pass muster, buy not Aryan enough for the patriarch. All the time, I was waiting for you to marry Jules. With a black in the family, I thought then I could bring home a Mideast terrorist and Father would not notice. By the way, when are the two of you going to tie the knot?"

Chris suddenly looked uncomfortable. He picked up one of his pictures. "See this woman."

"Oh my, the gorgeous Indian gal."

"I thought I was not supposed to say gal."

"You can't. I can. Wait, are you engaged to this woman?"

"No, but I am going to ask her."

"Well," Kat said with a bit of uncertainty, "strap on a pair and do it. Don't let this beauty get away. Jules okay?"

"Yes, we talked it over last night."

"I should chat with her. I miss her. And you and I won't be strangers anymore. You wanted to know about why I changed? Lots of things. The biggest is that I saw Father's empire from the inside. Chuck was totally unsuited for the role Father forced upon him as everyone knew except Father. No one knew but Chuck depended on me. I spent hours with him, like a shadow tutor. No one ever paid attention to me. I was the unseen younger sibling, quiet and observing. But I was learning all the time. Aside from the fact that Father's business practices suck, corporate culture really is set at the top, but where he funnels his money is horrendous. Think of any right-wing news outlet, advocacy groups, lobbyist effort, shaper of public opinion, and Father is helping them financially and thus calling some of the shots. He is real close to the Mercers and the Koch's. Where he used to just push his right-wing apocalyptic vision, now he is financing and shaping it along with his super-wealthy co-conspirators. Time to bring him down."

"Can you, I mean we . . ."

"Now is the time. I have been watching. You know he is a control freak, keeps a lot to himself, doesn't trust anyone. That is what makes this delicious, he trusts me because I am the good girl. Well, he is overextended, not keeping as good an eye on stuff. He is also distracted. With Bush the younger in the White House, he has kindred spirits in power. That is why he is in DC, to chat with the Neo-Cons running foreign policy. Time for them to take over the world . . . they are just looking for an excuse. Besides, he is not himself, not since Chuck passed."

"Kat, have I ever said that you amaze me?"

"Yes, just now for the first time, now let's get to work."

———

A prim black woman greeted Chris when he arrived at his parents' penthouse suite. He did not recognize her though she addressed him by name. "Your mother is awaiting you." He was ushered into a room that looked like a library. Three walls were covered with bookshelves. The fourth wall contained windows overlooking the city. It was a spectacular view.

Chris looked over to his mother who was sitting primly on what looked like a period piece chair. Chris could never understand this, why people would use furniture that demonstrated wealth but appeared so uncomfortable. Before her was a cup with what looked like tea. Chris was sure that it contained vodka but perhaps he was overly suspicious. Even from across the room she looked much older and frailer than she had a few months earlier. Her eyes were watery and red and her face trembled slightly, either from intoxication or nervousness. Chris was not sure. She rose unsteadily as he approached and leaned forward slightly to accept his perfunctory kiss on her cheek. Now he caught her smell. He was certain she had been drinking. It did not surprise him in the least, but the confirmation of his suspicion disappointed him nonetheless.

"Christopher, so good to see you though I wish you had given me more notice. Can I have Sylvia get you anything?"

"Oh," he said casually, "I will have whatever you are having." He immediately kicked himself mentally. That was unnecessarily cruel. But she seemed not to notice, just smiled and looked at the maid.

"Please take care of that, Sylvia." Then she looked carefully at her son. "How are you? You are looking very well. It has been so lonely here. I never see you. Kristen is God-knows-where now. I used to see Katerina often but now she is way too busy to spend time with me. And, of course, Charles is no longer with us. And your father . . . well. These are lonely times for an old woman like me."

Chris wanted to tell her that she was not that old. She looked the part of a declining dowager but she was, in fact, younger than her husband. He had been swept off his feet by her youth and beauty. Of course, her wealth did not hurt. She was a catch and Charles always got what he wanted. Chris could not imagine that he would have pursued her had it not been the wealth. He was calculating even then though she proved far more aware and savvy than he ever imagined, much to his later regret. Yet, in the beginning he had full-court pressed her with his charm, drive, and native intelligence. It was the same attributes that seduced her parents despite his lack of inherited wealth. He somehow conveyed a sense of aristocracy and entitlement even if it was tied to his Polish ancestry that could not be verified easily. He played upon his Catholic roots which appealed to Mary's Irish family. Somehow, it all fell into place until it didn't.

Chris looked at her hard. Somehow, the script he had written up in his head evaporated. Funny, he could weave his way seamlessly among movers and shakers in the world with ease. Over the past week or so, he had been answering tough questions at the Ford, Rockefeller, Casey, and several other foundations where officers seemed to be looking for reasons not to enhance their contributions to his effort. He typically found a way to parry their punches, walking away with their support and their resources. Now, however, he faced a wizened, craggy woman who also happened to be his mother. He melted just a bit inside, resolve dissipating in the face of ancient scripts forged in childhood.

"Mother, what is wrong?"

"What do you mean, dear? I am fine."

"Look at you." Now that he had taken the plunge, he might as well go all in. "You have lost more weight. I did not think that was possible. You look . . . frail."

"Oh, my dear, you know the old saying. You can't be too thin . . ."

"Or too rich," he finished the old truism. "Listen, I am sure that if I sipped your drink I would find mostly vodka. I don't mean to be cruel . . ."

"Then don't be."

"What, do you think I am trying to hurt you? Is that what you think? Listen, the easiest thing would be for me to stop by, make small talk, and head back across the ocean. Isn't that what we always did, dance around the elephant in the room."

She looked at him with cold, grey eyes. She struck him as a sculpture. Her bleached blonde hair was stylishly done, her clothes very expensive if dated, her makeup perfectly applied, if somewhat on the extreme side. He wondered if Sylvia had applied the surface covering to her skin, if his mother's hands would tremble too much for her to complete the task.

Chris had lived briefly with the horror of alcoholism. His mind wandered back to his first roommate at Princeton. The boy was brilliant, even standing out in a class of brilliant prodigies. Still, this young man felt pressure to be perfect, resorting to an ancient method for hiding insecurity. He understood the pains that addicts took to hide their affliction, the fear and terror of discovery, the games they played to maintain a charade of normalcy. He would awaken in the morning to find his roommate up and studying. At first, he was impressed, pushing his own game up a notch. But then he would catch a whiff of booze. This was not from last night's celebration. This was a fortification against the day's challenges, whatever they might be in his mind. Chris would say nothing.

Then, the initial grades started to appear, the first test of
worth against the best students in the nation. His roommate did
fine, Chris thought, but they were not perfect. Things deterio-
rated, the drinking got worse and the attempts to hide the problem more obvious. Chris would not only notice the telltale odor
in the morning, the signs appeared through the day. His new
friend appeared distracted, even disheveled some mornings, his
speech slower and a bit slurred despite his best efforts. When
he was absent, Chris would search his desk and belongings. He
would find booze hidden everywhere, particularly in bottles of
soda. Now, Chris knew that the boy had become a maintenance
drinker. And still, he said nothing.

As the basketball season approach, practice and classes became all consuming. He stopped paying attention. There was
nothing he could do, he told himself. He returned to his room
after a long day to find the young man curled in a ball on the
floor, crying hysterically. When he would not respond to his
ministrations, he called campus security and his parents. They
took him to a hospital and he would never see him again. He
should have intervened earlier, said something when he first
knew. Now, there was nothing to be said. That moment was
passed. He had said nothing once too often.

The memory pained him still. He looked inside himself
to see if he had accumulated any courage over the intervening
years. Speaking out was not mean or cruel in any way. It was an
act of kindness. But that did not matter, it was still very difficult,
particularly for a people pleaser such as him. That would never
change. "Mother, you are an alcoholic. Don't deny it. It was in

your family, though covered up nicely. Kay and I have talked about this at times. We have been very careful ourselves, there is a genetic component."

She puffed up for a moment. "Don't be dramatic, dear boy. Yes, I drink. I must. You have no idea what I must put up with. You were the one who ran off and to leave me behind, leaving all of us behind to fend for ourselves. Perhaps Chuck would still be—"

"Don't go there. Don't." He approached her so that she could not ignore him. "I was a coward. Everyone in this family has told me so. Since the diagnosis is shared by all, it must be true. I fully admit to it. But what would I have done had I stayed, become Father's lackey? Should I have joined his revolution? Mother, the man is a fucking Nazi."

"Christopher . . ." She seemed surprised.

"Don't stop me. You know better than anyone. The man is a virulent xenophobic, militaristic, racist, narcissistic sociopath. I have no idea if he was born that way or whether some trauma in his early days caused it, whether the family stories and crimes bequeathed upon him account for who and what he is. Whatever the roots, the man is now cast in stone. Each year he sees more demons to be attacked, using his wealth to plot against our very democratic institutions. He and his friends are going about manipulating the very foundations of society, buying political influence on a massive scale, gerrymandering voting districts, plotting ways to suppress voters they don't like, controlling media and the flow of information to the public."

"Oh, stop it. You are sounding like a hysterical child."

"Am I? Mother, look at me and tell me I am wrong. Look me in the eyes and tell me. You have been with him—"

"Forever," she said in a distant way. "Beyond forever. But what can I do, I cannot control him."

"No, Mother, but you can control how you react. You stood up to him before, you passed your own wealth to us children. He was furious, beyond furious, but you did not back down. Now you are passing your stock . . ."

She looked at him sharply. "You've talked with Katerina."

"Never mind that. That is not important now." He had gotten off track. "The thing is, alcoholism really is a disease. I had a roommate in college who almost lost his life. Maybe he is dead now, I don't even know. Anyways, I studied about it after the fact, when it was too late to help. I am not proud of that, I was a coward then as well. Damn, I am sick and tired of being a coward." He paused as if to make a personal vow and then continued. "I remember one thing clearly, though. Yes, events in a person's life, stresses, can trigger the disease. But the real disease is built into your chemistry. Alcoholics process the drug differently. No need to get technical but have you ever thought why the Irish, Scandinavians, or Native American's have a greater propensity to become drunks?"

"Of course not, but you are becoming tedious."

"Just listen to me, Mother. For once, please just listen to me. The point is that some ethnic groups have a much longer exposure to booze, which emerged in the Mediterranean area. Those with the wrong chemistry were selected out, they tended to die early."

"What in god's name has this to do with me?"

"You are Irish for God's sake."

She reared up slightly. "And so are you."

"Only half, perhaps I take after Father."

"Believe me, Christopher, you have nothing in common with your Father, absolutely nothing. I thank God for that every day."

"So do I, Mother, so do I. Here is my point though. It is hell living with that man. Anyone would seek relief. But for you, it likely triggered the underlying chemical issue. I want to help."

"For heaven's sake, how? At long last, how?"

"Glad you asked. First, we must get you into a medical program, rebalance your chemistry. Then we have to get you away from him."

"From Charles?" She seemed genuinely shocked.

"Don't look so shocked. The man is toxic. You stay with him and change nothing, I guarantee you will be dead within two years."

"Again, with the dramatics."

"Listen to me. I am deadly serious. Get cleaned out and then leave the bastard. Come live with me, or Kat, or go back to your family. Anything but here."

"Christopher, he is my husband. I made a promise to God."

"Oh for Christ's sake."

"Don't blaspheme in my house. I am a Catholic. I take my religion seriously. I am not modern like you kids. I cannot betray him, he needs me. He sees that he is losing his children and that is killing him."

"What? He never thought about us. You did. He cares only about his twisted version of reality."

"My dear son, you are not being fair to—"

"My God, the man is a monster, a monster! He raped his own daughters!"

That just came out. How did it happen? A secret kept close for years now seems to infuse every conversation. He had lost his composure, felt desperate to reach her. He is more disciplined than that. What is it about parents that sucks the composure out of the adult, turns them into a clueless child no matter their age. He watched her reaction. For several moments she stood absent any alteration in stance or expression. It was as if she were repelling the words away. Then he noticed some subtle changes. Her nostrils flared, her eyes narrowed slightly, the set of her lips suggested a grim purpose. "You said daughters, you used the plural."

Chris softened. It was out there but there was no need for cruelty. "Yes, he preyed on both Kay and Kat." Mary slowly turned and found a seat. It was as if the effort to stay upright would have been beyond her. "You didn't know, I thought you must have known. Well, the truth be known I only found out, but I guess I thought a mother would know."

Again, there was a long pause. Chris decided to wait, let her absorb what he had said. She took a drink from the cup next to her. Now Chris grimaced. He came to save his mother from self-destruction and perhaps all he was doing is driving her deeper into despair. Then she spoke, so softly at first that he had to strain to understand the words. "I knew about Kristen.

I knew about her. I could see something was wrong, in high school. She had changed, was less enthused about life. Even I noticed. Christopher, I was a terrible mother and yet even I noticed."

"Mother, for God's sake, don't beat yourself up. I didn't see it and I had been very close to her growing up. You want guilt, how do you think I feel? How could I have been so blind?" Chris walked over to the window and looked out over the city.

"Son, you were spending more time on sports and with your colored friends." Chris looked over at her sharply and she understood. She stood and walked to be next to him, intertwining her arm in his for support. "I should say your black friends. You need to forgive me. I come from a different generation, a different world. I never knew a col—black person until you brought that Ricky and that lovely girl."

"Julianna."

"Yes, lovely name, lovely girl. I see her on television now."

Chris wanted to go back his sisters. "You didn't know about Kat, did you?"

She held his arm even tighter, leaned her head against his shoulder. She seemed much older than her years, fragile beyond description. Chris wondered if a vaunted Chicago wind might blow her away. "No, I didn't know." She took a deep breath. "When I dug the truth out of Kristen I went to him. He denied it, of course. He told me that his daughter simply was a liar. I knew that was bullshit." Chris startled at her use of colorful language. "Your twin is an extraordinary woman, she was a wonderful girl. She would not lie about something that important. I finally confronted him, told him that I could not forgive such a sin, that he would never lay with me again. Eventually, he admitted it and gave me all kinds of promises that it would never happen again. He promised me. And I believed him. How foolish of me."

"Mother, don't be hard on yourself."

"No, I didn't protect my own daughters. What am I here for if not to protect my own children?" She sobbed softly and Chris wrapped his arm around her.

"What kind of brother am I? I could not save my own sisters. Worse, I ran away. Oh, I had good excuses but, at the end of the day, that is exactly what I did."

Mary suddenly spoke up with added strength, "We all should have stood up to him. He is a monster, a—"

"Sociopath," Chris filled in the word for which she searched. "He is a man who cannot think of anything beyond himself. He is without empathy, compassion, any human sensibility. He is the perfect conservative."

"No, Christopher, my father was conservative. My father, however, had honor. Your father is merely evil. He and his friends talk in front of me. They think I share their views. But they appall me, disgust me. You, my son, would be outraged. I am outraged. They all agree that they deserve whatever they have and that they should have more. There is no limit to their greed. But that is an old vice, obsessive greed. This crowd wants to create a society that tilts the rules fully in their favor. They don't want others to have a chance in life. It is even worse than that. They fear that they are losing control, that there are too many minorities, too many of *those* people. They can see that white, native-born voters will be a minority soon."

"But Father wasn't born here."

"No matter, he has no memory of anything else. He sees himself as one of the native-born elite, one of those destined to lead. They have spent hours here talking about how they will change things to ensure that they always run things forever. Most things you know. But they talk about things that really scare me, like somehow manipulating voting machines and rounding up the people they don't like and deporting them or planting false stories about anyone that stands in their way. They will do anything to stay in control, anything. They see themselves as waging some holy war against people they do not see as their equals. Christopher, these people your father works with despise democracy. They see most people as not worth having a say in the future of this country. And he sees no one strong enough to get in their way. He believes that the average American is simply too stupid to see what they are doing. He sees the political opposition as weak, concerned about things like fairness and justice. You were right, son, your father is a Nazi, his friends are no better than Hitler's henchmen."

"I fear we are right about him and what they will do," Chris said with a weary sadness.

"Christopher, do you know why I believe you are wrong, why he will fail when all is said and done?"

"Why, Mother?"

"Because of you and Kristen and now Katerina. He tried to capture your souls. In the end, he failed. I thought he might succeed with Charles Jr. He was such a sensitive boy but so weak. But Charles found a way to escape. It was not pretty but I understand. He had no choice. I think he felt that was the only way to get the rest of us to stand up and do the right thing. He could not say no to Father and he could not be what was demanded of him. In the end, he had too much integrity, too much kindness. I should have intervened. Just as with the girls, I should have seen. I should have responded. When Junior passed, when he passed . . . I was glad. He had finally found an escape . . . peace."

"I am not letting you go there. We all should have seen. This guilt is on all of us."

Then she became animated. "The point is, dear boy, that none of you turned out to be him. In one way or another, maybe at different times in life, you all rebelled. Think about that. He dreamed of you taking up his mantle, leading the revolution to which he was committed. In his twisted mind, life was a struggle to the end. Either the forces of light would win, or we would face Armageddon. Civilization, the kind worth saving, would be over. That, you figured out at some point, was an evil vision that repelled you. What you cannot appreciate was his obsessive devotion to bringing you and Charles on board even as you pulled away. The girls were not so important until later. But he saw the two of you, the male offspring, as the natural inheritors of the family mission. He would stay up talking about it. After a few years we had little to talk about. He and I were very different. He knew it. I was conservative, loved my faith and my church, but I was not what he was. He had a meanness that could not be quenched. What man could support policies that impover-

ish and exploit millions and somehow believe it is the moral
thing to do? I cannot fathom that. When that became apparent
to him, he no longer shared his dreams with me though I still
heard them often enough when he plotted with his close companions. It was foolish of him to let me hear but his arrogance
knew no bounds. I was no better than room furniture to him.
You should have been there when they would get together at
Vail or some private Caribbean island. The food and wines were
sumptuous beyond imagination. Then they would sit around
and complain how labor costs were destroying America. I swear
they would have brought back slavery if they could. I would listen to them, there were many sessions to which I and the other
wives were not permitted to attend. But I heard enough, enough
to be disgusted."

"I had no idea, Mother. I thought—"

"Yes, I know. You thought I agreed with him, the way I
stayed silent and seemingly supportive. No, inside I was seething." She looked up at her son. "You must remember, I am Irish.
Yes, through politics and business my family accumulated great
wealth. We were the Kennedys without any offspring to reach
national office."

"Sorry about that."

"Hah, you think Father would have permitted you any success. He would have buried you. You were an apostate in his eyes.
My grandfather would tell me the stories of what it had been
like when they all arrived in this land. There were the 'no Irish
need apply' signs, the crowding into Irish ghettoes. When my
father made it to the University of Pennsylvania, an Ivy school,

he thought his brains and ambition would be rewarded. He was slighted and embarrassed every day. If you were from the wrong stock, no amount of success could wipe away the stain. You don't forget those things. You never forget those things. You hand them down to the next generation."

"It was you," Chris said with emphasis. "It was you. I vaguely recall you telling Kay and I stories when we were young. You told us about the Irish troubles, the need to be kind to others, to understand others not like you."

"Well, I cannot take so much credit. That is not humility talking. Yes, I did tell you stories, the ones I was told. At the time, I never knew if you were listening. The thing is . . . the thing is, I believe the good stuff was already inside you. I may have helped it along just a bit."

He grabbed her hands. "I have thought on these matters so any times. How did we escape? He buried us in propaganda from day one. Yet, Kay and I would snuggle under the covers and talk about how we were sure he was wrong, they were wrong. He had all those famous right-wing nut jobs at the house. Later, I realized some of them were household names in right-wing circles, if not the whole country. Now, maybe I am beginning to get it. Without getting sciency on you, we are beginning to know that the brains of conservatives and progressives are structured differently. The two groups are wired in distinct ways. Now I get it. We reflect you, not him. We process the world through your internal architecture. That is the only explanation. It just hit me, Mother, you really are a Democrat, you just didn't know it." He embraced her. She startled a bit, affection did not come naturally to her. But she relaxed, let the warmth of his embrace surround her for the moment. "Thank you."

There was a discrete knock on the door which then opened. It was Sylvia. "Madam, Mr. Crawford has arrived. I told him that Christopher is here. He would like to join both of you if that is convenient."

Mary glanced at Chris who remained immobile. After a moment's pause she nodded approval. Within moments Charles Sr. entered the room and surveyed the two before him. Now that the emotion of losing his eldest son and heir apparent had passed, Chris thought that his father looked himself again, a tall, handsome man with elegant posture and demeanor who reeked of confidence and power. This was a man, Chris thought, who was blessed with the certainty of his position in life, his world views, and the personal convictions that flowed from whom he was. That must be a blessed condition, Chris thought, never to question anything. He wondered if his father had ever stayed awake at night wrestling with doubt, agonizing over a decision, struggling to find the truth in some thicket of contradiction and conflicted evidence. It did not seem likely. Life's purpose and meaning had been handed to his father as a given. Then Chris smiled inside. That really does take the enjoyment out of things. It is much better to figure all this crap out by yourself. It is harder but so much more fun.

"Well, son, good of you to drop in to say hello." He walked briskly across the room to give his wife a perfunctory kiss. She pulled slightly away from him. Undaunted, he took Chris's hand which he found unresponsive to his grasp. "And how is your twin? I have not heard from her since she has run off to join your little adventure."

"She is fine. I worry about her but she is very happy."

"It is remarkable . . ." Then Charles seemed to stretch his lean six feet two frame in an effort match the height of his son. He relaxed his frame when he realized he could not quite do it. "Yes, it is remarkable what some will do to avoid their responsibilities."

"I would hardly say that risking your life to help those in dire need is avoiding anything."

"Yes, yes," he said distractedly. "And to what do we owe this rare pleasure?"

"Usual stuff, Father, visiting the foundations that support my work and raising money from rich people, some of whom you consider friends and others who loathe you."

Such comments always grated on his father. Charles Sr. knew that many who had lost out to him in the business wars loved to support the work of his despised son. It was a way to get back at the hated and feared business titan. "You see, my son, I help you out even without giving you a dime for your silly hobby."

"Remind me to thank you someday," Chris emitted the words with undisguised venom.

"Happy to help, son, even though you disappointed me so deeply."

"Charles, don't . . ." Mary said with plaintive hopelessness.

"Oh, Mary, I think Christopher is a big boy now. He can accept his failings. Surely, a little truth won't hurt him now."

"Truth, what would you know about truth?"

His father's voice was well modulated, smooth and oily, the voice of someone who was seldom ruffled and used to the parry and thrust of deadly verbal conflict. "I just returned from Washington, as you know. It is so, what is the word, comforting, that is it. It is so comforting finally to have an administration who understands. Yes, we have been through such a rough patch with that clown from Arkansas in the oval office. Now we have real men. Of course, the President is a little weak, not very bright as you know, but he has surrounded himself with good men, good men indeed. The Negroes are rather weak, Powell and Rice, but Cheney and Rumsfeld and Paul Wolfowitz get it. They have the big picture. I spent a lot of time with Paul this trip. Of course, I did see Dick but he is a busy man, but we still had enough time to see that he and I agree on all the basics. Fortunately, Paul and I had a lot of time to lay out what needs to be done." His father gave him his best disingenuous smile.

"Congratulations then, Father, good to hear that your campaign for world conquest is on schedule."

"Yes, I am sure you are being very sincere. Too bad, really. You would have been a great ally. I remember looking at you when you were just a young boy. Already I knew that Charles was not cut out for the job. He was always sensitive, took after your mother. No offense, dear."

"Charles, really." She made more sounds, but they turned out unintelligible.

"Medicating yourself early, dear," he said to her before turning back to his son as he continued to flash his unctuous smile.

"Yes, even then I knew what you could be. You were the strong one, or so I thought. But it was not to be. You lost your way and you dragged Kristen with you. She had promise but you worked on her when she was too young to know better. I didn't have the time. If I had the time I could have saved her. I knew that you were corrupting her. Thank god you never got to Katerina. She has surprised me. I will bet you never saw that coming. None of us did but she is proving to be a wonderful ally."

Everything within Chris wanted to wipe that smarmy smirk off his father's face, tell him that Kat hated him as much as the rest of his children. But that would not be wise. He and Kat had plans and tipping off his father was not part of their machinations. "Yes, Kat has proved a big disappointment. I take it your world revolution will start soon."

"Soon enough. We just need the right catalyst. How I wish you were with me, Christopher. I tried to educate you, get you to understand."

"Understand what, for Christ's sake."

"That life is a struggle." His smile was now gone to Chris's relief. "There are some who are, by their nature and breeding, destined to lead. That is how progress is made. It is survival of the fittest. Catering to the dredges of society only diminishes all of us to the lowest common denominator. You think that is cruel. It is not. It is merely nature. To thwart nature is to deny destiny. These are natural laws, my boy. What you are doing is merely extending the miserable lives of people who will never contribute a thing to progress. Inequality and hierarchy are the natural order of things. That is why they occur everywhere unless man intervenes, typically with futile gestures. To believe otherwise is to engage in fanciful thinking."

"Well, Father, consider me a fan of Peter Pan."

His father smiled in that ingratiating way. "You think you are so clever with your Princeton and Oxford educations. But you know, even the founding fathers of this country knew that democracy would not work. That is why they limited voting rights, created the electoral college, and had appointed senators and not elected ones. They knew that people could not be trusted with governing, that the elite had to maintain control. Otherwise, the garbage out there would ruin everything."

"Well." Chris looked at him steadily in the eyes. "I guess that I prefer the garbage out there to the garbage I am looking at right now."

His father's anger suddenly flashed. "You are such a damn failure, just a loser, you threw everything away. Do you know how much that outrages me, to see promise squandered? I hate waste."

"As Rhett Butler once said, 'I don't give a damn.' I may never amount to much but at least I will never stoop to raping my own daughters."

"Goddamn it," the patriarch exploded. "You are insane. I loathe the very sight of you. The problem is that you are just like your worthless mother. You are just like her, soft and useless. And when you cannot win, you make up this vile crap. Why am I cursed with such . . ."

Chris was amazed when his father seemed unable to complete sentences. He had reached him. He started again with,

"The truth hurts . . . you fucking raped your own daughters, my sisters. Just admit it. Man up, at long last, man up."

"You want some goddamn truth?" Charles exploded.

Then his mother took over. "Just stop it, Charles, stop it." Mary walked up to her husband who stood moot. "You just listen to me. For one moment, shut up and listen. I am going into an alcohol treatment program."

"What, where is this coming from?" Now Charles was off his game. He had not anticipated this. "Which program?"

"Whichever program Christopher chooses."

"I should have known." Charles whirled to look at his son, his face flushed with anger.

"There is more, Charles. When I get sober, I am not coming back to you. I am leaving you."

"Don't be absurd. You can't survive without me." Charles sneered.

"No, you have that all wrong," Mary said with total control and dignity. "I cannot survive as long as I am with you."

Charles looked at her blankly. It was as if he was trying to make sense of a world that could not possibly exist. Then his hand shot out to slap his wife across the face. She shrieked and swung around but managed to stay upright. "Don't be a fool," he said but the words were uncertain.

Reality finally caught up to Chris. He wondered how often this had happened in the past. Three people looked at one another dumbly until Chris made his decision. His fist flew out and struck his father across the cheek. It was not a full blow but one strong enough to crumple the man to his knees. Then, the son stood over the father. "That was a love tap, you son-of-a-bitch. If you ever do that again to her, ever, I will beat you to a bloody pulp."

Charles Sr. struggled to his feet. A tiny trickle of blood seeped from his nose. "Never come back here again." With that, he turned and left the room.

"Will you be all right?" Chris asked his mother.

"I will be fine. He won't be back."

"Were you serious about getting sober and leaving him?"

"Yes, son, I have never been more serious about anything in my life." Mary looked at her son with conviction.

"Listen, I haven't asked her but would you mind if Julianna gets in touch with you, helps you out. I want Father to think that Kat is still his faithful ally."

"Kat, my God, I should call her and apologize for not seeing things." Mary's eyes moistened again.

"No, stay strong. Focus totally on getting healthy. The time for repairing the family will come. First thing is to get you sober and strong. Then we can get the family together. Got it?"

"So," Chris asked again, "you okay with Jules helping you?"

"I think so. She was always such a lovely colored . . ." then she hesitated, "I mean a lovely person."

"Yes, Mother, work on that colored stuff, will you?" Chris managed a smile. "I am so proud of you."

———

Two days later, Chris was awoken from a deep sleep. It was Jules, he realized he was in her guest room. They both found that sleeping in the same bed was way too difficult. She was rousting him. "Hey, what are you doing? If you are after a morning quickie, no dice. I am not that kind of guy."

"Not to worry, your virtue is safe. But get up. Something is happening in New York."

"Something is always happening in New York. It is New York for crying out loud," Chris responded sleepily.

"How late were you out last night?"

"Early this morning." He looked up at her annoyed.

"You better not have been out screwing some broad last night while I am going without." Jules looked even more annoyed.

"No, no, strictly business, raising money. I have sworn off sex." Then he looked at her. "Good thing, too. You look very fetching this morning."

"Up Romeo, you blew your chance, no pun intended. Come on, they are flying planes into the World Trade Center."

"They . . . who?" Now Chris was awake.

"Don't know yet. Lots of loose talk but mostly confusion and mayhem. I have been on the phone with my people, I am supposed to be vacationing with you, remember? They have a semi hands on deck situation."

"Meaning?"

"I just have to stay close to the phone. If they can get me to New York, they will. Right now, though, flights heading in that direction are being shut down."

"Jesus."

"Chris, the guys at network said there is chatter that this guy Osama Bin Laden may be involved. This has his signature, multiple acts of terrorism. Isn't he hiding in Afghanistan, with the protection of the Taliban?"

"Shit."

"There is more. The head guy of the Northern Alliance was ambushed. He was asked to a meeting with the Taliban, presumably to work things out and then blown up by a suicide bomber."

"Fuck." Chris jumped out of bed naked and rumpled through his clothes for his phone.

It took him a while to get through to London amidst several additional expletives. Ricky and he spoke for an hour as they reviewed the situation in detail and his senior team there updated him on all the intelligence he was receiving from the region. It was now almost a certainty that Bin Laden was involved, the messianic leader of the Northern Alliance was dead, and that the area was in chaos. Toward the end of the discussion, Chris was a bit relieved. It was becoming clearer that this might be a blessing in the long run. Bush and his crowd loved war. Taking on a backward place to rout the Taliban would be an easy target in their opinion and boost his popularity which had always been soft. Never mind that the area was known as the "graveyard for empires" most recently the Soviets. It was the short term that worried both Ricky and Chris.

When Chris turned to Jules after his call she handed him some coffee and a pair of his underwear. "You are worried about my attire, what is with that? You are not dressed yet either." He pointed out the obvious to her.

"And you are not dressed at all and I certainly don't need to see your junk," she responded. "In case you are wondering, I am not going anywhere. It is official, I am trapped in Chicago. They said I might as well stay home today until things clear up. Looks like we take care of your mother today."

"Oh my god, I forgot."

"While you were enjoying yourself, I was busy yesterday. I found an opening in a great program that is also very discrete, they treat a lot of important people. We can get her in any time."

"Good, I will call her. Getting her away from Father is my top priority here. I don't want to give Father any time to work on her. Besides, that will be better than sitting around worrying about things I can't do anything about. Did you know that this Bin Laden character has been trying to bait America into attacking him in Afghanistan?"

"Can't say that I did," she responded.

"Yeah, he went into hiding there sometime after the Taliban took over in 1996. Apparently, he thinks if he can lure the Americans into a war they will suffer the same fate as the Soviets. He went after a couple of our embassies in Africa and the USS Cole for that very reason. With this crowd in power, they are certain to go after our number one terrorist threat, with or without evidence that he is responsible. Perhaps this is the catalyst Father referenced."

"What?" Jules was not following.

"Nothing, just letting my paranoia run wild."

She sat down next to him and wrapped an arm around his shoulders. She kissed him on the forehead saying, "Chris, there is nothing you can do today. Let us focus on first things first. Let us get her into a program. And after that, I will look after her, make sure she is okay. I promise."

"Jules . . ."

"You can say it, you're a big boy now." She knew what was on his mind.

"Thank you, for everything. I—"

"Oh, I should make you blabber on about what a saint I am. I won't, though. That is because I am a saint and so modest. Besides, I do like your mother even though she thinks I am a nice colored girl."

"Oh my god, she didn't say that yesterday."

Jules laughed. "No, we had a good talk. She even told me that you made her promise to be politically correct. I will take good care of her Chris, trust me. I always thought she was cold, distant, but I sensed a different woman yesterday. We might just get along. She only called me a nice colored girl twice."

Suddenly Chris felt all the old affection for his oldest, dearest female friend. He remembered how they had teased one another and shared things in high school. He had been drifting a bit from Kay then and sharing intimacies with his male friends simply was not done. The taunting would be merciless. Jules would listen. She sometimes teased but always knew when it was time to listen and even comfort. He walked closer to her, leaning into her to kiss her gently on the lips. Then he pulled back with great effort. "Better put some clothes on. I can't decide if I think of you more as a sexpot or a sister and I would hate to confess that I slept with my ersatz sister."

"Good plan," she agreed. "even you are looking good me right now."

His phone rang. "Karen, glad you caught me. What do you know?" Chris made no effort to move away so Jules could hear the voice on the other end.

"Everyone is safe," Karen was saying. "As you can imagine, no one can figure out what will happen. Already, there is talk that perhaps the Americans and Brits will get involved, go after Bin Laden and the Taliban. Very early to say, of course. This is bloody crazy. Chris, I am going there."

"Going where?" Somehow his mind had stopped working for the moment. "You're not going to quit me and go work as a barmaid at the Hairy Whore."

"What? Don't be daft and it is the Hairy Hare by the way. No, I am going to Afghanistan. Don't you dare say no, do you hear me. You don't win these fights so forget it, buddy. Besides, this is personal, just like it is for you. As they say, I got skin in this game."

"Yeah, I know. I won't even try."

"What?" Karen was clearly put off her game by the easy victory. "I hate it when you go off script."

"Listen, kiddo, Kay needs you now, I am sure. But more than that I want some ears on the ground I can trust. Kay and Amar would not recognize danger if it slapped them upside the face. Okay, they would see the threat but ignore it. Can you promise to be brutally honest with me about what you see?"

"Yes."

"Even if it means pissing off Kay."

"I promise, on my family."

"Wait, you hate your family."

"Not as much as you hate yours." She chuckled at her little joke.

"Only my father. We have a lot to talk about when we can, interesting stuff on this end. Tell Ricky I approve of your hair-brained scheme. And Karen . . ."

"What?"

"Be careful, I don't want to lose you. You're a pain in the ass but—"

"Yeah, I know. You love me. All the guys say that. You really don't have anything to worry about, the mean never croak young. Besides, that is why I have been put on earth, to make your life a living hell. And Chris . . ."

"Yeah."

"That work has just begun."

CHAPTER 10

NORTHEAST AFGHANISTAN (FALL OF 2001)

There was a sound, irritating and persistent. Various alternatives passed through his mind, a fire alarm or that grating end of class alarm from high school or even the damn alarm clock. He considered the possibilities and determined it was none of these. It was his phone. He hated calls in the night. It was never good news. He checked the other side of the bed. It was empty. It was always empty these days.

"Yeah."

"Chris, thank god I have reached you. It's Karen."

Chris's heart leaped up to his throat. "What's wrong?"

"I am not sure. So much is happening here. Pamir's son, Majeed, was wounded. He is in bad shape. Azita and the whole family are distraught."

"Damn." Chris expelled.

"The fighting has picked up here. The military guys of the Alliance, I am using their communication system to reach you in fact, tell me that things are kind of screwed up. You know that the guy who was holding things together was killed the day before the towers were hit. You know his name?"

"Sorry, they all sound the same to me." Chris knew that was racist.

"Ahmad Shah Massoud. He was known as the Lion of Pan-jshir."

"Massoud? Wait, is Pamir and his family related to him?"

"Could be. It is a common enough name in that area but there might be a connection. Not sure the spelling is the same, but I should ask him. If the Taliban believe it so, you can put a big target on his family."

"Shit, don't let him or his family stray from the camp."

"I think he is aware. In any case, the Taliban are fired up. They smell weakness and confusion here. They are also panicky."

"Of what?" Chris asked though he thought he knew the answer.

"Well, on the one hand, getting the so-called Lion of the Alliance has jacked up the local Taliban. He was the glue holding the local warlords together. At the same time, pulling off the America attacks got the whack jobs all excited again with this jihad thing. Allah has blessed them, time to spark a wider war to punish the infidels. You get the picture. On the other hand, there is a lot of chatter that the West will invade any day now."

"I know. Tony Blair is on the tube all the time now making noises about standing with Britain's allies in the fight against global terrorism." Chris knew that emotions were running high on all sides.

Karen picked up the narrative, "Apparently, this is what Osama wanted all along and he just might get it. On the other hand, you should always be careful about getting your wish. No matter, they are psyched about killing Americans. And guess who the only Americans in the neighborhood here are."

"Fuck."

"You are eloquent this morning. One more thing. They have some prisoners here. They say that the local Taliban crazies are after two targets we care about. They want Pamir Masoud because he lied to the authorities in Kabul to escape to the other side. Maybe they just assume there is a connection with the dead leader. And get this, they are after Azita because she is a Muslim girl who is encouraging education of other girls, among other sins. Apparently, she has gained some notoriety, not a good thing with these crazies running loose. In addition, they are not too happy about what they term the foreign female devils. They would rather their people die than be treated by a woman . . . the bastards. You can guess who they are talking about. Kay and Amar are the female devils on their list. A British medical and intelligence team has arrived, more coming soon. So, I think we are safe here but with suicide bombers and the general uncertainty . . ."

"Shit. I am on my way."

———

Chris was exhausted. He spared no effort or expense getting to the Afghan camp. He was out of contact much of the time in route and worried constantly. What would he find when and if he got there? The drumbeat of war was in the air as Bush, along with some help from several allies, promised to push the Taliban from power as punishment for their abetting international terrorism. What did that mean, however? He could not shake memories of how badly the Soviets were beaten. Of all the countries in that troubled area, Afghanistan had proved the most resilient to conquest in the face of foreign incursions. There was the infamous nineteenth century incident where a British army attempted to retreat from Kabul back to the Indian subcontinent through the Kyber pass. Only one survivor made it, a doctor. Seldom had the empire faced such an embarrassing and total defeat. The Afghans might lose battles on occasion, but these fierce warriors seldom lost the war.

Now he slumped into a chair and looked over the faces opposite him. Karen and Kay were there along with two uniformed men he did not recognize. Karen started by introducing the unfamiliar men. "This is Captain James Whitehead. He heads the Brit medical team that just arrived and Major Salim Gupta, who commands a small security team to protect the medical and intelligence teams they continue to bring in."

Chris was relieved. For some reason, he was surprised at the major's ethnicity. That was silly, he concluded quickly. The British Empire had reached around the world. At one point, the sun truly never set on it. "Thank god you are here. I have been frantic with worry about my sister and . . . my staff."

"Yes," said the major. "Hopefully the Taliban will not make a final push before our operations are fully operational. We know they are infiltrating the area, desperate to create mayhem. They want to inflict as much pain before the coming air attacks are fully engaged. They may well feel their time is running out. Unfortunately, we are only a few, just an advanced unit to prepare for a more complete contingent. Our situation could be better." Though obviously Indian by background and, given his first name, possibly Muslim by faith, he employed the clipped expressions of a British educated soldier. He had little of the more singsong cadences of a native from the subcontinent. The way he expressed himself employed classic British understatement.

"Still, my thanks for your presence. What is the situation? Where are Doctors Singh and Masoud?"

Karen spoke up, "The thing is, Majeed passed away. His wounds were too severe. Perhaps if we could have gotten him to India, to better medical facilities. Even that would have been a stretch, he was touch and go from the beginning."

"I am sorry, how is the family?"

"Devastated," it was Kay who chimed in. "They insisted on bringing his body back to their village. We tried to stop them. Things are very uncertain now, at best the Taliban will strike back in the face of American threats, allied threats. But they insisted. They convinced us they would be safe among family. I am not so sure about that but what could we do? We could not arrest them."

"Wait, Amar didn't go with them. Isn't she a target, aren't you all targets, including Azita? I swear, if she—"

"Calm down, boss. Amar is over at the medical ward, working with one of Captain Whitehead's physicians. Business has picked up since 9/11. I don't know what we would do if the Brits had not arrived. Anyways, we put your stuff in the guest room which you will be sharing with the helicopter pilot who got you here." She looked at him with a meaning that told him not to say anything that might embarrass her. "You can catch up with her in the morning."

"Yes, of course," Chris said forcing himself to not convey any disappointment. Inside, though, he was confused and bitterly disappointed. He ached to see Amar again, to be with her.

Karen picked up before Chris could say anything more, "Here is what concerns us. We have not heard anything recently from the Masoud family. He promised to keep us informed. Frankly, we are worried."

Chris forced himself not to focus on Amar. "Okay, okay. I need to get to that village, the place where they entertained us when I was here last, right?" He did not wait for an answer. "In the morning, I am taking the chopper in there. I just need, what, a guide or some security."

"I can go with you," it was Karen.

"No. This time, finally, I am saying no. You can tear my balls off and I am not budging. You got that. I am feeling enough guilt about all this."

The two military men looked at one another with surprise. This was not the usual decorum. "Mr. Crawford, we are not sure how much help we can be tomorrow, we need our craft to continue supplying the base. We want to help, your organization's work here is helping us immensely, paving the way as one would say. We look forward to working together on the medical issues. Militarily, I cannot go into detail, but we are essentially an intelligence arm to help with the coming air strikes. In any case, we are grateful you and your team are here. Perhaps in a few days .

. . now, if we knew your people were in immediate danger, that would be different."

Chris raised a hand. "Do not concern yourself. I have my own transportation, the chopper that brought me in. Listen, everyone, lets convene as a group at nine in the morning. Would that be all right? I want to chat privately with my sister now, personal issues."

Everyone agreed. There was a consensus that additional logistical issues needed to be discussed between the new British teams and Chris's people. It was good that Chris was there to make immediate decisions. The morning would be fine. After everyone else had left, Chris and Kay looked at one another. Neither said anything.

"Walk with me," Kay broke the awkward silence. "It is lovely at the end of the day this time of year.

They found a bench away from any human activity and sat where they could look over the day's expiration. Darker orange and purple hues were descending over the surrounding mountains. At that moment, there was a hushed silence about them. Chris almost felt as if he were in a church. "Let me start with Amar. Is she avoiding me?"

Kay assumed a semi-disdainful smile. "My, my, we are full of ourselves, are we not? Not everything is about you, my dear."

"Don't patronize me," he snapped and then regretted it immediately. "It is just that I have been shot down by enough women to pick up on the signs."

Kay did not let him continue. "Let me cut to the chase here. Why do you care so much? I understand the Brits will bring in a few nurses. I am sure you can exercise your considerable charms on one of them for company."

Chris popped up and walked a few feet away. He was angry but not sure at whom, Kay or himself. "Okay, okay, I deserve that. I am a shit when it comes to women."

"Good, acceptance is the first step to recovery. Maybe we can get you into a program for sexual addicts . . ."

"Stop it, goddamn it, just stop it. Don't you see, I love her."

His words hung in the air. It was as if he had spoken them in some unintelligible tongue. Kay finally came back in a small voice. "What did you say?"

"I am in love with her. I told Jules. She and I didn't sleep together when I was in Chicago." Kay arose and came around so that she could look in his eyes. "I love her, goddamn it," he repeated.

Kay did not say anything at first. She looked at the pain that controlled his face. Finally, she smiled just a bit. "Sucks, doesn't it? Wow, I never thought you would get the disease. How is Jules with this?"

"Jules is good with it, at least I think so. We agreed about our love for one another but also that we never were in love, if that makes sense. She got that before I did. Oh my god," he let out a big sigh, "it sucks the big one. I never knew."

"It makes perfect sense. I get it." she murmured. "Well, finally, some karma in the world."

"Kay, do you think some of the women I—"

"That you screwed."

"Okay, did some of them feel like this toward me? Did I cause this kind of pain?"

"Are you really that dense?" Kay seemed incredulous. "Of course some of them did. That is what women do, fall for bad boys. But here is the more important issue, have you told Amar how you feel, does she know anything?"

"No, I suppose not."

"This is not quantum physics, you know, this is not Schrödinger's box. You did, or you did not." He was exasperating her.

Chris tried hard to recall the physics thought experiment she referenced. "I have not. It is harder than I thought. I am scared."

"I thought as much. She would have shared that with me." Kay grabbed her brother by the shoulders. "It is easy. Look, here is a newsbreak. Despite the fact you are a colossal shit, I love you. And the thing is, I am serious about that. I will never admit what I am about to say in front of witnesses but . . . you are a very special guy, rather one of a kind."

"Really?"

"Just shush and listen. The important thing is that I have come to love Amar as a sister. You don't spend time in hell with someone and not develop a deep bond. She is about the sweetest woman I know. Screw this up and you will be the sorriest sack of shit on the planet, in part because I will pick up where Karen leaves off in separating your balls from your body. Do you understand me?" She paused. When nothing came from him, she repeated more forcefully, "Do you understand me" She gave him a shake.

"I got it. Really, I got it." Then he pulled his sister to him. She resisted slightly but quickly accepted his embrace. "Thank you," he whispered.

"For what?" she asked, clearly puzzled as she rested her head on his shoulder.

"For saying that you loved me. I hope it is true."

She did not respond at first, just hugged him more deeply. Finally, she released him. "Yeah, it is true. There really is no accounting for taste. Tell me, you emailed that you wanted to fill me in on the home front the next time we were together. What is up?"

"You want the highlights first?"

"Sure," she responded.

"Here goes. Mother is in an alcohol treatment program. In fact, she should be finishing up the in-house portion of the treatment just about now. When she does get out, she is not going back to Father. Get this, she will move in with Jules. Your first question is why not with Kat. Excellent question. The answer is that Kat must maintain the fiction that she is on Father's side."

"Wait, the fiction."

"Right, she has changed, blossomed. You would not believe how she has changed. That shy, uncertain girl we remember has been replaced by a motivated, competent businesswoman. Suddenly she exudes confidence. The butterfly has emerged from the cocoon. She knows what she wants. Most importantly, she hates that bastard as much as we do."

"I still am not sure I understand. What happened?"

"For one thing, being on the inside, she sees just how corrupt and evil he is. She has seen the cycle firsthand. The more wealth that accumulates at the top, the more they spend on manipulating the levers of power to tilt things in their favor. Then they keep reinvesting the gains to gather more control. It is self-reinforcing. Who knows if it can be stopped now but you must start somewhere. But there is another thing, more important I suspect, your thing."

"I don't understand. My thing?" She wrinkled her brow.

"Kay, he raped Kat as well. When you got too old and could fight back he moved on to Kat."

"My god." Her face went blank. "I worried about that. I warned him. I wanted to warn her. I didn't. I couldn't admit it to her. Damn, that was so foolish. Why did I believe his promises?"

"Don't beat yourself up, so did Mother. She knew about you but failed to protect Kat, or so she believes. He had promised her he would never but, of course, he did. He is the guy who really believes the sun rises and sets over his navel. It is only now that Kat feels strong enough to talk about it. I think that was the final straw for Mother. Not even her Catholicism could assuage her rage."

"Anyways, the reason Kat has to keep on Father's side is that she plans on taking him down. She cannot afford to raise any suspicion in him until all is in place."

"Wait, take him down, you mean kill him? Jesus, I hope not."

"No, do a hostile takeover of the family business. Kay, we can do it. If we all pool our shares—Mother, Kat, you, and I we can get within striking distance. Kat is collecting some proxies and when I get the chance I will hit up some major shareholders who support my work. They like me if you can believe that. Either that or they are buying insurance in case there really is a heaven and hell. We can push him out as chair, clean up the place, and most importantly, stop him from using the business as an ATM for his hard-right causes. We can't stop the overall flow, too many sources, but at least our family won't be a major contributor to those Nazi assholes. There are outside shareholders that would support us just for that reason. They aren't necessarily liberals, but some are and some hate to see revenue wasted on any cause."

"I'm in," Kay said and then looked toward the mountains. They were becoming indistinct against a darkening sky. A pale moon had poked its presence over the western hills, a field of stars was beginning to emerge. "I never knew about Kat. Shit, how could I have been so blind."

"Don't beat yourself up, Kay, none of us talked. We can all agree now that we were not the Brady bunch. But you know what? We are getting there. Finally, we are becoming a family. By the way, you would have been proud of me."

She tried to smile at him. "I certainly doubt that but try me."

"I decked Father. He slapped Mother in front of me. I suspect he has been doing that for years. This time, he made the mistake of letting me see him do it. Boom, down he went. Wow, it felt good. I loved it. Of course, I am now banished from the kingdom for eternity as if I give a shit about that."

Now Kay hugged him again. "Chris, there is something I have wanted to say for a long time. I know I pulled away from you when we were in high school. You don't think very clearly at that age. I was in a blind rage. I am not sure I knew what to do with it. I wasn't strong enough to fight back, I was too guilty to tell anyone. You have no idea how many times I came to you, the words on my lips and just could not do it. When you drifted away physically, I went ballistic inside. I kept my loathing to low simmer, but I did entertain some evil thoughts about you. With all that I still could not get it out, could not tell anyone, not even you."

"Why not?"

"I don't know, I really don't. Now it seems silly, then it seemed impossible. Of course, that did not stop me from hating you when you never figured things out. I hate that, so typically female, right? We expect men to figure out stuff inside us that we won't reveal. Then we blame the guy for being a dunce. Well, you have heard me on that score before, no need to beat the horse again."

"Kay, it is okay."

"Fuck no," she burst out with real venom. "It is not okay. Can you forgive me? I want you to forgive me, if you can."

Chris wiped a tear that was slowly coursing its way down her cheek. "Kay, I am just as guilty. I felt you pulling away. Maybe I should have guessed but I suspect the truth was beyond my imagining. My real sin, I didn't ask, didn't insist you tell me what was going on. I wasn't confident enough. I thought you didn't like me because I just wasn't likeable, that you were better than me."

"You? Insecure? No way. I thought you felt the world revolved around you."

Chris laughed. "Maybe that was how it looked from the outside. Inside, so different."

"How about this?" she said as she ran her hand through his hair. "Can we be a family again? At long last, can we be a family?"

Chris held her as the darkness became complete.

———

The next morning, just as the faintest hint of light appeared behind the eastern mountains, Chris was up. He woke his pilot whispering, "It is time."

"Shit," came back from the semidarkness. "It is still the fucking middle of the night. You still want to do this?"

"Up and at 'em, I need to get out before my people are awake, they will go ballistic."

"That makes shit sense, they are your people. Don't you call the shots?"

"Are you married?"

"I was," the rough-looking middle-aged man said, "twice."

"Then you should know, a guy never is the boss of women."

"Good fucking point," he smiled.

Chris grimaced at the man's continuous use of profanity. It must be part of the pastiche for swashbuckling soldiers of fortune, the hard-drinking guys who satisfy their type A personalities by taking risks to make a living. He would get his chance today. They would fly into the unknown. A half hour later they had packed the gear they thought they would need and made their way to the newly created British medical unit area.

Major Gupta greeted them. "So, Mr. Crawford, you insist on doing this. I cannot lend you any of my soldiers since we have no confirmed evidence of problems. I do have a couple of local warriors who will go with you. They know the area and will get you to where you want to go. Do you have a weapon?"

"No, I hate guns."

"Well, sir, I appreciate the sentiment. Still, I would be encouraging you to at least take this." He gave Chris an automatic pistol with several extra ammo cartridges. "I am sure your pilot knows how to use it."

One of the local men sat next to the pilot guiding him over the hills, all of which looked the same to Chris. It was not a long trip by chopper but long enough for Chris to question what he was doing. This was a hairbrained scheme to be sure. Maybe they were just fine. Communications were always iffy here. Maybe they would look at him as if he were crazy when he ascended from the sky, trying to be a hero. More likely they would ignore his requests, make that pleadings that they come back with him. Still, no matter what, he would do his best to take Azita back with him. He had to admit, she had gotten to him. Her quick wit and impish smile had reached his heart. It was more than that. She did have a vision of what she wanted from life. Chris had wandered a lot, mostly affirming the paths his father desperately rejected. Eventually, he found a place that was as far from his father's world as he could get. Azita, though, desperately wanted to heal and to educate. It was her passion. Chris felt this strange need to make that a reality for her. He smiled to himself. At least he had figured out why he was doing this.

"They say it is the next valley," his plot said.

They emerged through an opening in the mountains to reveal below a long string of buildings stretched out along the valley floor. It surprised Chris. It was a decent-sized community. They found a place to put the craft down. Sand blew up around them as they landed. When they stepped out and the dust settled, Chris was surprised that no one was there. He thought curiosity would have attracted a crowd. After what seemed an eternity, two men slowly emerged from a nearby building. They engaged in a rapid conversation with Chris's two bodyguards.

One of the bodyguards turned to Chris. "You come. Not good."

"What is wrong?" But he soon realized he may be tapping the limits of the man's command of English. Soon they were in a building filled with men that Chris took to be the elders. He thought he recognized a couple of them from a brief visit he had made with Pamir earlier, at least vaguely.

"Yes," one of the vaguely familiar men said, "you visited with the good doctor. You are welcome but the news is not good."

"Oh? I have come after the doctor and his family. We are concerned about their safety." No one spoke for a moment. "Oh no, I am too late."

The elderly man looked worn even beyond his actual years. Chris wondered what tragedies he had witnessed during his life.

"I am sorry, Mr. Chris. I am so sorry. The doctor and his wife are dead. The Taliban came during the night."

Chris felt weak, dizzy. Where was he? What was this place? Why did he care so much? He did, though. "The girls, the daughters. What about them?"

"They are gone. They escaped, we hope. Maybe they are captured. Maybe they are dead and the Taliban took the bodies. We do not know. Sit."

The elder told them all he knew, the sudden screams and the shots, the confusion in the night. The Taliban had been making these raids among villagers. They had grown bold since the towers had been felled. The name of Bin Ladin was being raised as a renewed call for jihad. Actual and would-be Taliban were heeding the call before the infidels arrived in big numbers. Then, who knew what would happen? Finally, they discussed where the girls might be. Where should he look. The elders told him to wait, that men from other villages would be coming. But Chris said he would not wait. In the end, the elder promised a few men and wished him well. There was a place, some caves, that might be a place the girls had gone if they were still alive. The elder had one final request. Get the helicopter out of there. It would be a magnet for the enemy. They will start shelling and further endanger the village.

Chris pulled his pilot aside. "Go back. Tell them what is going on here. Take the guy who guided us here so you don't get your ass lost. Then come back this afternoon, late. Maybe I can find them by then."

"Are you fucking nuts? What are these girls to you?"

"Just do it." The expression on Chris's face silenced the pilot from further argument.

A half our later, Chris and a small security force were off, seeking a place where many agreed the girls might flee if they had not been killed. Soon, they were winding their way up into the hills that framed the community and served as stepping stones to the ragged mountains beyond. How could anything live in this godforsaken place, he wondered. It all seemed like hard packed sand and rock that had thrust itself to the surface. Whatever moisture had blessed the area seemed long ago sucked away, leaving a parched crust of barren ugliness. Yet, he could see flocks in the distance seeking out food from the scrub brushes and grasses that clung to life in what appeared to Chris as an excellent substitute for the landscape he would expect to find on the moon. The stubbornness of life is extraordinary.

They came across a young teenager herding some goats. His security people paid the boy no attention. He assumed he was known to them. Otherwise, how does one separate friend from foe? How can you determine who will help and who will send you to a final reward? The boy, however, was taken with the tall, unfamiliar man. Before his departure, the village leaders had forced him to put on local attire which was ill fitting on his tall frame. Still, from a distance it might hide the fact that he had no business in this part of the world. Perhaps he would be mistaken for Bin Laden, who also was tall. That would be rich. In the meantime, the Taliban would dispatch any American they could find. Osama had commanded such. It was total jihad.

The tall, wealthy terrorist had never forgiven the Saudis for turning down his offer to rescue the Kuwaitis from Saddam Hussein's hordes. Rather, Saudi royalty had turned to the West for help with America the most visible of the foreign devils who, in his mind, had polluted sacred soil. He had burned with resentment ever since, ratcheting up his terrorist attacks. The morning of September 11 was the culmination of his efforts. Now the Americans would come to him and his warriors would strike them down in this graveyard of empires.

They were now well beyond visual contact with the community. Chris suddenly felt alone and vulnerable. He did not know these men who were to guide and protect him. He had been told they would guide him to these caves that would have been a likely destination for the girls looking for immediate shelter. There were no guarantees though. Right now, they could be dead, captured, or being raped repeatedly before being dispatched to the next life. Mullah Omar, the one-eyed fanatic who led the Taliban, had turned his followers into sadistic killers. Azita would face a particularly cruel fate, she had offended Allah and the Prophet in their eyes. Chris's eyes searched each rock, outcropping, and crevice in the rugged terrain. Danger lurked with each step. He knew it was not his imagination, the men with him, veterans of much conflict were also uneasy. Evil had penetrated their world.

In early afternoon, they reached the caves. Chris was glad, he was winded, his soft life was catching up with him. The men around him looked as fresh as they had at the start. He would have to get back to the gym more often, if he got another chance that is. "Azita," he called out. "Deena." Nothing came back. He retrieved a flashlight and looked through each cave in the complex. Nothing. Chris was crushed, he could not believe how desperate he felt. He thought to himself, *If I ever have a child, I want her to be half as good as Azita.* He sat at the entrance to the cave while the other men ate. They brought him some food, he merely turned them away. He couldn't. His heart was too heavy, he could barely breathe. The woman he loved seemed to be rejecting him, the young girl who had captured his heart was likely lost forever, and her beautiful parents had been slaughtered without mercy.

He needed to move. He walked a few feet away to relieve himself. Then he decided to ascend to a higher point. The others would be angry at him for separating himself from the group. He must satisfy his curiosity, though. Maybe he could see something, anything. He came to a point above the caves from where he could look around. Nothing. He was about to descend when he heard a small sound. It sounded like a voice. It came from near a rock outcropping to his left. His heart stopped. He was a dead man, he was sure. What an idiot. Karen and Kay would spit on his dead body for his idiocy. As he fumbled for his pistol, a head popped up. "Mr. Chris?"

Chris stared at the image, disbelieving. "Azita?"

The girl rushed into his arms, crying hysterically. He got one word out "where . . ." when another head popped from around the rock. He could see another familiar face, Deena.

Chris brought the girls to the men who were shocked and happy. Deena began to chat rapidly in Pashto. The men nodded and looked gravely at one another. Azita translated for Chris. "She is telling them that the Taliban are in the area. We saw them coming and left the cave just in time. Eventually they left but it is not safe here."

Then she looked at Chris. "My parents, my brother, they are all gone." Her eyes brimmed with tears. Chris surmised she had few left to shed.

"Azita, let us get out of here. I want to take you and your sister away from here." Even in his own mind, he was not sure what the word "here" meant. "Tell them that we need to get moving. We simply have to take a chance."

They slowly started back in the direction they came. Each time a small rock was dislodged, or someone slipped in the hard sand, they stopped, scanning the terrain for any kind of movement. The tension was palpable, for Chris it was unbearable. Still, their journey back was uneventful. Chris was beginning to relax a bit. Perhaps they would be safe. His inattention resulted in his getting separated from the group. They had turned around a bend in front of him, were out of his sight. The path down was steep and the others were more experienced and adept with the terrain.

Suddenly, he sensed menace. At first, he thought his imagination was getting the best of him. No, the danger was real. Looking up he noticed a half-dozen men above him to his right, all waiving Kalashnikov rifles in his direction. Chris froze. Should he yell, run, plead, go for his gun. Against the Soviet made automatic rifles, his pistol seemed inadequate at best, more like useless. Perhaps he should pray. What was the perfect act of contrition his mother had taught him as a child? There was no way he would recall it now. He remained frozen in indecision as a small figure ran around the high ground blocking his forward view. It was Azita. His heart stopped. She was sacrificing herself for him.

"Get behind me," he barked at her. In response, she only looked at him with a bemused smile. What is wrong with her? She continued to ignore him. Instead, she grabbed his arm and started a rapid discussion with the men. He heard one of them say her name. This could not be good. The Taliban had targeted her, and they knew this was her. Suddenly though, the guns were lowered as the men smiled and then laughed. The remainder of Chris's group joined them and there was much praising of Allah and friendly banter.

"These are friends. Some of their daughters are in the school I started. They had come to search for Deena and me."

"I knew that," Chris said.

Azita only smiled at him. "And that is why you had this gun out. You know you would only shoot yourself." After a while this larger group reached a point where the terrain was less steep and the going a bit easier. Chris began to breathe easier. He still could not see the community but sensed it could not be that far away. Suddenly, the security men stopped, waving for everyone to get low.

"What is wrong?" Chris whispered to Deena.

"They are worried. Be careful. They have much experience." Her eyes were focused and intense. All was quiet, too quiet.

An ominous sense of impending doom settled over Chris. He strained to find something out there but nothing. "I don't see—" His words were cut short by the sound of a gun firing. The crack struck him as metallic and unreal until the surface of a nearby rock splattered apart. Chris froze until Azita grabbed his hand and pulled him to cover.

Now a firefight was in full force. Chris tried to raise his head to see what was happening. "No," Azita yelled. "I will die if I lose you as well." Chris laid back while looking at her, her eyes. Where there had been curiosity, there was fear. Where he usually saw laughter, there was anger. Where there had been excitement, there now was a form of despair. His heart broke.

Deena spoke, "Let the fighters do this. It is what they do. It is their life."

The air cracked with bullets, occasionally pierced with yells or even a cry. Slowly, the clatter of gunfire slowed. He would wonder if it was over but then a short burst would ensue. It was the not knowing that drove Chris to distraction. Were the good guys winning or losing? He had never felt so helpless in his life. Perhaps his dedication to pacifism had been misplaced. If these men who attacked them were to prevail, there was no dialoguing with them. His intellect and reason would be useless. His recognized charm would yield even less benefit.

They listened carefully. Nothing. Should they look? That seemed unwise. They stayed still while doing nothing. Suddenly a man jumped from the rocks above. He sprang to his feet and spun his gun in their direction. Chris had already reached for his pistol but could not find it. Damn, he was useless. The fierce man in front of them paused. Apparently, he wanted to enjoy the moment. Chris could see a smile form on his face, he would soon be favored by the Prophet, a hero for striking dead the hated infidels. Then, his demeanor changed, confusion and shock. From the corner of his eye, Chris noticed a quick movement and a pistol shot. The man's face registered surprise, then disappointment. Two more shots rang out and the man crumpled to the ground. It did not seem real to Chris.

"Deena!" Azita gasped.

Chris looked at the older sister and saw she was holding his pistol, the residual smell of gunfire hung in the air.

"I had to," she said in English. "I pray that Allah forgive me. Here is your gun, you had dropped it."

"I am sure he does, forgive you that is." said Chris as he took the pistol from her shaking hand. "If it helps, I forgive you."

She gave him a wane smile. Now the sounds of battle resumed. This did not sound good to Chis. The firefight sounded like a large battle to him but what did he know of fighting. The two girls huddled into his arms. He could feel their heartbeats but perhaps what he was sensing were his own.

"Do you know how to pray?" Azita asked him.

"I can recall a prayer or two."

"Then do it," she commanded him.

To Chris's ears another sound emerged. It was not gunfire, but something rhythmic and steady. He almost had it, lost it, and then it hit him with total clarity. It was a helicopter. Had his pilot come for him? That would be foolish, they will tear up the craft and the foolish pilot as well. The craft flew over him and they waved frantically. It was not his, too big. Then it was gone, their hearts sank. But the noise returned though they could not see it from their vantage point. The air suddenly shattered with new sounds, louder and more ominous. Cheers went up from some men near them. They could not tell whether from friend or foe. Explosions rocked the area and the ground under them convulsed with anger.

Two men appeared while Chris struggled to raise his pistol. "Friends," Azita barked, grabbing his arm. The men waived them to follow and they all scrambled. The chopper was landing about fifty yards away, again providing a cover of dust. They sprinted for it aware that machine gunfire was coming from the open bay sending bullets over their heads. Their other protectors were also firing away at targets unseen by Chris. Never had fifty yards seemed so far away. With every step he took, he waited for whatever a bullet felt like. Mostly, though, he focused on the small hands in each of his, Deena on one side and Azita on the other. He was happy as he felt them next to him, desperate in his fear that one or both would suddenly fall away dead.

After what seemed an eternity, they reached the open bay. He was dimly aware of two men in British military gear firing over his head at unknown dangers behind them. Someone reached out and grabbed Deena, yanking her in. Chris picked up Azita and literally threw her into the craft. A flash of recognition struck him, it was Karen who caught her and pushed her down to safety. A soldier grabbed Chris and yanked him in. As he fell to the floor he became aware again that an occasional bullet whizzed about him, clanging on the inside of the craft.

For a moment he thought he saw Karen wince but he must have imagined it. She continued to hover over Azita as if to protect her. Someone screamed "go, go, go! Goddamn it, go." His next image was one of the soldiers firing away to cover their escape let go with a profanity. His thigh turned red.

The chopper rose slowly. They kept firing at men who now seemed to scatter into the higher rocks. On one hand, he was comforted by the fact that the good guys would be okay. On the other, he still felt pure terror. Chris kept saying "faster, faster" to himself. He shut his eyes, just hoping that the staccato roar of the overhead propeller would keep going. It did, and the other sounds of fighting faded and then ceased. Someone shouted, "Everyone okay?"

The wounded soldier grunted something about getting one but that it was not serious. Then Chris noticed Karen. Her eyes were wide and unfocused. "You all right, kiddo?"

"No, I don't think so." Then she fell over on her side in slow motion.

———

Medical personnel were waiting for the craft to land. The two wounded were loaded onto stretchers. Chris walked along with Karen holding her hand. They had placed an oxygen mask over her face, he could not communicate with her. She had lapsed into unconsciousness in any case. When he could go no further, he stood with tears flowing down his face. Then he stuffed his grief inside and turned to go back to the two girls. "Let's get you something to eat," he said to them and took each by the hand.

The girls ate their food in silence. After a few bites, they mostly just stared at it. To Chris, they looked as if they were in shock, as if they could not comprehend the last twelve hours. Finally, they stopped, sitting there in silence.

"Can you tell me what happened?" Chris asked quietly.

"They are dead," Deena said. It was as if there was nothing more to be said. Chris stared at them. What a cruel land, it was not simply the landscape that was harsh.

Chris tried again, "I am thinking that it might be better if you talk about it. Maybe not, but try, for me."

Another silence. Finally, Azita began in such a small voice that Chris found himself leaning forward. "It was just before morning. Deena was getting up to check on some chickens we had, get some eggs for breakfast. For some reason, I could not sleep. I got up to help. I don't know why. I don't recall ever doing that before. I think maybe I was feeling guilty. Deena did most of the chores, I am such a lazy girl." Azita looked at her sister as if to apologize. "I followed her out to the coop behind our home. I had never done it before," she repeated as if the fact was a revelation. "Just as we started checking to see if there were eggs, we heard something. Men, dressed in dark clothes were running toward our house."

Deena then spoke up, "I knew they were Taliban, coming after our father and . . . my sister. I grabbed her hand and told her we must run far away. Maybe we could have hidden in a neighbor's house but then they would have been killed for hiding us. We did not know how many there were of them, perhaps they had come for the whole village. The only thing I could think of was the caves. I knew where they were, I don't think Azita did. They would provide some shelter until we . . ."

"I cannot get the sounds out of my head," Azita said softly. "These men crashed down the door. Then the screams. I could tell it was my mother, my poor mother. What had she ever . . ." The girl buried her head in her hands.

"It makes no sense," Chris said. "It never does. Hate is blind."

Deena took her sister's hand. "We decided to stay in the cave for the day and try making our way back in the evening, when we could hide better in the shadows. Then we heard men coming."

"Was it my group?" Chris asked.

"No, I could hear some of their talk. They were Taliban, I just knew," Deena said firmly. "I decided we needed to get out of the cave, they probably knew about them if they were that close and would be sure to check. We scrambled farther up the mountain, just in time as it turned out. I don't know how long we waited and then I thought I heard something."

"I did too," Azita said. "I decided to look, hoping it would not be the last silly decision of my life. It was you. I could not believe my eyes."

"Good thing neither of you had my pistol, you might have shot me." Chris tried a smile.

"What?" Deena seemed confused.

Azita looked at her sister. "You shot the warrior who was going to kill us. You had Chris's gun and you shot him when he found us."

"I did?"

Azita then hugged Deena. "I love you. I used to think you were a useless, silly girl. But you saved me today. You kept your head. I was the useless one."

"You saved all of us, Deena. Thank you," Chris said quietly, with meaning.

"But I could not save Mother, Father . . ." Deena could barely get the words out as both girls finally dissolved into sobs. They needed to get their feelings out at last.

Chris looked on for a while, his own heart torn. He knelt next to them. "Girls, listen to me. I cannot bring your parents back but, if I can, I am not going to let anyone hurt you, ever." They threw their arms around his neck.

Azita spoke up, "Chris, you are a good man. We love you as we would a brother or a favorite uncle. But you must leave one day. And we will not be permitted to go with you, not by our extended family."

"Why? I can offer you so much."

"Don't you see? You are a single man and not a Muslim. They would never let us go with you, no matter what you could promise us. I had great dreams. Still I am older now. I can see the difference between wish and what is possible."

"No, really," Chris wanted to argue.

"Please don't, you should never make promises that cannot be met." Azita had set her face but her lips trembled.

A young woman approached them. She wore a military garb, Chris assumed she was with the British contingent. Things were changing rapidly around him. "Dr. Singh sent me over. She wants me to put the girls in her room. It is all set up. I can make sure they have a chance to clean up and we have some new clothes for them."

Reluctantly, the girls let go of Chris. "Just go with this nice lady now. I will be here when you awake."

As they left, Chris called out, "Karen, she works for me. Can you say anything?"

The woman smiled. "The worst is over we think. There is much damage and it will be a while yet. But it is beginning to look more encouraging." She started to leave and turned back. "By the way, your sister is a marvelous trauma surgeon, as good as Captain Whitehead whom I thought the best I had ever seen. They saved her, that is for sure. They work very well together, a natural team."

He started to walk to the medical center. The nurse was right, though. They would be working on Karen for a while. He turned back, showered, and lay down on his bed. He suddenly realized how exhausted he was. He only intended to rest his eyes but quickly drifted off into a deep sleep. His childhood nightmares overwhelmed him, fantastical images of being surrounded by danger which took several forms. The setting mutated from jungle to desert and back. The basic theme remained unchanged no matter the setting. Evil was all about him, getting closer and closer. The worst were the reptiles, crawling steadily toward him until there was no escape. His panic rose and rose until it overwhelmed him. As they nipped at his ankles and began to crawl up his legs, he willed himself into the air. He could levitate, it was miraculous. Still, could he keep himself aloft?

Death, something worse than death, was within reach of him if he failed, if he were to fall back to earth.

From far away, he heard a voice, "Hey, wake up."

He looked up, groggily. It was Amar. As soon as his brain engaged, he jumped up before realizing he was only wearing his shorts. "Oops," he said.

She realized he was embarrassed. "You don't really think I care, do you?"

"Of course not, not thinking."

"Listen, Chris. I probably should have let you sleep but I thought you might want to know. Karen will be fine though the recovery will be lengthy. The captain and your sister are finishing up. Don't try to see her tonight, maybe tomorrow."

He almost told her that he already knew but simply thanked her. "Amar, I . . . I wonder if . . ." Then he realized he did not know what to say next. He wanted to ask her to stay but that did not seem right.

"Chris, you probably know that I had the girls put in my room. I knew I would finish up first and didn't want them to be alone. I should go to them, just in case."

"Amar . . ." Again, he did not know where to go next. He felt like a teen boy with his first crush.

"Tomorrow." She walked a few steps toward the door but then hesitated. Turning, she looked at him. Her eyes were without emotion, flat. "Thank you for the girls. I am grateful, we are, that is."

"Amar . . ." he started one more time with no better success.

"Listen, Chris. I know what you are struggling with. You think I am no different than your other conquests. You are worried that I will get weepy and clingy. But you listen to me. I am a big girl, understand? I won't fold up into some emotional basket case. Your sister told me all about you before we slept together. I knew precisely who you were and how little our . . . connection would mean to you. So, no need to get all apologetic and make up crap to keep me happy. I get it. We will just go on as if it never happened. Do you understand?" He didn't respond. "Do you?" she repeated with some vigor.

"I get it, totally."

"Great," then her voice softened a bit. It had all sounded better in her head when she rehearsed her little talk than when it came out. She did look a bit relieved. "We're good then."

"We are, totally." As she turned to go again, he called out. "One quick question though, if I might."

"Of course, a quick one. I am worried about the girls."

"Just a yes, no query." He paused, longer than he wished. She stared at him absent expression. Then he forced the words out, "Will you marry me?"

"What?"

"Amar, I am asking you to become my wife."

"Please, that is a very bad joke and I am in no mood."

"I am serious," he said walking up to her.

"My god, you would do anything to get laid." The words were out. She regretted them, not because she did not mean them but because they suggested a lack of control on her part. "Sorry."

"Listen to me. Do you remember the first time we met? No matter. You were holding a baby that was dying. I walked up from behind and something told me not to interrupt. I just stood there, watching. You were singing a song to the child. That was it. One tear made a path down your cheek. I can see it now, in my mind's eye. I could have asked you that very moment but that seemed a little impetuous."

"A little impetuous, how about totally nuts? You cannot be serious!" She tried to look angry but knew it was not convincing. She was not at all certain how she was coming across. She could not decide how she wanted to come across.

In fact, Chris was afraid she was about to laugh in his face. He was not about to back down though. "Amar, I have never, ever, been more serious about anything in my life. I've told everyone else about my feelings for you, even Kay. I have . . . have burned all my other bridges. I am more serious than you ever could imagine."

"Wait, I am the last to know? Perhaps I should check to see if there is a full-page announcement in the *London Times.*" Before he could respond she raised a hand. "Nothing more now. I am exhausted. Let me think on this. Tomorrow." Then she was gone.

He collapsed back on the bed. *Good going putz, that was clever,* he thought to himself.

———

He drifted in and out of sleep. He could not get Karen and the girls out of his mind. What if Karen had died? What would he have said to her parents? He knew she had a troubled relationship with them but it was far better than his with his dad. She had merely drifted away from their cultural roots. There was still affection there. He had met her folks once when they visited. Chris could tell they were proud of what she had accomplished. She, in her own irreverent way, adored them even if they did struggle with her lifestyle. *Dear Mr. and Mrs. Fisher, I went off and got your daughter killed because I was a goddamn idiot. I promise not to kill any of your other children.* He was going to have to be more careful with her, be stronger to keep her out of harm's way. Then he laughed at such a thought. Who was he kidding. He would, though, call them as soon as she was out of harm's way for sure.

Azita drifted into his thoughts. She was such a treasure, strong and smart and full of promise. He realized that there was more to Deena as well. She did not shine intellectually as her younger sister did but was very smart in her own right. More importantly, she was good at heart and brave beyond measure. Chris knew she would sacrifice her life for her sister's even as she criticized her sibling for being a useless child. But what could he do for them? Was Azita right? Could he not take them away from this hell? What would they do without their parents, the avuncular Pamir and the strong but loving Madeena? How would they survive? What would happen to Azita's dreams?

Then Amar would float into his mind. What had happened to him? Had he lost his bearings? Was she right that he had lost his mind? At least, if she was going to turn him down, as it seemed, at least she was doing it for a sound reason—he was nuts. The truth is that they hardly knew one another. He had known Jules since they were teenagers. They were the closest of friends, knew each other's thoughts, each other's physical rhythms, each other's dreams and ambitions. Perhaps that was the problem, they knew one another too well, there was no mystery left. That was not it and he knew it.

Amar had something special. She touched something vulnerable in him. Aside from her undeniable beauty, there were these conflicting qualities that made her unique. How could he know his feelings toward her with such certainty? They had not been together enough. In the end, that did not matter. He just knew it to be true. He loved her, desperately. He was in love with her. The human heart truly was beyond empirical calculation or intellectual understanding.

His on and off reverie was interrupted by voices outside his window. What time was it? Early morning? Who could be out this time of night? For a moment, he panicked. The Taliban? Had they infiltrated the camp? But no, the voices were soft and intimate. The language was English. The voices were female. He lay there listening.

"Okay, we can talk here without waking Deena," it was Amar's voice. She must be with Azita. Chris just knew it.

Indeed, it was Azita's voice that responded. "Yes, the hurt was not so bad when it was daylight, when we were busy trying to escape, to stay alive. But now, just lying there in the dark, my mind could not escape what I saw last night, what I heard—my mother's screams. What she must have thought, feared. She did not know we had left the house. I am sure, in her last moments, that she believed we were all lost."

"Azita, if you believe in God, they will know. They know you are fine."

It was not clear Azita heard her, she went on, "And Papa, he had such dreams for me, our dreams. Now they cannot be. A man such as that, so loving and kind and caring. He should never lose his dreams, for himself or for me. Never. But maybe it is me. I don't want to lose my dreams and now they are gone. Without him, I will never be a doctor, never follow him. I won't be what he wanted me to achieve. He deserved to see our dream realized."

"Are you sure? Are you so certain that your dreams are lost?" Amar's voice was soft.

"I cannot see how—"

Amar cut in, "Listen to me. I think you are old enough to hear my story. I wanted to be a doctor as a young girl. I am not even sure where that came from since girls were not encouraged in that direction. There once was a female doctor in my home area, however. I had an opportunity to befriend her, she was nice to me for some reason. Perhaps, even at your age now, I followed her around like a puppy dog. Back then, the lower-class women hated going to male doctors, a matter of modesty. She was a saint to these women and would get out of her office to work among the people as often as she could. Maybe, as a girl, I thought this was a way to be a saint. If I could only be like her."

"You are a saint," Azita offered.

Amar laughed lightly. "I think not, Buddha would not agree. But like you, my dream never left me even as I saw the world for what it was. I was lucky enough to study in England, most fortunate. I was permitted to study for my first degree at Cambridge where I lived with my aunt and uncle. But I was expected to return to India after that and get married. My family was quite old fashioned even though things were changing in my country. I was determined to go on to medical school and they were just as determined that I would be a good Indian girl. In their mind I was getting old."

"What did you do?" Chris heard Azita's soft voice. They must be sitting near his window, he thought, their voices were so clear. He strained to recall if there was a bench there.

"I was as obnoxious as hell. For a good Indian girl, I was a terror. Eventually, they relented, just a little. I could go to medical school if I married this man they thought suitable. He was the son of a family friend. Unfortunately, he lived in Canada, far from everyone I knew."

"Did you love him?"

Amar laughed. "I hardly knew him. But there is something I must tell you. I was innocent but also foolish when young. I believed a boy in college who got me pregnant and then was not to be found. I was close to finishing. They let me stay and my uncle arranged an abortion. However, I had embarrassed the family. Some girls are killed for such sins, they call them honor killings. My family was not nearly so primitive, but I had disappointed them bitterly. I was such an innocent to believe a boy who said he loved me. After my mistake, they kept a close eye on me. I deserved their suspicions I suppose. My family was not taking any more chances with me, I was to be married or return home."

"So, you did it. You married a stranger?"

"Well, that should not be such a surprise to you, in your culture. Many arranged marriages turn out fine, probably no worse than love couplings. Still, it was a disaster in this case. He did not want to be married. He hated that I was so ambitious. He wanted to chase after girls all the time and did. I did get to go to medical school in Canada, in Toronto, but he made my life a hell. He would hit me on occasion when I did not do all my domestic chores in addition to my studies or did not meet all his sexual demands. I will be blunt, it was like being raped all the time. But I did it until I finished and got my degree. Then I divorced him."

"Your parents were okay with this?" the soft voice inquired.

"He helped a lot," Amar chuckled. "He seduced my younger sister. Not even they could forgive that and then she became the black sheep of the family. This was a blessing for me though I did feel bad for her. After that, they let me finish my medical residency abroad. I think they felt guilty. But my point is that you need to sacrifice to reach your dreams. It is never easy, not even for me and I had so many advantages."

"Not easy, you say? It is impossible." Azita still despaired.

"Look at me, young lady. You say that again and I will put you across my knee. Did your father ever spank you?"

"No."

"Well, I will." But Chris thought Amar did not sound convincing. "Just trust me, I will figure something out, all right?"

Azita was far from convinced. "I already told Mr. Chris that it is impossible. My relatives must agree. They will not give me to someone not married and who is not a Muslim. They believe I must be a good Muslim girl."

"Chris?" Amar was surprised.

"Yes, he wanted to take me, and Deena."

"Chris, really? I didn't think . . ." Then Amar stopped, obviously confused.

"I think you should marry him," Azita said with enthusiasm.

"You are getting much closer to that spanking, young lady." The humor in her voice was obvious and Chris could hear Azita's laughter.

"No, you like each other. I know. I could see it when the two of you were together before."

Amar was obviously amused. "And when did you become an expert in matters of the heart?"

"It is natural," Azita asserted with confidence. "We girls just know such things."

"That's it, young lady, you are within an inch of being spanked. Besides, I think you should try to get some sleep." The voices got softer until they drifted to nothingness. The darkness lifted from Chris's heart as he drifted back to sleep as well.

———

Chris sprung awake the next morning. He sensed that it was later than he had hoped, the sun already was bright chasing away the night chill. *Damn,* he thought but caught himself. Where was he going in any case? It took him a moment to shake the cob webs from his brain. That done, he decided to check how Karen was doing. As he walked to the medical building he thought about the conversation he heard last night, the talk between Azita and Amar. He smiled to himself. He knew what he would do next.

From the door he could see the British doctor who headed their medical team, his name was Whitehead, right? He was talking with his sister as they looked at some charts. Something caught Chris's attention. They smiled at one another. Each of their eyes hung on the other longer than usual in polite discourse. Chris hung back, watching a bit longer. This was odd, something was wrong. Then he saw Kay reach out and touch the captain's arm. It seemed an unnecessary gesture, one totally uncharacteristic of her. The mystery deepened in his mind as he decided to enter. As he did, he cleared his throat in an exaggerated manner.

The two, who had been huddled over a medical chart, jumped back from one another as if caught in a tryst. *No,* thought Chris, *that was absurd.* His mind was playing tricks. "Oh, Chris," Kay said as she flushed a bit.

"Hi, sorry to bother you two, I was hoping to see Karen if I might."

"That should be fine, but not for long. She is still weak." Then Kay paused as if not sure where to go next. "Chris, you remember Dr. Whitehead, I mean James . . .Jamie."

"Of course, thank you, Captain, for everything. Your men saved us and you, well the two of you, saved Karen. I am so grateful. Karen is a pain in the butt but losing her, I cannot even imagine it." Chris smiled broadly at the medical officer before shifting his gaze back to Kay who still seemed rattled. Something was up.

He saw the captain about to say something when Kay took command of her situation. She strode across the room toward her brother, her face transforming from confusion to control in just a few feet. "First thing, Chris, thank you."

"For what," he was always thrown off when she was nice to him.

"For bringing the girls back. We are all grateful. In fact, the girls are at the school right now, the students are ecstatic to see them again and it is great therapy for them. Deena and Azita wanted to go back to their village, begged to go. But we refused and told them that was impossible, it is way too dangerous. They must stay here with us."

"I hope they are okay with that."

"They understand. They inspire me. So much grief and yet such strength, such resilience. This is such a harsh and unfor-giving place." Kay sighed. "Now, that brings me to my second point." Suddenly she began to beat on his chest and shoulders as he staggered back. But she kept after him, wailing away. "If you ever scare the shit out me like that again I swear I will rip your family jewels off and your career as a stud will be finished, do you understand me? What the hell were you thinking, pulling a stunt like that, by yourself, not telling us and with no support. Are you a total idiot?" She paused in the assault, waiting for a response.

"Hey, I just didn't want to put anyone else in danger, like you or Amar."

That did not seem to work. She began beating him again though with a touch less fury. "So, you go and scare the shit out of Amar and me. You are a fucking moron."

The captain sprang forward pulling Kay back. "Easy, dear. Don't kill the poor boy."

"Okay, okay." Kay managed to get out, panting hard. "I am fine now." But then she gave him one last whack before putting her hands up in surrender. "It is just that I . . . we . . . were so frantic. If I had lost you . . ." Tears formed in Kay's eyes, she could not finish the sentence.

The captain put his arm around her. "Why don't you go in and see Karen. I'll make sure to keep your sister away from all sharp surgical instruments."

Chris smiled at him. He might like this guy. He seemed to have a sense of humor. Then again, all the Brits did. He blanched at the first sight of Karen, there were tubes and stuff attached to her and she looked wane, without color. "Hey, kiddo, some people will do anything to avoid work."

"You! You are the source of all my troubles. Do you have the number of the Hairy Hare? The only thing I have to worry about there is some bloke trying to cop a free feel."

"Well, I wouldn't blame the horny blokes. It would be worth the try. Not going to work though, you are staying with me."

"Flattery won't work. I want a raise. Taking care of you is dangerous." She winced.

"Yeah, but I am worth it. Want me to leave you to rest?" he asked.

"No, no, I might as well get through all the pain at once."
She was not kidding.

"You are a funny lady, even when shot up all to hell." He
took her one hand that was free of tubes. "I should put you over
my knees for being so stupid but thank you. I am . . ."

"Oh hell, you would have done the same for me."

"I am glad you think so." He smiled. She followed suit.

She moved slightly and winced again. "Hey, Kay and Jamie
make a great team, don't they?"

Kay and Jamie? Chris turned that over in his mind. A good
team as surgeons or something more? Chris decided to take the
plunge. "Karen, how are you and my sister doing?"

"Glad you asked. I wanted to tell you, but I have been a bit
indisposed. Kay and I are no longer a scandal."

"Karen, I—"

Karen wanted to go on. "No, let me finish. It is fine, she really isn't a lesbian. I am a lesbian, which is why my family and
I are not, shall we say, close. But I knew from day one that your
sister wasn't. She was running from something, your father I
think. You can tell when someone is going through the motions.
I can at least, too much experience, I am afraid."

"Yeah," he said softly, "I know about all that now."

"Anyways, we talked it out. All is good." Her voice weak-
ened a bit. "You asked Amar yet?"

"She is thinking about it."

Her eyes flashed wide. "What the fuck is wrong with you?
You need to man up and strap on a pair. Just tell her the two of
you are getting hitched."

A nurse walked up. "Time for some medication, this will help you rest."

Chris leaned over and kissed her on the forehead. "See you later, kiddo."

"I better," she responded, eyes half closed. "I need an easy target."

Only Captain Whitehead was in the outer office. Chris wondered if he should say something, like ask the man what his intentions toward his sister were. But he remained silent. "Your sister is over at the school."

"Thank you, Captain. I hope I don't need a security detail." The doctor just smiled as Chris started toward the classrooms. When he arrived, he found a very large collection of girls and teens sitting on the ground outside the building. The number seemed larger to him than he recalled. He was surprised, thinking that the troubles in the area would keep the girls at home. He joined Kay, Amar, and Azita who, along with some teachers, were watching the proceedings. "What is going on?" he whispered to no one.

Azita now noticed he was there and, walking a few steps toward him, clasped her hand in his. He felt that Amar was paying close attention to Azita's movements even though she did not appear to be looking. "This is very special, Mister Chris. My sister is taking charge. She is talking with them about what these girls have been through to be here today and what we have just been through. Sharing our pain is good. It helps. We are not alone. Our grief is . . . universal."

"Azita, every one's grief is personal," Chris said with meaning.

"I am proud of Deena, of all these girls." Azita's voice wavered. "Oh no, the girls are wanting to name this school after me. No, they must name it after Pamir and Madeena." With that she dropped his hand and went to her sister's side to join the conversation which Chris, of course, could not understand. After some more back and forth, the student began to sing to the two sisters both of whom appeared moved.

Chris turned his attention to Amar, her delicate facial features, large doe-like eyes, and black hair that now blew in a stiffening breeze. She could not help but notice his stare but resolutely refused to acknowledge him. *That's it,* he thought to himself. He walked to her side and, grabbing a hand, pulled her away from the assembly.

"What are you doing?" She resisted his attempt to lead her away.

"Come with me. We need to get this settled."

"No, you cannot order me around."

"Yes, I can. Have you forgotten that I am your goddamn boss?" He was not to be deterred.

"But, but . . ." Still, she let him take her away from the assembled group.

He stopped eventually, sensing they were far enough away to ensure some privacy. "Amar, marry me."

"What, you drag me off like a cave man and expect me to say yes? Why don't you just club me over the head and drag me to your cave." She put on a firm face, but it was less than convincing.

"Don't tempt me," he barked. She opened her mouth to respond but never got the chance. Chris continued, "My turn now, so listen! I love you. I am in love with you. Don't ask me to explain it, I never thought myself a romantic. I know what is in my heart, damn it. You fill me up and complete me as a man. I cannot imagine not having you next to me for the remainder of my life. I can only promise you one thing. I will always treat you with respect and affection. Remember this, don't you dare judge me by your first husband." Surprise crossed her face. "By the way, I heard you talking with Azita last night. You were outside my window as it turned out. Hell, even she wants us to get married. Smart gal. We cannot disappoint her, not now, not after what she has been through."

"But you hardly know me," she stammered, not knowing how to respond but coming to the realization that he was deadly serious.

"I know Kay and I know that she thinks the world of you. Hell, she will break my kneecaps if I don't ask you. She knows what I need better than I do. Listen to me. I have wandered through life with things coming easily—prep school, Ivy League college, athletics, Rhodes scholarship, money, and now a position that gives me some stature and respect. Still, I never felt engaged. I was this glib guy who schmoozed his way with people and through situations. He has it all, they said. I am sure that is what they thought. But I was empty inside. I would look at some of these girls on the other side of my bed and could not recall their name for the life of me. We had nothing to talk about. The sex was empty release."

"And now?" She wondered where he was going with this confessional.

"Now, things are falling into place." He thought for a moment. "It is like the tumblers in a lock. You cannot open the door unless all falls into place. That is what it has felt like to me recently. I have connected with my mother, got her into an alcohol program. I know my younger sister for the first time and, frankly, she amazes me. Jules and I finally understand one another and what we have. Her brother Ricky is poised to take over for me which gives me options. Kay, dear Kay, I know she cares for me now. Hell, she beat the crap out of me this morning. If that is not love, what is? Even sweet Karen, such a treasure. Finally, the girls and you. You are the last tumblers. If you don't fall into place, the door cannot open. I will never see what is on the other side."

Amar seemed to consider this. "I have one question, it is hard to ask."

"Anything."

"What about Julianna, you say the two of you are good. I understand you and she—"

"I had asked her to marry me more than once. But she recognized something I never did. We are best friends, but it would never work beyond that. As I think back, I was relieved when she turned me down. That friendship will continue. Hell, she is looking after my mother right now. That is all it can ever be going forward."

Amar sighed. "I have one more condition. I want to find a way to adopt Azita, take her to England to be educated."

Chris smiled. "Well, I think you know how I feel about that. I want to take Deena with us as well, though we don't have to worry about any adoption. I just hope we can find a way to make all this work. Besides, Azita was the first to see that we were in love. I think she may be smarter than you. Hmm, come to think of it, maybe I should wait a few years for her?"

"She is way too smart to have you." Amar then sighed deeply but smiled. Chris knew it was over, in a good way. "You know, I am a proper Indian girl."

"Really, you could have fooled me after that first night."

She wagged a finger at him as he put up his hands in a gesture of surrender. "Down on a knee buster."

"What?" He was not sure he understood.

"Kneel," she barked with a smile. "I want a proper proposal."

"You're kidding?" Her expression did not change, however, and down he went. "Amar Singh, will you do me the honor of marrying me?"

"What, no ring?" she asked, a smile pushing the fake scowl off her face.

"Couldn't find an open jewelry store this morning. So, what is your answer?"

Instead of responding, Amar looked beyond him and laughed. "Did you get a picture, Kay?"

Chris stumbled getting up and turning to see his sister a few feet away. "Damn, no camera, but a memory for a lifetime—my dear twin sibling on his knees, begging." She walked up and hugged her brother. "This woman is a treasure. You have finally done something smart in your life. She, on the other hand is not nearly as smart as I thought."

———

That afternoon, the students were gone. Amar and Kay were back in the operating room, tending to some new wounded that had arrived from the fighting near the Masoud village. Chris briefly checked in with Major Gupta who amused him with the latest gossip. The Taliban offered an alliance with the Russians to gang up on the allies. Putin turned them down flat, the cold war was not what it used to be. Karen had been medicated again and was resting. Jets occasionally flew overhead, explosions could be heard from the far mountains. Chris next searched out Azita and Deena, asking them to walk with him.

"Tell me about this morning. I could not follow the discussion and then had to leave. The students were singing when I left."

"Yes," Azita responded. "It was very nice. They wanted to name the school after me, they thought it would not exist if not for me but that is not true. But I, we, told them that it would be much better if they honored our parents. We told them that they were responsible for our love of education." Azita looked at her sister. "Of course, some of us fell in love with learning later than others." Deena gave her an affectionate poke on the arm.

"That was nice. I am proud of both of you. And Deena, you did save our lives. I hope you have accepted that." The girl nodded but said nothing.

"The song you heard. It was an old Afghan song to honor our parents." Azita stopped and sucked in a big breath. She was on the verge of sobbing but fought back. "I keep looking around and expecting to see them. But it will never be. I cannot even think of the future. It is . . ." Then she stopped, lost for a way to express her dark vision.

"Sit down, girls." Chris found what looked like a picnic bench and sat across from the two girls. "Listen, I have something to say. Amar and I are getting married."

Azita's face lightened at that news. "That is so good. But Deena will be upset, she was hoping you would wait for her." With that, Deena gave her sister a sharp blow. "Ow, that hurt."

"Good," Deena said.

"But that is not the real news. We intend to take you girls to England with us. You need a future. It is not here."

They both looked at him for a long time without saying anything.

Azita stood and looked toward the mountains for several moments. "It is strange. This land is so hard. There is so much pain. Yet, I love it. It is all I know. In my dreams, I had my father taking us to England where I could go to a real school. Now . . ." She seemed to struggle with something. "This land is so difficult. Yet, it is also so beautiful."

"Remember this. Amar and I are not doing this just to be nice. The thing is, we love you, both of you." Chris stood up and walked around, putting his hands on each of the girl's shoulders. "Amar and I cannot replace your parents. No one can. But we can give you a chance in life."

More moments passed. The sisters looked at one another. Then Azita rose and put her arms around Chris's waist. "If only Allah wills it," she whispered. Moments later, Deena followed suit.

CHAPTER 11

THE THIRD HEGIRA

"Captain," Chris said as he sat down next to him in what had become their new and improved cafeteria, a clear sign of an expanding and evolving mission. "We need to talk."

"Only if you will call me Jamie. I will even respond to Jim or James, which the Americans usually prefer."

Chris smiled. He had gotten to like the man who, despite coming from a military family, proved informal, irreverent, and quite witty. He was a man after Chris's heart. "No, when I have serious business to discuss I think it better to use your official title."

"Medical business? Another sexually transmitted disease you want me to heal?"

"Why is it, no matter where I go, I am surrounded by comedians?"

"It might be you, ever consider that? You are pretty easy," Jamie said with a broad smile.

"Not bloody likely, I am just so serious all the time." Chris tried his serious demeanor to little effect.

The captain groaned, "All right, what can I do for you?"

"Sir." He put on his serious face. "What exactly are your intentions with respect to my sister? I am intent on preserving her virtue."

The captain smiled as he looked over Chris's shoulder. "Perhaps we can ask the object of your concern directly. Here she comes now with Amar." Kay sat next to James and Amar next to Chris. It had become a common arrangement. "Kay, your protective brother believes I am violating you with evil intentions and possibly obscene behaviors."

Kay smiled. "I hope so. Otherwise, I am wasting my best seductive wiles."

"So sad." Chis looked aggrieved. "And I did work so hard at setting a moral example for you. By the way, what seductive wiles?"

Kay started laughing despite herself and choked on the sip of water she had just ingested. "Says the playboy of the Western world."

"What?" inserted Amar. "A playboy? You lied to me. You told me he was a virgin."

"All right, I am putting an end to this right now. You, Captain, are not permitted to see my sister any longer and you, Amar, will get no sex from me until further notice."

Amar laughed out loud. She had gotten used to his humor though there were stumbles in the beginning. "Chris, think about this for a moment. I am surrounded by young British soldiers who enjoy very few opportunities for congress with the opposite sex. Any guess for how long I will be deprived?"

"Congress? Is that the same as screwing?" Chris looked at her for a moment. "All right, you are forgiven. However, back to serious business. What is with the marriage business?"

"I finally got a response from higher up. It turns out that I can marry you."

"Oh, Captain, this is so sudden," Chris said with a seductive voice. "Sorry Amar, I have a better offer now."

"Still don't get it, do you Chris?" Kay added. "Amar is the only person who will have you and I had to pay big to get her to agree."

The group laughed. They were laughing a lot these days. The extensive air campaign and more limited ground incursions were having better than expected effect. The Taliban had overreached, losing support among the local populations and creating many enemies who merely waited for an opportunity to strike. The time of the enemies of the Taliban to exact some revenge had arrived. The expected fierce resistance to allied strikes never materialized. In fact, the Taliban seemingly had disappeared in the northeast provinces, the Panjshir Valley and surrounding mountains now appeared safe and secure. Early reports suggested they were in retreat throughout the country.

"Hey, I am a catch," Chris responded as the women rolled their eyes and made gagging sounds. "However, let us not dwell on the obvious. Tell us, good Captain, you say that you are able to help me save Amar from her fallen state of sin and depredation."

"Well, she cannot be saved unless I can convince her what a mistake she is making. But yes, I have dug deep into the military regs and found that I can perform marriage services under certain circumstances. The rule was developed with male soldiers in mind, guys who were desperate to marry local gals in foreign lands, usually when there were children involved. You were not exactly what they had in mind, Chris, but the language is vague enough. The snags were arguing there were exigent circumstances and that Amar was a member of the British military. Getting your child out of the country satisfies the first condition.

"You mean Azita?" Amar asked.

"Yes, so we should make that a reality soon."

"What about the second?" Chris looked a bit concerned.

"Well, it really helps that she has British citizenship. And, all I need to do is put her on my payroll when the ceremony is performed. We contract with medical personnel all the time. The stretch was convincing them that a contracted employee met the letter of the law."

"Will that work?" Chris looked dubious and then confused. "Wait, you used the past tense."

"Amar, your intended is quicker than he looks," the medical officer smiled. He reached into his pocket and pulled out a piece of paper. "I pulled it off . . . here is the official permission."

Kay let out a small hooray. "I do so love you, Jamie." Then she realized what she said in public and blushed.

"Don't worry, Kay, so do I." Chris tried to cover his sister's embarrassment.

"We are not there yet. I would also love something that says you can have custody of Azita. With no functioning government in Kabul right now, I think getting permission from her extended family members will do the trick. Maybe I can parlay that into something that sounds official. Deena is different. Technically, she is considered an adult though barely."

"Jaimie," Chris smiled broadly. "I no longer care about your intentions toward my sister. Violate her at will, my friend. And we don't have to worry about the older sister, Deena. As an adult, I know what to do to get her into England."

"I want to put your mind at rest, sir. I intend to violate your sister every chance I get." The captain smiled until Kay punched him in the arm.

Amar leaned over to kiss Chris on the cheek. "Looks like your goose is cooked, or is it mine? In any case, we will discuss the details later. Jamie, we are due in the refugee camp now. Our customers await."

Kay then looked to her brother. "Walk with me to the medical unit. I am going to release Karen. She has been dying to get back to torturing you."

"I have missed that, really." They started out at a very leisurely pace. "I must be a masochist."

"Yes, self-abuse is a specialty of yours. Listen, Chris, if all this works out you will be leaving with Amar and the girls, or at least giving it the old college try."

"Yeah, I can't hang around forever though Ricky is so good I have become redundant I think. But I have liked spending all this time in the field including visits to the other sites in this part of the world. I have a much better idea of what people in the field face now. I have changes in mind."

"Yes, and I will give you my list. But listen, were you assuming I would go with you?" Kay asked uncertainly.

"To England?" he asked stupidly, thinking more about where she might be going.

She gave him her best look that said, "Of course England, you idiot."

"I just assumed we would all go. With the British team in place and things settling down I am not sure of our need to be here much longer."

Kay locked her arm in his as they walked. "Think of this. Their mission is military. They treat civilians when they can but that is not their priority. And the school, with the girls going and her mother passed, it will need tending to stay strong. In fact, I am not totally sure Deena wants to leave with you. She has grown so much in weeks. She . . . she wants to make sure that the school named after her parents thrives. She no longer obsesses about boys and marriage."

"Wow, that is a loss for the boys, she is a beauty. But tell me, how much of this is about medical need and education and how much is about Jamie. Kay, do you love him?"

They walked in silence for a while. He waited. Finally, she spoke, "The problem is, I am not sure what love is. For years I blocked everyone out, just a few lesbian connections and a couple of disastrous men. I never knew how much the whole thing with Father affected me." She paused again as if deciding what to say next. "I did like Karen a lot. We had little in common. Still, she made me laugh a lot. We would trade stories about you and laugh hysterically. I just loved the way she would mimic you. But I quickly knew our relationship was not the real thing, despite how comfortable it was. Trouble is, I don't know what is. She seemed fine when we broke off. I have felt bad, though. How does Karen seem to you?"

"She seems fine to me, but I wanted to ask you, get your take. What would a guy know? I also love that bugger even when she makes my life a misery."

"I know, and she loves you as well. But I think she guessed at where I was. I . . . I hated distancing myself from her. In any case, she made it easy, actually pushed me at Jamie."

"Yeah," Chris said, "she told me you were a fake lesbian."

"I wasn't very convincing I suppose. You know, you can only push human contact away for so long."

"I know. I really know. We are a pair, aren't we?"

"Chris, do you know why I beat on you that day when you returned with the girls?"

"I will admit to being just a little confused. I thought I had done a good thing, other than getting Karen shot."

"You did," Kay said emphatically. "I was not angry at you. I hated myself at that moment. I felt I got you into this. If I had not come here without permission, you would not have come. I got you here, got you into a situation where you were almost killed. I was panicked that day. If . . . if . . ."

"But nothing happened to me, right?"

"That doesn't matter. I was selfish. I did what I wanted. I have always been selfish. I shut you out for years, why? Was I punishing you, Father, all males? All I know is that I had a fierce, blinding anger. I don't even know why." She turned Chris around so that they faced one another. "Okay, you did run off and I did think you were a bit of a coward, maybe a colossal asshole. But I never looked at things from your perspective. Father would have been all over you, as a son in his male-dominated world. Chuck was not the natural heir, you would have been. I should have cut you some slack, but I didn't. You did what you had to do. I see that now. What did I do, though? I just stayed angry. I am so sorry."

"Don't do this, Kay, don't."

"I must." She heaved big sighs as if on the verge of sobbing. Her head bent into his chest as she fought for control. When she raised her head again, she was better. "This helps, it does. There were so many times when I wanted to pick up a phone, get on a plane, just tell you about Father and the abuse. But I kept it bottled up and it ate away at me. I am not sure how I got it out that day. It just erupted. Maybe it was getting it out to Karen. Or perhaps it was Chuck that brought home just how damaged we were, to all of us I think. We couldn't go on this way, all hiding in out private worlds."

Chris reached to the back of her head and pulled her to him. She wrapped her arms around him. "Kay, maybe Chuck died for us. That is silly, I know, way too dramatic. But think about how his death affected us all. He jarred us out of our private places, forced us to take hard looks at ourselves. Think of all that has happened in a few months. We are talking again, Kat has emerged from her childish cocoon to become a tiger. Mother is sober and independent. I am getting married. Of all the miracles, that's got to be the greatest. I mean, women throughout the Western world are on the verge of suicide. The great lover is no longer available. Hmm, perhaps I need to open a mission for grieving and distraught women."

Kay wiped a tear away and smiled. "I will give you credit for one thing. You do say the funniest things."

"What are you saying?" he protested with exaggerated hurt. "Surely my claim of superior sexual performance is no joke." Kay now laughed aloud. "Okay, Kay, no need to slit a gut, not that funny. One thing is true for sure, the Crawfords are now a family and we are not going to let that monster at the top dominate us any longer."

"Chris, just promise me one thing. Don't go off again on some stupid whim and get yourself killed."

"I will promise if you do one thing, tell me how you feel about Jamie."

"I need to work on that a bit. That is part of the reason I want to stay here for a while longer, to work that out. Is that all right?"

"Wow, you are reformed, asking permission."

"Careful, don't fuck this up by being snippy." Kay wagged a finger at him.

"Yes," he said softly, "you can stay."

"Of course I can stay. We may have reconnected but you still are not my keeper. I just want to make sure you keep supporting our work here."

"And I promise to pour resources into the school and the mission here. Kat herself gave me a bunch of money for your work. Besides, the Taliban has left this country in shambles. There is much rebuilding to do. I fear America will do what they did during the Soviet era, spend billions killing the enemy and nothing on the end game. It is what we Americans do best, kill people who look different than us. Now, let's go and free Karen from her hospital prison."

Karen was sitting in a chair, working on a computer. "Ah, the prison brass is here. Just in time, I was about to tunnel under the wall." A comely British nurse sitting next to her got up and murmured something about needing to get back to work.

Chris sensed something but decided he was imagining things. Rather, he immediately picked up on the rhythm of the exchange. "Yes, Doctor, I see what you mean. Significant physical improvement but continued personality deficiencies. I would say another month's confinement ought to do it."

"Funny man. With this new access to military communication systems, I am in instant touch with the world. The Hairy Hare wants me bad."

"What," Chris smiled, "they need another barmaid with a big rack and a small brain?"

Kay turned on her brother and whacked him in the arm. "Don't be such a sexist."

"Thank you, sister," Karen said. "He needs to be whacked at least once a day. It turns out that Ricky wants me back in England to work with him. This could be an offer I cannot refuse."

"I doubt that," Chris was dubious. "The man is way too discerning."

"Well, his exact words were something about missing me. Same thing. Anyways, he says that the initial reaction from immigration was ambiguous about permitting Azita to enter the country."

"What? What the fuck is their problem?" Chris was not happy.

"For Christ's sake, don't bite the head off the messenger. They are doing their bureaucratic thing. It is early in this action. They are concerned about a flood of asylum seekers. They need to develop appropriate policies. Blah, blah, blah."

"One fucking twelve-year-old girl, or is she thirteen?"

Kay looked at him. "I have two pieces of advice, dear brother. First, when you are talking with government officials, clean up your language and second, get your facts straight about your new daughter, like her age."

"Hey, I have been schmoozing with big wigs all my life. How do you think I have all this money to pay you guys?"

"I never thought much about that before. How do you con people out of their money? Extortion? Blackmail?" Karen said with an exaggerated smile. She had not been getting her Christopher fix every day. "Back to the matter at hand, whatever you do, get written documentation that the extended family is on board. Otherwise, they will throw you in the pokey for child abduction or human trafficking."

"Yes, next stop, her village. It finally is safe to go back again. And then, there is a plan for helping the girls into England percolating in my head, kind of a backup plan."

"Oh shit, Kay, your brother has a plan. I see a stretch in Kensington prison coming up for sure and, somehow, I will be the one nicked by the coppers for some stupid thing he does. You will visit us, right?"

Kay laughed. "I will certainly visit you, Karen."

"No, no, Kay will visit me with her baked goods. Believe me, solitary is preferable. If you have never experienced her baked goods . . ."

"Stop right there," Kay sputtered. "The next word you utter may be your last. Besides, that was when I was a kid. How was I to know there was a difference between dark chocolate and the regular kind. We had domestic help, remember, for all that practical crap?"

"Enough banter," Chris insisted as if that ever worked. "Are you getting ready for jolly old England?" he asked Karen.

She surprised him by not saying anything. Then with carefully paced words, she said, "Well, I am thinking on that."

"Okay," Chris said in the same slow cadence. "We can talk about that later. I guess life is complicated."

Karen continued, "I have been talking with Deena. In truth, she is a nice girl, she spent a lot of time with me during my convalescence. I taught her checkers and even chess. She is a bright gal, has been reading books I have lent her."

"Okay," Chris said slowly as Kay looked on with interest.

"It is just that she has been talking about staying and working on the school named after her parents. And she confided in me something else. She hopes to build a school in her dad's village. They don't have one, their kids have to travel forever to find a school and most don't stay long as a result."

"You promised I would build one, didn't you?" Chris asked without expression.

"Oh, promise is a strong word. I did say I might talk about it with you."

"I am sure," Chris said. "We will release you from prison but surely not for good behavior."

Kay added, "I'll send in that new nurse who was with you. What is her name?"

"Karan, but with an A, not an E. That could be confusing."

"With an A, not an E. Okay, I better do the paperwork." Kay grinned. "We are getting way too bureaucratic these days, damn British efficiency. How did you guys conquer half the world with all that damn paperwork?"

When they were alone, Kay looked at her brother. "That was strange."

"Does she know that you are staying, maybe she wants another shot at you."

"No, and no! I am totally positive there's nothing between us."

"What about Karan with an A."

"Perhaps," Kay mused, "but while I don't know her name I have already figured out Karan with an A is very popular with the guys."

"Enough of that," his tone changed. "I have some computer work to do and then a trip to the Masoud village to plan."

———

At 9:00 AM on a crisp fall morning, two British helicopters took off. In one of them, there was a contingent of security forces. All the intelligence suggested that nothing amiss would occur. Chris, however, was not taking any chances. He would have Azita, Deena, Amar, and Jamie with him. They probably could get by with one craft. Chris asked for two as backup. Gone were the days when he would fly off half-cocked, at least if he could help it.

This time, when they landed, there was a large welcoming crowd awaiting. As they departed the copter, each was welcomed as long-lost relatives. The greeting for Azita and Deena were incredibly warm. Much sympathies poured for them for the fate of their parents. When all had been formally welcomed, they brought the assembly to a makeshift shrine of sorts. It was constructed of bricks erected in a tower with pictures of Pamir and Madeena on it along with a poem in Pashto. Azita wiped a tear from her cheek. Then she began to read the poem.

> *The prophet blesses us with many gifts,*
> *Tall mountains, sweeping plains, rushing waters,*
> *With winged birds and soaring eagles and beasts of burden,*
> *With blue skies and fresh mountain breezes and bountiful offspring.*
> *Once in a while, he gives us a special gift, a teacher and a healer who,*
> *while amongst us,*
> *bestow upon us many precious and incalculable blessings.*
> *We have been so fortunate to know two so favored by Allah, at*

least for a moment on this earth.

After a time, they brought the group to an open place where carpets had been spread out. All sat on the ground in a large circle. One elder, a man with a worn, craggy face right out of central casting that Chris recognized from his earlier visit, spoke. Everyone listened attentively. Obviously, he commanded total respect. Azita then translated.

"He wishes to thank us all for this honored visit. He wishes to thank the honored British guest for all his help in driving the despised ones from the area. His planes and bombs have driven these people away to the White Mountains far away near Pakistan, near the Tora Bora caves, where the evil one now cowers in fear." Azita then quickly added, "I think he means Bin Laden."

"Tell him," Chris spoke, "that we thank everyone for this welcome. I am especially thankful for all that was done on my last visit which brought much misfortune on your village. I beg your forgiveness for that. You have been very kind."

The elder did not wait for a translation. He must know enough English to understand Chris's words. Apparently, he decided to see what he could do in English. "You have no blame, my son. Nothing was your fault. The despicable ones were all about us, waiting to kill us all. They know many warriors who fought them are from our village. But they are cowards. They came in the night, to kill our most honored ones and these gifts." He motioned to Azita and Deena. "You saved our precious ones here." He pointed to Azita and Deena. "They shall honor their parents by having children of their own one day."

Captain Whitehead spoke up, "on behalf of the British government I wish to extend my thanks and the hand of friendship." Azita now picked up the translation so that all the elders might understand. "Your people have been so helpful in our efforts to find the Taliban so that our planes might drop their bombs and drive them away. I know that they have taken great risks as they have gone about providing us with such excellent information."

The elder raised his hand, apparently deciding that Pashto was better so that all might understand. "Yes, and we are most grateful for the medical attention you have given our men who have been hurt in these days."

"Please, make sure all your people know that our medical help is available to all. Now, a toast." The captain raised his cup of tea, then wondering if this was a custom they would appreciate. "May peace and happiness be among you for a hundred years."

As all seemed to join in the toast, Chris looked over the group. He knew what he was about to propose might disrupt the bon homie that prevailed. He watched as they enjoyed the tea and sweets that had been laid out for them. Finally, Chris decided it was time. "There is something I want to ask of you. It is a great favor. I very much hope you will look upon it with kindness."

"Please ask, my friend," the elder said.

Chris sighed. "The good doctor," he indicated Amar, "and I are about to be married." He was interrupted with expressions of approval. "Thank you. Here is my favor I ask from you. We know that the Masoud clan from this village is prepared to take in Deena and Azita and raise them." He paused. "We humbly ask you to consider this. We, Dr. Singh and I, wish to bring Azita and Deena to England with us. We have come to love both girls and wish to give them every advantage, safety and a good education. Azita, as you know, wished to be a doctor like her father. It is what he wished for her. Deena recently has expressed interest in becoming an educator, like her mother."

Chris seemed poised to say more but was drowned out by a confusing chatter among the elders sitting in the immediate circle. Chris looked to assay the sense of the group but could not divine where they were going with their excited chatter. One thing was clear to him, unanimity of opinion did not reign.

The elder finally spoke up, "Many of us are concerned about this. We appreciate the offer. Some of us believe we have an obligation to the girls."

Chris raised his hand. "Let me say that we will ensure that they are raised in the tenets of Islam. It is the fastest growing religion in England and they will not be without many others who practice your faith, their faith. Believe me, we will watch over them with great care. What we can do is give them every advantage that my country offers." Chris suddenly caught himself. He said "my" country. He did not feel the need for a correction.

There was more animated discussion among the group before the elder turned and asked the girls a question. Azita responded excitedly while Deena barely nodded. That seemed to spark even more argument. This was not unusual in village decision-making processes. Discussions were often uncontrolled and vigorous, animated by emotional excess. The Westerners had no idea where the drift of the discussion was heading. Then, however, Deena began speaking loudly. She shouted the others down, which apparently shocked some of the elders. Then she spoke with great emotion. At one point, Azita yelled at her but Deena silenced her with a look and continued. Tears streamed down Azita's face. Whatever the girl said seemed to affect her sister and the larger group. The discussion continued for a bit with much more amity.

"We agree," the elder said with conviction. "Azita may join you and the good doctor once you are married."

"Only Azita?" Amar blurted out.

With tears still streaming down her face, Azita spoke in English, "My sister is staying. She says she wants to make sure the school is a success, that she wants to educate other Afghan girls. She now understands how important that is, that is what she says. And she told them how badly my parents wanted me to be educated in England, that I am to honor Father by becoming a doctor. She will honor our mother by working to educate girls."

Chris spoke to Deena directly, "Is this what you want?" He knew the answer. While Karen had warned him, Deena had said nothing about her thoughts until now. Apparently, Azita also had not known or had not accepted the reality until this moment.

"Yes," she said without hesitation, "I am not ready to leave. Maybe someday. But I must make sure the school is working well. That is what I can do for my mother and father."

"Do you believe her?" Chris asked Azita.

The young girl shuddered with emotion but nodded affirmatively. Chris guessed that the sisters had discussed this possibility. There was another pause, people looked at one another. Then the elder spoke in English, "I believe we are agreed then."

"Thank you," Chris said. "I want to say one more thing. This is a rather large community but you have no school. I want to build one here. The idea is not mine, really. It has come from Deena and from Karen Fisher who works with me and was wounded when I was here last. She has now recovered but we thought that she needed more rest. Karen and Deena will work on this school, and my sister will stay for a while after Amar and I leave with Azita. So, our presence will remain with you. We had made this decision before coming here but did not want it to look as if it was in exchange for your decision about the girls, about Azita that is."

"Thank you, my friend. We are most grateful. Your gift would not have won our favor in any case. We think only of the girls. It was Deena who was most persuasive. But the school is most needed. Allah will be very pleased."

After a while, and more conversation, the gathering dispersed. "You are certain?" Chris asked Deena as they mingled.

"Very certain, Mr. Chris. I thank you so much for everything. I only ask that you look after my dear sister. Perhaps I will join you someday, we will see. Now, I must help the captain with some paperwork that needs to be completed, explain it to the elders and my larger family. These papers will help you take

Azita to England. Can you look after Azita? I think she has
gone to our old house. She is sad."

Chris caught up with the girl in her old home. "Are you all
right? You looked so sad in the meeting. Did you not know that
your sister was thinking of staying? It looked to me as if she did
not decide until just now."

"I am sad. It will take some time. I knew she was thinking
about it. In the end, she saw the confusion among the elders.
Perhaps she thought it easier for them to let me go if she stayed
but she will never admit to that. I will talk to her again when
I can do so without crying. Mr. Chris, she was so good in her
arguments for me. You would cry as well if you could have understood her words." Azita wiped another tear from her cheek.
"Funny, we used to argue and spat like sisters do. She was older
and bossed me around when we were younger. I thought she
was jealous of me, of Father's affection. But she was proud of
me, I never knew. I never understood that. I will miss her so."

"I knew she was proud of you. I could see it in her eyes,
when you were not looking. You know what I think, in the end,
both of you will make great contributions to the world."

Azita did not respond but Chris was sure she had heard his
words. She continued looking through some books in her room.
Suddenly, her face lit up and she grabbed one. "This is the one I
wanted more than anything else. My father gave this one to me,
on the day the Taliban beat me so." She caressed it in her hands.
"There are other books I must retrieve but this is my favorite. I
was so afraid all would be gone."

Chris went to her side to look at the book. She let him look at it. He whistled. "Omnism? This is not easy reading, I know."

"That does not matter. I read a small portion at a time and then would think on it. I would go to my father and discuss what I did not understand. It has been getting easier of late, the understanding of the book, but not the loss of the lessons from my father. I miss him so. Sometimes, at night, I have this dream. I am wandering through a village, looking for someone. My panic keeps rising. That is silly, you don't need to hear this. But without him at my side, I just don't know . . ." she never finished the sentence. She did not have to for Chris to understand.

Chris stroked her head. "Azita, I want to say something. I will probably say it badly. I cannot replace your father. Neither can Amar replace your mother though the good doctor is the most loving and kind woman I have met in life. I still cannot believe she has agreed to marry me. Your father was a special man, from what I know he was loved by all and so full of affection and hope for you. He was so committed to his family, to helping you find your passion in life. I . . . I have never committed to anyone in life, not really. That wandering has ended. I now commit to you and Amar, totally. I . . . we shall make you a doctor, a teacher of the young, whatever you wish to be. You shall be the gift from your parents to the world."

Azita collapsed into Chris's arms, sobbing. "Being here," she finally got out, "it is so hard, the memories. I am so scared, Mr. Chris. I am afraid of the unknown, of failing the memory of my father, of being without my sister or any of my family. I fear I am not strong enough, good enough. What if I disappoint you? What if I fail in your schools?"

"What did your father do when you disappointed him?"

"Hmmm, he was always kind and gentle, he always had a lesson for me."

"Then I shall bury you in kindness and gentleness and silly lessons. Azita, look at me. I succeeded in all these places you feel are beyond your reach, like Oxford University. Think about that, how hard can success be there?"

She saw the crooked smile on his lips and laughed softly. "Thank you, Mr. Chris."

"One of these days, I want you to call me Dad, but only when it feels right. Okay, I will leave you to look over your stuff. Just forget the clothes unless there is some special significance in something. Otherwise, leave everything for the villagers. My guess is that it is the books you want. I am going to look over the village, maybe find a place to build that school." He started toward the door. "And Azita, come to me if you get stuck while reading that favorite book of yours. I am not sure I am as wise as your father, but I will do my best."

Soon Chris was joined by some villagers and then by Deena, Amar, and Jamie. "Well," Amar said, "we got a lot of papers signed. I even managed to convince Deena to include herself in the paperwork, just in case she changes her mind. For her, we mostly needed documentation of her age, that she is an adult now. They were surprisingly flexible once the decision had been made. Maybe Deena has a future as a lawyer, she must have been very persuasive."

"I hope not," Chris shot back. "I want her to do something useful."

They walked around, looking at various possibilities. As he paid attention for the first time, Chris was taken by one thought. How did Pamir Masoud rise from an isolated village like this to become a doctor and, in fact, a humanitarian? How could he attain such wisdom and personal character? Most from this wild area were warriors. They had fierce loyalty and were kind to visitors. At the same time, they could fight with an inborn ferocity. Pamir Masoud was so different. How could that be? This mystery reminded him of his own family where the children were so different from the father.

Several sites were suggested but Chris wound up rejecting them all. Each was fine but not special. Then he spotted some high ground just outside the village proper. It looked over the surrounding buildings and had two large trees that gave the site character. "This is it," Chris said firmly.

"But it is uneven terrain, is it suitable?" Jamie asked.

"No problem, I am sure I can convince you to bring in a few bobcats and stuff." Chris flashed his smile.

"I see you are a charmer, just like your sister."

Chris laughed aloud. "You must be besotted with lust my friend. It should be clear to all by now that I got all the charm in my family."

———

"This is highly unusual, highly unusual." Chris, Amar, and Azita sat across from an immigration officer at Heathrow Airport. "Let me review this. Your surname is Crawford and you are Singh. You claim to have been married by a British military officer just recently at some place no one has heard of in Afghanistan. You claim that this is your daughter but only have some papers as proof that no one has seen before. Her name is Masoud. One of you is an American citizen, one has dual British and Indian citizenship, and the girl has no passport at all but you claim she is Afghani, which is your alleged originating site. Let me ask you this, how did you even get here? How did any carrier let you on their plane?"

"Simple enough. We took a military flight out of Afghanistan to Rawalpindi and then used a charter flight to get to Heathrow."

"Whose military?"

"Yours. As you can see, a Major Gupta officiated at our marriage. He arranged the first flight."

"Gupta?"

"Yes, also one of yours," Chris said crisply.

Amar could not quite handle the subtle racist slight. "You might recall, sir, that India once was part of your empire. Many of us were educated here and still serve her interests."

"No need to be snippy, Miss. I am aware of our history." The official looked even more upset.

Chris nudged her lightly under the table and she quickly tried to smooth things over. "Very sorry, sir, you seemed surprised at the name of the British officer. I was trying to help."

The immigration officer clearly was unhappy. He looked at the papers in front of him. Chris decided to apply his charm. "I can appreciate your position. International terrorism is on everyone's mind these days, especially in my country where New York and Washington were attacked. You cannot be too careful, we surely understand that. But if you read the documents carefully, you will see that all is in order."

"The girl, the big problem is the girl. You claim she is your daughter." The officer looked at her suspiciously. "Does she understand English?"

"Oh yes, sir. I understand and speak English very well. This is my new father and mother now. You see, my biological parents were killed by the Taliban recently. My father was educated at Oxford, he loved your country. He was an esteemed doctor who helped my people. My mother was also educated and taught girls at the university before the Taliban came to power. My new mother and father have brought me to your wonderful country so that I might follow in my biological father's footsteps, I will become a doctor. I want to be just like my new mother, she is also a doctor." Azita took Amar's hand who fought off a tear.

The officer looked at her as if she had just dropped out of an alien spacecraft and looked relieved when the door to the room opened and another immigration officer entered. The two officials went back and forth for a minute or two in a *sotto voce* manner. Then he looked back at the trio. "Who are you people? Apparently, there are calls and emails from MPs and business-people, the American Embassy, and there is an American reporter doing interviews and live coverage out there in the terminal. What is her name again, Harry?"

"Julianna Jackson, from one of the American networks," the new arrival added.

"Really," said Chris with mock surprise. "How nice of Jules."

The immigration official did not look happy at all. He hated being pressured and he despised people using political advantage to get their way. "I must look more deeply into this. You remain here." With that, he scooped up the paperwork and left the room quickly as if he could not wait to escape.

"I don't think he is very happy," Azita opined with fear etched across her face.

Chris smiled. "He is just your average officious little . . ."

"Don't." Amar stopped him. "No need for colorful language."

"Bureaucrat." He finished with a broad smile.

Amar did not look happy. "I don't think we handled that well, including me."

Suddenly, Azita looked panicked. "Will they send me back?"

"Come with me," Amar said, bringing their two chairs over to the wall for a more private chat.

Chris checked his computer. His email box was lengthy with recent messages, all expressing support. He replied quickly to a few before composing a few texts. Then he stood up and leaned back against the wall, looking over at his instant family. His heart was full of anxiety and love. Despite everything he had arranged, he knew that immigration rules could be harsh, rigid, and even vindictive. That was especially true if they were trying to get into the U.S. There was no guarantee even here, however. He was aware of situations where equal pressure had been brought to bear with negative results.

On the other hand, he was with people he loved unconditionally. Whatever happened would mean little as long as
these two remained in his life. *How remarkable,* he thought. He
watched how Amar spoke with the young girl. She exuded such
love and caring as she calmed Azita down. The girl had been
through so much. Now, just steps away from taking a major step
to her life's passion, there was another hurdle. He could see the
young girl teeter on the verge of despair only to rally. Part of
this recovery could be attributed to Amar's soothing comfort.
But the rest lied within this amazing young girl herself. She
had such strength, resilience. She truly was driven by a sense of
mission, a personal conviction. Now, he also had a sense of passion and he was looking directly at it that very moment. It was
not that long ago that he knew neither of them, Amar only as
a distant employee and Azita not a part of his life at all. What
had happened to him?

His mind floated back to the morning he got married. He
woke early, it was still dark out. One small lamp lighted the
room just enough for him to make out the woman lying next to
him. Her long black hair played over her face, partially hiding
her undeniable beauty. He carefully pulled it back, hoping not
to wake her. He wanted to watch her without interruption. She
was a natural beauty, fine angular features dominated by doe-
like eyes and a sensuous mouth. Yet, that does not explain the
immediate attraction. He had met many beautiful women. His
wealth, looks, and easy wit and charm gave him access to many
females. Sure, like all straight males, he was sexually attracted to
so many. He would joke that he could walk across the Oxford

University campus or hit a London nightspot and fall in lust many a time over the space of a single hour. On first sight, he knew this woman was different, unique. He knew the name of this woman who shared his bed.

He often would go back to that moment in his mind, emerging from the back of the medical building where someone told him he could find her tending a small child. Was it her fatigued demeanor, speaking to the exhaustion of hours of labor to save and mend lives? Was it her casual and disheveled look that told him appearance meant little to her? How about the tear that slowly coursed down her cheek, revealing a level of caring against suffering and death? Of course, it could have been the lullaby she was singing to comfort a baby who was beyond help, sung in a language beyond the child's understanding? Maybe it was her voice, soft and choked with emotion? Many possible explanations, none that solved the mystery of that immediate and enduring connection.

It was still a bit early that morning of their wedding. He had leaned over and kissed Amar on her neck. She stirred and opened her eyes, smiling. "Remember, I am your prince charming and this is the big day. By big day, I mean when I make you an honest woman."

"Funny, in my dreams, my prince charming is so handsome and gallant."

"Ta da! Here I am," Chris said with an exaggerated smile.

Amar smirked. "Mother told me men would be so disappointing. Besides, you should leave. It is not lucky for the groom to see the bride before the wedding."

"Hah," laughed Chris. "I have seen everything the bride has to offer . . ." He was going to extend the joke but her grave expression stopped him cold. "Aah, bad joke?"

"Chris, I was awake most of the night, staring at the ceiling."

"Wedding jitters?"

"I guess," she responded in a low voice. "I still don't understand why you are doing this. I sometimes fear you are doing this only because of Azita, to save her. Before you say I am insane, you know all about my other marriage. That man did not like me much except to service him and make him curries. What I know about men and love is so little. What I know about sex comes from you. I feel so . . . inadequate."

Chris looked at her for so long she averted her gaze. Then he grabbed her by the hand and pulled her out of bed. "Come with me." He took her to the mirror on the wall. Taking her by the shoulders, he positioned her so that she faced the glass. "What do you see?"

"Me, and you."

"Do you know what I see? I see the most beautiful woman I have ever known in my life. I see a woman filled with kindness and love and sensitivity and wit whom, by the way, also happens to be a damn good doctor and I expect a discount on medical advice by the way. And about the sex, I see someone who has learned from the best, the well-known and highly-admired playboy of the Western world. Most of all, I see someone whom I love so unconditionally and so totally and so completely that any sanity to be questioned is surely mine."

"Well," she tried to smile, "we all question your sanity."

"There it is. Do you know how many women tried to impress me with their bodies or by batting their eyes? Rhetorical question, too many. You are genuine, and funny, and everything I have looked for in a woman and didn't even know existed until I found you. Azita is just a bonus. I . . . I . . . am in love with you. That's it, all of it."

"That's it. Then, so much the worse for you. I hope you realize that I will continue to make your life a living hell. I am taking lessons from Kay and Karen."

"I would not have it any other way. Let's greet the dawn rejoicing, shall we?"

Later, Chris recalled standing with Captain Whitehead and Major Gupta. Jamie laid out the plan the two British officers had concocted for the wedding. "The major will perform the ceremony and I will be the best man, only because I am the best man. And that way I can administer any needed drugs to keep you upright. We have the site set up. The major will say some bureaucratic stuff and then ask each of you to commit to the other. You can ad lib at that point but please don't nauseate me with a lot of romantic crap."

"Jamie, you will have to do better than this if you want a shot at my sister."

The sun had not quite made its way over the mountains to the east when the men and onlookers had assembled. From the building emerged five women, Amar, Azita, Deena, Karen, and Kay. The two girls were dressed in their finest native garb recently purchased by Amar who was outfitted in a native Indian Sari. The cloth was a basic white infused with brightly colored flowers and birds. With her black hair falling to her shoulders, she was breathtaking.

When the major got past the preliminaries required in a military wedding, he got to the core questions. "Doctor Christopher Crawford," using the honorific that goes with a doctorate from Oxford University which he thought put the groom on equal footing with his bride, "do you take this woman to be your legal and lawful wife?"

"Amar Singh, I had despaired of finding anyone to share my life with. Who could ever have predicted I would find such a woman here at the edge of the world, in this wild and magnificent setting. Yet, here I found the woman destined to be my soulmate. If there is some greater deity, I thank it. Major, to answer your question, yes, I take this woman to be my wife without reservation."

"And you, Doctor Amar Singh, do you take this man to be your legal and lawful husband?"

"I can recall my mother telling me that men were an evil necessity to be endured in life. For many years I thought she was right. But now I have met a man who has opened for me a whole part of life I did not know existed and which I had refused to accept. Thank you, Chris. And yes, Major, I do take this man as my husband, without reservation."

"Then, by the authority invested in me by the military authorities of the United Kingdom and by her Majesty Queen Elizabeth II, I now pronounce you husband and wife. I guess you may kiss the bride, now, though that part is not in the book.

Also skipped the part about anyone objecting, too much risk there."

In his head, Chris suddenly snapped back to reality, he was smiling at the memories. He was back in the immigration room at Heathrow. Amar was still huddled with Azita. They were playing a computer game which the girl was quickly learning to command. His new wife would make a great mother. He had never thought about children of his own. Perhaps that was not such an outlandish thought. His own unhappy childhood had soured him on the concept, why bring a vulnerable child into such a harsh world. But what he saw across the room was love and caring and sensitivity. This possibility was something he had never considered. They had married yet never even talked about creating life on their own. Did Amar simply assume he would be okay with that? No, she was sensible. She knew him better than he did himself. Once touched by love, she knew he would respond. Wow, he thought he was fortunate.

Still, the door did not open, no one appeared. What was taking so long? He knew from experience that bureaucracies were slow and cautious. That was his head talking. His heart was seized up with anxiety. These guys were used to pressure from the outside. They were trained to ignore it. They could act with considerable independence. What if they decided to make an example of Azita? What if they turned her away? How could he look her in the eyes and tell her he had failed her, her father, her mother? She would say that she understood and thank him for doing his best. But he could not handle that. He would probably lose all his remaining cool and wind up in prison. He was half Irish, he did have that damn temper. It did not show up often but . . . okay, it was time to think of something else. He forced his thoughts back to his wedding day. As he kissed Amar discretely at the end of the ceremony, she whispered to him, "I am a terrible Indian girl, I am thinking of you ripping this damn sari off me."

He whispered back, assuming onlookers had concluded they were sharing intimate expressions of their mutual love, "I bet all the nice Indian girls say that on their wedding day."

"In your dreams. I am afraid you might have married the one lusty, but still good, Indian girl. Does that even make sense? Anyways, it is a good thing we are in a public place." Then they broke apart to greet the others.

There were congratulations all around. Chris turned to a British soldier who was pressed into service as a groomsman, the same young man who had been wounded as they departed from the firefight on the day of the girls' rescue. "Thank you."

"My pleasure, sir. If that damn bullet had been an inch to the left it would have probably gotten me a trip home for some R&R."

"Better luck next time, then." Then Chris turned to Jamie. "Were you inspired? Give you any thoughts?"

"The issue is not with me. Do you have any influence with your sister? She is an independent lass."

"You are a glutton for punishment." Chris noticed other things that day. Deena and Karen spent a lot of time together, talking but sharing even more. It made him wonder but his suspicion seemed unlikely. Later, after they had eaten, he saw

Deena and Azita talking. There were tears in both of their eyes. Apparently, Deena had made it clear that staying was her final decision. She would remain for a while at least. That was not forever, though. He recalled thinking that they would be together someday. It must come to pass. Surrounded by people he had come to love, the mountains, the brisk, fall breezes, a sun that traversed a pure and blue sky, life was so good that day.

Once again, he snapped back to the immigration room at Heathrow Airport. What time had the officious bureaucrat left the room? He had not checked the clock. It seemed an eternity. He had enough, he was going to find out what was happening. At that very moment, the door opened. He was startled as a woman entered. She wore the uniform of an immigration officer. For some reason, Chris immediately knew she was from higher in the bureaucracy. She held herself with considerable assuredness and seemed more certain of herself than the angry man who first grilled them. After a perfunctory introduction, she indicated that Chris sit down.

The woman turned her attention to Azita. "Young lady, what do you want to do in England?"

"I shall study to be a doctor, as my father did before me." Her voice was clear and firm though Chris could see her anxiety.

"I did not think that Mr. Crawford was a doctor. Wait, I see he is has a doctorate, is that what you mean?"

"Oh, no," Azita announced. "I want to be a real doctor like my biological father. He was a great healer."

"I see." The woman smiled. Chris felt some relief even with the subtle insult of his not being a real doctor. Still addressing the girl, she asked, "So, you don't want be a fake doctor like your new father? Is that correct?" The woman cast a brief glance at Chris. Had she briefly smiled?

"Oh no, I love my new father but want to be a real doctor like my new mother." Azita thought she detected a shift in this woman's demeanor, a softening. Her own heart fluttered with hope for the first time.

"And you have no intention of blowing anything up." The official tried to remain serious without success.

"Oh, no." Azita seemed shocked at the mere suggestion. "I am here to learn how to heal people."

The woman then looked at Chris and Amar. "She strikes me as a bit young for medical school."

Chris breathed hard, the moment had come. "She has a great passion for medicine. She will get there though it is true that a hurdle or two still stand in the way. But mark my words, she will get there. You have no idea what she has already been through."

"I can guess and, like you, I do believe she will make it. Well, enough of this. I am here to tell you that I have overruled my subordinate who is most upset with me. He is not as bad as he sometimes appears, just overly cautious at times. We do have a lot of discretion but, unfortunately, we are judged mostly by our few mistakes and not the hundreds of sound decisions made every day. I suppose I cannot blame him. There are girls as innocent-looking as this one who wind up as suicide bombers. But that is not the case here, I am certain. Besides, you have generated quite a campaign on her behalf. Get ready for some cameras out there." The woman then picked up some documents that she had laid on the desk in front of her. "Ms. Azita Masoud, let me be the first to welcome you to the United Kingdom and good luck with your studies. Perhaps, someday, you can treat me when I am an old and sick woman."

Azita sat immobile for a moment. Then, she realized what was happening. She jumped up and ran around the table, hugging the surprised official. "I will treat you for free."

The woman embraced the girl despite her expected bureaucratic reserve. "Thank you but we have our National Health Service and I think your offer would be interpreted as a bribe." She laughed, and Chris thought he could detect a tear in her eye. For a moment, Chris considered giving the immigration official a hug himself.

"Thank you, thank you, thank you," Azita continued to murmur as Amar quietly went to rescue the immigration official.

Then the official turned to Chris. "Here is everything you need, passports, your original documents regarding the girl, and a temporary visitor's visa for her. Please start official adoption procedures for her if you will. That would head off any future issues."

"Absolutely, that is our intention," Amar responded.

"And Mr. Crawford, why not apply for British citizenship for yourself. I checked your background. You would be a welcome addition. Now I will lead you out." With that, she took Azita by the hand and walked out the door. She led them down a couple of corridors until they arrived at a larger concourse. At the end, Chris could see a crowd and cameras. The woman pointed in that direction. "That way to England. And keep a

good eye on this lass. There is much confusion and some prejudice out there these days. And good luck to you, young woman."
She leaned over and kissed Azita on the cheek. "If you were not
theirs, I would adopt you myself."

With Amar holding one of Azita's hands and Chris the
other, the three of them walked down the now empty concourse.

"Are you ready, my girl?"

With a deep breath, Azita responded, "I am, Papa." Amar
glanced quickly at her new husband while he fought back a tear.

As they approached the larger terminal, the roar from the
crowd rose. When they emerged, it was to a minor rock star's
reception. Cameras clicked. Flashes could be seen. As Chris adjusted to the confusion, he picked out Jules, talking into a microphone while a cameraman next to her recorded the moment.
Next to her stood Ricky, looking as dapper and successful as
ever. After what seemed as unnecessary interviews, they finally
made their way out of the terminal and into a waiting limo.

"I really hope you are not too exhausted." Ricky spoke first.
"Even more surprises await, at my favorite Afghanistan eatery."

"You have a favorite?" Chris could now laugh.

"I do now. Dr. Singh, Amar," Ricky added, "so nice to meet
the woman who is taking on one of life's most challenging jobs,
taming Chris. I feel we know each other but nice to meet face-
to-face. And you, young lady, so nice to meet the girl who won
my best friend's heart." Whatever tension and fatigue Azita had
felt was fading. She beamed and gawked at the buildings and
traffic about her. She was in a very different world.

———

The private room in the Afghan restaurant was a bit dark and it took Chris a moment to adjust his eyes. When he surveyed the assembled people, his mouth dropped open. Next to Jules were his mother Mary, his sister Kat, and his sister-in-law Beverly.

"Surprise!" Jules shouted.

"Oh my god," Chris was speechless for once. As he hugged all his family members in long embraces, Jules approached Amar.

"I really wanted to meet you," Jules offered. "In case you do not know, Chris and I have known one another since we were teens. I have some wonderful tips for you that might come in handy, you know, for handling him."

Amar visibly relaxed. "Yes, Chris has told me all about you. Can I confess something? I was very nervous about this moment, about meeting you."

"Yeah, I thought you might. Girl, let me tell you something. You are the best thing that ever happened to that guy. He and I wound up as best friends, but you are his soulmate. Everyone knows that."

They looked at one another for a moment and then hugged. "I am hoping we can be good friends as well."

"Oh no," they heard Chris say aloud, "first, Kay poisoned Amar and now Jules will work on her. I am doomed, doomed."

"Oh, don't be so dramatic," said his mother. "Women have spoiled you all your life, starting with me. But now I am healthy, so watch out." She smiled and then walked to Amar. "Welcome to my family. You are as beautiful as everyone said." After hugging Amar, Mary turned to Azita. "And you, young lady, I am your new grandmother. I am only hoping for one thing, that you allow me to spoil you rotten."

"I think that would be nice," Azita responded as everyone laughed.

There were more hugs before they all sat down. "I am stunned you are all here."

"Are you kidding," Kat spoke up. "When Ricky told Jules what was up, she let us all know. You could not keep us away. My brother got married and adopted a child. Are you kidding? I would have swum across the Atlantic. And look at this woman." She hugged her mother. "And, as you can see, Beverly is doing well. We have become closer, we all have. Of course, we are bonded in common cause, if you know what I mean. We will need to chat more about that while I am here. Father is still clueless as far as I can tell but there are some people I want you to discretely contact."

"Kat, I would climb Everest for you right now. Azita, look around this table. This is your new family. I love them all. I hope you will as well."

The young girl beamed.

———

It was early on Christmas day. Chris could not sleep and crept out of bed without waking Amar. On his second try he reached Karen. "Merry Christmas," he enthused, "it is the spirit of Christmas present."

"Bah humbug!" she responded. "Where are my presents? How come my Porsche didn't get here?" It was an old joke of hers, she was always kidding him about a Porsche that never arrived.

"It will be here when you get back."

"Yeah, yeah, that's what all the boys say and precisely why I prefer girls. But how's the season back in England, not the same here. I miss those 1930s version of Dickens's *The Christmas Carol* on the telly."

"Yeah, it is great. I never imagined celebrating Christmas with a real family. Nothing like it."

"So, things are going well? Has Amar broken you in yet?" Karen asked, realizing how much she missed Chris.

"Yeah, kiddo, really great. In fact, I have a great story for you. We wasted no time trying to matriculate Azita in one of your finer public schools for the spring semester."

"I see, you want her to avoid the rabble. You would prefer her to rub shoulders only with the snobbish elite."

"Not so much that, just want her to be intellectually challenged and avoid growing up to be like you. Besides, it is still easier to crack the better medical schools from a public rather than a regular school. I do worry about pushing her too hard, of maybe setting her up to fail but she is special. Don't lecture me on this, I spend sleepless nights on every decision."

"Tough being a parent."

"Toughest thing I have ever done but I love it. So, back to my story. I make an appointment with this crusty headmaster. He must have pretensions of being a scientist since he had equations written on his blackboard. Anyways, he looks down at Azita as if she were the parlor maid that just spilled the tea on a priceless Persian rug. He made a big point of her having no formal education. I explain how she had been homeschooled by her mother who had once taught at the university level and that her father had been a talented physician. He seemed totally unimpressed. This guy maintained an expression that positioned Azita as being the equivalent of Coco the Chimp who somehow learned the meaning of a dozen words. So, he asks her a couple of simple questions which she answers with ease. That threw him off his game. I could see his little mind churning away. He apparently decides to end this farce, which is what he thought it was, once and for all. This little urchin was not about to despoil his fine institution. He points to one of the equations on the board and asks if she has any idea what it represents."

Chris could not help himself and began to chuckle. "You had to be there. Azita got up and walked to the board. She looked intently and hesitated. I can see it in his eyes. He has her, she was toast. She is lost, he was sure of it. When he asks her if she is lost she tells him no but that one equation, as written, makes no sense. He started to tell me that there are other institutions where she might be a better fit. Or perhaps she could reapply after some formal preparation. I ignore him and casually asked her why the equation makes no sense. After all, I have no freaking idea. She picks up a piece of chalk and makes some corrections on the board. 'Now it is better,' she tells him, 'you had expressed the equation incorrectly.' He looked, looked again, got up and looked a third time. You should have seen the expression on his face. Then the two of them started talking so I excused myself so as not to embarrass him. About a half hour later he emerged with her and shook my hand. He tells me how happy they would be to have my daughter at their institution. You should have seen my daughter smile with total happiness."

"Oh my god, that must have been priceless. It was always awful being a working-class kid among those elite pricks." Karen did not miss that he referenced Azita as his daughter.

"I take it that is where you absorbed your refined language, hobnobbing among the elite pricks."

"Oh bite me. But damn, I miss you. I hate to admit that." Karen immediately regretted letting her guard down.

"Well, I miss you as well which brings me to my questions. What is going on and when is everyone coming back? "

"Are you sitting down?" she said.

"No, I am standing in the middle of Trafalgar Square."

"Don't be snippy, you want to hear this." Karen was obviously upbeat. "Jamie proposed last night."

"Did you accept?" Chris deadpanned.

"To your sister, asshole."

"So, hasn't he done this before?" Chris was not impressed.

"But this time she said yes."

"No freaking way! How, why?" Now Chris was impressed.

Karen now boasted. "I take all the credit. I wore her down. It drove me nuts that she kept putting him off. I would ask if she loved him and she would say yes. Then, I would ask what the problem is and she would say something like he is too old. So, then I would tell her that he is only eight years older than her, that is nothing. And then she would say but he has a child which he does by his first wife who died in a car accident and the kid is with his parents while he is here. To that I came back with that is BS since your worthless brother got married and adopted a teenager. That shut her up for a moment and then she comes up with something about him being married before. Then I lost it. You know me when I lose it. I shouted at her, telling her that she can really be dumb for such a smart woman. His wife died in an accident, she did not dump him because he was a serial wife abuser. It must have worked, she finally said yes. I mean, the guy is a catch, he really is. What is her problem?"

"Long story, kiddo, abuse and a dysfunctional family."

"I suppose. Anyways, they called England and talked with his parents and the kid, who is like seven or eight. When Kay got off the phone she was crying. Apparently, the boy wants a new mother, that touched her. But that is not all."

"There is more? Wait, don't tell me. You are getting a sex change operation." His jest was an attempt to push down the emotions welling up inside.

"Bite me again," came over the phone. "No, this is about me and Deena." Then she paused. "First, let me say the schools are going great. We have it fully supplied and now we have the resources to provide meals. Thank you, by the way, I must admit that you do know how to raise money. Anyways, you cannot believe the excitement among the girls. They are liberated and free and learning. You want an upper, be around them for a day or so. We are getting everything fully staffed, I am guessing all will be self-sustaining in a couple of months or so. Great, no?"

"But there is more, isn't there? I already knew the schools were doing well."

"A bit more, yes." Then, more silence.

"I get it, Karen. You and Deena are a thing."

"Wait, how did you know?" Karen was shocked.

"I am all-knowing, can't you tell? Here it is. While it is true that I fell off a turnip truck, I did not fall off last night. I thought I saw sparks even before I left. Then when you became tongue-tied just now, a rare event indeed, that was all the evidence I needed."

"Are you angry with me?" This obviously was important to her.

"Technically, she is an adult. If all this is consensual, of course not. Hey, I guess I would not be a good candidate for the morality police."

Karen jumped in, "Let me say this. I knew Kay was not a genuine lesbian almost from the beginning. By the same token, I knew Deena was. We danced around for quite a while. She had always made a big thing about boys and marriage. That was compensation I suspect. Can you just imagine a girl being at-tracted to other girls in this culture! When it happened between us, it was explosive, once she got over her shame which took a bit. I had experienced nothing like it before, not even with Ali-cia. But can you imagine coming out as a lesbian in this culture. The Taliban would behead her. Even the new regime, when one stabilizes, is not likely to be very liberal in this regard. The thing is, it is more than the sex. She is like Azita in so many ways, very smart but maybe not as brilliant. Then again, who is? But she is kind and sensitive and loving. She is just great with the girls, a born educator. She is her mother. I just love being around her.

She understands now that to be who she is, she must leave this country. She is ready for England."

"Karen, I can get her a work visa. She is an adult, it is not like Azita. I can make it sound as if she is the only qualified person in the world for a position here."

"Thank you, Chris. Have I ever told you I think you are great?"

"I think . . . never."

"Then I won't start now. Jamie rotates out in a couple of months. The education programs will be running well by then, Chris, we are coming home . . . all of us."

"What?"

"We are all coming home." Karen then paused for effect. "We will be together again."

Suddenly Chris was startled by a voice behind him. "Chris, I wondered where you had gone. Are you talking with your girl-friend? Kay warned me—"

"In fact, yes, I am." He handed Amar the phone.

After a moment, Amar's face brightened in recognition. "Karen, how wonderful and Merry Christmas. But what did you say to my husband, he is sitting here with tears streaming down his face?" Amar listened for a few more seconds before sitting down next to her spouse.

She put her arm around him. Her tears also flowed freely.

CHAPTER 12

PASSIONS REDUX

The university dignitary began, "Each year, we honor one graduate from among all our colleges to acknowledge the challenges they have overcome in the pursuit of their academic dreams. With some thirty colleges in our academic community and thousands of students annually receiving degrees, this is a singular award and an exceptional recognition. We have long appreciated that our undergraduate student body becomes more diverse every year. No longer is Oxford University an exclusive retreat for the elite and privileged. It is now the gateway to success for those of all colors, backgrounds, and social classes. Some of those on whom we have bestowed this coveted award have overcome extraordinary, sometimes touching, impediments to reach this day. We have an exemplary honoree this year, Ms. Azita Masoud, who has earned a first in pre-medical studies at The Queens College here at Oxford. Moreover, we are thrilled to announce she has decided to stay with us for her medical studies, turning down offers from Yale and Johns Hopkins Universities in the United States."

As the dignitary droned on about her accomplishments, Azita reflected on her past. She drifted back to when it all began, when she followed her father as he pursued his vocation. She winced at the memory of herself as an obnoxious, innocent child who hung on his every word and gesture. As he treated his patients, he would speak aloud, occasionally in English when he wanted the communication private between father and daughter. It was his way of imparting lessons to his young daughter. Even as a young child, he would let her do simple procedures on village women, watching closely as her steady fingers were applied to the task at hand. He only permitted this when treating females, and away from the prying eyes of the authorities. There was too much danger that a male would react to a female touching him, even a child. One always had to be careful. Her father would correct her at times but often merely praised her work. She picked up so much merely by watching him. Even from the beginning, she was so talented, so obviously gifted.

She recalled sitting at their kitchen table in Kabul. Her sister would be working with her mother on the household chores, occasionally looking in her direction and sticking her tongue out. Periodically, Azita would respond, telling Deena that her face would freeze with her tongue hanging out of her mouth. That would spark an exchange between siblings that would only be doused by their mother's exasperated intervention. Eventually, Deena would go off to the market and Azita's mother would sit with her to look over her lessons. The girl was a prodigy, her mother knew. She herself had been an academic star as a young girl but not even she was as gifted as her daughter. Still, the matriarch would be careful not to praise her student too much, better that she retained as much humility as possible in one so blessed.

Azita looked to the blue sky. How could she have been so fortunate. Shifting her gaze to the audience in front of her, she

could see Amar's angelic face. So many recent memories immediately flooded into her head where Amar would talk with her
about medicine just as her father once had done. She recalled
being so happy to see a female doctor apply her trade and to
be so successful. As much as she knew in her head that women
were as competent as men, years of being told differently took a
toll when she was young.

She had no female role models in medicine early in life outside her home, so doubt inevitably seeped in at the edges of
her head. Now she could watch her new mother ply her craft,
sometimes along with Aunt Kay. Everyone respected their professional skills without question. No one questioned their right
to be physicians. Her own confidence soared. Amar might sit
with her in the evening, talking about her own personal struggle
to become a physician from a conservative Indian family. There
were times when Azita would nestle against her, lost in her new
mother's lilting voice. She loved those intimate moments, on
occasion drifting off into a dream world where she would ac-
complish great things in Pamir's name.

The girl looked down at the audience. She could see her
loved ones in front. Searching quickly, she spotted her new father, Chris. As she grew more confident with him, she would
kid him that it was too bad that he was not smart enough to be
a doctor like his wife was and his daughter would be someday.
He never bit at her joke, readily agreeing that his wife had the
brains in the family but that he was so sexy that Amar was totally in love with him. Azita would laugh and respond that his
wife, her new mother, was only taking pity on him. She loved

thinking of Amar as her mother, she sometimes pinched herself at her good fortune. Then Chris would fake feeling hurt until they both would wind up laughing.

Their banter became a ritual that persisted for some time. As she matured, she would beg him to talk about the world, a world that she knew so little about when she left Afghanistan. He would mumble that she was like all women, she could never leave him alone. Then, he would rise to find his world atlas. He would open a page and talk about events and people from that part of the world. She marveled at his encyclopedic knowledge. He might even be smarter than Pamir, whom she had been convinced was the smartest man in the world.

She snapped to attention as the cadence of the introduction reached its natural conclusion. "Please give a warm round of applause to Ms. Masoud who has graciously agreed to share some comments on her personal journey."

Azita strode to the microphone wearing her academic garb. On this day, she was a young woman, no longer a child. She now possessed more confidence and maturity than the girl who walked down the concourse at Heathrow less than seven years earlier. She had been accepted into Queens College through an early admissions program and then completed her rigorous course of studies in science in only three years. All her fears of failure had been unfounded. It turned out she was her father's daughter. She was, in fact, a prodigy.

It was a delightful late-spring morning. The air was a bit chilly but the sun looked down upon the assembly from a bright blue sky. Oxford was a magical place on such occasions. The various colleges spoke of tradition, stability, and yet with an undercurrent of searching and newness. It held that tension between custom, continuity, and creativity with unique ease. Azita took a moment to look out over the crowd. She had sprung up several inches over the past few years. She no longer looked like a child but more like a young adult about to conquer the world. Her dark hair hung straight down to her shoulders. Her copper skin was set off by striking brown eyes. She was not as classically beautiful as her sister. To all who had known her over the years, she had evolved into a deeper attractiveness that was heightened by her incisive intellect and her quiet, unprepossessing demeanor that spoke of inner strength and purpose. How could she not be confident given all that she had endured.

Slowly, almost tentatively, she started to speak, first acknowledging the seated dignitaries as expected. Then she shifted gears. "I want to thank everyone connected to this award. Receiving this has been an honor which I will always keep close to my heart in part because it recognizes something beyond mere intellect and diligent study. It acknowledges passion, the sheer desire that propels someone toward an impossible dream, an unachievable goal. Such passion, if it can be found, is the greatest gift a person can have, other than an abiding love for God's creatures. I suspect that is what I most want to share with you today, just a little bit about my passion and how it came to be, how it was nurtured into something that could not be extinguished."

She gave a small laugh. "I am going to admit something right now. I am not quite sure what I am going to say next. I do want you to know that I had prepared a conventional talk. I even spent much effort on its preparation. In fact, here it is." She raised several sheets of paper in the air. "It was a fine speech, replete with big word and lofty sentiments. This morning, however, I realized it was not what I wanted to say nor what you needed to hear." She paused, lowering her head for several moments. "Last night, I had a nightmare, one that I have had many times over the past several years. It is one of those harsh dreams we typically associate with soldiers experiencing PTSD or post-traumatic stress disorder. I am sure you are looking at this perhaps too thin, maybe even delicate-looking girl and asking yourself how this mere slip of a child could suffer from such a debilitating condition."

She paused before answering her hypothetical question. "Perhaps, just perhaps, it has something to do with growing up in a country ravaged by constant war and turmoil. When did the killing start in the world of my youth? Some say when the Taliban took over in 1996. Others say when civil war broke out after the Soviets were expelled and the world looked away with studied indifference. Still others go back to the Soviet invasion or when the monarchy failed or even back to the days when all the local tribes were forced to unite as one fractious whole in our distant past. Of course, none of that matters to a young girl whose childhood was colored by endless conflict and killing. It is only the terror and killing of her daily experience that count. I would walk with my father, Pamir, to try and repair a little bit of the horror of those times."

She looked to the sky as if trying to decide where to go next. "Standing here, with a degree from one of the premier academic institutions in the world, is a small miracle. I can still feel the utter despair my sister and I, when I was just a girl of twelve years, felt as we huddled in a cave in the foothills adjacent to the Panjshir Valley. Early that morning, in the dark of night, our parents had been murdered by the Taliban. Why did they have to die? My dear, wonderful father, a physician, had escaped these monsters to heal those serving the Northern Alliance. These were the brave warriors who were holding out against the Taliban's complete domination of my country. It was also the area of the country in which he had been born and raised. These were his people, his tribe. All that was secondary, however. Mostly, my father had escaped their control to give my sister and I some hope for a future. For that simple and understandable reason, he and my mother paid the ultimate price. Even as I stand before you, I can hear their screams, the gunfire that ended their lives. Those sounds have been with me every day of my life since. My continuing despair is that their last thoughts focused on the fact that my sister and I might also be dead or were about to experience something worse. It turns out that these monsters were searching for me as well. The truth of this was determined from prisoners later taken by the British soldiers who were arriving after America was attacked."

She took a deep breath. "My sin? What was my sin as a twelve-year old girl? It was helping my father to heal the sick and wounded when girls were not permitted to do so, nor do anything else for that matter. Worse, in their unseeing eyes, my unforgivable sin was publicly advocating for the education of girls. How could such things be sins? I ask again, how could such things be sins? They were not sins in Allah's eyes, I have searched the holy writings. They are sins only in the minds of narrow men who live in fear and hate." Her voice elevated in genuine passion. "My sister and I cried that morning, our desolation was complete, our lives seemingly hopeless. We had lost our dear brother in battle to the Taliban. Now, they had tracked us down to murder us all, to slaughter the two most gentle and loving people seen in this world, our mother and father. Did evil know any limits? I am embarrassed to admit that I also cried that morning for a personal reason, a selfish reason. My dream of following my father into medicine seemed beyond reach. It could not be. My one burning passion in life would never be realized, there was no chance whatsoever. In my mind, I could not conceive of any possible way of escaping the fate of women in my country, or even if I could survive the next day. Yet, here I stand."

She could tell that the people looking up at her were listening. She had captured them. They were silent, waiting for her to continue. "There were other such moments. There came the day when I finally helped my mother by going to the market. As my sweet sister knows so well, I was not a good daughter when it came to our chores. I was spoiled and, frankly, pampered by our parents. I will say one thing to you, I shall not spoil my children that way if I am so blessed." She smiled, and people out there smiled back at her. "But on that one dark day, I felt guilt and insisted on going to the market. Being such a naïve girl, I stopped to read a notice that had been posted in the public square, forgetting it was an unforgivable sin. There were so many sins, showing an ankle in public, talking to a man not of your family, working in the professions, driving a car, learning about the world. The morals police saw this sin, my reading of this notice which, by the way, praised the destruction of one of the world's greatest iconic set of Buddhist sculptures. Seeing me, they went into a rage. They were beating me nearly to death, who knows the outcome if my dear brother had not arrived and, in a desperate effort to save me, took over the beating but employed only glancing blows. He saved my life that day. He thought me a silly girl, always my nose in a book, never doing anything useful for the family. At the same time, he would have sacrificed his life in a minute to save mine. I know that with total certainty. He would soon lose that life fighting these deluded people. He died seeking what he believed was right and good."

"I look down to my beautiful sister, so gentle and loving, who is sitting here with me this beautiful morning. She also saved my life, and hers, and the life of the man who would become my father. That day, in the mountains, when the Taliban had finally tracked us down, one of their warriors had cornered us. Right now, just in front of me, I can see the total hate in his eyes as he raised his weapon to kill us all. I can yet see his look of ecstatic anticipation that would accompany his slaughter of the infidels before him. Now, for certain, life was over. What does one think about in the final moment of life? Funny, I don't recall now. I did close my eyes with a final prayer to Allah, waiting for the death that could no longer be denied. All I heard, though, was a single shot next to me. Then a pause followed by two more. What I did not feel was any pain. Was death so simple? I asked myself. Had I seamlessly passed over to the other side? I then open my eyes and saw that the man who would kill us was on the ground. When I looked, my sister, Deena, was holding a pistol. Back then, I knew not where she had gotten it. She had shot this man in the heart, this man who would murder us with such glee."

She paused again, seemingly fighting back a tear. "My passion could be realized only if we fled from oppression. I, we, had several personal hegira's or flights to safety. I can so vividly recall our family taking flight from Kunduz, this was our second flight, the first being from Kabul to the north, to what they hoped would be freedom. We had originally started from Kabul. Now, however, we needed to escape the territory held by the Taliban. My mother, sister, and I hid in the back of a truck. If we had been discovered, we likely would have been killed on the spot. There would be no explaining our actions, not so near the front lines. The truck stopped on several occasions. We females, hidden under some supplies purportedly stored to help the Taliban fighters at the front, wondered if each moment would be our last. We could hear my father and brother making their arguments but not what was being said. Every moment was agony. At one point, a warrior thrust his bayonet, maybe it was a long knife, into the supplies. Likely, he was too lazy to unload the truck and look properly. His blade sliced between my mother's chest and her arm. That it did not slice into her was another inexplicable blessing. She uttered not a sound. Another thrust brought the blade an inch from my throat. I took courage from her and kept silent. We waited in terror for the next thrust, but it did not come."

She took another big breath. "Why do I talk of such things? It is not to secure your sympathy or your admiration. It is to acknowledge and praise the incredible courage and devotion of my biological family. I never had, until this moment, an appropriate opportunity to publicly thank them. Yet, that was not their greatest gift to me, not at all, not even close. What they really bequeathed to me was a love of learning, a dream, and a passion. My dear mother would sit with me every day and impart her knowledge to me. No longer able to teach girls in the university, she took me on as her student. And my father, dear man, would take me with him to see his patients whenever he could. He would instruct me in the arts of healing, of diagnosis, and medical problem solving with little thought to the risks he was taking. He nurtured an early curiosity into a full-blown love affair with medicine. No one can put a price on such things. No one can claim to understand the love I hold in my heart for them."

Azita looked down to her sister sitting in the front row and whispered the words, "Except you, dear sister." Moisture in Deena's eyes overflowed and ran down her cheek.

Azita looked up to the broader audience. "I also want to share with you another type of parental love. For the past seven years, I have been blessed with the love of two more parents, the ones who adopted me and brought me here to England. They have also showered me with affection and attention and possibilities beyond my early dreams. It was as if they were sent to me from some deity beyond my comprehension. I had met Professor Crawford, who is now on the faculty here at Oxford, but I thought he was back in England that day when my parents were slaughtered as my sister and I huddled in fear of our lives. We had fled the caves in which we hid when we heard the Taliban coming, hiding among the rocks until the sounds were gone. We waited, and then my heart sank when sounds returned. The tension was unbearable. Somehow, my sister and I managed to find some courage to look over the rock that sheltered us. My heart leapt. It was not the ones who came to kill us, but the man who would become my father. How could this be? I thought this must be some hallucination, a form of delusion. To my knowledge, he was here, in England. There was no logic, no explanation. But it was him. A miracle had happened, we were ecstatic. Unfortunately, that exaltation soon turned to despair as the Taliban found us again. They had not strayed very far. Bullets flew about us and all, one more time, seemed hopeless. Out of nowhere, a helicopter flew over and soon British soldiers were firing machine guns and rockets as we scrambled to the safety of their ship. It was as if I was living in a Hollywood movie script except that the bullets were real. I know they were real since my good friend Karen, now my sister's loving partner, was severely wounded and almost died." Azita found Karen in the audience and gave her a smile.

"Within weeks, I was on my way to England. Professor Crawford had married Dr. Amar Singh in the Panjshir Valley of Afghanistan, the ceremony performed by a British military officer. At the time, I wondered whether they had married only to get me out of the country. I felt guilty for a bit until I realized that my new father would never be able to get such a beautiful wife on his own. For sure, he needed my help to get such a love-ly bride." The levity brought a hearty laugh, a welcome respite from the harsh narrative she had been sharing. "But even then, the fears were not over. We were several hundred feet from my dream of being in your country so that I might study in a real school. And, at that moment when the journey seemed com-plete, there was one more hurdle. An immigration officer was saying no. I tried not to show my desperate fear to my new par-ents, I did not want them to share my despair but that is what overwhelmed me. I had let myself hope. It was one thing when you had only despair, quite another when your goal was within reach, when you can literally taste it. There were moments in that immigration room when my heart stopped beating, to be so close and then to be sent back. The cruelty was beyond my young mind to comprehend. If they had, I am not sure I could have gone on."

She looked directly at Amar. "Then, the woman who re-cently had embraced me as her own child took me aside as this official went off to decide my fate, or so I thought. My new mother consoled me, encouraged me, whispered words of love and affection into my heart. She told me that I would never be abandoned again. She saved me from one last descent into a personal hell. If I had not fully loved her up to that point, I did at that moment. Of course, I did not appreciate how many steps my new mother and father had taken to ensure I would not be turned away simply because I did not have the proper paperwork. There was a media circus taking place outside of our view. Well, as you can see from my presence here today, the immigration people relented." She smiled broadly as the audience applauded.

"And Dear Chris, my dear Chris, I never thought anyone could measure up to my biological father. And you, when I first met you on that day when I thought you had come to take your sister away from our medical work during the terrible days when we battled the Taliban. In truth, you did not get off to a good start in my eyes. Your reputation preceded you, and it was not at all flattering. You were described as the playboy of the Western world and you were there to take Kay away. That would have been unforgivable. And then I met you. What a shock. In truth, you were the kindest and sweetest man imaginable, next only to my blessed Pamir. Father, you have shown me love and encouragement and support every day since we met as you descended from the sky in your helicopter. One thing. I want to apologize for all the terrible jokes I have tortured you with, a wit I learned from my biological father. Of course, this public apology cleans the slate between us. I can start anew this afternoon." Chris laughed aloud while the audience chuckled at her loving irreverence. "How can I thank you for all you have done, for all you have meant to me. There are no words." She stopped, watching tears flow down his face, fearing she would lose her remaining emotional control.

"My message, in the end, is simple. If you are young, never abandon your passion. No matter how bleak things seem, most likely you will never face the despair I did. If you are a parent, love your children, nurture their hopes, make sure their passions in life are never extinguished. Our ability to bequeath what is precious to those who come after us is the greatest possible gift we can make to this world. I am confident of one thing. Our meanings are not what we do today. God is not some static concept, some eternal verity. The truths we seek are in the process of becoming a part of a universe still beyond our understanding but toward which each one of us can make some small contribution. Our children are small pebbles we drop into a vast ocean. The ripples they create eventually will find some distant shore and possibly transform the world as we know it. We can never trace the ripples as they make their way across vast distances. We can only set them in motion. We can only bequeath them our own passions and wish for the best."

Then she paused as the audience wondered if she had finished. She ended their uncertainty with the following words, "I only hope and pray that my parents, wherever they are, look upon me with favor, that the ripple they started so long ago is worthy of their memory." Her voice quavered slightly. "One last thought. Never pass up any opportunity to tell those whom you love how you feel. I thought I would have many opportunities to say such words to my biological parents and then, in an instant, they were gone forever." Now her voice cracked for a moment. "My father Pamir introduced me to your Shakespeare many, many years ago. I have always kept some of the bard's words close to my heart.

> *Who could refrain that had a heart to*
> *love and in that heart courage to make love*
> *known.*

I love you, more than words can ever express." She looked down at those looking back at her in the front row.

With that, she turned and walked back to her seat on the dais. For a moment or two, there was silence, she had ended abruptly. Then, a smattering of applause started that grew in strength as her words sunk in. Applause evolved into a standing ovation that went on for some time. She could not look up, she was embarrassed that people would see her tears. She need not fear. Many in the audience, and all those in the front rows who loved her, were drenched in tears themselves.

————

All the wetness had been wiped away by the time they had arrived at the Hairy Hare where Chris had rented the lower floor for a private party. There were more exclusive venues he considered but this establishment still held a special place in his heart. As they walked in, he grabbed Karen's arm. "Look, the same barmaid is still here. See, you could have had a lifelong career here. But you missed your chance now. You no longer have the goods, my dear."

"I don't know. I still have a damn good rack."

"Hmmm, I would have to check it out before I could pass judgement." He smirked.

"You will see my rack when they play ice hockey in hell," Karen shot back.

"On second thought, you still might fit in here very well. Customer service is not their strength." Chris murmured as he seemed to be considering some great mystery. "You know, the barmaid doesn't look as fetching as I recall. Maybe the work here is more taxing than I thought."

Karen gave Chris a smirk. "Well, it might be that she has four kids and is on her third husband. I wonder what passions her kids have, I can only imagine."

Soon, they were in the lower room and mingling among themselves before sitting down for the expected modest cuisine comprised of the best food that England offers in establishment more known for their drinking culture than the food. Not surprisingly, everyone seemed more interested in imbibing the Guinness and socializing. No one was in a rush to experience the culinary delights about to be offered. "Tell me again, dear husband, why didn't we select a great Indian restaurant like the Bombay Palace?"

"I will confess, dear, I lust after the barmaid here."

"Yes, she does strike me as your type. I will go and get her phone number for you." She gave him her best wicked smile. She had become so used to his sense of humor with time and proved a more than worthy foe for is jests.

"There is history here, sentimental memories, for me at least. Not the barmaid, mind you, the place." He added, "just humor an old man, okay?"

"All right then, maybe I will go and talk to the barmaid anyways. You are getting long in the tooth she might know some sexy, younger guys that might interest me."

"As if a good Indian girl would even think of that. Come, let's mingle."

"Jules," Chris said, "I am so glad you could bring your better half with you this time. Too bad the kids are at home."

Jules smiled broadly. "I didn't want to expose my young boys to you until they were older, like thirty. But Jim was anxious to come with me this time. He has heard about your terrible reputation with women and wanted to meet this famous womanizer."

Chris saw the man was about to defend himself, so he jumped in first. "No need, Jim, did Jules ever tell you that she was waiting to find a man better than me before getting married? You must be that guy."

"Okay," Jules offered. "Here is the truth. It was not that hard. There were dozens of them, really no end to suitable candidates. No offense, Amar, we all think you a saint for taking pity on him. Among the dozens better than you, dear Chris, Jim here was the best of the bunch."

"No offense taken, Jules." Amar laughed. "Hindus believe in karma and reincarnation. I did something terrible in my last life to deserve this character. I am hoping for a huge boost in my next cycle after this clown."

"Wait," Chris suddenly claimed, "I have to save my sister Kat from Ricky, I think he may have desires on her. Damn, he is worse with women than I am."

Amar took his arm and whispered in his ear, "I think you are way too late. Don't tell me you are the last to know?"

"Know what?"

Amar sighed. "He is your best male friend. Don't you ever talk?"

"All the time, but only about important stuff like Big Ten sports and how the Cubs are doing."

"Well, I hope you figure it out before you are standing there as the best man at their wedding."

"No way! You are bullshitting me." But curiosity captured him.

Before he made it to Ricky and Kat, however, Chris's mother caught them. "The talk your daughter gave this morning was wonderful. I could not stop crying, except to brag to people that she was my granddaughter."

When Chris recovered from a mother who had lost most every vestige of observable prejudice since she sobered up and left his father, he managed the question that was on his mind. "Mother, did you know that Ricky and Kat were . . . were . . ."

"Say it, son. They are going to get married. Everyone knows, except you apparently."

Kat approached him with a hug and a smile. "Tell me one thing," she said, "how can someone who is supposed to be so smart miss something so obvious? Ever wonder why Ricky was making so many trips to the States?"

"To raise money?"

"And he did a great job too. I will let you in on a secret. I had a crush on this guy from way back when you brought him around the house in high school. Finally, after all this time, I had my shot. I found that my attractiveness to men skyrocketed as my success in the business work grew."

"That is nonsense, Kat," Chris argued. "You became a real looker once you emerged from your cocoon. Confidence is sexy."

"Perhaps. In any case, I started helping Ricky connect with all those rich people I got to know after I took over the business as chairperson. My net of contacts had really expanded. We realized we liked one another. And I realized I could satisfy my high school fantasy. It was even better than what was in my head."

"Holy shit. Did not need to hear that, way too much information, way too much," was all Chris could manage before giving his best friend a punch in the arm. "You . . . you . . . shit, now I am going to have to call you brother for real."

"I think Karen wants to chat so let me quickly say something about Father. I did reach out to him. I told him everyone was going to be here, that we had all come when Azita first arrived and you had just married Amar. Now we all wanted to celebrate this milestone. I begged him to forgive and forget. It was no use. He is so hard and unreachable. Sorry."

"Kat, not your fault. Frankly, I am glad he is not here. What does he do these days?"

"I think he sits in his palace, makes voodoo dolls that look just like all of us and then sticks pins into them. I am still fending off his lawsuits. I am not sure why he is so angry. His wealth has increased since I took over, we anticipated the economic downturn better than others. You know, I cannot believe he never saw our coup coming. How could he miss it? My best guess is that, despite all the signs, he could not believe we would all betray him, turn on him. That was simply beyond his comprehension."

"Father cannot forgive." Chris mused. "We betrayed not only him, but we spit at his world view. That was an unforgivable sin."

"I really don't know why he is so bitter. After all, his right-wing friends are making steady progress toward taking over the world and grabbing all the money and power for themselves. Mark my words, one of these days we all will be employed as lackeys for a few international behemoths. Freedom will officially be an illusion. I guess Father is pissed that we are not helping him get there."

Chris chuckled derisively. "I agree. His passion, his vision, was to have a united family marching with him toward the new world order. Wow, he must have been crushed when a black man won the White House. But that is just a temporary blip on their march to total control. As I have said many times, they are on the winning side of a self-reinforcing cycle. As they accumulate a greater share of the economic pie, they have more to invest in further control of so-called democratic processes. It is only a matter of time. You know what the saddest thing is? The American people, most of them anyways, are way too stupid to get it."

"That's it, I agree." Ricky piped up. "Let's at least enjoy this day. Armageddon can wait for a week or two."

"Well, my boy, you will soon know what the end days feel like. Need any tips on handling a wife?"

Kat then punched him on the arm. "Careful, buddy."

Ricky laughed. "I would, but I have to find someone who knows something."

Amar pulled on her husband's arm. "Let me save you from yourself. And Kat," she called back as they headed toward Karen. "Don't worry, I will be sure to beat him up later, when he is naked and vulnerable."

"Gee, Amar, I don't think everyone heard you." Then he leaned over and kissed her on the cheek.

"Oh for Christ's sake, get a hotel room." Karen adopted her disgusted look. "You guys are like overheated teenagers."

"Now I get it," Chris intoned. "While my former best friend has been off seducing my innocent younger sister, my Judas of an assistant abetted his heinous sins by running things in his absence."

Karen laughed. "You really have not been paying attention, have you? You know we have new hired talent—Hans from Sweden and Carlotta from Spain. Ricky and I have been preparing them for leadership roles, which will be necessary when he spends more time in the States. And Deena is almost ready to run our education programs. My partner is amazing, so smart, such a hidden gem if you will. She told me that she did not study with her sister early on because she knew Azita was smarter. But she eventually found her way and found she was damn smart in her own right."

"You are good for her, Karen, and you know how much I hate complimenting you."

"You know, I must be good. As you have spent more time doing your professor thing at university, we have gotten bigger.

It is no longer a one-man road show which is good since that one man was always a bit suspect. You should be proud."

"I am but mostly proud of you, Deena, Ricky, and the whole crew. That is the satisfaction, building something and then letting it go." He hugged her. "But you didn't bring the girls, I love them."

"No, they are absorbing English like sponges, but we thought they would be overwhelmed here. Deena was ecstatic to find two girls from the same area as her own family. Of course, a lesbian couple adopting the girls was tricky. Good thing we have connections."

"And you two?"

Karen looked over at Deena who was chatting in an animated fashion with her sister and a tallish young man. "I can't believe it. I am in love. What else is there to say?"

At that moment, Kay wandered up with her two young boys who grabbed on to their uncle's pant legs. Chris tousled their hair as his sister shared her message. "I understand that they are ready to serve our wonderful repast. Better get everyone seated."

"One question, Kay." He pulled her aside. "What was the thing?"

"What thing?" She could not yet read his mind.

"Sorry, what attracted you to Jamie? You had shots at a lot of guys, why him? I never thought—"

"I know. You never thought I would get married. I still am not sure how it happened. It was slow motion. First, I was so impressed by his talent as a surgeon. Then I found out he was so funny in an understated way, that dry humor like yours. And he was nice, calm, and centered and . . . and . . . he loved me. Of course, being a dumb shit, I tried pushing him away. Thank Karen, she kept on me about what a dumb shit I really was. Good thing I didn't have family jewels like you. I certainly would have gotten the knee to the groin treatment. I don't know why he stayed the course until I finally got it."

"Got what, exactly?" Chris asked.

"That he is not Father and that I loved him. I think he is what I wanted in a father . . . what I had . . . in a brother. He has been great, Chris."

Chris leaned in and kissed her on the cheek. "Let's go eat now."

Soon, the task of gathering the crowd and seating them was accomplished. Chris rose and tapped his spoon on a wine glass. Everyone looked toward him. "Listen, the food will soon be here. There are a couple of things I want to say before that. Frankly, the food is so bad here that you may not give me a chance after you eat." Laughter as expected. "But I like it here. It was my favorite hangout when I was a student."

"Hell," Karen, interrupted, "what he really liked about the place was the barmaid. Unfortunately, for him, she would not give him the time of day."

"True enough and no more wine for this woman. First, I apologize that I could not get everyone front row seats to see Azita's amazing talk up close. Good thing, really, you would have seen her father bawl like a baby. Second, I want to make a very personal announcement." He took a deep breath. "Amar is pregnant again. We are having another child. In case no one has seen the pictures of Usha, I have several hundred. We thought her too young to be exposed to this crowd. I intend to keep her locked up until she is twenty-two."

There were expressions of surprise, congratulations, and then a robust cheer went up. "And as soon as I find out who the father is, I will let you know."

Kay threw a bread roll at her brother. "Amar, let me know if you need any help in punishing him later. I know some lovely torture techniques that I have perfected on Jamie."

Amar spoke up, "Thanks, Kay, but I have that covered. Anyways, yes, we found out recently and are thrilled. Truth is, my biological clock was ticking. We wanted another, and it was now or never. Hard to believe but Chris turned out to be a great dad. Just look at Azita and he gushes over Usha which, for those who did not know, was my mother's name. I still laugh when I think back to what I was told about him before we met."

"Those were bold-faced lies told by my malevolent sister, and Karen, and every other woman who knew me." Another cheer followed by more laughs. "Listen, before I shower my daughter Azita with deserved praise, is there anyone else with news they want to share?" He looked directly at Ricky and Kat.

Ricky stood. "A couple of things. Karen Fisher will be taking over primary leadership of the organization Chris built. Both he and I will stay involved as consultants and fund-raisers. But I will be returning to the States to marry his younger sister, Kat." Another cheer went up. "Funny, sometimes you look for something half of your life and it is right in front of you all the time."

"Ricky," Chris said with great seriousness, "anyone who marries one of my sisters will need much help. I know some excellent therapists." He paused for effect. "All right, enough jesting. I speak for the family when I say that we are thrilled to find someone to take her off our hands. To Kat and Ricky, all the best."

"To Kat and Ricky." The cheer arose from around the table as glasses clinked.

"Now to the business at hand, my daughter Azita."

But she cut him off, rising from her seat and holding up a hand. "Wait, Father. I know you are going to praise me and my accomplishments. In truth, that would merely embarrass me further. Rather, I wish to take the few remaining moments before our food arrives to make my own announcement, which only my sister knows, since I just told her. This is something I have not even shared with you, dear parents, something that was decided just this morning, after my talk. This is Benjamin Kaplan. We have known each other for about three years and now we want to say something publicly." She took a deep breath. "We intend to get married."

Amar and Chris smiled, they were not entirely surprised but had not anticipated such a public announcement at this moment. Deena clapped her hands. Karen gave a cheer, Kay a hearty laugh. Soon, everyone settled into a chorus of congratulations. Azita raised her hand to silence the crowd. "We have talked about this for some time. Somehow, it struck Ben after my talk that this would be a good day to finally go public, with everyone here and all. Maybe if I had given my original speech he would not have been so impressed. If I knew my eloquence would move him to propose, I would have given it long ago. Such a foolish boy." She smiled nervously at her small joke. She had Pamir's dry wit, and Chris's. "Mother, Father, I hope you are not mad that I—"

"God no, we are thrilled," Amar blurted out. "The world should know such wonderful news."

Then Kay asked, "How did you meet? How long have you known each other, did you say three years? When did you fall in love? We want all the sordid details. But the biggest question is this. How in the world did you keep this from your mother? Chris is always clueless, but Amar?"

"I suppose we have kept our relationship a bit quiet, well very quiet. I am a private person. I suspected that not everyone would understand us, to say the least. Not long after I started at Oxford, I had something happen, a very bad incident, that reminded me of that day in the Kabul marketplace. It was not as bad, just a reminder is all. A terrorist attack had taken place in London and that always brought out people who love to hate. I was walking through the streets one rainy day when some town boys began to follow me. I walked faster but they caught up to me, shouting 'Packey, go home' and 'we don't want your kind here.' I told them this was my home but that just enraged them even more. They pushed me. One struck me and I fell against a building, gashing my head. I saw no one around and felt panic when one sneered something about getting a taste of the Packey. Oh my god, I thought. They are about to rape me. And then, from nowhere, this tall, skinny boy arrived and began to shout at them."

"Did Ben drive them off?" someone asked.

"Not exactly," Azita smiled and the quiet boy seated next to her looked down at his salad. "One of these thugs hit him and down he went. But it proved a good tactic and seemed to work. His face was full of blood and they must have thought they had killed him because they all ran off. I managed to get both of us to the student infirmary, we must have looked like quite the pair, covered in blood. He insisted he would be fine. It seemed he was too embarrassed to talk about it with me, so I let him be. After, I felt bad, he was my hero and I did not thank him properly." She tousled his hair with affection and he looked up at her. "I kept looking out for him at university and finally spotted him one day. So, I followed him and got information about which college he attended and so forth. After that, I kept showing up in places he might be. In truth, you might say that I stalked him. It was not working. He would look at me but never approach me. I almost gave up, perhaps he thought me ugly. That seemed likely. Then one day, I said enough is enough. My biological mother told Deena and I how she met our father in school. She walked across a school yard and initiated a conversation with him, unheard of in Afghanistan. I thought I might try the same thing. I walked right up to him and said, 'I am Azita Masoud. Thank you for what you did that day.' I then had to ask him his name since he seemed to be mute. Finally, he said it was Benjamin Kaplan."

The young man next to her spoke up, "I thought at the time that she, as a Muslim girl, could not possibly like a Jew. So, I thought I would end things by telling her that I was Jewish. But she did not run away which surprised me. For a moment, I believed she had not heard me and I was going to repeat myself. She stopped me cold by asking if I was prejudiced against her."

Azita picked up the story, "He said 'no, I am not prejudiced.' Then he shocked me by saying he thought I was very beautiful. No boy had ever said that to me before. I was speechless but only for a moment. My knowledge of boys was, shall we say, very limited. I fell back on my intellect. I began rambling on about the first thing that popped into my head. I told him that I was an adherent of Omnism, which my biological father had told me about. I mentioned that my father had given me a book on that very subject when I had great doubt about my own faith. For those unfamiliar with this philosophy, it is the belief that all spiritual traditions have elements of truth in them. We can learn and profit from all faiths but responsibility for our spirituality lies within us. We must create our own moral compass. But I was perhaps a bit obnoxious and was totally convinced that this shy boy would not know what Omnism meant. Perhaps I was a bit arrogant, boys can be so stupid. I felt it necessary to explain things to him."

"And I stopped her," Ben cut in. "I told her that I was not as stupid as the boys she likely knew. I was aware of what Omnism meant. In fact, it had always made great sense to me. I added a few words about what it meant to me, personally. Then she looked at me with her wide eyes and I knew I was lost forever.

Later, I realized those wide eyes represented her total astonishment that I was not as dumb as a bag of rocks."

Azita smiled at him. "What this poor boy did not know is that I fell for him in that moment as well. Right then and there, I decided I would marry him one day. It was like my own mother, Madeena, and Pamir, in their schoolyard decades ago. Of course, I decided not to inform him of that fact just then. In my mind, he was still a definite flight risk. But he was doomed from that moment on. I think, I think he reminded me of . . . my father, my biological father." Then her voice faded.

"Since that day," the boy said in his own quiet voice, "we started to study together, go to lectures and concerts, share books and conversations. At some point, we knew we were best friends. Now we will make it official, or soon at least. I will have to break this to my parents and get a ring I suppose. This was sudden, listening to her this morning . . ." He did not know where to go next with that thought. "Listening to her this morning, my heart almost burst. Why wait another moment. Of course, my mother may have cardiac arrest, so it is a good thing that Azita has so many doctors in the family. But they have met her many times and do love her dearly. What is not to love? I think it will be all right."

The food arrived. People began to eat, though the buzz around the table continued. The cuisine was not as bad as Chris feared and he was spared the expected abuse. He looked around the table, small groups talking among themselves, and wondered at the assembly. They were a rainbow of colors, religions, ethnicities, and sexual preferences. Yet, they were bonded by love and a commitment to one another. They were his larger family, his tribe if you will, and he loved them all.

After a while, the pace of eating slowed, the relative silence turned to low-level chatter. Suddenly, one voice commanded attention. It was Mary, Chris's mother. "My dear," she was obviously talking to Azita, "I know you are too humble to accept much praise. But I am your grandmother and you must listen to me. You will find one day that demanding that people listen to you is one of the few blessings of old age. Besides, I think respecting the elderly is a part of your culture. Yes, I have been reading about your part of the world. I was so proud of you this morning. I bragged to total strangers that you were my granddaughter. Of course, they thought they were dealing with a doddering old fool. I suppose they were right." She smiled at her small joke.

Mary looked at peace as she continued, "But I realized something, how different I had become, what a better person. I was raised in wealth and isolation. We only associated with other rich people. Worse, I was raised Catholic. Others, just about everyone else, were to be viewed with distrust and suspicion. They were not part of the truth and probably going to hell in any case. I went from that to the isolation of my husband's world. That was a world defined by hate and measured by our ability to exploit the weak. It was a world I thought was totally natural, at least at first. Now, of course, I am now shocked at my callousness and disregard for others. In the end, the viciousness of my early world drove me to that Irish ethnic curse found in the bottle. It took my children to save me. How my children turned out so well totally mystifies me. They certainly did not get their goodness from me and certainly not from my estranged husband. I am embarrassed now as I think about how I treated Julianna and Richard when Christopher brought them into our house. I tried to be nice, at least on the surface, but I could not wait for them to leave. My son had his favorite joke that I would count the silverware after they were gone. Yes, I know about that. The problem was, that is exactly what I did. I knew no better."

"Mother," Chris called out, "actually that was a prudent action in Ricky's case."

"You shush, son, I can still put you over my knee." More laughter. "Then Julianna took me in when I was at bottom. I found out how delightful she is and why my son . . ." Then she looked at Amar and did not know how to finish the sentence.

Amar saved her, "That is okay, Mother, I know they loved one another. I love Jules as well."

"I am rambling, I am sure. But that is a privilege of age. I simply needed to say how much I love you, Azita, your sister, Deena, and Julianna, and my son-in-law to be, Richard. I am blessed beyond measure. But I still cannot figure out how my children turned out the way they did."

"I take all the credit for that," it was Chris, whose joke was greeted with a round of groans and jeers. "My sisters were a mess until I saved them. A miracle, really, my best work."

"Yes, son, no desert for you," his mother took back control. "Dear Azita, what do you intend on doing after you finish medical school?"

Azita seemed a bit surprised at the question. She thought deeply for a few moments. "First, I must successfully complete my studies, if I can." There was a murmur of laughter since success was assumed by all. "I think that I thought I might go back and practice as did my father. But I have been told by my professors that I can be a gifted medical scientist, that I can make contributions that might help benefit so many. Ben, after all, is also a scientist in training. That we might work together would be a dream. If that is possible, I could not turn away from such a life. Still, I will always take time to heal my people. I have never forgotten their suffering and I would find time to be there. The Taliban have not disappeared. The war in that poor country goes on and on. It tears me apart every day. My sister and I have talked about this. We have thought about how we might identify young girls like us, girls with great promise but few opportunities, and give them the same chances we have enjoyed. Whatever I wind up doing, whatever my sister does in her life, we simply hope to justify all the love and fortune that has been bestowed on us."

The room was dominated by a silence signifying admiration, perhaps awe. They were looking at a treasure. Chris admired his adopted daughter. Then he looked over the room. "Amar," he whispered to his wife, "I found my passion, at long last."

"What?" she asked, wiping a tear that was finding its way down his cheek.

Chris reached over and squeezed Amar's hand. She looked at him, her eyes moist. He then whispered to her, "Look around this room. Just look. I had no idea how lost I was when we first met."

"I did." She smiled at him.

Chris smiled at his wife. "You know, you could have done a lot worse than by marrying me."

"Wrong again, dear husband, but at least you are consistent."

"Wrong? How is that even possible?" Chris whispered his question to her.

"I could not possibly have married any better."

This time, this one time, he had no response.

ABOUT THE AUTHOR

Tom Corbett is emeritus senior scientist and an affiliate of the Institute for Research on Poverty-Madison, where he served as associate and acting director for a decade before his retirement. He received a doctorate in social welfare from the University of Wisconsin and taught various social policy courses there for many years. During his long academic and policy career, he worked with governments at all levels including a stint in Washington D.C., where he helped develop President Clinton's welfare reform legislation. He has written dozens of articles and reports on poverty, social policy, and human services and given hundreds of talks across the nation. In addition, Dr. Corbett has consulted with numerous local, state, federal officials on various issues in both the United States and Canada. Among other things, he has testified before Congress, worked with the Wisconsin legislature, and served on an expert panel for the National Academy of Sciences. His most recent books include *Tenuous Tendrils*, *The Boat Captain's Conundrum*, *Ouch, Now I Remember*, *Browsing Through My Candy Store*, and *The Other Side of the World*. Now retired, the author lives with his wife of forty-five years, Mary Rider, and their Shih Tzu dog, Rascal, in Madison, Wisconsin.

CPSIA information can be obtained
at www.ICGtesting.com
Printed in the USA
LVOW12*2251140318
569926LV00001B/5/P